In Scientia

L. J. BAINES

First paperback edition, February 2024

Published by *Not From Here Entertainment LLC*, 9000 Sunset Blvd, West Hollywood, CA 90069, USA.

The Cataloging-in-Publication Data is on file with the Library of Congress.

Cover art by Colton Giles, jacket design by Christian Storm, symbol and titles by L. J. Baines.

ISBN: 979-8-9897862-1-3

www.inscientianovel.com | www.lukebaines.com

~~To all my exes;~~
~~may you realize what you lost.~~

———

To the dreamers + lonely hearts:
may this fill you with hope
to make it through another day.

Contents

Prologue

L'homme et l'enfant

oonlight bathed the stairs of the Sorbonne in Paris. I was waiting with my mother. For what, I didn't know.

"Is it Dad?"

"What did I say about asking questions?"

"That *not asking them* was a stipulation of me being allowed to come," I groaned.

Her face broke into a smirk, instantly putting me at ease. She'd been cold since she picked me up from school in Manhattan and sped us to the private airport.

"What do you know about *stipulations*?" she asked.

"I'm ten. I'm not stupid."

She laughed. "No, my dear, no one could ever accuse you of that."

I desperately wanted to know more, but I knew better than to push it. For once I was being allowed along, instead of spying

1

through cracked doors or pretending-to-be-asleep eyes.

Before the wheels of the arriving town car had finished their final rotation, my father emerged from the back seat and was rushing towards us.

"Dad!" I accidentally shouted, as he scooped me up in his arms, my voice bouncing off the centuries-old university behind us. "I barely asked any questions," I lied.

Mom walked to his side and kissed him on the cheek. "We have to hurry," she said. "They know we left."

He lowered my feet to the ground. "You ready for an adventure?"

I nodded, trying not to burst with anticipation.

He took my hand and led us to a side door, where an elderly custodian was waiting. Before I knew it, the man was ushering us through a damp-smelling library, behind bookcases and false walls to reveal a labyrinth of limestone tunnels. After walking for what felt like hours, we arrived at a monolithic arch and ornately crafted bronze door: the entrance to Lutetia, a subterranean Roman city that resides beneath Paris.

My father turned to our guide who was trying to catch his breath. "Thank you. We wouldn't have found it without you."

"It was an honor," he said, taking a handkerchief out of his pocket to blot his forehead. "I pray it's in there."

"You're absolutely sure they'll connect you to this?" my mother asked.

"They already have," assured the man. "I've made the appropriate arrangements."

My father nodded, then focused his attention on me. "Turn around," he demanded.

Before I could argue, he doubled down. "I mean it. *Now*. There isn't time to explain."

I did as he said, my mother appearing at my side. I couldn't tell whether it was supposed to reassure me, or encourage compliance.

Behind me, my father began speaking in a tone I'd never heard him use. "Your chest is constricting," he purred, his voice pitched far lower than normal.

Hissing filled the cavern, as if air were escaping a ruptured tire.

"You cannot feel pain. You cannot breathe," continued my father.

I turned around in time to see the old man fall to the ground, the horror of the moment blanketing my body in shock.

I ran to help him, but it was too late. His lungs had given up.

I looked to my mother, then to my father, the ones who had taught me right from wrong.

"You… killed him," I uttered, the gravity hitting me as the words fell out of my mouth.

"Him, and many more," bellowed a stranger's voice from the partial cover of darkness. He was wearing a hooded robe with a crucifix around his neck, emerging from a barely standing temple. "The time for contrition has finally come."

My parents moved in front of me, like chess pieces blocking an attack.

"My son's innocent. You cannot—" My father's desperation echoed around us, as more men dressed the same stepped out from the shadows; seven in total surrounded us.

"They set us up!" proclaimed my mother, her icy façade strengthening.

"Harm him and the treaty will be over! You know that! *This will mean war!*" My father was pleading now.

"*Crux sacra sit mihi lux!*" the men chanted.

He spun around to face me, crouching down to my level. "Find my parents," he demanded.

My mother joined him, pulling my face toward hers. "This isn't what it seems. Nothing ever is. Trust in what you know of us, trust in what you know of you!"

"*Exorcizamus te, omnis immunde spiritus!*"

Bright, white embers of light began rising from the palms of the men in robes, their eyes reflective in its glare. It was as if they were seeing into another time and place.

"We'll never stop loving you," said my father, his eyes welling up. "One day you'll understand."

"Wait," I exclaimed. "Why are you saying goodbye?" I could feel my clammy hands clutching onto their arms, but nothing felt real. They looked to one another, an unspoken exchange only they understood.

"Daddy, I'm scared! Stay with me!"

"You are stronger than you know, my boy," my mother urged, tears dulling the sparkle of her eyes.

"No, I'm not! I'm not strong like you." The words would barely come out.

"Listen to me, *you* are our miracle," my father said. "One day you'll find your own miracle and the world will no longer be a scary place."

"*Vade retro Satana!*"

The men moved in closer, as my father's voice purred once more.

"*Run. Find my parents.* Do not look back. Do not stop until you are safe."

As soon as the words left his mouth, I felt them infect my body. I tried to stop myself. To overpower my mind. To coerce my body into submission, but it was no use. I'd lost all control.

Against my will, I turned away from the people who'd brought me into the world as they stood to face an impossible tidal wave of light.

The last image I have of them is of their backs, fighting for their lives as my legs forced me away — out through the tunnels and catacombs, and into the car still was waiting outside.

It would be almost a decade before I'd meet the men in robes again. This time, however, they'd come for me.

ONE
GRAVEYARD GIRL

I stared at the faded-yellow glow in the dark stars on my ceiling, willing them to give me the energy to get out of bed. My grandma had surprised me with them when I was four, after a particularly bad round of night terrors. She'd told me they were magic, a sign that my dead parents were watching over me. *Classic.*

Now, thirteen years later, I looked at them like the phosphorescent powder they actually were. A chemical compound of alkaline Earth metals—strontium, magnesium and calcium. Not magic, but an illusion. Basic chemistry masquerading as a lie.

"Eva, are you up?" my grandma called out from downstairs. She said it like a question, but her tone gave her away. "We have to be gone by six at the very latest!"

"Coming!" I lied, before banging my hands on the ground to mimic footsteps. I needed another minute to stress myself out about the enormity of the day that lay ahead.

As usual, the weather in Spring City, Pennsylvania was doing the opposite of what it was supposed to do. Late-summer rain pelted against my window, as an insidious wind tried to break

7

through. I couldn't help but root for the weather as I watched the leaves of our maple tree struggle to remain tethered to their stems. That is, until I pictured my granddad having to rake them off the lawn by himself in the weeks to follow. He was entering his early-80s, and while he was still able to do everything he'd always done, I knew that wouldn't be the case for much longer. Had I not been awarded a scholarship to complete my senior year of high school at one of New York's best boarding schools, the guilt that was dancing in my chest might have shackled me in place forever.

I sat up on the edge of my bed and took a deep breath, if only to prove to myself that I could. I hadn't had a panic attack since elementary school, but the soul crushing fear that oxygen wouldn't be there when I needed it still rang true in my head. And in my body.

I threw on the outfit I'd laid out the night before: black jeans, boots and a white tank top. As I looked for the bomber I'd pre-selected—black with cherry embroidery that read, "kindness is an act of rebellion"—a rhythmic knock sounded on my door that could only be my gramps. I opened it to find him standing there, smile on his face, proudly presenting my freshly ironed jacket.

"First impressions are everything," he said, grinning. "We don't want people to think you don't take pride in your appearance."

"Solid point, Gramps," I said, choosing to ignore the fact that he'd made the material shiny from ironing it on a setting that was too hot. "I'd be crushed if someone made a judgement about me based on the wrinkles in my clothing."

"Come down and eat some breakfast. Your grandma's making those meatless sausages you pretend are food."

"I can't," I blurted out, when what I really wanted to say was *stop being nice to me or I may never leave*. He must have sensed it. "I'm okay, honestly."

"I know you are, but do you?" he asked, to which I rolled my eyes. "You're going to do great, Eva," he said. "We're so proud of you."

Talk about twisting the knife. Ray and Annie Nelson are the kind of people who are impossible to hate, which isn't to say I didn't give it my best shot. They'd raised me since birth, and in spite of the pain from the death of their son and daughter-in-law, they loved me in a way that left no doubt. Even when their grief had a way of lingering behind. We may not have had the most money, or the most in common—their ideal night out is the Senior Special at the Royersford Grille (any entree and one canned vegetable for $9.99. *Kill me*)—but they did everything they could to make up for the gaping hole left by my parents.

Interrupting his attempt to hug me, I grabbed the jacket from him and stuffed my arms into the sleeves as quickly as I could. Sincerity makes me monumentally uncomfortable. Especially before coffee.

"I'm gonna say bye to Paul and Edie—"

"You don't have time, dear. You'll miss your train and your gran—"

"Then I'll get on the next one. Cover for me. She'll have a fit," I said, kissing him on the cheek and running out the door, so he didn't have a chance to stop me.

As I rode my rusted bicycle down Main Street, turning onto Bridge, I said a silent goodbye to a town I was sure wouldn't miss me. In seventeen years, I couldn't think of a single interaction that wasn't marred by either pity or disdain. "Eva-Annie," as certain people liked to refer to me, was a regular feature on the revolving marketplace of gossip, where opinions were traded like stocks. It's always fun to learn new things about yourself, especially from people whose names you can't remember.

The rain had eased as I pulled into the grounds of the cemetery, a gentle fog disappearing before my eyes. Had I not been there every week of my entire life, the gloomy scene that lay before me might have turned me back around. Instead, I was distracted by more emotion than I'd anticipated as I approached my parents' graves. After all, it was goodbye. At least for a little while.

"Hey guys... so... today's the day," I said, my voice threatening to break. "I'm finally getting out of here... I'm really gonna miss..." Before tears could escape from my eyes and betray me, I tried my best to laugh it off. *Nope. This is stupid. I am not crying over inanimate objects.*

I picked a couple of wildflowers off the wet grass and placed them on their shared headstone.

"My train leaves for Manhattan in an hour. Sixty minutes more of this hell hole. Weird, huh?" I said as I fiddled with my mother's necklace. It was the only thing of hers I had: a dark red, raw crystal on a thin gold chain. "Gotta be honest, I'm scared to death, no pun intended. What if it's not everything I've made it out to be, you know? Like, what if I'm the small fish in the big pond, and that little voice inside me that says I'm destined for something great turns out to just be a very elaborate delusion?" I let that hang in the air, the stillness making me uneasy.

"This would be a great time for you to do that parental thing, where you fill me with false confidence and tell me I'm being stupid and that everything's gonna work out..." I half joked.

"Okay, well great chat guys... as always."

Before I stood up, a laminated section of newspaper I'd stuck there years earlier caught my eye. The three-line article that described my parents' deaths was the first piece of news I'd ever read, and probably the reason I hoped to be a journalist someday. I could never work out if it were the laziness of the piece, or the lack of information surrounding the crash itself, but being raised without answers caused an insatiable thirst for them. Some kids want dolls; I wanted a subscription to *The New York Times*.

"I promise I'm gonna do better than this," I said, peeling it off the stone and sliding it inside my jacket pocket. "If I ever get the chance."

A car horn sounded that I immediately recognized it. Fearing I'd miss the train, my grandparents had driven up to the cemetery to collect me. Knowing how hard it was for them to be there, I quickly kissed my hand before touching it to my parents' headstone. "Love you, Mom. I love you, Dad," I said, with an accidental heavy heart.

As I turned, a dragonfly swooped by my face and landed on their grave. The realist in me knew it was most likely hunting the mosquitoes that had started to appear after the rain. But the little girl, who believed in the stars on her ceiling, wanted it to be a sign that her parents were wishing her well. Funny how logic rarely prevails.

Placing my bike into the back of my grandpa's pickup truck, I felt like I was being watched. The local chaplain, Father Michael, had appeared at the entrance to the church that presided over the graveyard. He surveyed me with a judgmental gaze, not even trying to hide his disdain. I couldn't be sure if it were my outspokenness over the years (faith through guilt doesn't do it for me), or my frequent visits to see my parents and infrequent visits to his services, but he'd made it clear I was no longer welcome. An unspoken arrangement I was more than happy to oblige.

MY GRANDMA barely spoke during the forty-minute car ride into Philadelphia. She only occasionally broke her vow of silence to ask me if I'd remembered various items that I had, indeed, packed. I chose to believe she was trying to be strong, but it felt like she was angry that I was abandoning them after everything they'd done for me. My grandpa, on the other hand, didn't shut up, regaling me with stories he'd already told a million times.

"I can't remember the name, but it was a little movie theatre in Greenwich Village. Your dad had just gotten back from deployment in the Arabian Sea after 9/11, and your mom had moved to New York from England days before. She couldn't believe that in one of the most vibrant cities in the world, a serviceman was using his time off to see a revival of *Casablanca*."

"Wait, he was on furlough?" I asked, a detail I hadn't considered before.

"He was supposed to go back. Instead, he met her."

"She asked him why he wasn't uptown, drinking and celebrating with his buddies. He looked her in the eyes and said after everything he'd seen—"

"All he wanted was 'to be reminded of what love was supposed to look like,'" I said, quoting my father. "What a line."

"It wasn't a line. That was *him*."

"Your mom told me she fell for him right then and there," added my gran, emotion filling her voice.

"Question time, I think," my grandfather announced. A tradition of his I usually despise. "One thing you're grateful for?"

"You two," I said reluctantly, but I meant it.

I heard my grandma start to cry, as Gramps reached out his hand to comfort her.

"I'm going to be less than three hours away, guys. It's not like I won't come back to visit."

"You say that now," she interjected, "but you're going to be having the time of your life, and that's great by me." She turned around in her seat to face me. "But if you don't check in with us at least once a day, I'll be on your doorstep quicker than you can say homeschool."

I thought of a rebuttal but nodded my head instead.

"Second question. Something you're proud of?" asked my granddad.

"Getting out of Spring City," I said, a little too quickly.

"Eva," warned my grandma.

"Joke, Gran. I just can't wait to live in the city."

"Better," she responded. "But I still don't understand why we can't just drive you there."

What I couldn't tell her was that I didn't want everyone looking at them, then looking at me, wondering why my parents were so old. Or worse, looking at our truck and making assumptions about the kind of person I was based on it.

Grandad broke the tension, once again: "Final question. What's something you're excited about?" I took a second, trying to give them some of the honesty I so desperately craved in others.

"I can't believe I'm about to admit this, but... school. Two of my teachers used to be actual journalists. At legitimate newspapers. And the school's own paper—"

"Is one of the best in the country and has won all sorts of awards," he said, amused. "Before you know it, you'll be at NYU."

"Don't," I snapped. "I don't wanna jinx it."

"Didn't you say that every senior who graduated from Anderson last year got into their first choice?" asked Grandma.

"That's what it says on their website."

"Then that's what'll happen."

"We'll see," I murmured.

I'd only just begun wrapping my head around the fact that I was attending Anderson. Let alone my dream college. I wanted to embrace the excitement, but I was terrified that I wouldn't be able to deal if it were taken away.

We pulled up to the curb and as everyone predicted, I was late. Fortunately, a signal failure was holding the train in the station as I said a quick goodbye before grabbing my things to sprint to the platform. Granddad slipped money I knew he couldn't spare into my bag before I ran off. And Gran, who wasn't able to get any words out, gave me a letter, which I stuffed into my pocket.

I didn't have the heart to look back at them as I squeezed through the mechanical door just in time. I knew they'd be waiting, waving until the train disappeared, and I couldn't deal with that image lingering in my mind. Especially if anything were to happen to them while I wasn't there. I knew I was being overly pessimistic (even for me), but I couldn't stop my thoughts from trying to unravel.

I could, however, pretend to search for a seat as I pulled my luggage farther into the carriage, and out of their sorrow-filled sights.

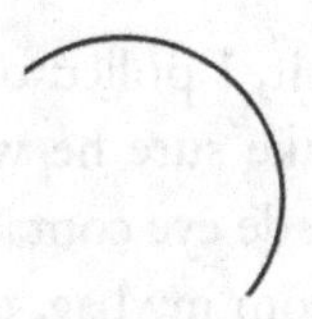

TWO

YOU ONLY GET WHAT YOU GIVE

Butterflies burned holes in my stomach the entire train ride into Manhattan, arriving just before 10 A.M. at Penn Station. The irony that I desperately wanted to leave Pennsylvania and ended up at a station named after it was not lost on me. I smirked as I got swept into a sea of impatient people, who funneled like sheep toward a lone escalator.

Beads of sweat formed on my hairline as I rose on the stairs, my body's sadistic protest to the humidity and stale air. On the sub-level, people scattered like worker ants hopped up on sugary soda. I knew better than to stop for directions in the path of New Yorkers walking, so instead, I opted to follow strangers in front of me, hoping they'd lead me to the subway. Or at least the street.

Three dimly lit tunnels and a fight with a ticket machine later, I arrived at the station entrance, greeted by an endless number of stairs. Dragging my luggage through a deluge of angry passengers who'd much rather shove me than help me, I found the platform just in time to make the next train. I'd almost composed myself when I accidentally made eye contact with a guy opposite me. He smiled, and out of habit/politeness/stupidity, I smiled back, internally begging him not to start a conversation.

Not wanting to risk it, I pulled out my phone to look busy, glancing up again to make sure he wasn't still staring. He was. *Damnit*. Realizing I'd made eye contact twice in under a minute, I took my headphones from my bag, casually placing them in my ears as a social, 'sorry we're closed' sign.

When I got off the train, to take in even more stairs in front me, the man appeared in my periphery. He was speaking but I couldn't hear what he was saying on account of The Radio Dept. crooning in my ears. I pulled a single headphone out.

"Need a hand?" he repeated himself.

"I'm good, thank you," I responded, while he was still getting the words out.

"You sure? It looks heavy."

"I need the exercise," I said bluntly, turning to power up the stairs.

Arriving into the bright sunlight, a wave of fresh air settled over my sticky skin. It felt like freedom, made even more special by the sight of the Chrysler Building peeking through others in the distance. I knew how lame it was to be impressed by it, but I didn't care.

Everywhere I looked, people were rushing to take care of seemingly Earth-ending affairs, zipping through cars and cross-walks with laser precision. Adjacent to me, guys my age were playing football in a park, their obnoxious taunts toward one another rising above the city's hum and its cacophony of honks and sirens.

I understood how Manhattan could be too much for some, but to me it was exhilarating. As if its chaotic energy were conta-gious, positively charging every ion in my body.

"Can I get your number?" the guy from the train asked, appearing behind me. "I can help you with your cardio." He grinned, clearly proud of his extraordinarily skeezy one liner.

"No, I'm good," I said. "I prefer to work out alone."

His face lit up. *Ugh*. He thought I was flirting.

"Truth is… I'm not allowed to date. On account of my probation agreement. Ya stab one guy and they wanna punish you forever," I said, with a deadpan expression on my face.

The look on his was priceless.

"You're…" he laughed uncomfortably. "Joking, right?"

"*I wish*. You can search me if you like. Amy-Beth Martin," I said, challenging him. *I mean, why not? I had the time.*

He looked at me and then to his phone.

"It's fine, I don't mind. The price of fame. Or is it… infamy?" I mused aloud with faux wonder. He opened his phone and typed in the search bar. As he scrolled through article after article of '*Child Accused of Stabbing Man Seventeen Times,*' I took my cue to leave, crossing the intersection before he had a chance to look back up. The left wheel of my suitcase, however, had other ideas, flinging off its axle as I pulled it up onto the sidewalk. Dragging the overstuffed canvas rectangle another two blocks was the icing on the cake I did not need.

Anderson Preparatory's building took up half a block in the Lower East Side. The 22-story tower included an aquatic center, a library, a full gymnasium (joy), three floors of student housing, and, of course, a ballroom—*because what high school doesn't need one?* Its history stretched back to the 1700s, boasting notable alumni that included famous politicians, authors, businesspeople, and celebrities. However, with yearly tuition and accommodation totaling almost $100,000, the luxury of attending was reserved for very few. That is, unless you were a charity case, like me.

I was attempting to drag my suitcase through the aggressively heavy glass door when I heard the guy from the train.

"Let me help you with that!"

"Wow, you really wanna get stabbed, don't you?" I said, turning around, ready to explode.

To my surprise, it wasn't the world's most annoying man, but a Brad Pitt lookalike, minus 40 years. He stood holding a bicycle over his shoulder, his sweat-soaked-shirt revealing a body so defined it didn't look real.

He backed up. "Uh, sorry... just thought you could use some help?"

"Oh," I said. At least I was succinct. "Wrong, umm... you go here?"

He was so handsome I couldn't look directly at him.

"As of yesterday," he said, pulling out a student ID as proof.

"I'm not actually psychotic. There was a guy on the train."

"Guys on the train are the worst," he teased.

"You're not from here." There was a Southern drawl to the way he said 'guys.'

"Alabama."

"Ah, old money," I said like I'd figured it out.

He laughed. "No. No money. I'm on scholarship."

"Oh," I said. Again. He was still holding his bike, and I was still blocking the door. "Sorry, did you wanna get by?"

"Sure, but I could also, ya know, help you?"

"Why, do I look feeble or something?" I probably did, but I wanted to hear him say it. Instead, he looked away, abashed.

"Not at all. Just tryna help out. My momma always said, if you can help someone out, you should."

I looked him up and down, trying to figure out what his angle was.

"So, he's a gentleman... I've read about those. Fine, you can help me with my bag. But only because my upper body seems to have gone on strike. And, perhaps most importantly, because it seems to be stuck under the door."

His expression brightened as he pulled it free with one tug. Before I knew it, we were climbing the arduous 86 steps to the girls' dorm. I was thankful I let him carry it; I was perspiring enough as it was.

"We're not supposed to go in. Boys, that is," he said, stopping abruptly outside the door.

"We're still doing the gender thing, then?"

"Apparently."

"Well. Thanks for your help."

"Anytime. Seriously, whenever you need it." There was something clumsy about him that made his attractiveness more tolerable. "Maybe we could hang out some time? Get food or something?"

"Huh?" I asked. Out loud. "Why?"

"Some people find the process of absorbing nutrients to be beneficial."

"Oh, right... I think I saw a TED Talk on it once."

He looked at me earnestly, waiting for an answer like he'd never experienced rejection before.

I couldn't help but be distrustful. *Who was this guy and why was he so sweet and so... sincere?* "I'm gonna have to get back to you on that. It's been a long..." I looked down to my phone to check the time. "Wow, it's still morning."

"Yeah, of course. Sorry. I'll leave you to it," he said unaffected, disappearing around the corner while I tried to figure out how anyone who looked like that could be interested in me. Perhaps I was already the target of a make-over bet. Or perhaps I'd just watched too many 90s movies.

The common room of the girls' dorm was clinically beige. Grey couches with lime-green cushions (*why?*), surrounded by black and white pictures of flowers. It smelled like artificial vanilla and microwaved food. I waved hello to two girls who were watching TV, as I followed a sign toward my assigned room: 13.

I took a moment to mentally prepared myself. I'd been dreading meeting my roommate as soon as I found out I'd be sharing a room. There was just too much potential for it to go wrong and, where I was concerned, it had been my experience things generally go wrong.

My plan was to be polite, but not overly friendly. I wanted to set a boundary that BFF wasn't in my vocabulary, that I required space from society in order to function amongst it. But as I opened the door I was almost bowled over by a girl hugging me. Worse, it felt like she meant it.

"I'm Delilah! You must be Eva!" She was warm, maybe even authentic.

"And you're a hugger," I said without thinking.

Luckily, she found it funny. I just hoped she wasn't laughing at me.

"Oh good, we're gonna get along. Thank God!" she said, walking back over to a wall collage she was making out of Polaroid photos. "I'm new, too. Got in last night. Hope you don't mind, I snagged the bed closest to the door?"

Her dark skin and high cheekbones framed intensely-green eyes that were impossible to look away from. "No. The window's great," I said, kicking my suitcase over to the far bunk bed, which had a desk underneath it.

"You're from Louisiana?" I asked, unzipping my bag and throwing my clothes into the drawers.

"New Orleans. How'd you know?"

"MSY bag tags," I said, pointing out her suitcase in the corner.

"Woah, you scared me! I thought you could tell by my accent. I wanna be an actress, so that would *not be good*."

"An actress? Cool."

"Yeah. Or a lawyer, whichever comes first. What about you?"

I was nervous to say it out loud. Perhaps in case she shut it down.

"Oh, um, a journalist. I know print's dead and everything, but I—"

"No, you'll be a great journalist. You're so quick, like with the tags."

"It's probably got more to do with my inability to let things go, but thanks, I'll take—"

Delilah picked up a Polaroid camera and took a picture of me to add to the wall. I knew I was going to look shell-shockingly bad, but I pretended not to care as I waited for it to develop in front of me.

As she began hanging string lights across the room, I took the opportunity to take in the other photos. There were multiples of a stunning Asian-American girl who dressed too well not to work in fashion.

"My girlfriend," said Delilah, as she caught me looking at a photo of them together. "Well, I think... That's not going to be weird for you, is it?" she asked in a way that implied if it were, I was rightfully the problem.

"No, I dislike everyone equally," I joked. "But wait, you only *think* she's your girlfriend?"

She threw her waist-length braids from one side to the other, with a dramatic exhale. "*Well...* She just started at college and asked for 'space,' also known as seeing if there's anyone better out there. Good luck to her. I'm a ten plus." I couldn't believe her confidence, or her openness. Seventeen years of living in a small town had conditioned me to feel like a freak for listening to Bowie, instead of Bieber. Five minutes with Delilah and I felt basic.

A text tone beeped, temporarily distracting her.

While she looked at her phone, I pulled out mine to answer the three texts and two missed calls from my grandparents.

> In my room safe, already unpacking. Love you x

"So, you met Dylan...?"

"Who?"

"The Calvin Klein-looking model *from Alabama*," she said the last part extra-Southern.

"Is that his name?" I'd never asked.

"Yeah, he texted wanting to know if my roommate just arrived with a blue suitcase." We both looked toward my blue suitcase.

"Guess we have no choice but to confirm it," I said, as she texted back. Three dings immediately followed, prompting Delilah to let out a belly laugh.

"What?" I asked, feeling self-conscious.

"He likes you."

"Why?" I blurted out. "Not to bet against myself or anything, but I really don't—"

"Okay, I'm going to slap you."

"No, I mean... I was kinda rude to him, not to mention sweaty. I'm not sure I trust someone who'd still be into me after that."

"First of all, who hurt you? Secondly, your version of rude is definitely cute." I wanted to be offended, but I knew she meant it as a compliment.

"Eh... I don't know."

"Look, I only met the guy yesterday on the shuttle from the airport, but he seems nice enough. Definitely not like the other snobs who go here."

"You met some already?" I asked in a hushed tone.

"At the library. Let's just say, they put the P in privileged."

"*Great.*"

She lifted her phone to ask how she should reply. "So?"

"What if it goes bad? I really don't wanna make this year any more brutal than it has to be."

"Alright," she said. "But just be prepared, he's probably gonna ask you out again."

"I honestly doubt that."

"No, he will," she cackled. "He already texted he would."

We chatted a little more before I decided to explore the kitchen and bathrooms. After all, I was happy with how I'd performed; I didn't want to ruin it by continuing to speak. A rare feat for someone who struggles to control her mouth around new people. Sure, I didn't establish the boundary I had in mind, but I'd take a friend over an enemy any day.

THE AFTERNOON PASSED as I wandered the school, meeting two other boarders in the common room on my return: Daniela from Mexico City and Yun from Shanghai. They seemed nice enough, if not completely unbothered to make friends. I had to admire their resolve.

As the light began to fade, casting a golden hue through the hallway, I found vertical windows that opened up onto a fire escape. Remembering I had my grandma's letter in my jacket pocket, I tried to investigate whether it was structurally sound enough to hold my weight while I read it.

The window opened easily (an excellent feature in an emergency exit), so I considered it my invitation to step out. Hesitantly, I crawled across the metal landing that was covered in decades worth of grime, finding a spot that perfectly framed the Manhattan Bridge.

The sight of my grandma's handwriting alone made my heart sink. It wasn't so much that I missed her already, but rather the thought that she might be missing me.

As I unfolded the lilac stationery, three hundred-dollar bills fell into my lap—no doubt from her personal 'rainy day' stash. Including what my granddad had given me, and my savings, I had enough money to get through to the end of the year without having to get a part-time job. It was the difference between throwing myself into studying or slaving away over a coffee machine, and I appreciated it wholeheartedly. My eyes started to glisten before I'd even read the first line.

My dearest Eva,
I wanted to write as I knew I wouldn't be

able to say everything I needed to say before you left. This is such a wonderful time for you… Your grandfather and I couldn't be more proud. I know you'll worry about us because your heart and thoughtfulness are so much bigger than you'll ever admit, but I want you to know that we'll be just fine. I will miss you, of course, but every time I do, I'll be reassured knowing that you're out in the world doing exactly what you're meant to be doing. I know life hasn't always been kind, and I know we haven't always been able to give you everything you need or deserve, but our love for you is beyond measure. You are a gift, and have been the brightest light on our darkest of days. Now it is your time to shine, my sweet girl. The world is yours, and everything in it. You have your mother's beauty and fierce tenacity, and your father's all-consuming heart. Never, ever, forget that. Let them guide you, for they are always watching. We love you, Eva.

Your proud and adoring,

Grandma

Tears trickled down my cheeks, as I looked up into the dusk sky. I could just make out a handful of stars that had broken through the smog of the city.

I knew better than to depend on dreams. If life had taught me anything, it was that as comforting as they may be, it was impossible to live inside them forever. When you wish and pray, plead and scream, for things that never materialize, giving up on hope isn't a choice. It's just something that happens. But as I sat there with my grandma's words fresh in my mind, I realized that for the first time in a long time, I actually wanted to believe. I wanted to hope. I wanted to get swept up in the excitement of the unknown, instead of anxiously dreading the bad before it arrived.

Maybe it was my time? Maybe the rejection, and the loneliness, and all the horrible things people had thrown my way over the years had happened for a reason. Maybe, things really were about to change... It almost felt too big to even consider. Almost.

THREE

SWEET HOME ALABAMA

Armed with lukewarm coffee and a half-eaten bagel, I walked so fast to my first day of classes that I almost started skipping. Thankfully, I caught sight of myself in a glass door and snapped myself out of it. Just because I was excited didn't mean I needed to act like one of *those* people. Besides, I already looked ridiculous in the Anderson Prep uniform, potentially the worst ghost outfit of all time: a tartan skirt, collared shirt, tie and a blazer. It was all of fashion's least desirable elements wrapped up in a four-hundred-dollar price tag... or just under one fifty if you got it secondhand on eBay, like my gran did. Aside from the tacky rhinestones I had to pick off from the previous owner, it appeared barely worn.

"Come in!" sang out a man's voice, which I assumed to be Mr. McKenzie's. He was the head of the Language Arts Department, ex-*San Francisco Chronicle* journalist, and the reason I'd been given my scholarship.

He sat behind a solid wooden desk that took up most of his office, surrounded by floor-to-ceiling books. The leather-bound kind, that I'd only ever seen in movies.

"Hi, I'm—"

"...'For us statistics trapped below the poverty line in small town America, *living is no longer the struggle. Existing is.*'" He looked up through his glasses with a trained smile, his sandy-blond hair making him appear younger than the fifty-year milestone I knew he was approaching. "Your words, Miss Nelson?"

"Yes," I confirmed, somewhat proud. I was still confused that he'd picked my essay out of everyone who'd applied for the Language Arts scholarship, but I was trying to let myself have it for once.

He looked back down at the folder he'd been reading from.

"I was just going over your file. Eight classes. That's a hefty workload."

"I think I can handle it."

"Especially for someone coming from the public school system. Your electives are Advanced Journalism and Media Studies. You're set on journalism, then?"

Huh? Of course I was. That's the whole reason I was there. My stomach began to sink, as if it had known the whole time it was too good to be true.

"Uh... yeah, that was the plan."

He grinned again in a way that was starting to feel patronizing.

"Why?" he asked. Striking fear into my chest. I wasn't prepared for an interrogation.

"Well... I've wanted to be a journalist for as long as I can remember. There was always something about reading the newspaper. Like it was a gateway to the world."

"If you want to see the world, be a flight attendant."

"Well, it's more than that... *obviously*. It's about the news. It's about the facts."

"The facts?" he mused, clearly growing more unimpressed by the second.

"No. It's..." my voice was getting louder and I wasn't sure I was going to be able to keep it in check much longer. "It's about being in the dark. About not knowing things. *About unanswered questions that keep you awake at night.* I've felt them my whole life. Gnawing at me, *taunting me,* and if I can prevent other people from having to feel that way, then that's what I want to do. I wanna search out the news, present it to the public. No matter how hard, or how tough the truth might be." I was breathing in too much air, or perhaps not enough. I tried to compose myself, wiping the moisture that was appearing on my palms against my skirt.

"That," he said, pointing at me pompously. As if he were giving me a gift. "That we can work with."

"Thank God, there's something," I said more sarcastically than intended. I motioned for the door, but apparently, he wasn't finished.

"One more thing before you go," he said, taking off his glasses to clean the lenses. I couldn't tell if they were dirty, or if it were just part of the show. "I know you were hoping to be part of the school paper—"

"Yes. I need a published article for my college—"

"Sadly, all the positions were assigned at the end of last year. The editor, Annabel Monteith, has full discretion over features though, perhaps you can submit something to her."

"Oh, okay," I said. Even if it didn't feel like it was. Any misconceptions I had that he was going to be on my team were quickly dissipating.

"You have all the *potential* in the world to succeed here, Eva. It's up to you if you do."

The way he said 'potential' made it sound like a poor people's disease. Internally, I rolled my eyes. Externally, I smiled.

"That's... wow. Thank you."

"Don't mention it," he replied. "Unless of course it's in an acceptance speech."

Fortunately, his phone rang and he excused himself to take it.

I gestured that I was heading out, thrilled at the prospect of my getaway until I remembered that he was also teaching my first class. I just hoped that his ego matched his effectiveness as a teacher.

Subbing my blazer, I pulled a hoodie over my head to keep out unwanted attention, which meant any and all. It wasn't that I hated small talk, it was that I was allergic to it. My body couldn't process it, much like wheat to a celiac's stomach. Mercifully, no one attempted contact, and I made it to a seat in the back corner out of McKenzie's line of sight.

He entered the classroom like a pop star arriving to a meet and greet.

"Hello, hello. I'm Mr. McKenzie, and this is Advanced Journalism. If you are not here to *advance* your journalism, now would be a great time to use the door. It's located to my left." He chuckled, as if to signal he was making a joke. I knew better.

He unstacked his books and walked around from behind the table to sit on it, hamming up his approachable vibe.

"You all know what journalism is by this point. I'm not here to go over the basics or hold your hand. This is an AP class, so I expect you to know how to present facts and find credible, well-researched sources." I could have sworn that he looked at me when he said that last part, but I was willing to overlook it on account of the fact that it might have been my cunning insecurity.

"I'm not interested in correcting grammar or sentence structure. If you're incapable of constructing active sentences, then this class is most certainly not for you." The room collectively gulped. "I am, however, here to make you the best writers you can possibly be, to take you from students to journalists. A primate could write a top-down news article, but writing for the news is so much more than that. So let's kick things off with a simple question. What makes a good news story?"

A girl in the second row, mousey but serious, raised her hand.

"It should be new. New information, or a new take on old information," she said with an assuredness that gave the impression she was stating fact, rather than answering a question.

"Good, Annabel. Example?" He pointed to a guy with jet-black hair, who looked immediately flustered, but my attention was fixated on Annabel. The editor of the school newspaper. There wasn't much I could tell about her from the back of her head, but from how tight her pony was scraped back, she appeared to be a very serious individual.

"Uh, well... new information would be if... contaminants were found in a city's water supply. A new take would be if someone proved that those contaminants were good for you," the guy said, seeming more and more sure of his answer with every word.

"Sure. What else?"

"Good news satisfies multiple elements of newsworthiness, such as impact, conflict and interest," said a guy in my row. I was keeping up, but the intellectual volleyball was making me dizzy. Not to mention stirring the lingering feeling that I had no business being there.

"Absolutely. Example?" said Mr. McKenzie. This time I was almost certain he was looking at me. I turned around to check. "Yes, Miss Nelson. You."

Could he smell fear? I wanted to die. Or evaporate. Whichever was quicker. My cheeks flushed as I threw out the first answer that popped into my head.

"Impact would be if the containments in the water supply affected the entire country... and conflict would be if they posed a serious health risk. If a public figure or a 100-year-old man died because of it, that would satisfy interest."

"Good." He winked.

I could have burst out of sheer elation, until I realized that was probably his intent.

"But... good isn't great, is it?"

I thought he was still addressing me and I nearly had a coronary, but before I could pass out, he turned to the rest of the class and said, "Who can tell me what makes a story *great*?"

Silence, as the professor looked around the room.

"Prominence? The first or the most or the best," said Annabel, as if growing unsure of herself.

"Prominence is only part of it. You're still thinking on a macro level. How are you going to get your reader to buy into this? What's at stake for Mary-Jo Baker in Oak Grove, Missouri, with her high school education? Why's she going to care about contaminants in the water supply? Does she even know what contaminants are?"

Students began writing hurriedly, so I joined them, but I rejected his 'common folk' analogy in my core.

"What's the image you're creating? What does it feel like? Can you touch it? That's how we get Mary interested. Not just by telling her about the contaminants, but by having her experience them on a level anyone can understand, through depth and color."

I wanted to raise my hand and ask whether respect for the reader was optional. I've never been able to understand intellectual elites who view the working class as beneath them but are more than happy to profit off their backs. I continued to take notes, but my heart wasn't in it. 'Mary-Jo Baker' was my grandma, and the money she spent on her newspaper subscription was the reason people like McKenzie had a job.

The remainder of the class played out in the same vein—important information that I needed to pass, hidden within layers of ego and classist superiority. But, like a good girl, I put a smile on my face and listened with attentiveness. Reminding myself that whether it was fair or not, society rewards those who are educated.

Our first assignment was to write an ethnographic article on a significant New York City location. I had to Google it to figure out it was just a stupidly long scientific term for people watching. *Literally*. I had two weeks to do it and I already felt like I was behind.

Annabel was one of the first out of the room, presumably to get a front row seat in her next class. I managed to catch up with her in the hallway, as she swapped textbooks in her locker.

"Hey, do you have a second?" I asked, my head bowed like I was approaching a bear.

"Not really," she said, rummaging around in her bag. She looked up to see me. "Oh. Sorry. You're one of the new girls, right?"

Her stare was robotic. "Uh, yeah. I'm Eva."

"The journalist."

"Well, wannabe."

Damnit, Eva. Just say yes.

"Yes."

She nodded. "Nice. I'm thinking about it, too… if I don't do international relations or biomedical engineering."

"Cool," I said, stuck for something insightful to say. I felt dumber just having heard the sentence.

She shut her locker. "Was there something you needed?"

"Oh, yeah. *The Anderson Advocate*. I was hoping to write for it."

"I'm sorry. All the positions have been filled."

"McKenzie said I could maybe submit a feature?"

She started walking, so I followed her.

"Sure, you can submit anything you like. If we have the space, we'll publish it."

Her words were friendly; her tone not so much. "Are there any topics you're particularly interested in?"

"Whatever works!" she sang out, walking into a classroom. "Nice to meet you!"

"It was a treat," I said, knowing full-well she couldn't hear me through the door that had already closed.

I remained in a state between dazed and resentful for the rest of the day, each hour deepening my sense of inadequacy until it peaked in AP Chemistry. I'd anticipated it being a challenge—I'd only taken it to prove to colleges that I wasn't a lightweight—but it was like trying to dissect a foreign language. I skipped lunch to catch up on what I'd missed, but by 5 P.M. all I could think about was food. So I grabbed a bowl of cereal and made the awful decision to climb into bed to eat it.

The setting sun streamed in through my window, as it dipped behind the buildings downtown. It felt so warm and cozy against my skin I had to close my eyes for a moment. To rest them before all the intense homework I was about to do. Or so I told myself.

Two hours later I woke up in pitch darkness, drool seeping from the corner of my mouth. My phone was ringing from an unsaved number, so I let it ring out. As I fumbled to look up the 504 area code, a text from Delilah came through.

It's D! Did you eat?

Not yet. Fell asleep

Hurry. They stop serving in 15

I jumped out of bed and threw on the lights to assess the trainwreck that was my face, when another text came through.

ps. Dylan's here

He's excited to see you haha

In my own personal protest, I gave up trying to look good, throwing on sneakers and heading downstairs in my drool-stained hoodie and jeans. I didn't even bother adjusting the ridiculously lopsided ponytail I was sporting.

. . .

THE CAFETERIA WAS PROBABLY the most relatable thing about Anderson. Like every school in America, it smelled like boiled broccoli and bleach. Rows of long wooden tables occupied most of the room, while serving stations lined the far wall, leading to the kitchen. The lights of the city twinkled through large windows, that at the right angle revealed the East River.

Dylan stood up as I entered, as if to greet me, but Delilah interjected. "Get food before they take it away," she said, gesturing toward it. The three of us were the only ones there.

I grabbed a plate of what looked like congealed spaghetti and two desserts—Jell-O (dependable) and strawberry shortcake (high risk, high reward)—and returned to the table.

Dylan got up again as I approached.

"Hey. Hi. How's it going?"

Delilah laughed at his awkwardness. I managed to refrain.

"It's good," I said, sitting down. Then I remembered it wasn't. "Wait, what am I talking about? I had the worst day. This place is..."

"*A lot*," Delilah added.

"Yeah, that's an understatement," I agreed. "Like is it possible to be failing before we've even been tested?"

"You better believe they're testing us," she said. "Every one of my teachers reminded me that if my GPA falls below 3.8, I'll lose my scholars—"

"Same—" said Dylan.

"Wait, we're all on scholarships?" I asked.

"We both are," he said.

"And so am I. How many do they give out?"

"A handful, but only to seniors," said Delilah. "It's so transparent. It's like you wanna brag about giving a free education to people who need it, but you'll only expose the paying students to them for a year."

"Never thought of it like that," said Dylan, crestfallen.

"We still earned our place here," she continued. "We got the grades, and we did the work."

"Exactly," I joined in. "Maybe they didn't wanna bring us in before SATs were done in case our scores were higher?" I was shocking myself with my optimism.

"Most of my med-school competition all have the same SATs at this point anyway," said Dylan.

I sliced through the slab of spaghetti on my plate. If the texture hadn't ruined my appetite, the topic of conversation was starting to.

He could tell. "Was there anything good about your first day?" He asked, hopeful, like I could turn things around.

I racked my brain, wanting to give him something. Even if it were just a crumb. "For a brief moment I thought my mentor might actually *like* my writing?"

"I'm sure he did!" he beamed. I felt myself mirror it.

Delilah must have caught it because she stood up.

"Meeting Katie for coffee," she said. "I should get ready. Tell them I'm in the bathroom with cramps if I'm not back before checks."

"Have fun," said Dylan.

I looked at her to say; *I know what you're doing, stop it.*

"No, really I'm meeting her at eight," she said, laughing as she left.

Dylan was oblivious.

"I should go study in a second," I said, establishing my exit.

"For sure." He was so earnest it was unnerving.

I took a scoop of both desserts, mixing them together as I chewed.

Dylan picked up a piece of leftover bread, putting it in his mouth.

"Hey, look," he said. "We're eating. Together."

"So?"

"So it's kinda like we're on a date."

"Except we're not," I said. "That would require my consent, which I'm a pretty big fan of." I was making a joke, but with about ten percent sincerity.

"Me, too," he declared. "Huge fan of consent. *No is a complete sentence.*"

He looked at me amazed. I couldn't figure out why he seemed so interested in me, or why I was acting so mean toward him, but nevertheless, I persevered. "What's your deal? You're too handsome to be this unassured."

The crystal blue of his eyes lit up. "You think I'm handsome?"

"That's what you got from that?" I quipped, which only seemed to make his grin grow bigger. "It was less of an admission. More just stating a fact," I added. "If we did a straw poll of seniors, four out of five would agree that you're good-looking."

"Only four?"

"You gotta factor in the homophobes who'd vote no because they think admitting another man is attractive means they're gay."

He laughed, continuing to stare at me with hypnotic fascination.

"What?" I asked. "Does every girl just throw themselves at you or something, and I'm like interesting 'cause I don't?"

He was sheepish. "No... you're... interesting cause you ask questions like that, and because you make me think about questions like that. If you really want to know." He wasn't backing down and I had to respect his courage. "I just think you're cool."

"I assure you, once you get over the semi-witty one liners, there really isn't much else."

"I'll be the judge of that," he said. "If that's okay with you?"

"Are you asking me out?" I teased.

"Yeah, I guess?" he said, completely unsure. "Eva, you wanna get dinner with me?"

"Sure," I said.

"*Outside* of the cafeteria?" he clarified.

He was onto me, I had to nod yes. *Or maybe, I wanted to.*
"Sure, Dylan. I'll go out with you."

I sounded reluctant (by design), but the truth was I'd be lying if I didn't admit to having been a little intrigued. Perhaps the all-American country boy was finally making a resurgence?

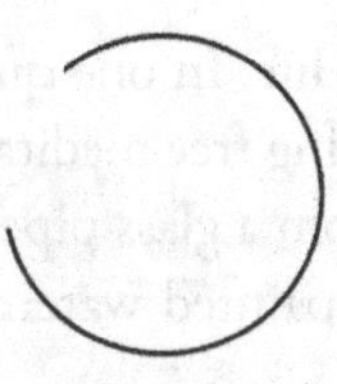

FOUR
LOVEFOOL

The best part about Anderson was being able to take study hall off-campus. The first chance I got, I raced out to Washington Square Park. Arguably my favorite place in Manhattan.

Clusters of green and gold leaves hung over the curb of Waverley Place, camouflaging the urban sanctuary from the twenty-plus story buildings that surrounded it.

It was known for hosting some of the city's most prominent protests, including the women's suffrage movement and the borough's first ever labor marches. The park also served as a stomping ground for notable figures such as Mark Twain, Henry James and Buddy Holly—plus, I was almost certain, some incredibly talented women whom history had classically excluded. As I walked past the sprawling fountain, framed by a seventy-foot marble arch dedicated to the first president of the United States, I wondered what my place would be among its many visitors. If my presence would register even a drop.

The smell of incense and chlorine, carried by the humid breeze, dizzied my senses as people crisscrossed around me. There was more life in the half-block loop than I'd seen anywhere in the city. Perhaps anywhere in life. In one quick scan, I could see a girl and a guy in sarongs offering free meditation classes, a man hiding in the bushes smoking from a glass pipe, and a woman in a pirate outfit dancing while she painted watercolors on scraps of parchment. It felt electric.

Motivation hit hard, so I took a seat under a giant elm and started taking notes for my ethnography assignment. Shorthand descriptions for the things I was seeing and ideas on how to develop them into the article I needed for class. As I was scribbling, glancing between my notebook and my surroundings, I realized that not a single person was looking at me. Not one. It was a visible departure from Spring City, where I always felt like 'that girl,' and not in a good way. There was something freeing about feeling invisible. Something promising even, to know that I could fail and no one would care but me. I closed my eyes at the thought, letting the last of the summer sun wash over me, basking in the tinkling of keys being played on a piano to my left.

When an unfamiliar peace settled over my body.

I felt... light.

Dreamy, even.

That's why when I saw him, I couldn't be sure if he were real.

It didn't help that time seemed to be standing still, suspended in a sticky state of limbo.

I blinked hard. Trying to force my irises to adjust to the brightness of the day.

As colors morphed back into their rightful place, so, too, did my sense of reality.

He wasn't an illusion. He was, in fact, real. Sitting on a bench opposite me that had previously been vacant. Pieces of dark hair kept falling onto his tanned, olive skin as he read from a ragged book. He looked to be around my age, maybe a year or two older.

I was transfixed. In awe. Not just at his beauty, but at the enigma of who he was. I tried to make out the name of the book he was reading, to piece together any kind of clue to who he might be, but the language seemed foreign. Sunshine bounced off his high cheekbones as he took an unlit cigarette from behind his ear, then held it to his mouth.

Overtaken by whatever haze I was in, I felt myself almost get up to approach him, when the man I'd seen in the bushes sat down in the middle of the pathway that separated us. He was talking to himself as he inhaled again from a lit pipe. Almost immediately, he began coughing loudly.

"Damn! No one can take a hit like me!" he screamed. "No one!"

His laugh was maniacal, and even though he was no longer covered by shrubs, as I'd first seen him, he was acting as if he still were—peering around, then retreating behind thin air. It would have been comical were I not worried for his mental health.

Apparently I wasn't the only one concerned; the mystery guy was also keeping watch, glancing up between sentences with empathetic eyes.

"I'm the champion!" shouted the shoeless man, before breaking down into a fit of sobs. "I don't wanna anymore. Don't make me, I don't wanna," he cried.

He was beginning to attract more attention, including that of two NYPD officers standing guard near the arch, who began walking in our direction.

"Please! Please! Make it stop!" the man begged. He was banging his fists on his head, growing more and more violent.

I wanted to do something—what, I wasn't sure—but before I could, the guy from the bench stood up, walked over, and pulled the man's arms away from his face.

Surprisingly, he didn't fight back.

His arms fell limp, as if he'd been instantly pacified by whatever the guy had to say. Gratitude spread across the man's face as he accepted the folded bills being offered to him.

Pocketing the money, he stood up and quietly exited the park, seconds before the police arrived.

As I tried to make sense of it, the guy collected his iced coffee and book and began to head west out of the park. It happened so quickly, I barely registered that I'd gotten up to chase after him.

It took me a block, but I caught up to him on Washington Place.

"Hey!" I shouted. To no response or reaction.

"Umm, hi! Sorry to bother you," I said, increasing my pace. I didn't know what I was doing, but there was a feeling of urgency running through my body that felt impossible to ignore.

"Hello? Sir?" I was within arm's reach; *he had to know I was addressing him*. "Okay, I know you can hear me on account of the fact that I'm making sound and you've got nothing covering your—" As soon as the words came out, I regretted them. Barring the plethora of legitimate personal reasons he had for ignoring me, I was also assuming his ableness. I was just about to turn back when he stopped walking so abruptly that I almost ran into him.

As he turned to face me, it felt like my heart had forgotten how to beat.

I wanted to speak but my mouth refused to form words.

I just stood there, staring at him like a robot whose power had been cut, increasingly aware that with every passing second, I was making myself seem even weirder. I wanted to run away, but it was as if something were holding me to the spot, magnetizing me to him.

"Can I help you with something?" he asked, his face unread-able. His voice was deeper and huskier than I'd imagined. Wiser somehow.

"Umm..." was all I could get out. My brain had given up, and I couldn't remember why I'd raced after him in the first place. If I had a valid reason to begin with. I had to admit, at least to myself, that maybe I just *didn't want him to leave.*

Self-doubt had almost enveloped me when I remembered the man.

"The man! What happened with the man?" I asked, too enthusiastically.

Up close, his eyes were the nearest thing to enchanting I'd ever seen. They were a sweet caramel-brown that grew slightly darker the farther they radiated out. A defined black line circled his iris, framing a chasm I felt myself falling into.

Had he not blinked, I might have stayed in them forever.

"He was having some sort of episode," I said, trying to recover. "You talked to him, and he just... he was calm. What did you say?"

"You chased me down to ask me that?" he asked with a smirk. I couldn't figure out if he were flirting, or trying to distract me.

"Yes, actually. I did," I said, snapping into business. Well, faux-business. "I'm a journalist and I—"

He bristled, visibly uncomfortable. I could tell I was losing him.

"Or, more like I want to be a journalist. Someday. And I was just... I am... intrigued by you." I wanted to edit the last part, but I'd already spoken it aloud.

He searched my eyes with such probing confrontation I had no choice but to look away for fear I might get lost in them again.

"I gave him some money," he said, his tone gaslighting me into feeling stupid. "He's probably gone to score."

"No," I said, with mounting courage. "You said something to him *first*, then you gave him the money. It was what you said that calmed him down, not the money."

When he smiled, I almost felt my knees buckle.

"You don't miss much, do you? What's your name?"

"Eva. Eva Nelson," I said, almost physically stumbling. "And you?"

"Well, Eva... off the record, of course, I reminded him that he was already on a rollercoaster, so he may as well enjoy the ride." There was an air of mischief to his voice that made it sound like it was a lesson he'd learned firsthand.

"That's it?" I prodded without hiding my suspicion.

"The guy was having a bad trip," he said with finality.

"Sure. Yeah," I said, actually considering what he had said. The realization that I'd run after a stranger to give them the third-degree was setting in. My face flushed so hot it felt as if my skin was about to peel off.

"Well, that was a really, umm... a really nice thing to do," I said, wanting to disappear.

"Sure," he said, breaking eye contact with me. "If there's nothing else, I've gotta get to work."

"Where do you work?" I asked reflexively. "I mean, sorry. There's nothing else. Thank you. Sorry."

He nodded, and without so much as a goodbye, turned around and walked away.

I, on the other hand, stood there in shock, afraid to move a muscle for fear I might further damage my ego. Instead, my brain involuntarily replayed every second in a jumbled fog. I couldn't fathom how any single interaction could go *that wrong*, especially one I'd been present for.

By the time I finally managed to mentally and physically unstick myself and walk the five blocks back to school, I'd decided that it wasn't so much a single nail in the coffin, but rather many, many tiny ones that had contributed to my demise.

Delilah was sitting at her desk, busily typing away on her laptop when I zombie-walked into our room and face-planted on the mattress.

"Hold up," she said. "I'm supposed to be the dramatic one."

"Help," I whined.

"For real, or are you just committing to the bit?"

"I made the biggest fool out of myself in front of the hottest guy alive."

"So, the latter," she said, holding back a laugh.

"No," I said through gritted teeth into my pillow. "You didn't see him. He was *perfect*."

"Pull yourself together. No one's that hot," she said, with such certainty that it made me temporarily doubt my memory.

"No," I said. "This guy *was*." I sat up, trying to pull myself out of the tantrum. "I'm fine, I'm just embarrassed. And whatever, it's not like I know him, or will ever have to see him again." As the words left my mouth, I felt strangely sad.

Delilah must have sensed it because she sat down on the bed next to me. "Wanna talk about it?"

"I didn't know people could be like that," I said, as though I needed permission to say what I'd been trying to verbalize. "Like, actually magnetic, not just in the hyperbolic sense." I couldn't believe how pathetic I sounded, but I'd never been so drawn to someone before.

"Energy's a real thing," she said, like it was a universally accepted fact. "Anyway, I'm sure you weren't anywhere near as bad as you think you were. You have a certain charm."

"I do?" I asked, hopeful, willing to believe anything to quell the negative thoughts that were having a dance party in my head.

"It's not my personal taste, but I can see why it drives a lot of people crazy," she said with a cheeky grin.

"Well, lemme tell ya, it's been my personal experience that is *absolutely untrue*."

Delilah laughed. "Wanna go sit in the sun and buy food we can't afford?"

Part of me wanted to. To drown out the unfavorable memories in overpriced calories, but the thought of being in public and having to form sentences felt like too much.

"No. I can't," I said. "I need to evade the world for a minute, bury myself in these..." I lifted up my textbooks.

"Alright," she said. "You do you, but if you dig too deep, holler and I'll throw a ladder down. Or some chocolate."

"Thank you. I may very well need that."

. . .

It was a full week before I saw him again. Seven long days of non-stop homework and tests. Not that I was keeping track, or hanging out in Washington Square Park unnecessarily every chance I got, or anything.

In my defense, I did finish two assignments long before they were due. In my offense, it was the trade-off I gave myself: I could sit there and be a borderline stalker, but I had to write; otherwise, I would be an actual stalker.

I'd turned the papers in before I left for the park, or rather, uploaded them through the school's submissions website that scans it for plagiarism. Not that I'd ever cheat—the knowledge would haunt me forever—but I couldn't shake the low-level anxiety that I'd subconsciously copied someone else's work.

Walking through the shade of the towering sycamore trees that guard the southeast entrance of the park, I realized it already felt like a second home.

It was strange to be so comfortable amongst such chaos. There was no denying that it was a circus: constant yelling, music, chanting and—of course—protesting, in every form and fashion. But somehow it calmed me, grounding me in the best possible way.

It was around four in the afternoon when he entered the park and sat on the same bench, a black iced coffee in hand. He had a leather jacket on, so I couldn't see the definition of his arms like last time, but somehow he was better looking, especially against the crisp white of the partially unbuttoned shirt he was wearing.

He was further through his novel, and this time, I was close enough to make out part of the title: *Odes*. I searched it on my phone, and found the winner: *Horace: The Odes*. I didn't speak Latin (*who did?*) but the internet told me it was a collection of exceptionally old poems. I was busy trying to decide if I really wanted to lie about having read it just so I could talk to him, when my legs made the choice for me.

As if compelled by an invisible force, I stood up and walked over to where he was sitting. My heart racing so fast, it felt as though the beats were colliding into one.

He was more beautiful than I remembered. Dazzling, even. Like my brain had blocked some of it out as a measure of self-preservation. He was softly biting the nail of his middle finger as his eyes flicked from left to right. I sat down next to him, losing my breath slightly, as I spoke.

"Good book?" I asked.

He didn't respond and I thought he was going to ignore me like he'd tried to last time. I wanted to be sick. I couldn't figure out how I ended up back there again. Tongue-tied in Washington Square Park.

"Uh-huh," he said, after a viciously long delay.

"Do you exclusively read in..." I paused, pretending to analyze the cover of the book. "...Latin?"

"No one does romance like the Romans," he said, matter of fact.

"Yeah," I responded, completely unsure of what he meant. But ashamedly impressed.

And then he said nothing. Not a word. Not a sound. *Just cold, uninterrupted silence.* Continuing to read like I didn't exist.

Was I supposed to take that as a hint that the conversation was over? Or were the poems written before Christ just *that compelling*? I wanted to leave, but I couldn't bear him thinking he'd dismissed me.

"Anyway, I just wanted to say sorry, for the other day. I don't usually chase after strangers."

"Don't apologize," he said. Again, without looking up, which made it all the more impressive a few moments later when he did. His brown eyes bored their way into mine. "Enough people in life are gonna do that for you. Don't do it to yourself."

I felt an urge to laugh but I wasn't sure why. Perhaps because it sounded like bumper sticker logic, or perhaps because it rang so true it unsettled me.

Quick, deflect, I thought.

"Oh, so he's a therapist?"

"Just some free advice. Yours if you want it."

"Unsolicited advice," I said under my breath.

Something about that amused him.

"Is something funny?" I asked, fury rising. He took the cigarette out from behind his ear, and held it between his index and middle finger.

"You know, you have to actually light those things if you wanna inhale the cancer."

"Is that so?" he said.

"Just some free advice. Yours if you want it."

"You're relentless," he said.

"Thank you," I retorted.

He laughed again, putting his book down to give me his full attention.

Exhilaration surged through me, sending tremors into my limbs.

"Where are you from, Eva Nelson?" he asked, remembering my full name, which made me giddier than it should have.

"Bowery and Delancey," I said.

He raised a questioning eyebrow.

"Spring City, Pennsylvania," I relented. "Where middle class dreams go to die."

"But not yours. You got out." He surveyed me. "All the way to the big, bad city. *Impressive*." I couldn't work out if he were being patronizing or sarcastic.

"Thank you, it is. Especially when you're not just handed everything," I said, taking a massive stab in the dark. "What was it like to grow up here?"

"What makes you think I did?"

"Your indifference to it all."

He smiled. *One point for me.*

"Park Avenue, with all the things," he said. "It was *perfect*."

There was sadness to the way he said 'perfect.' I couldn't tell if it were because it evoked an unrelated memory, or if my careless stab had hit a vein. I didn't know what to say, so I averted my gaze trying to think of a segue.

"I should get going," he said before I could come up with anything.

"To school?"

"To work."

"Where do you work?" I asked again, reflexively.

"Always with the questions," he said, stirring up my insecurities. He must have seen it flash across my face because he followed up with, "A bookshop. On Avenue A."

He stood up to leave.

"I never got your name," I said.

"I know."

Then he left, leaving me once again staring hopelessly into thin air.

I had no way to contact him. No way to follow up, or to find out anything else about him, but he knew that. It was intentional. As much as I wanted to believe the interaction was flirtatious, I knew it couldn't have been; if it were, I would have had his number, or he would have asked for mine.

As miserable as I felt, I took solace in the fact that I wasn't an actual stalker. At least I knew when to quit.

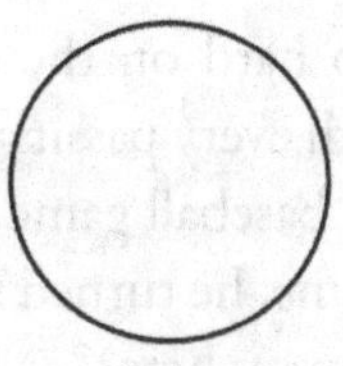

FIVE

JUST LIKE HEAVEN

I was just about to crawl under my duvet (for eternity), when I remembered that somewhere within the haze of the mystery guy time warp, I'd agreed to go on a date with Dylan. *That night.*

I felt terrible. Dylan didn't deserve to be going on a date with someone who forgot about him. No one did, but especially not someone so kind.

I had to be upfront and cancel. It was the right thing to do.

I picked up my phone to draft a text:

> Hey! Really sorry to do this so last minute, but I'm feeling sick. Won't be able to hang tonight. Sorry!

Immediately, I felt queasy. At least the text was turning into the truth.

Realizing how cowardly I was being, I threw my phone onto my chair and ran up to the boys' dorm. All I had to do was be honest: *now is not the time to get distracted by boys. Any, and all of them. I was in New York to study, and that was exactly what I was going to do.*

I knocked a little too hard on the door, anxious that I was going to lose my nerve with every passing second.

A student watching a baseball game on his phone opened the door. Without looking at me, he turned to walk away.

"Um, hi? Is Dylan Lawson here?"

He looked up briefly. "Oh. Yeah."

Without another word, he turned back disappearing down the hall.

I wasn't sure if I were supposed to follow or not. I'd taken a single step forward when a female teacher appeared from out of nowhere. She was around my height, with curled golden hair to her shoulders, wearing overalls and Doc Martin boots. She beamed at me, but it didn't register. I was too preoccupied internally, panicking about being caught somewhere I shouldn't be.

"Sorry," I said, turning away. "Wrong floor."

"Eva?" asked the woman, who appeared to have an accent of some kind. Southern, I guessed. She was upbeat, but relaxed. The opposite of confrontational.

Did I have class with her and somehow my goldfish brain had forgotten?

"It's probably too late to deny it, right?" I asked.

A man likely in his late fifties appeared behind her. He was dressed in a bright paisley-patterned shirt and wore an ear-to-ear grin.

"It's so nice to meet you. I'm Dylan's mom, and this is his dad," said the woman, reaching out to hug me before I could escape.

My mind was spinning. *Why did they know my name? What had he told them about me?*

"I..." I said, rooted to the spot. "I'm actually... not supposed to be on this fl—"

Dylan appeared behind his dad. A family picture in the making. Thankfully, he looked as mortified as I felt.

"Eva, sorry! Hi," he said. "My parents just surprised me. They wanted to make sure I'd settled in, even though I told them *not to come*." He was even more nervous than usual.

His dad chimed in, tipping his head toward his wife. "She insisted."

"We didn't know he had plans tonight," said his mom.

"Mom—" said Dylan.

"It's all good. I was actually just... we can hang out another time," I jumped in. "I'll be here all year."

"No," the three of them said in unison.

Dylan took the reins. "They're gonna be in town for a few days. It's really not a big deal."

"That's true, we are," she said, in an almost singsong manner. I could tell she wanted nothing more than to spend time with her son, but because she knew he wanted to be with me, she was willing to sacrifice her own happiness for his.

It was in that moment that I must have blacked out because I heard someone say, "We can all go?" and it sounded like it came from me.

Before I could retract it, to turn back the clock on my temporary insanity, his mother was already accepting my offer.

"We'd be thrilled!" she exclaimed.

"No, it's okay," said Dylan, the color draining from his face.

His dad leveled the vote. "Dinner on us. Anywhere you like."

Shellshocked by my own behavior, I retreated to change my clothes, beating myself up on the journey back downstairs with all the things I could have said. *I'm sick. I can't. I don't want to. No.* Instead, I'd either invited myself to their dinner or invited them to ours. Neither was an option I felt particularly good about.

"What are you doing right now?" I asked Delilah, as soon as I walked through the door.

She was on her bed watching something on her laptop.

"Knitting a sweater," she replied sarcastically.

"I mean, tonight," I said hurriedly, as I tried to find something to wear. "I could really use a buffer."

"Does it involve leaving this bed?"

"Yes. But. It also involves free dinner."

I pulled out the only dress I owned. My grandma had made it for my graduation.

"Is this acceptable?" I asked, holding it up against my body.

"For a dress-up party?"

"Ouch. For dinner with Dylan."

"Oooh," she said, her face lighting up. "I love this for—"

"And his parents."

"*No*," she said, as though she were expecting it to be a joke. When she realized it wasn't, she followed up with, "But why, how?"

"Umm... I offered," I admitted. "I'm putting it down as orphan trauma?"

"Oh, love..."

"So you'll come?"

"I can't. Katie's coming over."

"But... but my parents are *dead*."

She looked mortified until I laughed.

"Woah, you almost got me there. But no, I'm still not going."

"I think I hate you."

"So you don't want to borrow an outfit, then?" she asked, getting out of bed to pull a little black dress from the wardrobe.

It felt far too tight, but I reasoned it was better than being mistaken for a costume party attendee.

I WALKED OUTSIDE to see Dylan's parents already sitting in a taxi, his dad crammed awkwardly upright in the front seat.

"I'm... so sorry about this," said Dylan. His back to his waving parents. "I'll do anything for you to pretend it never happened. Seriously, anything."

"It's okay," I said. "They're beautiful." And they really were. And so was he, a perfect extension of them. "I don't mind."

Mostly I didn't. Growing up without parents, it was something I'd never experienced. It felt like a cozy blanket. Even if it was wrapped a little too tight.

They took us to a steak restaurant with red leather booths and bread rolls so soft I could have sworn they were made from cotton candy.

"I'll get the garden salad, please," I said to the huffy waiter.

"That's all?" he asked.

"Please, order whatever you want," his mother interrupted. "This is a special occasion."

"Honestly, the salad's fine..." Everyone was looking at me. My worst nightmare.

"I'll do the cheeseburger," said Dylan to the waiter, trying to take the heat off me. "We can split it if you want?"

"Sure," I said, just wanting the conversation to be over.

"Let's do two burgers," said Dylan's dad. "And I'll do the sirloin."

"Actually..." I wanted to cover my face in the tablecloth, so I didn't have to see them. "I don't eat meat, so the salad's fine." I tried to say it as quickly as possible to not further add to the drama.

Before all three of them could put words to the horrified looks on their faces, the waiter stepped in.

"We actually have a meatless burger if you'd prefer?"

"Oh, sure. Yes. Thank you!"

Welp.

It wasn't until before dessert—they insisted on ordering a bunch to share, which I was secretly hoping for—that the conversation took a turn. Dylan had gone to the restroom, and a brief silence settled over the table as his mom checked if it was safe to speak. My throat immediately went dry.

"We're so sorry about this! Hijacking your date," she apologized. I didn't know if it were because she was an artist and it just came with the territory, but aside from being sweet, she was also genuinely cool. Someone I'd want to hang out with outside of the situation I was in. "It all just happened so fast, and we didn't want him to miss out cause we'd planned some silly surprise."

"It's okay, honestly," I said.

"He doesn't usually bring his parents on dates. Not that he's been on very many—"

"Darlin—," Dylan's dad interrupted.

"No, it's okay. I enjoyed it. *Really*. You're both definitely in the pro column."

His mother beamed, then leaned in close. "What's in the con column?" she asked, like a girlfriend prying for gossip. "Cause I betcha we can fix 'em. We like you almost as much as him."

"*Mom*, what are you talking about?" Dylan asked, returning from the bathroom to save me.

"We weren't talking about anything," she said.

"Then why were you leaning in like you do when you're being sneaky?"

"I am *not sneaky!*" she squeaked. "When am I ever sneaky? Take that back. I don't want Eva thinkin' I'm sneaky!"

Dylan leaned in, impersonating his mother. "Dylan, honey. It's your dad's birthday tomorrow. I bought him speakers from Best Buy and put your name on it, so just pretend you got them for him." He laughed, as did his dad, nodding knowingly.

"*I never!*" she protested. "I'd never do anything like that." Her lie shining through.

They were white picket fence wholesome, and it felt impossible to resist.

"It was great to meet you," I said to his mom, who hugged me outside the restaurant while Dylan hailed two taxis. "Come visit us anytime. Dylan's back for Thanksgiving—"

"Mom!" Dylan yelled as he opened the door to one of the taxis. "Leave her alone."

"What?" She raised her hands in guilt, joining him.

"Thank you for dinner, Mr. Lawson," I said as he hugged me.

"Seriously, anytime," he replied, echoing his wife's sentiments. "I've never seen Dylan so uptight. It's hilarious to watch."

In front of us, Dylan was proving his point, talking animatedly with his mom. I stepped in to mediate.

"It's only that I baked them special and we won't have time to stop by in the morning."

"Just leave them with the front desk. I'll pick them up tomorrow after class."

"If they're not refrigerated—"

"In or out!" the cab driver yelled as I approached.

"In," Dylan said. "Mom, I should get Eva home."

I intercepted. "No, no. Go with them and I'll take this cab."

"No!" they both exclaimed as I went to get in the taxi.

His mom tried to interject. "Honestly, Eva it's—"

"Please, *I insist*," I said, proud of myself for finally getting out the words I'd meant to say earlier. "I don't mind in the slightest."

"Are you sure?" she asked.

"I'm fine, I promise!" I urged, getting into the car and rolling down the window.

"Text Dylan when you get home?" she said. "Otherwise, I'll worry."

"I will."

"Thanks, *Mom*," he said, sternly; she got the message and departed.

Dylan tapped on the passenger side window and handed a twenty to the driver, who'd already started the meter. "Forsyth and Delancey. Make sure she gets in okay."

He returned to my window looking defeated.

"Well..." he said. "That was... even more embarrassing than the time she drove three hours to summer camp 'cause she was worried I didn't pack enough socks."

"Had you?"

"What?"

"Packed enough socks?" I asked seriously.

He hung his head pathetically. "No."

"They're great," I said. "You've got nothing to be embarrassed about."

"I wish that were true," he said. "Text me when you get home."

"I will."

"You really are something," he said.

"So are you," I replied, smiling and winding the window up.

I kept my eyes on him as the driver pulled away. I understood, of course, why he was embarrassed. If the roles were reversed, I'd feel the same. But as someone on the outside looking in, I was fascinated by the relationship he had with his parents. It was the kind of familial affection I'd only ever seen on network TV. Not that my grandparents didn't try to shower me with love, but it somehow never felt the same, coming from eyes that looked nothing like my own.

Sorrow trickled in as my mind went to my own parents. Wondering how different I would be if I'd known them. *Would we have stayed in Spring City, or gone back to England where my mother was from? Would we have been close like the Lawsons? Or was I better off somehow?*

As the taxi reached the end of the block, a red traffic light brought us to a stop. To my right, the glow of a small neon sign, emblazoned simply with 'a bookshop,' captured my attention, awakening a flutter in my stomach.

"What street is this?" I asked, though part of me didn't need him to tell me. My heart pounded as if it were trying to break out of my ribs.

"Ah, it's... A and twelfth or eleventh," the driver said trying to find the sign.

"Avenue A?" I smiled.

"Yeah," he said checking out the signage. "Eleventh. Avenue A and Eleventh."

"A bookshop on Avenue A," I thought aloud, shaking my head.

The light turned green, but before the driver could accelerate, I screeched, "Stop!"

Flinging the car door open, I leaped onto the sidewalk.

"I forgot something, keep the money."

Like an insect in the dark of night, I felt myself gravitate toward the light. Thoughts of Dylan and the feelings I'd had just minutes before disintegrating with every step. I wanted to stop myself, to turn around and walk as fast as my legs would carry me, or better yet, get back into the taxi. But my logical mind wasn't in control anymore.

It felt like the kind of fate I couldn't turn my back on.

I lied to myself that I had a choice. That I could leave, but my hand was already outstretched, about to push the door open.

If I went in, I reasoned, the third time would have to be the last. Any action past that point would be masochism. Or insanity. If he gave me nothing again, I had to forget about him for good and stop torturing myself. Literal (neon) sign, or not.

The shop was long and narrow, with new and used books crammed into every area of available space. I snaked my way through the shelves toward the counter, my temporary high evaporating, when I saw a raven-haired woman in her late 20s. She was wearing a cutoff T-shirt that read: 'Jane Austin was a witch.'

I was about to leave when he entered the room with two boxes stacked high in his muscular arms. I must have caught him off-guard because I saw his expression change when he noticed me. I couldn't be certain... but it might have been the start of a smile.

A song I couldn't name played as he put the boxes on the counter.

Standing tall, he took me in.

His twinkling eyes made my knees unsteady.

Not only that, but I'd lost the ability to speak. Once more.

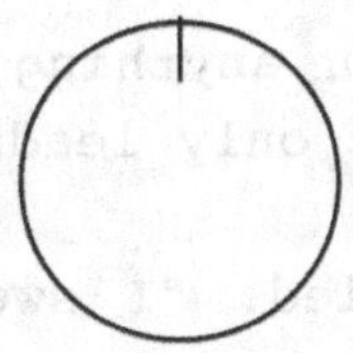

SIX

LOVER, YOU SHOULD'VE COME OVER

The moment I saw her standing there, I knew I was in trouble.

It was different from the first time, or even the second. She was wearing a tight black dress that clung to the curves of her body, her light brown hair pulled back from the sides of her face. It made her delicate features even more pronounced.

Her eyes, though, her sapphire blue eyes, were as intense as the first day I'd looked into them.

She was staring at me, as if studying my reaction. I hadn't realized it, but I was smiling.

Instantly, I shook the thought from my mind. The last thing I needed was for this girl to think I was interested in her. Sure, she was attractive and intelligent — actually intelligent, in the way that matters. But if my life had proven anything, it was that any kind of attachment only leads to trouble.

"You," I said.

"Me," she replied. "I swear I was driving by and…"

She looked down to break contact, but it only made me want to find her eyes even more.

I could see Rachel pretending not to listen from behind the counter.

"Don't you have a break you need to take?"

She feigned confusion. "Who me?"

I gave her a look I knew she understood.

"Guess I'll be taking my break."

"Pretty sure if the roles were reversed, this would be considered stalking," I said.

"It's messed up that it isn't. I mean, obviously I don't pose the same physical threat as you pose to me, but if you turned up where I was reading and then again where I work, I'd be pretty freaked out," she said, speaking so fast I found it hard to keep up. "Except in the way that I probably wouldn't be freaked out. If it was you… which I guess, is why I'm here."

I couldn't let her go on. If she did, I might catch feelings in a way that could hurt us both.

"It's not a big deal," I said, leaving no room for interpretation. "I don't care if you're here." It was the furthest from the truth, which is why I had to say it.

I opened one of the boxes with a utility knife to unpack our latest order. I needed to occupy my hands, to distract my mind until she left. I knew I was being unkind, but in the long run, it was for the best. Resisting her was already hard enough; another minute longer, and I might snap.

"Wow," she said. "Okay… message received. I won't bother you again."

I heard the door open slightly, then she doubled back.

"You know what?" she said. I didn't *want to know what,* but it didn't seem like she was going to give me a choice. "I think the lady doth protest too much."

"Excuse me?" I asked, taken aback.

"It's a saying. From *Hamlet*. It means you're overselling it. Your… disinterest."

"I know *Hamlet*," I said, like it was an achievement.

"Well, I don't buy it." She looked at me with seriousness, her arms folded. "Are you married?"

Now I was confused. "No."

"Girlfriend?"

"No."

"Are you into women?" she asked like she'd discovered the reason.

"Yes," I said, with a smirk.

"Then, what's your problem? 'Cause there's no way you can dislike a stranger this much. I mean, spend some time with me, then hate me. It's what everyone else does."

Rachel returned, rocking on her heels before I acknowledged her. "I just remembered; I already took my break."

"Then take another one," I said.

"I'm good. I don't need another—"

"Clock out early, then. It's dead anyway."

"But boss—"

"Said I was in charge."

She analyzed her options. "Alright, but I better get paid 'til nine." She left for the backroom and I returned my attention to Eva.

"You seem… I'm sure you're…" I said, trying to find words that wouldn't set her off.

"I am," she said. "I'm all the superlatives, but we're not talking about me."

"Let him have it," said Rachel with a sly expression as she put on her patchwork jacket.

"Appreciate the support," I said, wishing she'd leave.

"Shouldn't have sent me home then, idiot," she said. "Woulda had all the support you could handle."

I waited to hear the front door close before I continued, her departure aligning perfectly with the last bar of the music.

Piercing stillness filled the room, before a Jeff Buckley song crackled out of speakers decades past their expiration date.

"A bookshop," she said. "Funny."

"The owner thinks so."

"Was I supposed to be able to find it? Or was that just part of the weird mind game you seem to be playing?"

Of course it wasn't. The last thing I'd ever do is manipulate someone like that. But I couldn't deny that on some subconscious level, maybe I did want her to find me. I'd moved onto unpacking the second box when I snuck a glance in her direction.

Her head was hung, despair on her face. It was an emotion I didn't know how to handle.

"Would you like me to go?" she asked.

"No," my mouth responded, a knee-jerk reaction. I tried to recover. "I don't care if you're here."

"Yeah, we've established that," she said. Her shoulders sank even lower.

I couldn't bear it.

"I'm not looking to date anyone," I said.

"Neither am I," she responded. "I don't think."

"Then why are you here?"

"I don't know." She was looking away, as if trying to find the answer. "Maybe the same reason you don't want me to leave."

I let out an uncomfortable laugh because I knew it was the truth, and so did she.

"Relentless," I said.

She picked up a pen from the counter, then reached for my hand. Instead of pulling away, I let her take it.

Her touch was soft, like expensive silk. I had to stop myself from thinking about how it would feel to press my lips against her skin. To kiss the back of her hand.

To kiss her face, in the spot just above where she was frowning.

To find her lips.

She turned my hand over and started writing on it. I could smell the sweetness of her breath as I forced my hand not to tremble.

"My number," she said, placing the pen back in its place while still holding onto my hand. I felt a kick in my gut. "If you ever figure all this out, feel free to use it."

She released her grip, as I scrambled to find words. What I wanted to say was: *yes. Yes, you beautiful human. I want to use your number. I want to call you all the time just to hear your voice.* But I knew against all hope that I couldn't. That I wouldn't ever allow myself to do that.

Instead, I stood there mute, as she turned and walked away.

If there were ever a moment frozen in my mind, it was that one. I wanted to run after her, chase her down and tell her all the things I have to carry. All the things I have to hide. How I thought I'd noticed her before she'd noticed me that day in the park. That I saw her standing by the fountain, writing in a notebook. Transcribing the world, flicking between her paper and reality, analyzing every detail. I'd wanted to approach her. Not to interact — I knew better than that — but to be in her vicinity. I reminded myself that life was a game of chess. Why play the queen if you know you're going to lose it? That was a type of recklessness I couldn't afford.

Everything would have been fine, had she not chased after me. I knew immediately it had to be her. The timbre of her voice a perfect match for her intense stare. I'd wanted to stop in my tracks, to take her in, but I kept marching forward, steered by the knowledge that I was saving us both. I only relented when she left me with no other choice.

The second time was entirely my fault. I'll rightfully accept the blame. I knew she'd be in the park; that's why I stayed away for a week. But I slipped, typing her name into my phone's browser. Eva Nelson, 17, was from Spring City, Pennsylvania. She had a relatively sparse online profile. No social media and no retouched selfies, which only made me like her more. When I found her writing and couldn't stop reading, blog after blog, I knew I was tiptoeing into fire just to see how hot it was. I'd had one conversation with her and I was already too interested in the prospect of her. Even if she did seem safe. I knew from experience that such a thing didn't exist. Especially for me.

She'd written a profile on her grandparents, who couldn't have seemed less threatening — good people who raised a good person. I wanted to believe that. None of the information I found online indicated she was a risk. I suppose that's why I returned to the park that day. Not to see her or to interact, but because the threat didn't seem imminent. I realize now I let a feeling I couldn't even identify cloud my judgment. I'd succumbed to the most pathetic of emotions: lust.

I lied to myself that I had it under control, even when I saw her walking over to me, as I hoped she would. For a minute, maybe I did. I could tell I was upsetting her, frustrating her, which I thought would make her leave. When she didn't, my curiosity got the better of me and I wanted to know why. I searched her eyes, looking for warning signs, and was temporarily lost. She caught me off-guard by asking about my home. A place I tried never to think about.

That's why I surprised myself when not even five minutes after she'd left me in the shop with her number, I pulled out my phone to use it.

She picked up on the second ring.

"Hello?"

"Hi," I exhaled.

Her gentle breath filled the earpiece.

"I was thinking," I said, though the truth was, thinking was the last thing I was doing. "If you're free tomorrow night…"

"I am," she said.

"Cool. I'll pick you up after work. Around eleven."

"Sure. Eleven." She laughed, but I didn't get the joke. "Anderson Prep. I'll meet you outside."

"Good night."

I'd almost hung up when I heard her say, "Wait!"

"Yeah?" I answered, scared that she'd changed her mind.

"I never got your name."

"Max," I said.

"Max…" she said. "Nice to meet you."

"Goodnight, Eva Nelson," I said, trying to wipe the smile off my face.

I'd never felt so truly torn between my head and my heart. I knew what I should be doing, but for reasons I couldn't process, it felt so much better to run in the opposite direction. It was like glass breaking in slow motion — no matter what I did, I was bound to get cut. The conclusion was forgone, the bullet had left the barrel.

I was on the verge of breaking one of the two promises I'd made to myself after my parents were killed. I was falling for someone, and I didn't know how to stop it. I just prayed I didn't take her down with me.

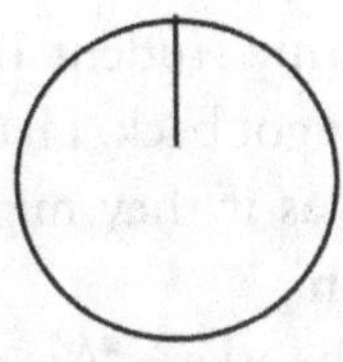

SEVEN

IF IT MAKES YOU HAPPY

I was on my way home in a taxi, somewhere between unconscious and catatonic as a result of what I'd just done. I couldn't believe the words that had come out of my mouth. The only thing I could be proud of, the only hope I could cling to, was that I hadn't cried.

I had a feeling I was about to, when my phone rang; the number withheld. My heart ached for it to be him, and for one of the first times in my life, it got what it wanted.

His name was Max and I was seeing him the following night. I was buzzing with anticipation, I wanted to run through the streets screaming until I lost my voice. Or at the very least, text everyone I'd ever met—

Then it hit me, as I arrived back at school.

Dylan.

I was thinking of how to let him down easily, when I turned to see his taxi pull up. He was stepping out of the car with tinfoil-wrapped packages, looking just as surprised to see me.

"Eva!" he exclaimed, shutting the taxi door with his foot. "Did they lock us out?"

"No," I said, swiping my student ID against the after-hours card reader. "I actually just got back. I had to..."

I looked to my shoes as if they might have the words I was looking for written on them.

"Is everything okay?" he asked. "Are *you* okay?"

"Um... well."

"Eva?" he asked, sounding worried.

"It's not that I don't like you," I said. "But—"

"Oh."

"Yeah... I'm really sorry. It's just..."

"It was too soon to meet the parents?"

"I kinda met someone and it's probably nothing, but that's kinda where my head's at."

"*Oh.*" He nodded, in a way that made me want to cry.

Time lagged, as if the universe were dragging the moment out so I could feel every inch of his disappointment. It was a dagger to my little black heart.

"We're still friends, though, right?" I asked meekly.

"Well, that depends... on how much pumpkin spiced banana bread you can eat," he said, handing me two loaves.

"Eating has never been a problem for me."

"Tell me you don't wanna come home with me for the holidays after that."

A smirk appeared across his face. Then on mine.

DELILAH MUST HAVE HEARD the haphazard clanking of my beginner heels down the dorm room corridor because I could hear her chanting "Kiss and tell, kiss and tell," before I'd even opened the door.

She was sitting on her bed cross-legged, scrolling through a website on her laptop. Papers and books scattered all around.

"Need me to send up search and rescue?" I asked, as I collapsed on the floor like a sack of sand.

"If you're referring to all this?" She gestured with dramatic flair. "It's just all my hopes and dreams crashing down around me."

"Seriously?"

"No, but yes. The head of Drama, Mr. Jenkins, emailed to say that all the roles in both the winter *and* summer plays were already assigned. Last year. Can you believe that? What school auditions for both plays *at the end* of junior year?"

"Maybe it's a rich people thing? They do the same with the paper."

"If I'm not in the play, Yale Drama's out. I was counting on their scout seeing me. It's the whole reason I came here."

"They won't even let you audition as a substitute?"

"An understudy," she corrected me. "And no, apparently all those are taken, too."

"Well, that's kinda suspect."

"Right? It'll mean I'll be the only drama major who didn't get to audition. Hence, this mess. I'm trying to find a way to argue that I should be given a chance to at least audition. I've been through the school's bylaws back and forth, and even looked up what's left of Affirmative Action laws."

I walked over to look at her research.

"Maybe you need to come at it from a different angle?" I wondered aloud. "Can I?" I reached for the laptop, which she pushed toward me without hesitation.

"What do you know about Mr. Jenkins?" I asked, while searching his name in the browser. "It's ultimately his decision, right?"

"Yeah. He's a lifer. Been here longer than the limestone."

I browsed through web results that showed Peter Jenkins had been at the school since the early '80s. There were only a handful of sites that mentioned any real information about him, but there was no shortage of photos.

"He loves any chance to jump in front of a camera, doesn't he?" I said. Clicking through images of him at various events.

"Yep, total showpony. He can't get through a single lesson without dropping at least one famous alumni's name." Then her voice changed into that of a showy New Yorker: "*As my good friend and former pupil, Kelly Prescott, once said to me... Yes, yes. That chair. Declan Bancroft sat in that chair.*"

"So, he's after prestige? Interesting..." I said, continuing to scan images. "We can do something with that. Hmm, maybe this?" I'd landed on a group photo. It was from the wedding of Broadway star, Shelby Sarpy.

"I don't get how—"

"If you can't get someone through logic, get them through emotion. Or credibility. Or both."

"Okay, *ethos, pathos, logos.*"

I opened up Gmail to create a new account.

"I have an idea. Gimme a man's name that sounds important."

"Barack Obama."

I rolled my eyes, opening a second tab. "Better yet, who's the biggest acting agency?"

"CAA."

I searched the company and found the name of an agent, Jason Finkleman. I pulled up his IMDb, then his Instagram.

"Wait, wait, wait," she said, like she was coming out of a fog. "What happened with Dylan? Kiss and tell."

"His mom kissed me on the cheek. Does that count?"

"Only if she was hot," Delilah joked.

"Sure, but not my type."

"Did you at least want him to?"

"Umm, I..." I thought about Dylan, how cute he'd looked bantering with his parents, the look of wonder he'd given me across the table all night. I thought about how I enjoyed being with him; there was something so warm about his affection. And then I thought about Max. His lips, his eyes, the feeling of his hand in mine—how strong and gentle it was all at the same time. How I wanted to reach out and grab him.

"I have no idea," I said. "But I just told him we're better off as friends, 'cause, well... I saw the guy from the park. His name's Max and he's taking me out tomorrow night." I glossed over the last part as fast as possible in case saying it out loud made go away.

"You saw two guys in one night? I'm solidly impressed."

"I'm not."

"Okay, so, Dylan's done. We don't like Dylan?"

"I do, but I already like Max way more."

"So, date them both. Guys have been doing it for centuries."

"No, I couldn't lead Dylan on like that. I mean. I just had dinner with his parents."

"Fair point," she said. "You were in weirdly deep for one date."

"Okay. I think I've got it."

I'd created a new Gmail account for Jason Finkleman. "How's this sound?"

Peter,

    Great to see you at Shelby's wedding.

    One of my junior agents tells me you have a student we might be interested in representing — Delilah Landry? Another feather in your cap, I hear.

    When can we see her perform?

    -JF

"No, there's *no way* he'd fall for that," she said. "What if they know each other?"

"I already checked. They don't follow each other on socials, and there aren't any links between them online. Not even a group photo. Plus, this agent's based in LA."

She read it again. "I don't know..."

"It's your name on it, so you're the one who should be. Why don't you think about it?"

She looked at me, thinking.

"Nah, life's short," she said, reaching over me to click send.

I crossed my fingers and tried to pretend I wasn't nervous. I wouldn't forgive myself if it backfired. "*That* was badass."

I climbed up to my bed and collapsed on it. "I'm beat."

"Same." She collected the books and papers from her bed and threw them on the floor, before turning the light off.

I loved that she got social cues.

"Wait, tell me about the cute boy!" she said, jumping into bed.

"But I'm *so tired*—" I protested in a child's voice.

"Fifteen words or less."

I thought about it, counting it out on my fingers as I said it. "Name's Max. Works at *A Bookshop*. On Avenue A." I made sure to stress the A, unlike how he had said it to me. "Too pretty. Might be a trap."

"All the fun ones are girl!" she said. "Sweet dreams."

As exhausted as I was, it was impossible to sleep that night, which made it even harder to concentrate in class the next morning. To say I was annoyed at myself was an understatement. Media Studies was the class I was most looking forward to. Thankfully, my anger woke me up long enough for me to at least be present. Even if my hormones (my best excuse) kept pulling me back into thoughts of Max... and Dylan.

The frigidity of the room didn't help. According to the weather app, it was going to reach the high 70s, but the overnight chill that starts to happen in September had leached into the building and was protesting departure. I pulled the hood from my sweater over my head. The warmth of the fleece cradled my cold ears.

Sheila Marshall was every bit the icon I'd imagined, brilliant in the bad way, and mad in the good. Dressed in an off-white blouse with an oversized bow on the neckline, she should have looked chic. Instead, accessorized with her naturally curly hair and smeared red lipstick, it came off as eccentric. She'd "cut her teeth" in tabloid journalism in Britain, her penance for which she said was "having to teach ethics to hoity toity high schoolers for the rest of eternity." She smiled though, when she said that, in a way that made me believe Anderson was exactly where she wanted to be.

She changed the PowerPoint slide that was being projected at the front of the room to a news story about Leighton Diggs, a famous football player I'd never heard of who'd been shot in a robbery. The headline read: *Football Superstar Slain.*

"At the time of his death, he was the third highest scoring kicker of all time," she said. She clicked to another article with the headline: *The Death of a Legend.* "Which accounts for headlines like these," she continued.

She moved on to the next slide: *NFL Star Diggs, Two Others, Die in Robbery.*

"But this is the actual story, isn't it? This is the best representation of the facts of the day. There was a robbery that claimed the lives of three people, and one of them was a famous person. And that famous person is the reason it was national news."

She then clicked to another slide: *Hero Dies Hero*, which recounted a tabloid exclusive that described Diggs as having attempted to save the life of one of his fellow victims by crashing his car through the gas station.

"Now, various outlets are going to find different angles of the news story to get people to buy their... I was almost going to say newspaper. Remember those? To get people clicking on their links."

A few people laughed.

"But what about this?" she asked, as she flicked to another slide: *Leighton Diggs, NFL Player, Convicted of Sexual Assault.* "Twelve years prior, Diggs was convicted of assaulting a woman he went to college with in Texas. Does this bear any significance to the way we tell the story of his death?"

"It shouldn't," said a guy in the front. He sat slumped, his arms hanging over the back of his chair, legs widely spread. As if the amount of space he took up was proportional to the size of his ego.

"Why not?"

"It's not relevant," he continued. "You said it yourself. The story is about a famous kicker and two people who died."

"And what are the ethics of reporting this story?"

"To be respectful of his family, his fans, his legacy."

"It's to tell the truth," I said, without meaning to. Everyone was looking at me, so I had no choice but to hold strong. "Our job is to tell the truth, to give readers the entire story."

Annabel Monteith stared at me like she was shocked I had brain cells. I hoped it worked in my favor as I'd emailed her the night before in my insomnia haze, asking to be considered for a feature. I smiled, but her attention was diverted to the front of the room.

Miss. Marshall changed the slide, subtle gasps cannoning around the room. It wasn't so much the headline, but the photo that accompanied it. Multiple emergency vehicles surrounded a taped-off area around the gas station. In the center you could see the car that had crashed through the store windows. Amongst the glass and shrapnel was a white sheet that outlined the shape of a body.

"Is this part of the entire story?" she asked.

The room was silent.

I wanted to look away but couldn't. A burning pain was growing behind my eyes.

"No," I said, clearing my throat. "That's sensationalism."

"Why?"

"Because it's not necessary to tell the whole story." I kept my emotions in check because I couldn't not.

"Excellently put, Eva," she said, not seeming to notice the single tear that escaped my eye. "As for Digg's past, you're both right. It's about telling the truth and being respectful. I would however add, Mr. Strider, that we must also consider respect for the victim's victim. Perhaps it shouldn't be the headline, but erasing it from his life erases it from hers."

The bell rang shortly after, so I fled to the fire escape off the girls' dorm. I was so worked up, I accidentally looked down as I climbed out onto the metal grate. Vertigo pummeled me in the face, as I tried to take in fresh air.

"Take a breath, Eva," I said to myself. *You got this.*

And I did, sucking in oxygen until I felt my chest relax.

I tried to close my eyes, but it only brought me back to the crime scene photo. I opened them quickly, blinking hard to instead focus on the Manhattan Bridge in front of me.

It wasn't as if the dead body was even visible, but the tableau it created was enough to incite my imagination.

My dad had died on impact. My mother, who was in labor with me, died in the hospital shortly after. If my grandparents hadn't been following closely behind, I would have joined them.

Thinking of them made me want to pull out my phone.

"Hello?" she answered on the third ring.

"It's just me."

"Eva, dear. Is everything all right? Are you okay?"

"Yes." I laughed, trying to cover the sound of my tender voice. "I'm totally fine. I'm just calling to check in and say hello."

I could hear my granddad in the background asking, "Is that Eva? Is she okay?"

They both got on the phone. I could imagine them sharing the handset between them.

"Eva, are you okay? Do you need money?"

"No, Gramps. I'm good, thank you. I appreciate it, though." I wanted to say I missed them, but I couldn't find the words in my mouth.

"How's school? Are you managing?" Grandma asked.

"I'm doing okay. It's different, but it's..." I didn't know how to tell them that I was sorry if my actions had hurt them in any way. I knew they must have, but it had never been my intention.

"Eva, dear, are you still there?" Granddad asked.

"It's cutting out slightly," I lied, recovering. "Anyway, I was just saying it's all good. The weather's still warm enough, so that's nice. I've been hanging out in the park, writing a bit."

"Be careful in the park, dear, that's where all the crazies hang out."

"I'm one of those crazies, Gran," I said as a joke, but with an undercurrent of years of feeling like I'd never belonged. She must have felt it because Gramps stuttered into a topic change.

"Do you think you'll be back for Thanksgiving?" he said.

"Depends on school, I guess. I'll have to see what the workload's like."

"Okay, well, let us know and we'll buy you a ticket. We'd really love to see you."

"Thanks, Gramps," I said. My heart was sinking. It's crazy how a little geographic distance can help you appreciate people.

"Just let us know," my grandma said.

"I will."

"Okay, we love you," she said.

"Yes we do. We love you!" repeated my granddad.

"Thanks, guys. You, too," I said, hanging up the phone, feeling slightly better. I might not have been able to say what I wanted to, but at least I'd called. That was something.

DELILAH WAS a breath of fresh air as I walked into the room. Or rather, a tornado of it.

"Your backwards ass, sneaky ass plan worked!" she said, hugging me.

"He responded?" I was kinda surprised myself.

"*Yes*. And I got an email asking me to audition! I can't believe it!"

"That's incredible! I'm so excited for you," I beamed.

"I've been working on the scenes all afternoon. They're really good for me. I think I have a shot."

"Of course you do," I said encouragingly and I meant it.

"You're right I do," she said, reassuring herself. "And I'll tell you what else I got? I got news. For a Miss..." She mimed reading from an invisible letter. "Ev...a, Nel...son."

I was immediately nervous. "Oh God, what?" I asked.

"No, it's good. Mostly."

"Oh God," I said again.

"Well, I asked Katie about your mystery guy cause she and her friends know everyone who hangs out in Washington Square Park."

"I'm not sure I wanna know..."

"Your face says different," she said. I felt myself blush. "But actually, that's the thing: no one knows him. They knew exactly who I was talking about, even sent me a screenshot, but they said he's a total loner. They've never even seen him speak to anyone."

"Oh," I said, getting embarrassed. "So maybe it's not a date, then? Maybe it's just like, a friend hang?"

"There's no way to know for sure—"

"So I just go in there blind?" I asked like a sullen tween. "While secretly preparing for the worst, while even more secretly hoping for the best?" I was trying to be matter of fact, but I could feel myself starting to spiral.

"Or you could just be present," she tried to interject.

"No, you're right. I'm making this a thing when in reality, it could be nothing. And maybe that's okay... maybe we're just supposed to be frien—" Delilah cut me off for my own good by holding up a photo on her phone. "One of the boys sent me this."

It was a picture of Max on Instagram in the bookshop, a worn novel in his hand. A bright flash lit up his face, curiosity in his brown eyes caught mid surprise. The caption read: '#HotBoysReading.'

I stared at the photo for too long, my heart melting.

Delilah laughed, pulling me out of the trance.

"Help," I gulped.

"He's a total babe. I get it."

"No, it's more than that. He's... being around him... it feels like..." *Nothing I've ever felt*, I wanted to say without sounding like a total psychopath. After all, I'd known the guy for a collective 20 minutes.

"Ooh, you've got it bad," she jabbed.

"No, it's just—"

"Yes?" she asked, with an expression that said 'try me.'

"It's just... that... damnit, maybe I do."

Her laugh forced my face into a smile.

"Well, good! In the immortal words of Sheryl Crow, '*If it makes you happy, it can't be that bad.*'"

I shook my head, more than amused, as Delilah returned to her audition.

I wanted to get behind the sentiment of the song but I couldn't stop running through all the things that made me feel good in the moment but were actually bad for me. Like sugar, cutting my own bangs or social media. Things that had me feeling great for a moment, before bringing me even further down minutes later.

I hoped against all hope that Max wasn't going to be one of those things, just another temporary high. If he was even going to be that. I didn't want to dwell on the worst-case scenario, but high school heartache and rejection had taught me it was better to be prepared. So I let my mind wander to the bad, with some Sour Patch Kids on hand to pull me back whenever I felt tempted to veer completely off-course.

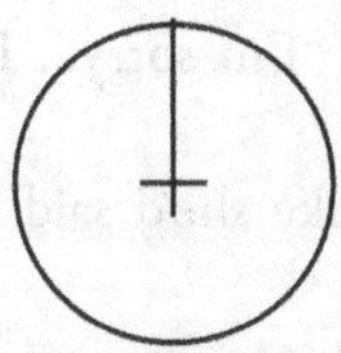

EIGHT
IN A SENTIMENTAL MOOD

Eleven PM is such a ridiculous time to meet someone. I'd already eaten dinner (twice), got ready, then got unready, took a nap and looked at the same page of a textbook for two hours. I'd never be able to remember a single word that was printed on the page, but every line of the accompanying cartoon will be etched into my mind for eternity.

Much to Delilah's protests, I wore jeans, my favorite Bowie T-shirt and a leather jacket. If I had to find out the date I thought I was on was just a "friend hang," I wanted to at least be comfortable. She did, however, convince me to put on lipstick.

"You can still look chill and relaxed, and like you don't care," she argued. "But a lip says, I'm here, I'm alive, kiss me."

I was already applying the deep red wax to my lips. "I'm doing it, aren't I?" I reassured her. It wasn't as if I didn't like how it looked. I just didn't want to attract attention. Then I remembered, on a date that was kinda the point.

"And maybe lose the necklace. It's not the vibe," said Delilah, assessing me with her eyes.

"I never take this off," I said. "It was my mother's."

"Oh, crap," she said. "I'm sorry... I didn't mean it in a bad way."

It was clear she felt like she'd said something wrong, but it didn't upset me.

I looked at myself in the mirror and could see what she meant. It didn't really go with the outfit. There was something about the unfinished stone, and the minimalist way the chain wrapped around it that made it skew crafty when sitting upon a vintage tee.

"It's okay. It's not like I knew her," I said, undoing the clasp.

"Oh, love, please don't take it off. I didn't mean it."

"No, you're right," I said, putting the necklace on my side table. "I can see now, objectively, that it is *not the vibe*."

"No, really. I didn't mean—"

"Honestly, it's fine," I laughed. "It's a good reminder that when I need to make tough unemotional choices, I am fully and competently capable of doing so. I just wish I wasn't so nervous. My mouth is so dry I can barely speak."

"You're gonna do great sweetie," encouraged Delilah. "It's not as if it's your first date."

"Exactly," I said, shrugging. "Except that it kinda is."

"What?" she asked, like I was a Martian. "Seriously?"

"If you'd met the people I went to school with, you wouldn't be asking me that. I was beginning to think I was asexual until—"

The thought was interrupted by the sound of an aggressively loud motorcycle revving its engine down the side of our street. It seemed to turn the corner, and... stop. Right out of the front of the school.

Delilah and I shared a look, before climbing over my desk to peer out the window. "Is that him?" she asked.

"I think... maybe?"

I wasn't sure if I was embarrassed, or something else.

"Good choice on the jeans."

"I'm not riding on that."

Delilah laughed. "*Yeah, okay.*"

I grabbed my jacket and went to prove her wrong.

The upside of living on the fifth floor was 86 steps to think of a rationale for why riding on a motorcycle was a terrible idea. I'd decided I was going to tell him that I was still down to hang but that I'd meet him there. 'Coma patient' just wasn't on my goal list for the evening. If I said it in the right way, it might even come across as amusing.

I walked out the door, ready to present my case.

He was sitting atop a vintage black and silver bike; his helmet off, a few strands of hair falling onto his stupidly kissable cheekbones.

"Hey," he said.

His demeanor was cold, but he was addressing me, so that felt like an improvement.

"Hi," I said, approaching him. Already feeling shy.

He handed me a helmet. "Get on."

My heart started to race.

I took a deep breath, readying myself for my opening argument.

"Okay," I said, shocking myself.

I pulled my hair around to one side of my head and placed the helmet over it like I knew what I was doing. Part of me wanted to be angry for not standing my ground, but the other part, the louder part, was sick of caring about every little thing. Maybe it was the time of night, or maybe it was him, but I felt like being reckless.

I locked the helmet in place and stood up on the passenger footrest to swing my leg over the other side when my foot slipped off the peg almost bringing him down with me. As quickly as I could, I repositioned it, instinctively grabbing his shoulder for support; electricity buzzed through my arm.

I pulled away to settle myself on the saddle, trying to sit on its highest part to put as much distance between us as possible. The curved padding had other ideas though, sliding me forward toward his body.

"You might wanna hold on," he said, moments before he kicked the stand and revved the throttle to accelerate.

I didn't have time to think; my fight or flight response triggering my arms to throw themselves around his middle. The exhilaration of speed lurched forward at me, the night air whipping down the insides of my jacket, covering my body in bumps. Even the hairs on my neck stood up, as if they were mini conductors of current.

We rounded the corner onto Houston, and that's when he really opened up the engine. Dodging cars and racing traffic lights. It made me want to scream, and for once, it would have been out of sheer excitement.

We sped north onto FDR Drive as I watched the lights of Williamsburg and Greenpoint sparkle like embers across the river. Exiting in Harlem, he zipped down a few more streets before pulling up into a dimly lit alley.

He'd turned off the engine but wasn't getting off the bike. I tried to look around us, the reality of how deserted we were beginning to close in. Perhaps getting on a motorcycle without asking where we were going hadn't been the smartest idea. I wasn't scared exactly, but I did wonder if I could reach my phone to send Delilah my location without him seeing.

He took off his helmet, and tried to turn around to mouth something to me. I flipped open the visor to see his lips.

"You have to get off before I can."

"*Right*."

"Use my shoulder," he said patiently. I was sheepish nonetheless.

"Right." I did as he instructed and by some miracle managed to dismount with only a small stumble. He, on the other hand, did it in a single swoop, putting me to shame. It gave me the urge to push him, but I refrained.

"Need a hand?" he asked, pointing to the helmet *I was still wearing*.

I wished I could disappear into the wall. Instead, I wrestled with the clasp and squirmed my head out like a crumbling cork being removed from a bottle, the tight padding all but ripping my nose off.

Handing him the helmet, I quickly brushed my hair back to hide the perspiration that was gathering on my forehead.

"Thanks," I said, as he masked amusement.

I looked around at the overflowing dumpsters. "You should know my roommate has my location."

"Noted," he said, walking farther down the alley.

I had to jog a few steps to catch up to him.

"Like jazz?" he asked.

"Sure. It's great to listen to while you're on hold with the bank."

He looked at me fearfully. "I hope you're kidding." Abruptly he stopped, knocking twice on a graffiti-strewn black door that was built into the side of the alley's brick façade.

A man appeared, holding the door partially-ajar. His slick hair and face tattoos suggesting he wasn't to be messed with.

"Password?"

"Mingus."

The man opened the door wider to assess me. "The girl's gonna have to answer a question."

"C'mon, she's with me," said Max. *Was I?* The thought momentarily distracted me from the ridiculousness of whatever was happening.

He looked me up and down. "I'll make it easy. Favorite standard."

"As Time Goes By," I said without hesitation. It's the title song from *Casablanca*, the movie my parents were watching when they met, and the record I grew up listening to on repeat.

The man sneered. Max looked away.

"Jazz standard, not movie musical."

"Oh, come on," I protested. "If it was good enough for Billie Holiday, it's good enough for you."

I didn't know what I was fighting for but there was no chance I was backing down.

"I'm only letting you in 'cause that's my wife's favorite movie," he said. His expression softening. "Go learn something."

He motioned behind him, as Max slipped him two twenties.

"She should have picked Bogart," he snickered as I walked past him.

I paused. "If only she were given a choice." I was indignant and he seemed to find it comical.

As I stepped inside, I could hear the faint tinniness of cymbals and the muffled vibrations of piano chords. Max led the way down a set of stairs that opened up onto a small basement landing where a black velvet curtain hung.

He pushed the drapes aside to reveal a stained glass door, which when opened, allowed the full volume of the music to escape the ragged, soundproofed seal. Our entrance coincided with the arrival of a double bass, which plucked its way into a lower key.

There was barely any light, the only source coming from the farthest side to us, where contrasting rugs outlined a stage. Three men played, while a fourth sat on a seat among them, bopping to the beat. Mirrors hanging above their heads showcased their laser-precision skill, effortlessly controlling their instruments like they were extensions of their limbs.

The room itself wasn't much bigger than mine and Delilah's. Rows of mismatched chairs were arranged against exposed brick walls, adjacent to a wooden bar that was so worn it appeared to be sinking.

Max ushered me toward two empty seats nestled in the back corner. I wasn't sure if it were the warmth of the crowded space or the obscurity of the darkness, but something was lulling me into a sense of ease and I was trying not to fight it.

The fourth musician stood up and put his mouth to a shiny silver saxophone. Bright sound slid from its end, as though it had been waiting hours to escape. I was transfixed, each note piercing perfectly through to the next, sliding so freely through the melody that it left the rest of the band having to chase after it.

Out of the corner of my eye, I could see Max studying me like arithmetic he found entertaining. I wanted to react, or care, but I couldn't summon the energy. The melancholy of the music had taken hold. It felt like the kind of old New York people always talk about, and for once, I didn't wanna cheat myself out of the moment by overthinking it.

I was so immersed, so in awe, that I grabbed Max's hand without thinking when the pianist started playing what sounded like the first line of as *"As Time Goes By."* If it weren't for the static electricity that sparked off us, I might have accidentally kept holding it forever.

I felt myself blush, but before I could feel the true weight of it, the room plunged into total darkness.

"What happened?" I asked, a little too loudly as the band abruptly stopped playing.

It sent a shiver down my spine.

"Blackout, I guess." Max whispered.

It felt like something more.

As people around us arrived at the same conclusion, using their phones as flashlights to illuminate the room, Max stood up. "You hungry?"

I shrugged. *Sure.* I wasn't, but I can always eat fries.

We got up and climbed the stairs, the sharpness of the cold air shocking my body into the reality of where it was. I threw on my leather jacket as we walked past the doorman.

"Hey, Casablanca," he said. "You have fun?"

"I did," I replied, still in a daze. "It was almost as good as seeing a mov—"

"Don't you dare finish that sentence," he said.

"No, for real, it was magic."

"Well, good," he beamed. "Come back anytime."

"Thanks," I said, feeling like I'd achieved something.

As we reached the exit, he spun around to a wall covered in flyers.

"Hold up," he said, searching for something. "They play that awful movie down by the Central Railroad Station in Jersey."

He pulled a sheet of paper off the wall and handed it to me. "Here. Take it. The wife makes me go every year," he said, winking at Max.

"'Makes you go?' Yeah, right." I smirked, taking the banter one step too far as usual. Aside from it being confrontingly sweet, I also didn't want Max to feel pressured to commit. "But thank you. This is cool," I said, in a way that was so far from it.

"Yeah, thanks," said Max, saving us. "See you round."

A few blocks away was a 24-hour diner that made me feel like we were in Edward Hopper's *Nighthawks*. Most likely designed after it, the yellow lights of Suzy's were a beacon among the grimy greens and blues of the city.

"Is that right?" I said out loud, glancing between the clock on the wall and my phone.

It was. 1.47 A.M.

"Woah," I muttered, immediately texting Delilah I was alive.

"You got lost for a second back there." A hint of pride in his tone.

"No, I didn't. Did I?" I asked, feeling self-conscious. "Yeah, well, light deprivation will do that to a person."

He laughed. "There's nothing wrong with getting a little

lost," he said, flicking his eyes to mine, before returning to read the menu.

Blood pulsed to my face, making me acutely aware of the sterile, unforgiving halogen that flickered ever so slightly above us.

"More free advice?" I shot back.

"Yours if you want it," he said, his eyes never leaving the page.

The waitress came to take our order. He got steak and eggs, and a black coffee. I got fries and a chocolate milkshake. As soon as she left our table, he said: "You order like a 12-year-old."

"Yeah, well... you order like a caveman."

He pulled a face.

"To think I was gonna let you try my shake," I said.

"I prefer strawberry anyways."

Of course he did.

"So, Max..." I said, forcing myself to look him in the eyes, thanks to an article I'd read about dominant people responding well to assertiveness, or something like that. I only got halfway through. "Aside from reading in Washington Square Park and A Bookshop on Avenue A, what do you do with your time?"

"This and that," he said.

And then nothing.

"Oh yeah?" I said. "Such as?"

"Such as... lots of things."

I laughed, this time out of frustration. "Are you intentionally making this hard?"

"Not intentionally, no."

"You just blinked!" I said.

"So?" he responded. "I'm not allowed to blink?"

"Blinking's a sign of lying. Everyone knows that," I answered flatly.

He shook his head as he looked at the table and then up at me. Full eye contact, zero blinks. "I am not intentionally trying to make anything difficult, your honor."

Happiness overtook my face. "Good. Then would you like to answer the polite, conversation-starting question?"

"I could..." he began. "But I'm not sure it's wise to divulge how I spend my time with... you know, someone who has a habit of showing up where I am."

"Yeah, I hate you," I said. Unable to believe I'd fallen for his trap.

He leaned in. "Then why are you still smiling?" If I was, so was he.

"You're relentless," I said.

"Thank you."

"So it *is* a compliment? Good to know."

"Sometimes."

"You're re-lent-less," I said, stressing the syllables.

"Yes," he responded. "Like that."

We stared at one another, my heart fluttering.

"Is this where I'm supposed to throw down your corny 'no one does love like the Romans' line? Cause I'm not sure I have the stomach for it."

He sat up straight. "That wasn't a line," he said. "That was the truth. They were the first to write about love like it actually is."

"Oh, yeah? And how's that?" I asked sarcastically.

"Rare. And fleeting," he said with a look of complete seriousness. Zero blinks.

"So, he's a pessimist?" I inquired genuinely.

"I'd say, a realist."

"But you think love is unattainable?"

"I never said that, but sure. For most," he said. He gestured around the room. "You think anyone in this room knows real love?"

"That's a bit arrogant, isn't it?"

"I was including myself."

I looked around the room and thought honestly about what

he was asking.

"Yes, I do," I stated indignantly. "I think everyone in this room knows, or has known, a certain type of love."

He thought about that.

"Exactly. I'm not interested in 'a certain type of love.'"

I wanted to let the subject rest, but my stubbornness wouldn't let me. "Does that help you? Keep people away?"

"Apparently not," he said, eyeballing me. "Besides, it's not about keeping people away."

"Sure it is," I replied. "If it's elusive, then it can be kept at a distance. That's why you read the Romans. To reinforce the idea that love is... rare and fleeting," I said like I'd stumbled upon the answer to unlocking him.

"Now who's the pessimist?" he shot back coyly. "I read them 'cause they remind me of what love's supposed to look like."

I froze. Had he really just said those words? My head was spinning and I could have sworn I was losing my hearing. I tried to catch my breath.

"Are you okay?" he asked, concern growing across his face.

"Yes," I mumbled, the noise of the room coming back to me. "I just... where's our—" I looked around the diner to find the waitress who was walking toward us with our drinks, as if on cue.

After she placed them on the table, I took a long sip of the shake, relishing the rush of sugar.

My eyes flicked to him as he sipped his coffee.

"Good?" he inquired.

I nodded, peeling my lips away from the straw.

"Mm hmm," I murmured.

My mind was racing and the brain freeze didn't help. What were the chances he'd say the same thing my dad had said to my mom? Maybe the words were different, but the intention was the same. *What were the actual odds?* I tried to do the mental tally in my head, until I considered the thing I didn't want to consider for fear of getting my hopes up: maybe it really was some kind of fate.

It was a concept that was becoming hard to deny. The thought filled my chest like a warm breeze.

It wasn't until we'd paid for our check that I realized the importance of what he'd said. He was open to love, maybe even looking for love, and he was there... with me. I ran through the conversation in my head as we left the diner and walked back to his bike. Perhaps it *was a date* after all? The thought alone made my hands tingle. Had I ruined a potentially romantic moment with all my probing? Had he been flirting and I didn't volley back hard enough? I had to say something so he knew I was on the same page.

"Hey, Max," I said, at the entrance to the alley.

He stopped and turned to face me.

"I've never met—"

"Anyone like me?" He teased, finishing my cliché of a sentence.

Good one, Eva. Super original.

"Well, same," he said, seriously. Like he meant it. "I've never met anyone like you either."

Tiny dimples appeared next to his perfect lips.

"So, what do we do about that?" I asked, attempting to recover.

A conflicted look settled upon his face.

"You got anywhere to be?"

I shook my head.

"Cool. There's some place I wanna show you."

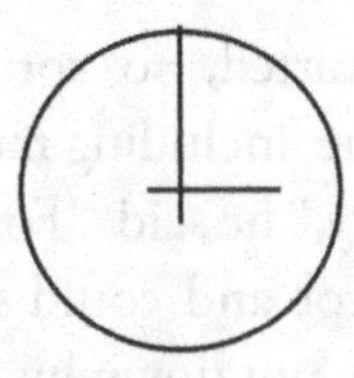

NINE

KISSING YOU

It felt different riding back downtown. The closeness was inviting, as if our bodies were each other's missing half.

We pulled off Broadway and stopped outside an elaborately constructed gothic skyscraper, just blocks from the World Trade Center, which loomed impressively above. I wondered what my dad would have thought about the colossal tower, rebuilt even more impressively than the last.

As we got off the bike, Max pulled open the seat to rummage around for something. He still had his helmet on as he took mine and placed it inside a reusable shopping bag.

"Follow me," he said, walking towards ornate gold doors. As we reached the handle, he added, "I'll distract the doorman. You go straight to the elevator."

What?

He was already inside before I had the opportunity to protest. Immediately, I crouched down, mostly out of panic.

"I've got a delivery for the penthouse," he said.

"Deliveries 'round back," an old man's voice croaked from behind the reception.

I duck-walked my way toward the counter. Figuring at that

point, I'd already committed, so springing up unannounced would only shock everyone, including me.

"This is a food delivery," he said. "For Mr. Corvus."

I'd reached the elevator and could see the man in the shiny reflection of the doors. He put down his paper to take Max in.

"Apologies," he said. "Go right on up."

Max nodded and turned toward me. I was so nervous about getting caught, I closed my eyes for a second thinking that if I couldn't see him, he couldn't see me.

I opened them in time to see him walk into the elevator closest to me, so I slid in after him seconds before the doors shut.

"A heads-up would've been nice."

"I wasn't sure you'd do it."

I looked around the embellished, mirrored box. "What are we doing here?"

"You'll see."

"I'm not really into surprises," I said.

"Is that so?" He laughed, stepping out of the elevator and making me feel like a petulant child.

In front of us was a single door, marked with the letter 'P,' which I assumed indicated the penthouse. Realizing we were outside someone's home ignited the kind of fiery feeling that comes from being somewhere I knew I wasn't supposed to be.

Max must have felt the panic; he grabbed my hand and swung me around to a hidden door on the other side from where we'd arrived. A gold sign read: *Maintenance Access*.

I stepped inside to see iron stairs that trailed off, up into the dark spire. Max followed, closing the door behind him, taking out almost all the light.

"We're going up, aren't we?" I asked, scared of the answer. The only thing lighting up the tight space was a red Exit sign that loomed above us.

Confirming my fear, he started on the first few steps, taking them three at a time.

I pulled the elastic I had on my wrist around my hair, and followed him up. "But not... not all the way up, right?" I said, trying not to sound like I wasn't my losing breath, when, in fact, I was. "Right?"

Max just laughed. *Helpful*.

The higher we got, the smaller the steps became, until a ladder appeared before us. I was petrified to think where it led, let alone to what height. The elevator showed 56 floors in the building; we'd walked up at least an additional four or five flights.

My terror was realized when Max opened a manhole, and all I could hear was the wind howling above.

"Are you sure about this?" I asked.

He squeezed through the exit, then turned around to offer me his hand.

One look was all it took. He gave me one look, and the fear washed away, as it had been doing all night—my legs willingly taking the additional steps, my hand reaching up for his.

He pulled me through the opening, and before I knew it, I was gazing into the night sky from a height so high it felt unnatural. There were only a few buildings taller than us, but our 360-degree view of Manhattan was almost completely unobstructed. Max replaced the manhole cover and guided me to stand on top of it.

"This is where I am," he said.

"What now?" I asked, trying to listen and not die.

We were in a turret of sorts—the only thing separating us from the many, *many* feet to the ground was a waist-high stone wall I was clutching desperately. The wind roared around us, strands of my hair escaping from their bond as Max moved closer.

"When I'm not reading in the park... or at the bookshop. This is where I am."

"It's beautiful," I said, properly taking in the view for the first time. "Once you get over the fear of plummeting to your death."

"Nothing like great heights to give you a different perspective."

I looked down. I shouldn't have. "Park Avenue didn't come with a view?" I joked, referencing our first meeting.

"It did," he replied, the same sadness from the park clearly infecting him.

I released my clenched hands from the stone wall and tried to focus my attention on him. "When did you leave?"

"I was ten."

"Oh," I said, confused.

"That's when my parents were... they died."

"Both of them?"

"Yes."

"I'm sorry," I said. Feeling an all too familiar pain.

"It's okay... they... it is what it is, right? I mean, you just get on with it. Your life changes, you adjust. Maybe you don't ever get over the memory of how it felt to have them around, but the more days that go by, the easier it all gets."

"I'm sorry," I repeated, processing what he'd said. "I've never thought about it like that before. I always wished I'd known my parents, but maybe knowing them would have been harder."

"Both of them?" he asked, an understanding look of sympathy crossing his face.

"Yeah."

"I'm sorry," he said.

"I was a baby," I said, dismissively.

"Doesn't mean it doesn't hurt just as bad."

"I guess."

A silent knowing passed between us, like we'd just unlocked some secret language only we knew.

"I have this memory of my mom holding me. I know it's not real 'cause she died as they were taking me out of her," I said, trying to escape the sense of self-blame that was always undoubtedly bubbling under the surface. "But sometimes, I pretend it was true. I imagine her holding me... and think about how different my life would have been if she—"

"Don't," he said, softly. "I promise you, there's nothing helpful down that road. I've been there so many times I thought about camping out forever. But there's no happiness there. You just have to play the cards you're dealt."

"Is that what you're doing?" I asked. *"Playing the cards?"*

"I don't have any clue what I'm doing," he said.

I could recognize his damage so well. In many ways it was an exact replica of my own.

I looked out across the city. The sun starting to rise in the distance, slowly turning the high-rises from monochrome into color.

"My granddad has these questions he always makes me answer," I said. "You wanna hear them?"

"Shoot."

"Something you're grateful for?"

"Uh... my health," he said, throwing it away like the act of answering was more important than the answer.

"Okay," I said. "Something you're proud of?"

"I haven't smoked a cigarette in three months."

"That *is* something to be proud of," I said, like a mother. "And here I was thinking the unlit cigarette thing was just for show."

"I don't do anything for show," he said. "Having it and not smoking it is the best kind of discipline there is."

"If you say so," I said, eyeballing him. "Lastly, something you're excited about?"

A smile crept over his face. "Hold on, I've done two questions and you've done none."

"You haven't asked me any," I said defensively.

"Something you're grateful for?"

I looked around. "Being in this city." My face lit up. "And I don't remotely care how lame that sounds. It's magnetic and I feel lucky to be here."

He was analyzing me again like I was hard to figure out.

"My parents met here," I said, trying to open up the way he had with me. "At a screening of *Casablanca*. My dad was on leave from the Navy…" I could feel my voice start to break, emotion infecting it. "Anyway, they fell in love and nine months later, I was here… and they were not."

"How?" he asked, sensing I wanted to talk about it. Most people are afraid to ask.

"A car accident," I said. "They were on their way to the hospital. To deliver me."

"I'm so sorry."

"Thanks," I said. "From what I've heard about them, they would have hated going out in something as generic as a car crash."

He laughed. The fact that he knew it was okay to made me feel even more connected to him.

"At least something great came from it."

"And what a consolation prize," I said, hitting the sarcasm a little too hard for it to be passed off as humor.

"No," he said. "A prize. Period."

It made me smile in a way that was too big to hide.

"Something you're proud of?" he asked.

That I managed to trap you into a conversation, I wanted to say but didn't want to kill the mood. "Keeping it together. I'm always pretty proud of myself for that."

"It can feel like your whole existence some days."

"Yeah. It really can," I said, eyeing him. "Something you're excited about?" I asked before he could.

"Sneaky," he said.

"Ya snooze, you lose pal."

He laughed.

"Go on. Something that you're excited about?"

He was amused as he moved his face closer.

His eyes bore straight into mine. He was so close I could feel my breath rebound off his skin. Slipping one hand around the back of my neck, he cradled my face in his other. The warmth of his skin melting my frozen cheek.

Then he kissed me. Softly, tentatively. Like his lips were discovering mine.

Pulling away slightly, he hovered mere millimeters from my face, offering his kiss again. It was as if the world stopped, just for a moment. The air kicked itself from my lungs, my heart soaring, as if the butterflies that had been fluttering in my stomach all night were finally taking flight.

I kissed him back, grabbing his neck and his waist. I needed to be as close to him as possible, anticipation rising through every cell in my body. Every molecule.

We were intertwined, as one, our weightless bodies enveloped by the dawn breeze that danced around us.

It felt like nothing else in the world mattered. Only us, and only that moment.

My mind imagined neon light emanating from around us, intertwining with us, as Max began to spin me.

Around.

And around.

Higher, and higher. Lighter, and lighter...

Until *thunk*. I felt myself fall against the rough, cold stone, Max's arms the only thing stopping me from collapsing completely.

"Ow." I laughed, trying to recover, disoriented. Furious at my knees for betraying me.

My hand reached to where I'd hit my head. "Well, that was..." I pulled myself up, my train of thought interrupted by the ghostly look on Max's face. "Are you okay?" I asked.

Worry washed over him. "Am I okay? Are you okay?" he responded, clearly concerned.

A tidal wave of embarrassment careened over me. "Yeah. I seemed to have... fallen," I said. "Fainted?"

"Yeah, I'm not sure." He looked just as confused as I felt, but reality was starting to sink in and along with it, the horror of the fact that I might have actually... *Fainted*.

"Oh God," I exclaimed. "I'm so sorry."

"It's okay." He assured awkwardly. "As long as you're alright?"

There was no doubt he was concerned, but he seemed different, cold almost... like the feelings he'd displayed just moments ago had been finite, and were now eroding before my very eyes.

"I'm totally fine," I lied, still out of it.

I stood up to face him, hopeful things could return to how they just were.

"Good," he said, his tone failing to convince me. "It's late. We should get you home."

The words ripped like a knife, but I did my best not to show it.

"Yeah, of course," I answered. "I've got class in a few hours."

Every rung, step and landing to the penthouse floor felt like an eternity. I didn't know what to say, so I didn't speak; the sight of Max's back striding off in front of me didn't fill me with confidence that he wanted to hear from me anyway. What I couldn't work out was why.

When we finally got to the elevator, I made eye contact with him and when he didn't smile back, I had to know for sure.

"Do you find that all girls pass out when you kiss them... or am I... just lucky?" I asked, teasing myself.

He nodded, like he was discovering it. "No, Eva. Just you."

"Happy to be a first," I said, trying to lighten the mood.

By the time he dropped me home, I was ready to put my insecurities behind me. I'd decided that even if I had freaked him out a little, I wasn't going to be the one to act differently. Things happen in life that you can't control, *like apparently I faint when hot boys kiss me*, and if he wasn't mature enough to appreciate that, then I'd dodged a bullet.

Dismounting the bike in a single swoop, I had the helmet unclasped and removed before he even had a chance to touch his chin. I was learning. I just hoped he was paying attention.

"I had a really nice time," I said, trying to force myself to speak slowly when all I wanted to do was run. "Thanks for letting me see a bit of your world."

He nodded. "I had fun, too."

"Let's do it again."

"For sure," he said. Looking away, fiddling with his helmet strap. He was acting like he didn't want to be there, yet he wasn't leaving.

"Next week?" I challenged him.

"Didn't you say your grandparents were coming in then?"

"No," I said, baffled by the left turn. "They hate the city. I never would've said—"

"Sorry. Must've gotten mixed up."

"It's okay."

I couldn't work out if he were trying to avoid making plans with me, or if he was trying to restart our earlier conversation.

"They're your dad's parents, right?" he inquired.

"Yeah," I said. "Why?"

"What about your mom's?" he doubled down. "Where are they?"

"I don't know. I never knew them," I replied, which was the truth. "They died when she was a kid."

"Sorry," he said.

"It's all good. Seems to be a theme in my family. So, next week?" I asked one last time. Any and all pride I formally had was long gone.

"For sure," he said again. "Let's."

He leaned in, so I bought my face to his.

"Don't faint," he joked.

I laughed, and he kissed me.

Soft.

Passionate.

Convincing.

Perhaps everything was okay.

"Goodnight, Max," I said, pulling away. "Call me."

"Goodnight, Eva," he said.

I turned and felt like I was floating again. Five flights felt like one, and before I knew it, I was staring at my ceiling, trying to piece the night together. The jazz, the diner, the bike, the skyline... the kiss. Aside from the way it ended, it had been a perfect night. Joy overwhelmed the shame, so I let it. Within moments, I was drifting off, a goofy grin plastered across my face.

When my phone alarm went off 45 minutes later, I wanted to break it and the promise I'd made to myself the night before that I wouldn't miss first period, no matter what. So, I rolled out of bed with my eyes still shut, showered, and took myself to class. I may have fallen asleep for most of it, but I was there, and I even took a note:

Stories are never finished.
They're just published.

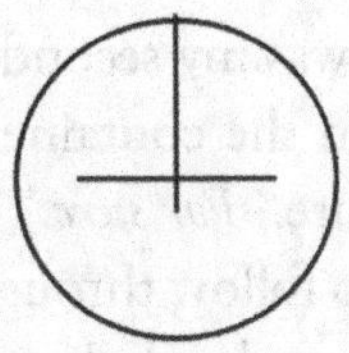

TEN

I Belong in Your Arms

It's not that I was expecting him to call right away. He's far too much of a cool kid to do that. I never saw his phone, but I imagined it to be the kind of thirty-dollar burner that's sold at gas stations—his own personal act of rebellion towards 21st century tech addiction. But knowing and hoping are two very different things. Hope, in these situations, can spiral out of control, much in the same way negativity can. Once you let it in, it's not long before every thought becomes infected.

It was Friday night, about 36 hours after seeing him (but who was counting?) that I let my mind drift into thoughts of how our interaction would go, whenever he did decide to reach out. Would he be cold like he'd been in the park? Or would he speak to me how he did on our date? Like I was special, or somehow remarkable? But before I knew it, Sunday had arrived and my phone hadn't seen any action.

I tried to shut off the evil part of my brain, but I couldn't shake the sinking feeling that something was wrong. It probably wasn't helping that I kept falling asleep to *The Smiths* almost every night.

"I don't understand," I said to Delilah in the cafeteria, mid spoonful of ice-cream. It was my second pint and I felt nauseous, but there was still more in the container. "I said let's hang again next week, *he said*, 'For sure.' *For sure.*' Why would he say that if he wasn't actually going to follow through? It's just dumb."

"Well, guys by nature are dumb."

"Just say no," I ranted. "When I said call me. He could have said, *no*, I'm not going to call you. It's not that difficult. At least then I wouldn't have stared at my phone for five days straight waiting for it to ring."

"Yeah, it's not hard," she reasoned. But I had a feeling she just wanted me to shut up. This wasn't our first Max hasn't called conversation.

"And who doesn't have Instagram? It's weird—"

"You don't have Insta—"

"Exactly! *I'm weird!*" I exclaimed, about twenty decibels too loud. "I should just call him. Shouldn't I?" I said. "That doesn't seem overly desperate, right?" I could hear the shrillness in my own voice but I wasn't about it to let vanity hold me back.

"Do whatever you need to do," she said.

"So that's a: you don't think I should, but you think I'm gonna do it anyway, so you're not gonna bother talking me out of it?"

"No," Delilah said, with as little judgment as possible. "It's a: if you need to call him 'cause you can't *not call him*, then call him. But if you can wait... without going completely insane... then wait."

I thought about it very seriously. For all of two seconds.

"No. I can't wait." I'd done almost a week of it and was already a hop, skip and a jump away from being committed. "I'd rather know now so I can I move on," I said, like I was living in my own telenovela.

I pulled out my phone and called his number.

It rang seven painstakingly long times before diverting to an automated message bank.

"Do I leave a voicemail?"

"No," she said. But it was too late.

"Hey." I stood up and started wandering around the room to try and ward off my nervousness. "It's me. Eva. Eva Nelson. From...well, the other night." I looked to Delilah for help, but she shrugged her shoulders, looking baffled, in awe of my stupidity, no doubt.

"Anyway, I just wanted to say hey... and that, well... I was thinking about spontaneously fainting again this week and I wanted to know if you'd be around to watch? Ya see, it's kind of a spectator sport. It's only fun if someone's there to point and laugh."

I looked to Delilah, who was on the verge of cracking up.

"Lemme know," I said, then hung up.

We stared at each other in complete shock.

"Wow. That was a lot," we said in unison.

"Oh God, it was, wasn't it?" I asked, knowing the truth but needing it to be confirmed by an independent source.

"I mean, yes," she said, apologetically.

"It wasn't even a little cute?" I asked.

"It was very you."

Horror befell me.

"No," she said. "In the way that if he gets you, he'll get that, and... he'll love it. If he doesn't, then—"

"Yeah, I don't think he will," I said, confirming the answer to myself. I was sad at the thought, but I also realized that there was truth to what Delilah was saying. I didn't want to be around someone who didn't want to be around me. "Maybe it's for the best. If he doesn't get me, then... he doesn't get *all this*," I said, gesturing toward my ice-cream-covered face.

"Look at you getting the hang of it!" Delilah said, like a proud stage mom.

It wasn't complete closure, but I managed to feel somewhat resolved for two moderately productive days until I tricked myself into believing that he wasn't the type of person to ever check his voicemails. I knew it was a stretch, but having grown up glued to rom-coms, where plotlines revolved around missed connections, I decided I had nothing to lose by sending one final text. If he didn't respond, then I was done. For good.

> Hi! Wasn't sure if you got my voicemail, so figured I'd text… I think you're great :) Let me know if you wanna hang again sometime x

He didn't respond, of course.

No reply, no call. Nothing. And ashamedly, it broke me. Harder than I knew was possible.

I'd unlearned how to do even the most basic task without crying, like falling asleep. The darkness and silence terrified my lonely heart. I was overreacting, I could feel that. I knew it wasn't possible to have such strong feelings about a person I barely knew, and yet I had them all the same. The truth was, I missed him. I missed the way I thought he saw me. I wanted to know what I'd done wrong, what about me had turned him off. I tortured myself, replaying every moment, constantly on the hunt for clues. I had to know so I could fix it, or at least prevent it from happening again. Something, anything, to make sure I'd never repeat hitting rock bottom.

It was Sunday night, twelve days post-date, when a thought struck me I couldn't shake. I'd been studying at the library, also known as thinking about Max in a different location, when I started to panic that something was wrong with him. It was just after 8 P.M. when I arrived at the horrible theory: what if he never made it home? Motorcycle accidents happen all the time. What if he were hurt and lost his phone, and or my number? Or worse…

I couldn't figure out if it was just another inventive way my mind was playing tricks on me, using my anxiety as a means to justify seeing him, but by around 9:30 P.M. I decided that my fear of looking stupid didn't outweigh an alternate situation where he needed my help.

Within minutes, I'd packed my things and found myself standing in front of the bookshop. Through the window I could see that it was open, but it wasn't until a customer walked out of the door that I saw he was there. He was sat at the counter, book in hand, wearing a faded denim jacket with shearling around the collar.

I struggled to catch my breath, just as I'd done the first day in the park. His signature strand of hair was exactly where it should be, strewn across his forehead. I felt my hand wanting to brush it off, to tuck it behind his ear, so I could look into his eyes.

The door finally closed but, before it did, he glanced up. At least I thought he did. I couldn't be certain he saw me but anticipation swirled in my stomach nonetheless, the elation of seeing him immediately erasing any fear that he was hurt.

I stood there, waiting to hear him call out my name. Praying that he would run out onto the street to find me.

When he didn't, reality crashed down on top of me. The rush I was feeling meant it was wrong for me to be there. Perhaps for a moment, I'd been truly concerned about his wellbeing but, if I was honest with myself, I'd just wanted to see him.

As soon as the realization hit, every ounce of happiness drained from my body. I had to leave. No going in. No excuse for saying hello. *No asking where it all went wrong.* I had to put one foot in front of the other, and walk.

I'd made it all the way to 6th Street before I finally managed to catch my breath.

It was in between inhales that I realized how late it was, and how few people were out. I looked around for a taxi, but the roads were dead. Worried that if I didn't maintain momentum I'd return to the bookshop, I pushed forward into the chill of the night. My theory being that if I were quick enough I could bypass any potential danger. The wind had picked up since I'd left the library so I kept my head down, focusing on the sidewalk. Putting as many steps between Max and me as possible.

I'd just crossed Houston, heading to the Lower East Side, when I noticed the rhythmic clack of boots behind me.

Click clack. Click clack.

If I really thought about it, whoever was walking behind had been there for at least four or five blocks.

Click clack. Click clack.

I took off my gold-plated rings, and tucked my mother's necklace into my shirt. They weren't worth anything but a stranger wouldn't know that.

Hoping a few of the restaurants that lined the street would still be open, I took a right down Rivington. As I turned the corner to look back, I saw the outline of a man all in black: coat, boots, pants, shirt. I thought for a second it might be Max, but he walked differently. Something about the way he moved was... *off*.

I increased my pace but the man's steps sounded closer and closer. I tried to brush it off as paranoia, but I couldn't shake the sickening feeling that he was following me.

Click clack. Click clack.

As I turned the next block, my heart swelled to see people outside a bar, drinking. I crossed the street toward a group, only to sidestep behind them as the man strolled past without so much as a backward glance. I let out a breath, realizing I was gravitating further and further away from sanity. I was only four blocks from home but still moderately scared, so I called Delilah. She picked up on the second ring.

"Heeeeeyy," she said.

"I didn't wake you, did I?"

"No, love, you're good. What's up?"

"I'm walking down Ludlow and Rivington. Can you watch my location? The park scares me," I said, too ashamed to tell her about the episode I'd just had.

"Of course. Want me to come down?"

"No, but I appreciate it; 172 steps. That's friendship."

"Don't you forget it," she laughed. "See you in a sec."

My shirt was sweat-soaked by the time I got home, despite it being 60 degrees outside. I couldn't be sure if it was the heartbreak of seeing Max, or working myself up over a stranger, but I felt a spiral coming on and I knew the only way to escape it would be with sleep. I managed to disassociate from the feeling entirely until I found myself in Advanced Journalism the following day. The $6 coffee I'd bought myself as a bribe to leave the comfort of my bed had done more than just alert me to my surroundings. It had stirred the beast in my head and I was losing my grip on being able to drown it out.

Thoughts infested my mind. The knowledge that Max was alive and well meant that he was actively choosing not to contact me. I had to confront that what I'd thought of as mutual and real was actually a one-sided fantasy. Then the thought dawned on me: what if he had seen me, and he didn't like what he saw? What if all my flaws, all the horrible things I secretly believed about myself were true? *What if I was too much, too needy, too depressed?*

"Don't you agree, Ms. Nelson?"

I looked up to see Mr. McKenzie and the entire class staring at me.

I didn't know what to say. I hadn't a clue what he'd asked me, let alone the topic.

"Ms. Nelson?" he repeated.

"I'd love to agree, but I'm gonna have to be honest and say that I might have zoned out for a moment there...so I missed the question. I apologize," I said, hoping he'd take the truth as an offering.

He smiled. "But you're back with us now?" he asked.

"Fully and completely," I nodded.

"Good," he said, pausing for effect. "The rest of us have been discussing Lawrence J Philip's "Hierarchy of Communication," which ranks written documents as the least effective way of approaching or interviewing a source, and *what* as the most effective?"

"Oh, umm…" I actually knew this. I'd read it last week. "Face to face!" I blurted out. "He says it's the only form of communication that allows you to use all of your senses, instead of just one." *Man, did I feel smug.*

"Indeed. He also says that a source is more likely to divulge information they wouldn't over the phone or by email, because?"

He looked around the room for someone to answer, and even though I could have, I was ready for the attention to be off me. Instead, I slid down in my chair and took a breath.

A guy whose name I thought was Felix answered, "People are more likely to trust you if they can see your face. It taps into their empathy."

"Exactly. Our brains are hardwired to mimic other people's actions. If they smile, you feel at ease, and so forth." He looked at his watch and continued: "And that is about all we have time for. Please remember the first exam of the semester is next Friday."

I started packing up my things as the bell rang.

"The result of which will be added to your marks from the assessment that's due today. Or," he added, looking back at the watch, "in four minutes if you want to go by the syllabus, and I have a feeling some of you are. Christopher, Gleb, yes. I watched both of you typing away on your phones all class and it's been mentally noted."

Panic pierced through my body. I'd completely forgotten about the assignment. I felt my blood pulsate, but I refused to give into the anxiety. I couldn't, not in front of so many people. I would never recover. I forced my mind to name as many shades of color in my head as I could, a trick I'd learned from some YouTube therapist. The idea, she said, was to distract the mind from whatever was triggering the episode.

Onyx, ink, ebony, midnight… I thought to myself.

Obsidian, coal...

I tried to focus my mind, but I couldn't formulate a solution quickly enough. I hadn't even started the assignment and it was impossible to write something in four minutes. I ran through potential options: I could tell the truth—I was having an emotional week and I needed an extension. Or, I could lie and blame a computer problem, but at best that would buy me time to get my laptop, which was literally two floors away.

Then I remembered. There was stuff I'd written that he hadn't read, things that hadn't been posted online; assignments from Spring City. They weren't the best—I'd learned so much already in the few weeks I'd been at Anderson—but it was better than nothing. I pulled out my phone and searched through my emails. Mr. McKenzie's assignment was 1,000 words on a human-interest story, and I had just the piece... if only I could find it. I'd written it up the previous year, as an interview with a woman I'd met volunteering at our local nursing home. She was a doula, who helped terminal patients prepare to die.

I scanned it as everyone started filing out of the room. My word choice could've been better, and the lead-in wasn't the catchiest, but it was the only viable option.

"Everything okay there, Eva?" McKenzie called out.

The last few people were making their way out the door, and I was the only one left in any of the rows.

"Sure, yeah," I said, picking up my bag and moving toward the front of the room. Still unsure of what I was going to say.

"I really respect you. So, I want to be honest," I started.

"Lots of honesty coming from you today."

"Yes. Sorry again about before. I guess that's linked, actually, to what I—"

"It's okay, of course," he said. "I do understand, but you also have to understand that if you respect me, as you say you do, then your behavior is demonstrating the opposite. I don't think I'd be remiss to say, I expected more."

"Yes," I agreed. Pressure was building up behind my eyes, my chest rising and falling quicker than ideal.

"You have so much potential, Eva..."

And there it was again, my least favorite word. The one I'd been hearing my entire life.

I couldn't control it anymore, a tear fell from my left eye. Then from my right. Then another. And another.

Before I knew it, I was crying. In front of my supposed mentor.

He turned to pick up a box of tissues, offering them to me in a gesture that felt more human than I knew him capable.

Reluctantly, I took one, blowing my nose as quietly as possible.

"We've really thrown you in the deep end here, haven't we?" he offered.

I wanted to disagree; I didn't want him to think I couldn't handle the workload, because if my head was in the game, I would have been fine. But reluctantly, I needed his sympathy.

"It's been an adjustment," I confirmed.

"There's no shame in accepting defeat. If anything, it allows us to—"

"I'm not sure I'd call it defeat," I interrupted. "I just need an extension. Just a day?"

"Ah," he said, sounding even more disappointed. "I'm afraid I can't help you with that. It would be unfair to the students who did the work on time."

"Of course. I get that," I said. "I do have something, it's just not as good as I would like it to be."

"Any decision you make is yours, but don't lose sight of the big picture. I know how bad you want it to work out here, but we're only a few weeks in. You still have time to return to your previous—"

"No," I said defiantly. I couldn't even hear the sentence out loud. "That's not an option."

"Well, just give it some thought. Because it is an option. Graduating at the top of your class there would be much more advantageous than failing here. After all, your scholarship is dependent on your grades."

Fury rose to my face. I was late with one assignment. *Why was he ready to discount me so quickly? I hadn't given up, why had he?*

"I'll be fine," I said, trying to stand to my full height. "But thank you. I appreciate the concern."

I was about to leave when I paused momentarily.

"Was there something else?" he asked.

I wasn't finished embarrassing myself, apparently. "I've emailed Annabel a bunch of times about submitting a piece for the paper."

He chuckled in the most patronizing way possible. "Perhaps you should focus more on the work you've already got on your plate, Eva. Writing for the paper is a privilege."

I didn't know what offended me more. That he was right, or being lectured on privilege by a white-collar white guy. Either way, it was clear he wasn't going to help me.

"Yes, it is," I said, as I backed out of the room.

It was one minute to noon as I uploaded my old assignment to Anderson's submission site. If he were going to give me elitist tropes, then I was well within my right to give him reused work.

I kept it together through the busy corridors, passing students down three flights of stairs, and all the way into the girls' dorm, so I was surprised when I walked into my room and burst into uncontrollable sobs. Delilah had asked how my morning was and instead of a response, I gave her a waterfall. I slid down the wall feeling lost and humiliated.

She knelt beside me on the worn vinyl, gently rubbing my back, trying to infuse life back into me.

"It's okay, love," she said. "Let it out. You got this."

I didn't wanna hear it, but my body did. Like I had no choice in the matter. So I let myself cry.

I cried for the two men who'd let me down, but mostly I cried for myself. I cried because I couldn't believe I'd put myself in a situation where I let a boy who didn't even like me derail what mattered to me most. *I was supposed to be smarter than that. I was supposed to be stronger.*

"It's going to be okay," Delilah said, still at my side. "I'm here."

"I'm sorry, I didn't mean to unload—"

"Babe, quit it," she said. "This sorry excuse for a room is your home, and I am your friend. If you can't cry here, where can you cry, huh?" she asked, ever so sweetly.

"Mm hm," I muttered.

"Is it the boy?" she asked. "Still nothing?"

"No, but yes," I hiccuped. "I mean, sure, it's him too. It's everything."

"How many days has it been?" she asked.

"Twelve," I said. "And I know," I added, anticipating her response.

"Babe…"

"I know," I hiccupped again. "He's gone."

"I'm sorry," she said. "I think so."

"But he… he was just so…"

"It's so much harder when they seem promising and then they disappear. The almosts."

"I don't like dating," I said.

"No one does," she responded. "That's why people put themselves through the agony of marriage."

"That's bleak."

"Correct."

"It's fine," I lied. "I don't know why I'm so upset. I barely knew him."

"Don't do that. Feel whatever it is you feel."

"Sure, yeah. I get that, but also, practically speaking, I spent like six… or seven… hours total with him. How sad can I possibly be?" Hearing myself say it out loud made it all the more pathetic.

"I only knew Jack Dawson for three hours and I still cried when that ship went down," said Delilah.

I laughed.

"Okay, enough of that," I said.

"Want some good news?"

"Please," I recovered, wiping the mascara from under my eyes.

"I got a part," she said, smiling.

"*What?* In the play?"

Delilah giggled. "Yes."

"*You got a part in the play!*" My enthusiasm sounded forced, but it was genuine. "Delilah, that is amazing!" I went to hug her too fast and ended up pushing her over.

"Thank you!" she screamed, kicking her legs under me.

"Why did you let me go on and on?"

"Because you needed to."

That hit. I really had. "Thank you," I said. "Really."

"You got it."

"Alright, this is big." I couldn't cry anymore and I was about to. "We should do something special!"

"You know what, I agree," she said. "What are you thinking?"

"Whatever you want." A pang of grief flooded back into my chest. "This is your celebration."

"Eva, love…" said Delilah, noticing. "You just made it through your first dating encounter with a New Yorker. This is just as much a celebration for you."

I wanted to disagree, but before I could, she got a mischievous twinkle in her eye and said, "Let's go dancing. I know *just* the place."

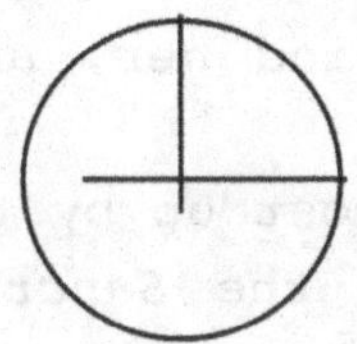

ELEVEN
PRETTY PIECE OF FLESH

The rage that coursed through my body was so vicious, I wasn't sure I could hold onto the handlebars of my bike without ripping them clean off. It bubbled and spasmed inside of me with such ferocity, I wanted to explode. To decimate myself and everything in my vicinity. Or better still, to close my eyes and let speed do its job.

It would've been better for everyone. My recklessness had not only put my life in danger, but hers too, and no matter how I tried to spin it in my head, I knew I could never live with myself if I dragged her down with me.

I needed to figure out a plan. Immediately. If the men in hoods didn't already know what happened, they would soon. Every impulse in my body was telling me to run, to find the farthest place and hide out for as long as possible, but I knew if they couldn't find me, they'd find her, and I couldn't let that happen.

The sun was almost up by the time I arrived home, and just as the *Sancti* had once waited for my parents, they were outside my apartment door now, waiting for me. Their clothing was more civilian this time, perhaps an attempt to blend in, but their air of pageantry and righteousness was impossible to mistake.

A middle-aged man with a shaggy, graying beard stood in front. Next to him, a younger man with sharp cheekbones and even sharper eyes leaned against the wall. Expressionless, they stood aside as I put my key into the lock.

"To what do I owe the pleasure?"

"Inside," instructed the older one, clearly buying into his own cloak and dagger routine.

I complied, opening the door and flicking on the lights.

The two men followed me in, quietly surveying every inch of my living room. I tried to not let it rattle me, but my hands were starting to shake.

"People know we're here," stated the younger one. "If you attempt anything, our brothers will be alerted."

I chuckled. How little they knew.

"Not if it's done right," I said, adding quickly, "fortunately, I don't practice."

"I pray that's the case, for the sake of your soul," said the older one. "I would imagine the slightest temptation would unhinge you."

Something about the cruelty in his eyes made me recognize his face. He'd been there the night my parents were killed, standing alongside the man who'd done the talking.

I exhaled, but refused to drop my gaze. I had to let him know I wasn't intimidated. Weakness of any kind could, and would, be exploited.

"Father… I assume?"

"Gleason," he said, puffing out his chest.

"Well, Father Gleason, this has been fun. Let's do it again in another ten years."

"Why aren't you displaying your symbol?" asked the other one, almost earnestly. He was no more than 35, still boyish in appearance and, every so often, demeanor. His calculated stare was made acceptable by his overt politeness, the combination of which unnerved me to my core.

"He's not the brightest, is he?" I asked Gleason, returning my attention to him.

"Brother Berinati asked you a question."

"Berinati? As in The Cardinal's—?"

"Son, yes," he answered for himself. It was a name I hadn't heard in years. Not since I'd researched the man responsible for my parents' deaths. But it made me feel the same, like a terrified child.

"As I just said, I don't practice. I don't have a need for it."

"So you have no knowledge of the energy

surge that just lit up half of Manhattan?" prodded Father Gleason.

"What energy surge?" It was clear they didn't know much or they wouldn't still be asking questions. I had to play as ignorant as I almost certainly was.

"The energy surge coming from this building."

He stepped forward, brow furrowed.

"No idea—"

"If it wasn't you, then it must have been the young woman you dropped off at Forsyth and Delancey. Correct?"

My mind raced to Eva. I couldn't imagine them doing anything to her without evidence, especially in a dorm filled with students. The *Sancti* practically invented staying out of the public eye, but there wasn't a world where I would've anticipated them knowing about her already.

I had no choice but to take responsibility. I felt myself slip into damage control; a skill I'd come to perfect. The scars of a kid forced into adulthood years before I should have been. I needed that coping mechanism if there were any chance of getting out of the apartment alive.

"He didn't like that," said Berinati, flatly.

"Huh?" I asked, pretending to snap out of it. "No, I was just trying to remember her name. It makes them feel less like a one-night stand when you drive them home."

They both stared at me, their eyes

dissecting mine. I knew they didn't believe me — what intelligent person would? — but the question was whether they had any evidence to back it up.

"Be sure we'll look into it," he warned.

"I don't doubt it."

"Still doesn't explain the surge," added Gleason.

"Did it harm anyone?" I inquired, thinking perhaps I'd found my loophole. "This energy surge?"

"Let's not deviate from the point."

"That's the whole point, is it not?" I asked, not looking for an answer. "That's what all your rules are for, *correct*?"

Berinati went to speak, but Gleason stopped him with a look. Their hesitation added to my confidence.

"Well, Father? Did it?"

Gleason stared into my eyes, looking like he'd caught me. "So you're admitting it was you?"

"*Admitting* to practicing without proper identification?" added Berinati, as if the semantics mattered.

"I admit to being out of control with a woman whose name I don't remember. If you need me to explain further, your holiness, I can," I spat.

"You're claiming she contributed no part?" Berinati continued.

"All she knows is that she had a good time," I replied, my heart breaking a little. I despised lying at the best of times, but referring to her with such disregard made me feel sick.

Gleason must have sensed my pain, sliding his face even closer to mine. "That's a lot of power for one person."

"I wouldn't know. I've never had to test it out. As I told you, I don't practice."

"It seems you have an answer for everything," he relented, his musty breath enveloping me.

"No," I said. "There are certain things I'll never have the answers to. But I know better than to stir all that up."

He pulled back and started pacing the room. Arms crossed behind his back, he looked as if he were about to deliver a sermon.

"Did you know that during the Shang Dynasty, 1,600 years before Christ's arrival, familial exterminations were the norm? It was thought that if one apple were rotten, the tree should be taken out entirely. Their belief in 'guilt by association' was deemed sufficient enough to warrant death to the entire bloodline," he said.

Actually, I did know that, and they weren't the only ones.

"Didn't they also believe that if you swallowed the whole egg of a blackbird, it would result in a baby? Behind you isn't always the best place to look when you're trying to move forward."

"Your depraved parents thought themselves smarter than everyone else, too," gloated

Father Gleason. "I trust you recall how that turned out?"

Anger seared through me like lightning. I wanted to hit him unconscious; instead I whispered through gritted teeth: "Like you said, a lot of power for one person."

I was mistaken if I thought it would intimidate him. He smiled, glee igniting his irises.

"Anthony, my bag."

Berinati obliged, picking up a small, leather medical bag and handing it to him. He opened it and fished around for a small knife and portable blowtorch.

"Restrain him," said Gleason.

The younger priest stepped toward me. As if it would be a match.

"That won't be necessary," I interjected. I'd rather be killed at their hands than humiliated. "Do I at least get to know the crime?"

"Use without identification. Lucky for you, you'll never have that problem again."

He lit the blow torch, moving the flame up and down the knife, heating the blade. I understood what he intended to do; I also understood how futile it would've been to fight. I could have run, but only temporarily. I could have made them forget, but others would be close behind. Instead, I unbuttoned my shirt and braced my arms behind my back. After all, it was the least I deserved for being so stupid.

The knife began glowing red, heat ricocheting off my skin from an arm's length away. I clinched my hands in anticipation. Beads of sweat, trickling down my body.

Gleason stepped forward, and without notice, began searing the Symbol of *In Unio* into my chest. A circle, cross and triangle inside a square — a physical representation of what I'd been running from my entire life, branded into the skin above my heart.

The pain was almost unbearable, but nothing compared to how disappointed I was in myself. After everything my parents had worked so hard for, after everything they'd sacrificed. I'd willingly put myself in the same danger.

My consciousness began to flutter as Gleason traced back over the lines he'd already created, digging the knife further into my flesh.

I was holding my breath for so long, doing anything to stop myself from making noise; I didn't realize I was running out of air. I gasped through locked teeth, as blood dripped down my stomach, and began seeping into my jeans.

"Dominus vobiscum," Gleason said, as I fell back against the wall. *God be with you.*

I held it in until I heard the elevator doors close. Then, I finally screamed.

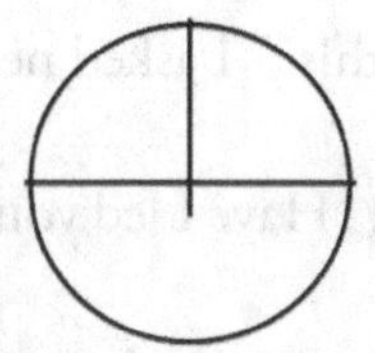

TWELVE
UGLY HEART

"Excuse me sir, do you have an aux cord?"

Apparently Delilah had a song for me.

The man grumbled in what sounded like Russian, before digging around his front seat to find a worn cable.

"This one's for Casper," she said, as I opened my window. "Can you turn it up please, sir?"

The sound of an acoustic guitar blared, as we drove up Bowery, the setting sun intermittently visible through skyscrapers to my left.

I put my arm out the window to feel the wind rippling through my fingers. My hair whipped against my face as I reclined back into the headrest. I felt happy, if just for a moment.

We arrived at The Clarence Hotel in the Meatpacking District to a block-long line. It didn't matter that it was a Monday; everyone was trying to get into Le Toit.

"Um, that's a lot of people," I said, feeling nervous and like I was the only one wearing fabric. Delilah had described it as an 'old school, rooftop vibe' but the crowd was skewing far more 'adult entertainment.'

"Are you sure about this?" I asked nervously. "No one's going to buy that I'm 21."

"Relax," said Delilah. "Have I led you wrong yet?"

She had a point.

"No," I said. "But all great empires must crumble."

She laughed, pulling me out of the car and to the front of the line. If I hadn't been riding a temporary high from the drive there, I would have insisted on going home.

I kept my head down, focused on the concrete, to limit any and all confrontation. When we stopped, I looked up to see a woman so glamorous it made me pause. She had flawless black skin and stood over 6ft tall—Grace Jones, with Audrey Hepburn's style. She looked me up and down, before nodding to Delilah and then to a security guard who let us straight in. No ID, no list, nothing.

"She's—"

"They," Delilah corrected me.

"They are *stunning*."

"Right? And don't ya just love it?"

"What?" I asked, as we made our way past neon graffiti wallpaper to an elevator that took us 17 floors up.

"The irony," she said. "That someone from the most targeted minority, is the one of the city's most powerful."

Ding. The elevator doors opened to the first level of the club. There was a bar, DJ, dance floor and seating area filled with people leaning over tables. Toward the back of the room was a jacuzzi surrounded by black leather loungers that overlooked the city.

"What *is* this place?" I asked, feeling incredibly self-conscious and out of sorts.

"It's the last of New York's nightclubs."

"It's not even 5."

"That's what makes it so fun."

She grabbed my hand and guided me through clusters of

bored, beautiful people. No one was rude, or gave me any reason to believe I didn't belong. If anything, people caught my eye, but that's exactly what I didn't trust. It reminded me of an eighth-grade sleepover I went to where I surprised myself by actually having fun. Until I overheard someone ask why I was there and the birthday girl responded: "I don't know. I didn't want her to come but her grandma told my mom we had to invite her." Needless to say, it was the last party I ever went to. Not that the invitations piled in.

A hidden staircase in the back corner of the room, lined with bright pink wallpaper, led to an open-air roof. The sun hung low in the sky, the lingering heat giving the illusion of a second summer. Delilah stopped in the middle of the dance floor, so I did my best to sway to the techno beat. All limbs, no style. Singing the lyrics to *Ugly Heart* on repeat in my head.

I managed to make it through a few hours without giving in to the waves of sadness that kept trying to wash over me, but as the moon rose so did my grief.

"You okay?" Delilah asked, as I walked to the railing to get some air.

"Just needed a second."

"You're doing so well, babe. It's okay if you wanna talk about it."

"No, I'm good. I've said all I need to say. I liked the guy, he didn't like me. The end."

She nodded understandingly. "I'm sorry."

"It's okay," I said. "I'm okay," I lied again.

"You will be. You just gotta accept that some boys are ghosts, and you'll never know why."

"I'm trying," I said, half-believing it. "It's just... why ask to hang out again, or say he was going to call if he had no intention of doing it? I just don't get it."

"Maybe he felt it in the moment," she offered. "And something spooked him?"

I thought back to his face as he held me after the kiss. The look of terror strewn across it.

"Trust me, I've been over every minute in my head. More than once. The fainting thing definitely freaked him, but he seemed fine when he dropped me off." Then realization struck, how he'd asked about my grandparents. I'd brushed it off as confusion, but he didn't seem like the type to mix up details. It was an itch inside my brain I couldn't scratch.

"He asked about my grandparents," I said.

"How sweet," she joked.

"No," I thought out loud. "He asked about my mom's parents completely out of nowhere. It was bizarre."

"The guy sounds a little bizarre. Maybe... like I keep saying... you're better off?"

I knew she was right. Logically. But I didn't want to accept it. Not just because I liked him, but because none of it made any sense, and I desperately needed it to.

We got home around eleven, and I lay in bed, wide-awake, until after two the next morning. My inner voice spiraled out of control, its volume so deafening that by three, frustration forced me out of bed, and I reached for my laptop.

I'd already searched extensively for information about Max online, but what I hadn't searched was myself. At least, not in a very long time.

I opened a browser.

'*What about your Mom's parents?*' he'd asked. '*Where are they?*'

He didn't ask if I still saw them, or why I didn't talk about them. He asked where they were. It hadn't felt significant at the time but, thinking back on it, something about it was off. Maybe it wasn't even the words, but the way he said it.

I entered a search term I'd used a million times: *Edith Edie Becker, June 4 1985.*

My mother's maiden name.

As soon as I figured out how to Google, I was typing in her name. I'd read everything there was to read about her, which unsurprisingly wasn't much—she'd grown up in a different technological decade—but I'd never thoroughly searched for information about my maternal grandparents. I knew they'd died when my mom was a little girl, near her twelfth birthday. She'd been born at home in London, but the exact place I wasn't sure of.

Finding nothing I hadn't already seen, I changed the search to: *Ernest and Irene Becker, London.*

I'd seen their death certificates before, when I had to do a family tree in the fourth grade, but that was about it. I pulled up their records on The General Register Office of Great Britain's website:

E. Becker, married to A. Becker, died of natural causes on the 14th day of March, 1996. A. Becker, widow of E. Becker, died 6 December 1996.

That was pretty much the extent of the information I knew about them. I clicked through a few more results before stumbling onto something I'd never seen. E Becker's obituary:

Ernest Becker passed away at his home in Harrogate on Saturday, March 14. Much loved by his wife Irene, family and friends. Private cremation.

I highlighted the word 'family.' Why wouldn't the notice mention his only child, his daughter? I changed the search terms: *"Irene Becker" obituary "Ernest Becker 1996".*

It was the second result on Google.

Irene Becker, beloved wife of the late Ernest Becker, died peace-fully on 6th December 1996. In lieu of flowers, donations to St Michael's Hospice.

Again, no mention of a daughter, or any children for that matter. I tried: *"Ernest Becker" "Irene Becker" Harrogate daughter.* Nothing related came up, so I removed the quotation marks and put: *Ernest Irene Edith Becker death.*

Only my parents' obituary came up:

Paul James Nelson and Edith Nelson, nee Becker, died February 16, 2006. Beloved son of Raymond and Annie Nelson, beloved daughter of the late Ernest and Irene Becker. They leave behind their only child, Eva.

I couldn't figure it out. I lay on my bed running through (and ruling out) potential reasons why my grandparents' obituary wouldn't mention my mom until it was early enough to call my grandparents. They were usually up by 5.30, but I waited until six just to be sure, climbing out onto the fire escape with my laptop and a blanket, so I wouldn't wake Delilah.

Gran answered after the first ring.

"Hello?"

"Hi, Gran. Everything's okay," I said, before she had time to panic.

"Eva, hi." I could tell she was caught off-guard. "Your grand-dad's just gone out to the grocery. I can call you when he's back?"

"It's okay, I just had a quick question."

"He'll be sorry he missed you."

"I've gotta get ready for class," I lied. "This'll just take a second."

"Okay... what's on your mind?"

"Mom's parents?" I asked.

"Yes."

"Ernest and Irene Becker."

"Mm hm."

"Why wasn't Mom listed in either of their obituaries?"

"What, dear?" Her voice was croaky, like she'd just woken up, which only made me feel more ridiculous for having called. Yet, I persisted.

"Neither of their obituaries mentioned my mom. Isn't that strange?"

"Is it?" she asked.

"Yes. Usually it would say, *survived by his wife and daughter*, or *she leaves behind her beloved daughter*."

"I'm not sure," she said. "They were English, so they might do it differently over there."

"It's death. They do it the same everywhere."

"If you say so," she replied with a forced yawn that told me she was trying to end the conversation. Of all the topics, death was her least favorite.

"It doesn't matter what I say; it's what everyone else's obituaries in the world say when someone dies and they have a living child." I knew I was being hostile, but she was being avoidant, even more so than usual. I tried to rein it in. "I'm sorry. It's just strange, is all."

"It's alright, my dear," she said. "I know it's hard for you."

"It's not *hard for me*," I snapped, getting immediately agitated again. "I'm just tired of nothing ever making any sense."

"Sometimes things don't make sense, Eva," she said, as though it were a battle she'd already fought. "And no matter what we do, nothing can change that. We just have to accept it and move on."

"What if I don't know how to move on?"

"Hush, now. You can do anything you put your mind to."

"I just wish I knew more," I said, trying to contain my frustration. "Sometimes I feel like part of me's lost forever because I didn't know her. And it's just like... no matter what I do, I'm always going to be chasing after that."

I let that hang in the air. After all, it was the truth, and I'd never said it out loud before.

She didn't say a word.

"Gran, are you there?" I asked.

"Yes, dear. I'm here."

"You have nothing else to say?"

She took a long breath, perhaps also trying to contain her frustration. "I wish there was more I could tell you—"

"Can you just have a think? There's nothing else about her parents that you know? She never mentioned her mother's maiden name, nothing?"

"You know everything I do, sweetheart."

"Egg delivery!" my granddad exclaimed from the background.

"Ray, it's Eva!" She called out, before returning her attention to me. "Though she did sign another name once."

"What?" I asked, dumbfounded. "*Seriously?* Why didn't you tell me?"

"I'd completely forgotten until you—"

"What was the name? *Tell me you at least remember that?!*"

"Eva, please don't speak to me like—" Her voice was breaking, shattering my heart. But years' worth of fury was working its way into my chest. *How could she keep such a crucial piece of information from me?*

"*Do. You. Remember. Or*—" My raised voice echoed off the buildings opposite Anderson. I was certain people in the dorm could hear me, but I didn't care.

I heard my granddad enter the kitchen where I knew my gran was.

"Annie," he said. She must have been crying. "Is everything—"

"Sinclair," she uttered. "Like the gas station."

"I can't believe you kept this from me!" I exclaimed, feeling betrayed.

"She said it was a mistake. An old boyfriend's last name."

"What's going on?" asked my Granddad, who sounded as though he was by her side.

I entered a new search in my laptop:

Edie Edith Sinclare born 1985 Deceased 2006

Google corrected me with *Sinclair*. I selected it.

"I've gotta go," I said.

"Eva, hold on a minute," my grandma asked.

"Honestly, Gran. I don't really wanna hear anything you have to say right now."

Numerous hits lit up my screen. I clicked on the images tab and was struck by a photograph of a couple holding a baby. The woman had fiery red hair with my mother's cat-like eyes. The man was classically British, but with my mother's high cheekbones.

My grandma whimpered, as my granddad took the phone.

"Eva, this is your grandfather," he announced. "What's going on here?"

"Not now, Gramps," I said, then hung up on him. I was completely captivated by the photograph in front of me.

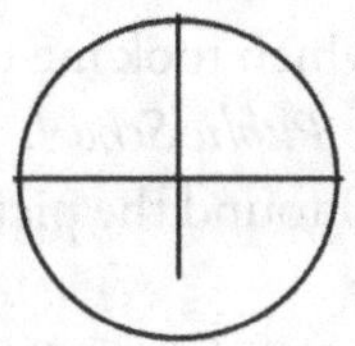

THIRTEEN
DAMAGED

I'd never seen pictures of my mother as a child, much less a baby, so it was hard to tell if it was her or not.

I clicked on the link and was taken to an archive of a newspaper article. *Gem Heirs Welcome Daughter:*

Atlantic Mining and Minerals Heir Terence Sinclair and his wife, Alida Sinclair-Dubois, welcome the arrival of their first child, Edith Sophia Sinclair.

I pulled up a new window, and searched: *Edith Sinclair Terence Alida.*

The vibrant red of the woman's hair caught my eye immediately. I clicked on a thumbnail, which took me to another photograph. It was of the couple, slightly older, but not much, walking their daughter to school. She looked to be almost a teenager.

I got closer to the screen. Unable to stop staring.

It had to be her.

She had dark brown hair, the piercing blue eyes of a cat, and features that were almost too big for her face. I clicked on the link for the picture's source, which took me to a news article that read: *Classes Commence at Elite Public School.*

I scrolled down until I found the picture and its caption:

Ernest and Alida Sinclair bid farewell to their daughter, Edith, 13, who begins class today at the Windsor School.

I clicked back to the previous page to see if I could find more. There weren't any more photographs of them, just listings of articles about the gem and mineral company and its CEO Terence Sinclair, plus, a few equestrian news articles about Edith Sinclair's wins at various European championships.

I typed in *Terence Sinclair*. Google stated:

Terence Sinclair is a British businessman, philanthropist and the chairman of The Atlantic Mining and Minerals Company. He is married to Alida Sinclair-Dubois, an heiress from France's prominent Dubois family.

I clicked on the first news article: *AtMin Stock Rises 80%; Is It Still Under Valued?*

There was an image of Terence, now older—early 70s, dignified white hair, tailored suit. He was being interviewed on a cable news program about the company's quarterly earnings. I clicked to return to the search, as I saw my phone light up.

It was my grandparents. I knew I shouldn't have hung up on them, but I was too angry to say anything productive so I let it go to voicemail.

A news article farther down the page caught my eye.

Britain's Priciest Home: Sinclairs Buy Neighboring House for £118m. The article from 2003 stated:

One of Europe's richest families is set to own the most expensive house in Britain. Terence Sinclair and Alida Sinclair-Dubois, who already own a historic neo-Georgian mansion on London's so-called Billionaire's Boulevard, are expanding next door for £118m. Once completed, experts estimate that 22 Kensington Palace Gardens will be worth well over £200m.

I felt like I'd been hit by a tidal wave. *Who were these people?*

I had to know more.

I searched for their company, *Atlantic Mining and Minerals.*

They had operations in thirty-six countries but were head-quartered in London. It was noon there and without hesitating, I dialed the switchboard number.

As the automated message played, "Hello and welcome to Atlantic Mining and Minerals. If you'd like to be connected to a dial by name directory, press one," I tried to figure out what I was going to say.

"*What are you doing, Eva?*" I asked myself out loud.

I pressed the star key for an operator.

Immediately, I was connected with someone.

"Atlantic Mining and Minerals," said a female voice.

"Hi. I... uh..."

A terrible idea came to me, and I typed London alarm companies in the search bar of my laptop.

"Hello?"

"I need to be connected with Terence Sinclair's office."

"Thank you. One moment," said the voice.

Orchestral music played as I scrolled through the web results.

"Executive Office, Olivia speaking," said a younger, more energetic voice than the last.

I flicked to a new browser page and typed *Atlantic Mining and Minerals Olivia London.* Nothing of note came up.

"This is Michelle, with Security Solutions International," I lied. "I need to speak to a Mr. Terence Sinclair about his property at 22 Kensington Palace Gardens."

"I'm afraid he's in a meeting," she answered automatically. "May I ask what it's in regards to?"

That was as far as I'd gotten in my head. I had to freestyle.

"Uh... are you an authorized user?" I asked.

"I'm not sure," she said. "Possibly."

"I can't give out any information unless you're an authorized user on the account. Your full name?"

"Olivia. Mager," she said.

I typed it into the search bar.

"M-a-g-e-r?" I asked, even though I was already looking at her LinkedIn profile:

Olivia Mager, Executive Assistant, Atlantic Mining and Minerals. One year, two months

"Yes," she confirmed.

"Hmm. I can see here you were added to the system." I had to try and do the math. "July of last year?"

"That would have been when I started," she said.

"Okay, great," I replied. "Can I have the four-digit number on the account?"

"I'm not sure what they would be. I can have someone call you back?" she said, sounding like I was losing her.

"Of course, only, I'd consider this information time sensitive."

"May I put you on a brief hold?" she asked. "It will only take—"

I cut her off by pretending I was divulging information. "Between you and me, I'm the same. I can never remember any numbers. We can try it up to three times before it kicks us over to the security questions."

"Okay, sure," she said. "Try, seven four seven one."

Rolling my eyes, I pretended to type.

"I'm afraid not. The system was set up by Mr. Sinclair

himself, if that helps at all?" I said, pretending to be accommodating.

"Try, two zero one zero."

According to Google, that was his wife's date of birth. *People are so predictable.*

"Unfortunately, not. Would you like to try another?"

"Zero four zero six?" she added, sounding flustered.

It took me a second to realize, but it was a number I knew by heart. My mother's date of birth. I almost threw my laptop off the fire escape in shock. It could be a coincidence. Or could it? I argued with myself while trying to remain present. "Unfortunately, not," I said. "How about we try the security questions." I had no idea if it was gonna work, but I figured the worst thing I could do was hang up and hope they didn't use caller ID.

"You know it's probably best if I transfer you to Ms. Akande, our—"

"Let's start with the home address and phone number for the main account holder?"

"Oh, umm... it's 22 Kensington Park Gardens and the number is zero two zero, seven nine three seven, six six eight three."

Bingo, a direct line to the Sinclairs.

"Fantastic," I said, pretending to type on my laptop. "I can see here that the system is showing a power outage, but I've actually just seen an alert pop up that we've contacted someone on the premises and an engineer is en route. We won't need your help after all," I said.

"Oh. Oh, well. Okay then."

"Thank you for choosing Security Solutions International. Have a great day," I said, hanging up before she had a chance to say goodbye.

I stared at the number in my notes, and without pausing to think or plan, I found myself entering it on the keypad of my phone.

It rang three times before a woman answered in an extremely over-pronounced British accent. "Sinclair Residence, how may I help you?"

"Edie Sinclair," I said, without thinking.

There was a short pause before she responded in a flat tone: "Ms. Sinclair is deceased."

I felt my world shake, just slightly. I knew she was dead, of course. The exhilaration of discovering new information had just made me forget for a second. Hope is a dangerous seed.

"I know," I clarified. I'm writing an article on her—" The phone clicked. "Hello?" I pulled it away from my ear to check. She'd hung up.

I went to my call log and called the number again.

After three rings, the lady was back on the line. "Sinclair Residence. How may I help you?"

"I'd like to speak to someone about Edie Sinclair, if I—" She'd hung up again.

I dialed back immediately, adrenalin taking over my brain.

"Sinclair Residence. How—"

"You may help me by telling me about Edie Sinclair!" I yelled.

Another voice came on the phone. A friendlier one, still refined, but with an unmistakable edge. She had the hint of an accent other than English.

"*Her name* was *Edith*," said the woman.

"Sure," I said. "Edith."

"What is it you'd like to know?"

"Uh, well... I'm writing an article on her and—"

"All media requests must go through our—"

"I'm not," I said. "I'm not the media, well, not yet," I added, unsure of where I was going. "I plan to be one day, but... the truth is that Edie... that is, *Edith*... taught me, when I was a kid. In New York. She was my au pair, and I always wanted to get in touch with her. I didn't realize she'd died."

"Ah," said the woman. "Well, I'm sorry I can't be of more help."

"It's okay," I replied. "I'm sorry to have..." I changed tack. I needed to give her a reason to speak to me. "It's just, I have some of her things," I lied. "Some books and stuff that she left behind."

"Give our housekeeper your address. She'll arrange to have everything picked up."

Damnit, not what I thought she'd say.

"Can't," I said, making it up as I went. "On account of the fact that I'm on my way to the airport. And to be honest, I'd prefer to do it in person." I thought back to McKenzie's class: *Face to face is the only way to understand the whole story.* But how? The idea was insane—the farthest I'd ever traveled to was Florida. I pulled up a new search. The cheapest flight to London that night was eleven hundred dollars, and I only had a thousand in savings.

"I can bring them by," I said, shocking myself. "I'm sure she'd want you to have them."

There was a long silence. So long that I checked my phone twice to see if the call had dropped.

"I could be there Friday morning," I offered, though I didn't know how.

"I'm not sure I'll be in to receive you," she said. "But you're welcome to stop by mid-morning and leave the items with our staff."

"That won't work," I blurted out.

"Excuse me?" she inquired, the politeness disintegrating from her tone.

"I insist on giving it to you personally. *Edie...*" I stressed her name how I knew it, "would've wanted it that way." Of course I had no idea what she would have wanted, but I said it anyway and hung up before she had a chance to contradict me.

I didn't have a clue how I was going to get there, but something was telling me the answers I'd been searching my whole life for might be on the other side of the Atlantic.

I worked through various solutions in my head, but my thoughts were racing away from me. It wasn't until Delilah tapped on the fire escape window, miming a question about whether I would join her for breakfast, that I realized my hands had been clenched since I'd hung up the phone.

I exhaled sharply, attempting to stop them from trembling.

Delilah pulled opened the window. "You okay?"

"Yeah," I managed to mutter.

"Want me to wait for you to change?"

I looked down at my pajamas. "Sure." I was out of it, and feeling nauseated from not having slept. Food sounded smart.

I climbed through the window, pulling my belongings through with me.

"I won't be a second," I said, heading into our room.

I quickly changed into my uniform and, as I walked down to the cafeteria with Delilah, attempted to detangle my hair.

She was talking about Katie while I ran scenarios in my head for how to get my hands on cash. I wanted to tell her but didn't want to risk being talked out of it, or worse, getting her in trouble if anything went wrong. Flying to another country, where I didn't know anyone, was the epitome of foolish. But not going wasn't an option. I had to get there. I was more certain about that than I'd been about anything.

I was so distracted that I almost bumped into Annabel, who was hanging up a poster advertising tickets for winter formal.

"Woah, sorry," I said, turning my shoulder at the last second to avoid hers.

"Oh, hey! It's o—"

"Holy blazer," said Delilah, referring to Annabel's rhinestone-decorated lapel.

Staring at it, I realized it was the only other one I'd seen at

Anderson, aside from mine. I looked down at the circular glue marks on my lapel, where rhinestones once were, then to her

"Thanks. My way of trying to brighten up Tuesdays!"

As she said it, her eyes darted to me, and then down to my jacket. We were both arriving at the same conclusion: *I was wearing her old blazer.*

My face flushed red.

"Wait, you're Annabel?" Delilah asked, leaving no doubt she knew the answer. "The editor of *The Advocate?*"

"Yours truly," Annabel confirmed, a hint of worry between her eyes. We could both tell Delilah was about to say something spicy, and while I wanted to myself, my priority was to get away from her.

"We should go," I said, before Delilah could finish her thought. "See you in class."

I grabbed her arm to lead us away.

"See you there," Annabel said, before adding, "Eva, you're coming to the winter formal, right?"

"I wasn't planning on it."

"Because I was thinking..." her eyes lit up as though she were about to present me with a giant Lotto check. "How would you like to cover it?"

"Huh?"

"Yeah. Portia's supposed to be writing the feature, but she's flowery at the best of times. Why don't you write one too, and I'll publish whoever's better."

I didn't know what to say; my mind was at max capacity.

"Sure, yeah. Let me think about it," I said.

"Great! I'll email you the link for tickets!"

She bopped off down the hallway, ponytail flinging from side to side.

"Is she always that..." she took a sharp inhale of air.

"Uptight? Yes."

Ding.

My priority email sounded as we walked into the cafeteria. It was from Annabel, a link to buy formal tickets.

"She's efficient, though," I said, taking a fruit salad from the counter.

I clicked the link.

"No. *Stop*. This can't be right."

"When you say it like that, it probably is," Delilah snickered.

"Tickets are three hundred and fifty dollars. Each." I was in shock.

"Surely they'll let you in for free if you're covering it for the school paper?"

"I guess not if she's sending me a link to buy tickets?"

We sat down at our usual table where Dylan was already eating.

"Morning," he said between chews of Rice Krispies.

I gestured hello, while Delilah continued to rant. "And she's not even guaranteeing they'll use it? That's basically pay for play, which is illegal."

"Except I actually think this is her trying to be nice."

She sectioned off a piece of clementine and ate it. "Oh, hey, next Monday we have our first run through of the play," she said. "And I'm super nervous. Can you guys come watch for moral support, 'cause all the other drama kids are... well, drama kids?"

"Of course," I said.

"I'm there," agreed Dylan, before looking to me. "Hang on, you're gonna go to formal? That's what y'all were talking about right?"

"Are you insane? I can't afford that," I laughed.

"I could take you?" he offered, attempting to act casual. Like he was trying not to spook a horse.

His sweetness melted me a little.

"That's... really kind," I said. "*Seriously*, thank you. But even if I did go, which I don't think I can, I'd have to write something for the paper, so it'd be more of a work—"

"I could put it on my mom's card?" Delilah added. "She'll never know as long as you pay it off before—"

"I'm so stupid," I said as I got up to leave. "Thank you! You're the best!"

Before I knew it I was taking two stairs at a time to get back to our dorm room.

I opened my laptop to find the flight options still on my screen. The cheapest took me to SvalbardAir.com, where I began filling out my passenger details.

"*What are you doing?*" I asked myself aloud, pulling my hands away from the keys as if they were hot coals.

Was I really going to get on a plane, fly halfway across the world, and knock on some stranger's door? I took out my wallet from my backpack and dug around in it until I found what I was looking for: my grandparent's credit card.

Reserved for emergencies, I'd never used it, but this seemed like one. I knew there were probably other ways I could find out more information, but the urgency in me threatened to explode if I didn't do something right then and there.

I flicked the Internet browser back to the picture of Edith Sinclair at thirteen, and then back again to the flights. My mind may not have known what was happening but my hands seemed to, as they typed out the remaining details.

Submit.

The webpage went bright white, receiving data to load another.

Congratulations, Eva Nelson. You're headed to London!

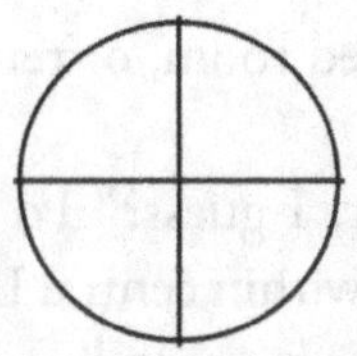

FOURTEEN
LONDON CALLING

I spent the first five hours of the flight panicked about lying to everyone. But by the ninth hour, and after a surprise (to me) layover in Norway, I was too tired to even think. I'd told Delilah I was going upstate to visit distant relatives, but to tell anyone who asked that I was sick. I'd told my grandparents I needed the weekend to process what happened, that I'd call them when I was ready to talk. If everything went according to plan, I'd only miss two days of school. Not ideal, but nothing I couldn't catch up on.

The Underground train took me from Heathrow Airport into the city; that much I was cognizant for. It was mid-morning, but I couldn't see the sun on account of the cement-colored clouds, which suited me just fine. All I wanted was sleep.

"Passport and credit card please?" said a girl with purple hair who didn't sound like she was from England. She was sat behind scratched Plexiglas, as she checked me into the hostel.

I handed over the card and my passport, thinking about how disappointed my grandparents would be if they knew how I'd used it for the first time. It was the only birthday present I'd asked for when I turned sixteen.

"You wanting a six-bed room, or ten? Both female only, with shared bathroom."

"Whatever is cheaper, I guess?" I'd never stayed in a hostel, but it was the only thing within central London I could afford.

As if on cue, "That card was declined," said the receptionist.

Terror prickled through me, like ants finding a home. "Oh... ummm...."

"Happens all the time," she said, clearly feeling bad for me. "You call your bank. It's no problem. I wait."

"My phone doesn't actually work yet. I have to set it up." It was the truth, but I also couldn't call the bank for obvious reasons.

"You have other credit card?"

"I have a debit card?" I wanted to cry so badly. The stress was heightening the exhaustion.

"We take a £150 deposit. Is that working for you?"

"Sure, that's great," I said. *If the card even works.*

As the receipt printed, I prayed it would reveal good news.

"That worked," she said. "Let me get you key."

I watched her program a keycard as I clung onto the counter, fearing the jelly feeling in my legs was going to take me out.

Within minutes, she was leading me toward a room that could only be described as sour—both in its strong vinegar smell and the involuntary way it made my face react. I held my sleeve over my nose as she pointed toward the back of the cramped space, where a window looked out onto a brick wall.

"By the window is best. It's cold, but no smell."

I did as she said, walking over to the corner bed and climbing to the top bunk (the farthest from any potential rats). Fully clothed, hood up over my head for sanitary reasons, I lay down.

It felt so good to be horizontal, with my legs completely extended, that I almost fell asleep immediately. With one eye open, I grabbed the shoulder strap of my bag, and looped it around my wrist, in case anyone tried to steal it.

. . .

IT WASN'T until two Brazilian girls accidentally turned on the lights around nine P.M. that I realized I'd slept all day. My stomach was tied in knots of hunger, my throat so blisteringly dry I could barely swallow.

I forced myself up on a mission to find food, speculating it would be the remedy I needed to sleep through the rest of the night. As I walked out the doors of the hostel, the brisk night air alerted me to my surroundings, making me feel as though I'd finally arrived in London.

Dampness cloaked the city in a way that it didn't in New York: A sweeping mist, visible only across streetlamps, fell endlessly from the black sky. It was like moving through a raincloud; the constant sense of moisture impossible to evade.

The breeze picked up as I turned south, heading toward the River Thames, where I found an all-night bakery. It was too cold to sit, so I ate a savory pastry while I followed a cobblestone road that led me into Trafalgar Square.

Clutching my jacket even tighter, the sharp chill burning my hands and cheeks, I looked up at the National Gallery and across at the giant monuments and statues that filled the relatively empty plaza. I thought of the millennia of history I was surrounded by, and the many millions of people who had been there before me— the electricity of their memories lingering behind. I wondered if Jane Austen or Shakespeare had strolled through the King's Mews, as it was known then, or if Sir Isaac Newton had stood where I was, ruminating life's greatest questions.

I felt both completely insignificant and somehow special for having made it this far. I may not always get it right, or be the most likable person. I may be difficult, and... *relentless*... but at least I was doing something with my life. At least I refused to stay in my box, in Spring City Pennsylvania, where it wouldn't have been everyone else's thoughts that ended me; it would have been my own. I was perhaps more lost than I'd ever been, but I was lost because I chose to be.

Leaving the square, I noticed something that took me back to Manhattan—the unmistakable sound of boots, clacking against the pavement.

Click clack. Click clack.

The metronome was different from last time, but the fear that shot through my body was identical. I was only two blocks from my hostel when I crossed the road to see if the person behind me would follow.

To my dread they did, the sound of their walk unnerving me to my core. There wasn't a soul in sight, and every light was out except the ornate lamps that illuminated the anguished sky. I turned to look behind me. The person was dressed in black, head dropped, watching the ground as the gap between us closed.

Click clack. Click clack.

Suddenly, I stopped. I couldn't fully comprehend why, but I knew I had to. I was tired of running from things, from people, from my problems. I was tired of hiding. So I did the dumbest thing imaginable and turned around, ready to face whoever was following me.

There was only about 25 feet between us, and I could just make out the shape of his face. He was thin, white, nicely dressed, tall—almost six foot, I guessed—but his features remained obscured. It wasn't until he raised his head to look at me that I realized the ridiculousness of my fears: I saw the white collar tucked under his chin, and the long crucifix around his neck, seconds before he walked into me.

"Evening," he said, angular features giving him a striking look.

"Evening, Father," I said, blushing.

Sure, I was embarrassed for creating a situation entirely in my head, but I was also proud of myself for confronting something that scared me. It made me feel powerful, like I was ready for whatever the following day had in store. Good, bad or ugly, I was facing my fears, and I was certain that had to count for something.

My alarm woke me at eight the next morning to a stale blanket of heat hanging over the small room. Too many people and a militant radiator gave the air a thickness that only seemed to encourage the groggy, confused state my body was in. As I pulled off the free eye mask from the plane, flutters of worry and excitement filled my body, running down into my hands, as if the energy were trying to find an escape. I jolted upright and jumped off the bunk bed, knowing that if I didn't start moving I'd start overthinking.

I had three hours before I wanted to be at the Sinclairs' and there was somewhere I wanted to stop by on the way. Alida had said mid-morning, which to me meant eleven. I showered, tried to style my hair in a way that didn't make me look like a drowned rat, and applied some mascara and lip-gloss. I'd brought a red floral sundress that made me look moderately presentable (for them) which I wore with my Docs and a leather jacket (for me). After all, it didn't matter what I was wearing, I was bound to stick out in a house that cost more money than my entire town and, potentially, the two towns over from it.

The Windsor School that Edith Sinclair attended was a twenty-minute walk from the hostel. I had no idea what I imagined I'd learn, but something was telling me to visit. After all, in journalism it's the people around the subject who often tell the most interesting story.

The sun had managed to momentarily break through the clouds as I picked up a coffee and muffin, and marveled at the architecture wherever I looked—from Her Majesty's Theatre to Banqueting House, to the only remaining part of the Palace of Whitehall. I arrived at the Houses of Parliament and Big Ben, gawking in awe at the significance of where I was, only to turn around to find the glorious and gothic Westminster Abbey, and beside it, Edith's former school.

It was a four-story, stone building that resembled a castle of some kind—no doubt at some point it was. I approached the entryway and was greeted by a metal gate that prevented access from the public.

A kid a few years younger than me approached it to leave.

"Hey! Hold the gate," I called out, crossing the road.

He stared at me, perplexed.

"I forgot my pass," I lied.

"You don't go to this school," he said, looking me up and down dismissively.

"Excuse me?" I replied, pretending to be offended. "Of course, I—"

"No. You don't. If you did, I'd *definitely remember*."

It wasn't even the sentiment that made my breakfast want to come back up. It was the fact he was looking at my chest.

"Ha," I pretended to laugh. "Ya got me, I'm surprising my cousin. It's her birthday."

"I knew it," he grinned. "Maybe I'll see you around?"

"We can only hope," I said, walking past him before he could question me further. He held the door open like he was impersonating a doorman. I nodded, pretending I understood the joke.

If the exterior of the building were impressive, the other side was intimidating. A church that looked older than Westminster, presided over an open-air courtyard, with medieval buildings towering above.

I walked past a plaque engraved with the Latin words *Per Ardua Ad Alta*, which I assumed was the school's motto. Getting on the guest Wi-Fi, I pulled up Google to translate it when I realized the last time I'd done that had been in Washington Square Park, trying to figure out how to talk to Max. How things had changed. The euphoria that was once there, now replaced with sadness.

"*Nope. We're not doing that*," I said to myself, flicking my hands as if it would shake the feeling out of me.

I looked back to my phone. The phrase translated as '*through effort, great heights are reached*.' I scoffed. The concept that hard work alone resulted in success was a lie perpetrated by the wealthy. Effort wasn't a guarantee for success. Take my grandparents, who both had jobs since they were sixteen and yet wouldn't be able to survive without partial government assistance.

From the research I'd already done, I knew success was a common theme among its alumni—three Nobel laureates and six prime ministers—but with costs of over eighty thousand pounds per year, it seemed fair to assume that anyone fortunate enough to attend had already been blessed with a distinct advantage.

"Can I help you, Miss?" A gruff man had appeared behind me. A security guard.

"I'm just waiting for a friend," I said, anxiously.

"Where's your visitor's pass?"

Great question.

"Umm, I didn't check in," I said. "Cause my friend said she'll be here in a second."

He looked at me like I was stupid.

"It doesn't matter how long you're here, you still have to check in." He sighed. "What's your friend's name?" he inquired, pulling out a tablet computer.

"It's fine," I said. "I'll wait outside."

He started to look at me suspiciously. "Who are you here to see?" he asked again.

"Edith Sinclair," I said, panicking.

He looked up from the tablet.

"The same Edith Sinclair that building's named after?" His tone was sarcastic as he pointed to a structure over my shoulder.

Turning to look at it, I was baffled why there was a building with her name on it.

"Miss?" he demanded.

"Sorry... sa... someone must be playing a prank on me," I said, dropping my head in pseudo-sadness.

"Ah..." he mumbled, uncomfortable.

"People can be so cruel," I added, continuing with the charade.

I excused myself and quickly left the grounds, run-walking down the block until I was far enough away to sigh in relief. I couldn't believe I'd almost gotten caught. *Trespassing. On private property. On a tourist visa.* If I hadn't needed to be at the Sinclairs' within the hour, I might completely have freaked out and gone straight to the airport.

Instead, I made my way on foot to Kensington Palace Gardens. Dubbed by the tabloids as "Britain's priciest row," it housed everyone from billionaires and diplomats, to business leaders and royalty. Backing onto Kensington Palace, the street had long been associated with Europe's most elite, and was even rumored to have tunnels that connected to the royal residence itself.

A grand archway, with cream plaster and gold embellishments, announced the entrance to the street. I stood watching for a moment, waiting to see if the armed police were stopping pedestrians from entering. When I could tell they were only checking cars, I slipped through the green metal fence and headed toward their address.

Forty-foot trees lined the storybook street, swaying gently in the wind. Overhead, a storm was gathering strength, readying itself to roll in. I hoped it wasn't a sign of what was to come as I marched forward, anticipation rising high in my throat. Bright white three-and-four-story houses looked even brighter against the dark grey clouds, highlighting the enormity of where I was.

These were not ordinary homes, and neither were the people in them. It was another world. One with incredible means, and no doubt extensive connections. I needed to be careful.

Since I'd called them, I'd been trying to devise some sort of plan. I bought three of the oldest-looking books I could find from a used bookstore in Chinatown, which I planned to pass off as Edith's. I felt horrible for toying with their emotions, but I didn't know how else to get access to them. They were a guarded and well-protected family, for understandable reasons; they weren't just going to volunteer information when they didn't need to.

The closer I got to their house the wider the street became, with each property more palatial than the next. The buildings were set back from the street, their driveways adorned with different luxury cars. Glancing through windows, I could see lavish furnishings, including what appeared to be a room where everything was covered in gold. But nothing compared to, or could prepare me for, 22 Kensington Palace Gardens.

The mansion loomed like a grand fortress. Its central structure was flanked by four-story towers at each corner, standing guard as regal sentinels. Surrounding it, manicured lawns and vibrant gardens turned the grounds into a private paradise, insulating it from the roughness of the outside world.

The house itself was built out of large blocks of pale stone trimmed in marble, matching the color scheme of the street, or perhaps having been the one to initiate it. I'd read online that the stone used came from surplus material from the Houses of Parliament, and the marble from the Taj Mahal. It blew my mind the many ways people with too much money chose to spend it. If I were ever faced with the decision of whether to cover my house in rocks from another continent or feed several thousand children, I hoped it wouldn't even be a choice.

I pressed the buzzer on the outside gate, then attempted to tame my wind-trashed hair.

"Sinclair Residence. How may I help you?" It was the same woman from the phone. At least it sounded like her.

"Hi..." I said trying to find my voice. "I think we spoke the other day."

"I remember," she said.

Then, nothing.

"Well, good chat," I mumbled. "I'm here to see Terence and Alida."

"Mr. and Mrs. Sinclair," she corrected me sternly, and then buzzed me in.

Honestly, I was expecting far more of a fight.

With a shaking hand, I reached out to push open the gate. Impeccable ivory stone steps led to the house, where gas lanterns and marble balustrades framed the façade.

I couldn't tell if I was imagining it, but it felt like someone was watching me as I walked up the stairs. The hairs on my arms raised as I looked up into the large windows of the towers to see nothing but blank spaces.

Something inside me was screaming out to run. Unsure if it was intuition or fear, I reached for the handle anyway. Before I could turn it, a petite woman I assumed to be my phone nemesis opened it.

Her face was more motherly than I'd anticipated, which threw me.

"Follow me," she ordered.

She sounded different in person, but just as cold, walking off so quickly that I didn't have time to ask her if I was supposed to remove my shoes or not. I had to half-chase after her, navigating through the foyer, dining room, another room, and finally reaching a sitting room at the back of the house. Panting, I couldn't help but think about how far I'd have to run if the need arose to escape.

The place itself wasn't scary. Just the opposite.

There weren't any pictures online of what the house looked

like inside, but it was far more modern than anything I would've ever imagined. The 20-foot ceilings were framed by intricate moldings that looked original, with stark white walls that melted seamlessly into the shiny marble floors.

Chandeliers, multiple per room, dangled above lush furniture swathed in neutral upholstery. The only colors came from a freestanding glass elevator in the center of the house that gleamed like a captured rainbow, dispersing light from the floors above.

"Wait here," she said. "Don't touch anything."

I turned around to sardonically ask, "Am I allowed to sit?" but she was already gone.

There weren't any personal items in the room, no trinkets or photos, leading me to wonder if it was used to meet with guests, or if the rich just looked down on that sort of sentimentality. They were, however, fans of expensive candles and palm-sized rocks, which lined the fireplace mantel, each of them a deep red or dark blue. I almost reached out to touch one, curious if they were genuine sapphires and rubies, when I heard approaching footsteps.

A serious woman in her late forties, carrying a leather folio and an air of superiority, had appeared.

"Sit," she said, walking over to the couch opposite me.

I did as she instructed. Something about the way she spoke made me feel like I'd been sent to the principal.

"My name is Vivienne Akande," she announced. "Chief Counsel for the Sinclair family."

My stomach sank. They'd sent a lawyer.

I didn't know what to do. Suddenly flying to a foreign country without telling anyone seemed like a colossal misjudgment. Regret hung in the back of my throat. Every reason I had for not being honest with Delilah seemed more frivolous by the second.

"I didn't realize they needed a lawyer to have a conversation,"

I said, with a hint of mockery. I stood up. "This was obviously a mistake."

"You're absolutely right it was," she replied, unreadable. Her eyes flicked up to mine. "Fortunately, I'm prepared to overlook it upon return of Ms. Sinclair's property to her Estate's trustees. Forfeit the property, and you have my word, no charges will be pressed."

"Charges? What *charges*?" I asked in a way that sounded like the concept was ludicrous, even though I knew people with money didn't need legitimacy of any kind in order to litigate.

"Trespass, fraud, blackmail..."

"Alright, calm down," I said, faux-laughing. "I haven't asked for a single thing. Do you need me to define blackmail to you? And by the way, I can't trespass in a place I've been explicitly invited to. It's a good job I recorded those phone calls."

I took the deepest breath possible without giving away my desperate need for oxygen. As long as she didn't poke any holes in what I said, I might just be able to get out of the room without the police being called. *What had I gotten myself into?*

"Everyone's recording everything these days, aren't they?" she said, looking at me like she'd just caught me in a game of chess. She unzipped her portfolio and leafed through it. "In homes, in streets... even in schools, which I suppose makes a lot of sense. They need to know the name and face of every single person in and out of their property. The Windsor School, for instance, has some very high-tech equipment. Crystal clear pictures," she said, turning over photos that showed me trespassing on private property not even an hour earlier.

I wanted to vomit. Sweat instantly covered my body, my knees feeling as though they were about to lose their structural integrity. I couldn't understand how everything had gone so wrong, so fast. *Was trespass a misdemeanor or a felony? Did it even work like that in England? How was I going to explain it to my grandparents?* I thought I was going to black out.

"You've had someone following me?" I asked, trying to sound outraged to project my innocence.

"Would you like to have a seat?" she asked.

"Standing works for me."

"The school informed us. The Sinclairs are trustees of—"

"So money does buy everything," I interrupted bitterly, trying to remember which way I'd come in, wishing desperately I had a phone that worked without Wi-Fi.

"We'll see," she said. "Turn over everything in your possession that belonged to Edith Sinclair and we won't press charges."

That's all they wanted? Relief washed over me, but I tried not to show it. I didn't want to tip my hand. Instead, I unhooked the bag from my shoulder and pulled out my only leverage: three used books.

"I'll need it in writing," I said, putting them down on the table.

"Of course. And the necklace."

What necklace? I thought. Until she stretched out her hand toward me. Gesturing to my neck.

"What?" I asked confused. "No... this was my..." As the word almost came out of my mouth, I realized what it meant. It was my mother's necklace and *they believed it was their daughter's.*

I tried to take in air, but my quivering diaphragm restrained me. It was the proof I needed; they were my grandparents. But if they knew about her... then they must also know about me.

My head spun, any glimmer of hope for a happy ending crumbling in my chest.

"The Sinclairs are prepared to offer you a one-time payment of twenty-five thousand pounds for the necklace, the books and your signature on a non-disclosure agreement. Consider it a gesture of goodwill." Her demeanor remained as steely as when she first walked into the room.

"I'm not for sale," I said, tears betraying me as they rolled down my cheeks. "And neither is my property."

"I take it you have proof that it belongs to you?"

I knew immediately that I didn't. My mother never had a will, so my grandma hid the necklace for me per her dying request.

"It was given to me," I said, fighting every urge not to fall completely apart. "I have witnesses."

"I think we both know that unless it's notarized, it's not binding."

My heart throbbed; my own flesh and blood couldn't care less about me. I wanted to run out and never look back, but not without the only thing I owned of my mother's.

She pulled out a copy of a contract and handed it to me. "This is a one-time deal," she said. "As soon as you leave the Sinclair's residence, I will no longer be able to help you."

Something about her tone irked me.

I replayed the sound of the words in my mind as I pretended to stare at the contract.

"It was you..." I said. Beginning to understand. "Who answered the phone when I called here... you were the one I spoke to first."

I could see her playing through my line of questioning in her head. "Yes. When someone claims an alarm has gone off at one of our properties, I am informed. When that person claims to work for a company that isn't one of our approved suppliers, I am very much *involved*."

"Huh," I said, wiping the tears from my eyes. "So it wasn't fraud, then?"

"Pardon?"

"Fraud has to deceive, doesn't it... or it's not fraud. You knew the truth all along."

She looked at me, as if momentarily confused.

"Maybe the Sinclairs have a legal dictionary you can borrow," I shot back, pulling myself together. "You'll never be able to press charges for fraud or blackmail, especially after my lawyer proves it was coerced. Tell the Sinclairs they can keep the books, and their offer. Consider it a gesture of goodwill."

"Why don't you tell us yourself?"

I turned around to see Terence Sinclair. He was a young seventy, with piercing eyes that looked like he was reading my soul. He held himself in a way that demanded a certain kind of respect. Respect I didn't have any intention of giving him.

"I told you," said another voice behind me.

It was Alida Sinclair, who was more vibrant and beautiful than any picture could capture. With fiery red hair and refined features, she had the face of a supermodel from a Fellini film. She was smiling at me, but talking to her husband.

"She sounds identical to her," she said.

"You look just like her, too," he said addressing me. His voice softer, more kind than his appearance would suggest.

The room was starting to spin. "What is this, round two?" I asked. "The reserve team? Get her with the one-two punch?" I didn't know what I was saying.

"Surprises like this don't usually happen to us," she said. "You have to forgive—"

The accent I'd sensed over the phone was slightly thicker in person. Eastern European for sure. She continued to stare at me, almost in awe.

"I don't have to do anything," I replied. I was trying to steady my feet, readying myself for another attack. "You knew about me."

"Not until you called," he said. "And even then, we still had so many questions."

"The money?" I asked, horrified. Still catching my breath. "The contract?"

"My insistence," said Vivienne, looking at me. "A prominent family such as this—"

"That's okay, Vivienne," ordered Terence.

She was being dismissed, but she seemed upbeat about it.

Almost cheerful. "If it's any consolation," said the lawyer, leaving, "it was a pleasure sparring with you."

I was shaking with anger.

"Would you like to sit?" Alida asked.

"*No*," I said, more firmly than intended.

"Can we get you anything to—?" she tried to ask before I stopped her.

"So it was what, a test?" I asked, finally voicing what I knew to be the truth. "The money?"

"No," said Alida. "Nothing like—"

"In a way," said Terence.

"My love," she hushed, in a tone contrary to its sentiment.

"You're a very smart girl," he said to me before turning to his wife, "there's no need to sugar-coat it."

Blunt silence filled the room.

"You're going to be waiting a lot longer than either of you have left, if you're looking for me to thank you for finally being honest."

Terence's face grew enormously wide, breaking into a chuckle. "You're just like her," he said, nodding. "Your mother." He looked me dead in the eyes as tears started to form.

"Oh, Terence," Alida said, walking over to comfort him. She, too, was tearful.

"I have to go," I said, walking around them to leave.

"Wait, please," Alida begged. "Please."

Her pain stopped me in my tracks. It was an agony I knew too well to ignore.

"Losing Edith…" she said. "It almost killed us."

I turned around. "Yes," I said. "I remember hearing about how distraught you both were at the funeral."

"*We didn't know*," said Terence, sternly.

His eyes told me he was telling the truth. But how could I trust them?

I looked to Alida. She, too, was visibly shaken. We all were.

Gently, she spoke. "Can we start over?"

"I don't know," I spat. And it was the truth. I was still trying to wrap my head around everything that had just happened.

"Some tea, then?" Terence asked.

"Or a Scotch," Alida joked.

Words escaped me. I was in a daze.

"Sure," I finally said. "Both."

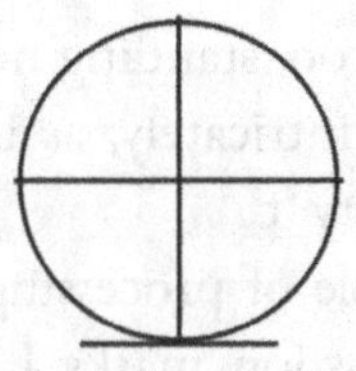

FIFTEEN

UNTITLED

We moved to a room at the other end of the house, where the exterior walls had been replaced with glass. It showcased a sprawling view of the backyard, complete with Kensington Palace in the distance. The looming storm outside was on full display, the trees whipping back and forth in a frenzy. Terence was supervising a fire being lit, while Alida went to retrieve something from upstairs.

I hid in the darkness of the powder room, trying to collect my thoughts. The only light radiated from flickering candles set in antique gold hardware, all emitting the same fragrance that permeated the rest of the house. I ran my hands under the tap, splashing water on my cheeks. My mind raced so fast I couldn't decipher my feelings, but I knew I had to feign composure. I marched back outside, ready to confront my demons.

By the time I returned, Alida was sitting next to her husband, a shiny dark wooden box on the couch opposite them.

"I thought perhaps you'd like to see some photographs."

Unable to resist, I walked over and opened it. Inside were old pictures of my mother as a toddler, with jet-black hair and giant, doll-like eyes. Then, a little older, playing in the snow. There were pictures of her as a teen too, standing next to a horse in dressage, the horse's hair braided intricately, as if done by someone who took pride in crossing every 't'.

I was numb, incapable of processing what I was seeing. The answers to so many question marks I had about her life were staring back at me. But none of them matched the stories I'd made up in my head, weaved together between the facts I had, or thought I had. Part of me felt like it had imploded.

Overwhelmed, I pushed the box away and looked up at the people who had kept me in the dark for so long.

"How did you... not know?" I asked. "Let's start there."

"We lost touch with Edith for a few months," said Alida, stiffening. I noticed she wore a geometric pin of small diamonds in the shape of a triangle and circle, sitting within a cross and a square.

"She left," said Terence, more bluntly. "Ran away."

"It wasn't the first time, so we weren't worried," Alida added. "It was a habit of hers. A way to let off steam." I could relate, which both excited and hurt me, like a jagged knife being extracted from flesh.

"But when she didn't show for..."

"Christmas," Terence added.

"We knew something was wrong."

"What year was that?" I asked.

"2005."

"The year before you were born," said Terence lightly, like he was helping me arrive at the news.

Nevertheless, it hit hard.

"She was with my dad that Christmas," I said. "In Pennsylvania." I was trying not to cry again. "They met in New York over the summer."

"She was living in one of our properties there," said Alida.

"We tracked her that far. And then she disappeared."

I realized what it meant. "Because of me," I said. "She'd met my father and was running away because she was pregnant. You wouldn't have supported it?" I stared them in the eyes, tears welling up in my own.

"If I'm honest, no. I can't say that we would have," confirmed Terence.

"We don't know that," contradicted Alida. "*We do not know that.*" She was regretful. Perhaps even heartbroken.

I wanted to run and hide under the nearest set of blankets, but the weight of her words pummeled me in place.

"We never got a chance to figure that out," said Terence. "We never got the opportunity." The way he said it was drenched in whatever guilt his wife was harboring.

"If you didn't know where she'd gone, how did you know she'd died?" I asked, unwilling to let emotion cloud my rational mind.

"I felt it," Alida said, with indignation. The tension in her voice indicating her conviction. "I knew she was gone."

"Like I said. We knew something was wrong when she didn't come home for Christmas," said Terence, as if attempting to add logic to what she was saying. "It's something she'd never missed."

"They were living with my grandparents while they looked for a..." The thought of them, how they'd react to this news, how much I missed them, started hitting me. But before the sadness could consume me, I realized how much more I would've known about my life if my grandma had been forthcoming with me. I bristled. "She'd told them it was the happiest she'd ever been. They died—"

"We know," said Alida, cutting me off to spare my pain. Or maybe her own. "Vivienne provided us with all that information yesterday."

"Once you called, she did some digging," said Terence.

"Multitalented," I quipped.

Terence laughed. "Yes, she is," he said. "We pay her a lot of money to do a lot of worrying for us."

"That's the secret to staying young," said Alida. "Paying people to stress, so you don't have to."

I wanted to laugh, but I was on the working-class side of the poverty spectrum where the joke wasn't as funny. "Cool," I said, signaling that I was ready for the conversation to be over. "Well, you know the rest then, so I should get going." I stood up to leave. I didn't know why, but it felt like the absolute right choice. I couldn't sit still any longer.

"Stay," said Alida. "Please."

"For lunch," said Terence.

"Or forever," she added.

"My love." He was cautioning her not to push me.

"For as long as you want," said Alida. "After all, we're your... you're our..."

"Yeah, I get it," I said. "You're my *family*'... and you've come to help me just after I've finished needing help. Where were you when my grandparents had to bury your daughter and almost went broke doing it? Where were you and your literal castle when all we could afford were fourteen cent noodles and whatever the local food pantry had to spare?"

"You have a right to feel angry," said Terence.

"Oh, thank you. Exactly what I've been waiting for. Your permission."

"We didn't know, Eva," he said desperately.

"All we can do is go from here," said Alida. "We'd love to get to know you."

"Now that you've checked I'm not here to rip you off?" I said, biting back at her potential kindness. "Thank you for your time, but I have someone waiting on me," I lied, not entirely sure why.

"We already lost our daughter..." said Terence, his voice breaking. "We'd like the chance to know you."

"That's something I'm going to need to think about," I said.

"There's also the matter of the extended family, and Edith's trust," said Alida.

"Alida," warned Terence, again.

"It obviously belongs to her—"

"I don't want it," I said without hesitation, something in my body answering for me before I had the chance to think it through. I may have been naïve about the world, but I knew that people didn't just hand money over without a catch. "I already told your lawyer once that I can't be bought—"

"She only meant—"

"*I know what she meant*," I insisted.

The room grew quiet once more, easing and exacerbating the tension.

I turned to leave.

"We're having a small dinner party tonight for our dear friend's birthday. Your great-uncles, and great-aunt will be there —" explained Alida.

"Distant family," Terence interrupted, downplaying it.

"Some of your mother's cousins will also be here. Your cousins too."

"I'm sure there will also be time in the future when... if," he corrected himself, "you're ready."

"We'll eat around eight," she said. "You're welcome... always."

I nodded so they knew I'd heard them, but I didn't have any words left to say.

"At least take the car. It's pouring!" She called out, but I was already out the door.

I couldn't speak. The burn that had been sitting in the back of my throat since I saw the photos of my mother had finally given way to tears. I pulled their front door shut, running out into the rain. I got three houses down before I let the convulsions take hold of me, sobbing uncontrollably. My whole body ached, just as my heart did.

Perhaps it wouldn't have hurt so badly if they'd just been upfront. If they'd told me the truth, instead of testing me with games and torment. Maybe the blow of information wouldn't have packed such a brutal punch. But the lies made the truth that much harder to reconcile. I was furious, and sad. Most of all, I was exhausted.

As I turned onto Bayswater, the main road, I spotted a double-decker bus stop opposite me that was headed for Piccadilly Circus. It felt like a sign; my cue to escape the rain.

I climbed the stairs to the top deck of the bus, where the least amount of people were—if the mascara smeared across my face wasn't enough, the fact that I was completely soaked certainly wasn't helping.

I'd almost managed to compose myself, when I felt my phone vibrate through my bag. It must've connected to the bus's Wi-Fi.

"Tell me you're not in *London*?" It was Delilah.

"Umm..." I responded, looking out at the storefronts on Oxford Circus that needed to be lit up during the day because the weather was so miserable. "Yeah, I kinda am."

"Oh my God... *what?* Not that I'm not solidly impressed, but—"

"Wait, how did you know?"

"Don't freak, but the credit card company called your grandparents, and they called me when they couldn't get in touch with —," she said as quickly as she could. Spitting out the news like it was live ammunition.

"No," I said, in disbelief. "No. *No, no, no, no.*"

"Wait, it's okay," she said, interrupting my almost meltdown. "I totally covered. Told them it was a scam going around. Just to check their statement when it comes in."

"Did they buy it? Do you think they bought it?"

"Definitely. They weren't even thinking you were there. They thought the card got stolen."

"Woah," I said, realizing the near miss.

"But you need to call them. I told them you'd been sleeping a stomach bug off. They sent soup."

As if my body were rejecting their kindness, I started sobbing again.

"Oh, babe," she said.

"I'm okay," I lied, trying to pull it together. "It's okay. It's just... it's been a weird day... a weird couple of days. Couple of weeks actually."

"You didn't follow him there, did you?" she asked, sounding truly alarmed for the first time since she called.

"*No!*" I said, between hiccups. "I'm not that psychotic... I don't think."

"Good. *Good*. 'Cause that would be intervention territory."

"I found my grandparents. The dead ones. Turns out, they're not so dead."

"What?!" she asked, in a way that made me feel like the way I was behaving wasn't a complete overreaction. "How was it? Were they nice?"

"Well, they offered me twenty-five grand for my mom's necklace and my... *silence?*" It sounded way more James Bond having said it out loud.

"You didn't sign anything, did you?" I could tell she was processing. "Who are these people? Are you safe?"

"I'm fine," I reassured her. "I told them to shove it and I bailed."

"Good girl! What did they say to that?"

"Come over for a dinner party tonight. Meet your relatives."

"Oh, so they're like that," she said, as though she knew exactly who they were.

"Yeah, it was a lot."

"So, are you gonna go?" she asked.

I laughed until I realized she wasn't joking.

"*Hell. No.* I don't want anything to do with them."

"Okay," she said in a way that didn't sound like it was.

"What?"

"It's just... you're gonna go anyway, aren't you? Like, it's you.

And this is your family... the thing you always talk about not having. Plus, you're already there. In London."

"Okay, I get it," I said.

"I'm not saying you should, I'm just saying—"

"I know what you're saying."

"Look, don't go if you don't want to. It's completely your choice. Whatever makes you happy."

"Honestly, I'm not sure what makes me happy anymore," I admitted. "I think I'm just exhausted. I really need to sleep." I pressed the button to get off the bus. There was a building I recognized; I figured I could walk from there.

"Okay, well I support your choices. All of 'em. Forsyth for life."

"Forsyth for life," I agreed, wholeheartedly.

"When do you fly back?"

"Sunday," I said, realizing it was the following night. My head jolted at the thought of having to take those flights again.

"Okay, well, text me updates so I know you're safe."

"Will do. Thank you. *For everything*."

"Of course. Love you!"

"Love you." It felt somewhat unnatural to say, but I meant it, so I knew I had to express it. I hung up, stepping off the bus, back into the unforgiving rain. It was ten blocks to the hostel, and when I returned, I peeled off my clothes and replaced them with a hoodie and sweats that had been sitting next to the radiator all day. It was heaven on my cold, wet skin.

I climbed up to the top bunk and almost instantly passed out, before remembering I had to call my grandparents.

I stared at their number in my contacts, unable to press the call button. Instead, I sent a text:

Sorry I haven't called you back. Thank you for the soup you guys didn't have to do that. Think I just need to sleep it off. I'll call you Monday when I'm feeling better. Love you both x

I heard the text tone ding back, but my eyes were already shut.

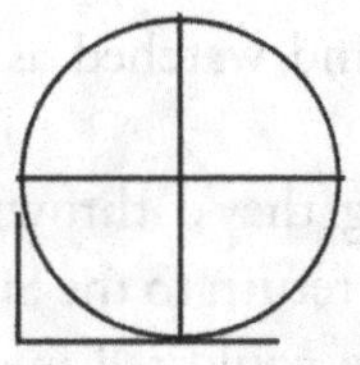

Sixteen

We Are Stars

I awoke five hours later, covered in a thin layer of sweat. Certain it had only been minutes since I passed out, I reached over to check my texts and discovered it was almost seven P.M. I read gran's reply:

> I'm sorry, Eva. I shouldn't have spoken when I didn't know what I was talking about. I stirred up old wounds. Please forgive me and call us as soon as you can. Feel better. We'll worry until we know you're OK.

I wanted to call her, but I knew I couldn't until I was back in New York. If I did and she asked where I was, I wouldn't be able to lie again, and the truth would do the opposite of alleviating her concern.

I wrote back:

> I'm safe and feeling so much better. Don't worry. I'll call you soon. I promise x

It was the best I could do.

I locked my phone and watched as the clock rolled over to seven.

Even after everything they'd thrown at me that afternoon, part of me still wanted to return to the Sinclair's. To meet my relatives—I wondered if they could tell me anything that mattered. Like why she ran away, or chose to keep me a secret. Or better yet, who she really was and what she liked. *How could I, of all people, walk away from all those potential answers?*

Delilah was right, I thought, sitting up. I was already in London. When would I have this opportunity again? It was a temptation I couldn't resist.

After a quick shower, I tried my best to blow-dry my hair on a tiny built-in unit, but after ten minutes of flustering and not much drying, I gave up, opting for a top knot I was certain I'd be judged heavily for. Dressed in black jeans, a matching top, and my leather jacket, I figured I'd at least blend in. Most likely with the waitstaff.

I was walking out of the reception doors, trying to zip my jacket up to brave the three blocks I had to walk in the rain to the Underground, when I heard my name being called.

"Eva?" inquired a brunette woman in her early forties. Her voluminous blow-out framed sparkling green, almond-shaped eyes. Beside her stood another equally striking, equally aged woman. She had slick blonde hair down to her chest and sharp blue eyes that combed over every detail of my face.

"Without a doubt," said the blonde. Her accent was polished, if not overstressed. "She's a replica. In every way."

Men in black suits held umbrellas over the women, shielding them and their floor-length dresses from the rain. The brunette's Grecian gown featured clusters of beads running down the neckline, but the real stars were her three-tiered ruby earrings. The blonde was understated, yet was equally showstopping in a high-collared black dress with an even higher leg slit. Around her neck was a diamond-encrusted pendant—a circle, cross, and triangle inside a square, the same symbol I noticed on Alida earlier that afternoon.

"I take it the Sinclairs sent you," I said, smug I'd made the connection.

"Something like that," said the brunette. "Your mother was our cousin."

"You're sisters?" I asked.

"No," they laughed. "Second cousins," continued the blonde.

They looked at me in a way that made me want to run, like predators eyeing prey.

"Oh, well, I'd love to talk to you about it some more, but..." I gestured to the rain.

"Of course," said the blonde, ignoring me. "We just wanted to stop by and make sure you were okay. Your mother was like a sister to us."

"Our condolences," added the brunette. Almost making me believe she cared.

"Thanks," I replied. "But if we could just speed this up?" I wasn't being covered by either of their umbrellas.

Shock spread across both their faces, as if I was the first to see through their façade.

"We just wanted you to know you have options," offered the blonde. "For instance, if you wanted to get away, anywhere in the world you'd like, you could take our plane. She flies almost eight thousand nautical—"

"Eva!" A voice called out from behind me.

It was Alida, waving me over from the back seat of a Rolls-Royce limousine.

"Speak of the devil, and she shall appear," said the brunette, sliding up next to me.

The blonde mirrored her on my other side. "We're here for you in any way that you need," she said, too close to my ear. I felt like I was in a movie. Or rather a pantomime.

"Money's no object," added the brunette. "We could set you

up with some of that too, if you needed." *Why did everyone related to this family assume I could be bought?* As if I were defined by what they clearly regarded as my lowest attribute.

Alida's driver had stepped out of the car and was leading her towards us, umbrella over her head.

"Forcing me to get out of the car is below even you two," she said approaching, before turning to me. "What did they say to you?"

"Nothing," said the blonde, interrupting.

"They were in the middle of trying to convince me to leave. So far I've been offered a plane and cash," I said. "I'm crossing my fingers a pony's next."

"Well, I hope it didn't work," said Alida. "The rest of the family—"

"No, just the opposite," I said. "If anything, they've piqued my interest."

In truth, they hadn't. All I wanted was to go back inside, take another shower (I was soaked again) and go back to sleep. But my ego refused to give them the satisfaction.

Pride flashed in Alida's eyes. "Let's go then, shall we?"

"Yes, let's," said the blonde, marching forward. "We can all ride together."

"You can tell us the story, on the way, of how you happened to find us after all this time," the brunette chimed in. "We're dying to know." Her tone reeked of accusation but of what, I couldn't tell.

Alida extended her arm, gesturing for me to join her in the car. Just as she was about to get in, she turned and warned, "Be careful what you say in front of them. They're as cunning as snakes."

"Funny," I said. "They implied the same thing about you."

I climbed into the plush backseat, with Alida sliding in beside me. The two women sat in seats that faced us, the confined space stretching out the invisible tension even further.

"Dry off, darling," said Alida, handing me a blanket with H's all over it as we accelerated forward. "You don't want the damp getting into your bones."

I did as she told me, but only because I wanted to know what it felt like to use cashmere as a towel.

"I see you've met my niece, Elizabeth," she said, pointing to the brunette. "And Terence's niece, Nicole," gesturing to the blonde.

I nodded, unsure what to make of them.

"Though I don't remember inviting either of them," said Alida. "As usual, I'm disappointed, but not surprised."

"I don't remember inviting any of you," I said, turning my attention to her. "Why were you outside my hotel?" I asked, defensively.

"Can you call that a hotel?" Nicole slipped in.

"I don't appreciate being watched."

"In case you wanted to come tonight," replied Alida. The lights of Piccadilly Circus reflected off her jeweled bodice as we drove by. "The weather was terrible, and I felt so bad letting you go out in it this afternoon. I didn't have your number to call you... so I came along. Hoping."

"I'm fairly certain Ms. Akande has my number, or could find it very quickly if she didn't. Along with my social security information and the name of the last boy I *kissed*." As if just saying the word summoned the memory of Max, I felt my body go back to our date. Bliss, followed by an agonizing blow.

Alida smiled at me as I shrugged off the thought. "We've missed out on so much, Eva. We just want a chance to change that."

I didn't know how to respond. The words themselves were beautiful. The fairytale kind that every parentless kid dreams of hearing. But I didn't trust a single syllable, which in my mind rendered any potential feelings null and void.

I sat back in the seat, holding onto the wet cashmere.

"We came because we wanted to represent both sides of the family."

"There is only *one side* of this family, Nicole," shot Alida. "The sooner you learn that—"

"Easy to say when you and Terence are the ones dictating the terms."

"Rules are rules. We have them for a reason," dismissed Alida. "And that is the last I want to hear of it this evening. It is vulgar to air private business in front of one's guests," she stated with finality, as we pulled into an underground carpark, beside a loading dock.

Watching her shut them down, especially when they were clearly so in need of it, should have made me happy. Instead, it filled me with dread. The political stakes in the Sinclair family were just too high, and I had no experience playing their game.

Realizing where we were, Elizabeth's mood improved. "Oh, good I've been meaning to—" she began.

"At this hour? It's going to be mayhem," interrupted Nicole.

"I asked them to close early," said Alida, confusing me as she stepped out of the car. "But you two can wait here. This isn't for you," she added.

She was already gliding across white carpet that had been rolled out across the concrete. I got out after her, managing to refrain myself from pulling a face at Nicole and Elizabeth. Antagonizing them further seemed idiotic.

A man in a dark, double-breasted overcoat, bowler hat and a bright yellow tie was waiting to greet us. He stood beside a plaque that read: *Selfridge & Co.*

"Good evening Mrs. Sinclair-Dubois," he said.

He opened double doors to reveal an art-deco elevator, adorned with bronze and cast-iron figures representing each sign of the zodiac. I was mesmerized.

"Marvelous, isn't it?" she said, stepping in. "They put the

other ones they had in the Museum of London. But they kept this one, secretly. For special customers."

We traveled three levels up, arriving to the bright lights of a department store floor.

An intense woman in a tight black bodysuit and leather skirt emerged in the hallway. Her face lit up in fake delight.

"Mrs. Sinclair-Dubois," she said. "A pleasure as always."

Stepping out onto the white marble tiles, I could see every high-end designer imaginable. Gucci, Louis Vuitton, Dior...

"We have your room ready, but would you care to browse the floor?"

"I trust what you've pulled will be sufficient," said Alida striding forward.

The entire level was deserted, except for a few employees, each patiently stationed within their respective brand areas. We veered off the main floor into a room decorated in monochromatic blue, its carpet so plush and heavy beneath my shoes that I was certain it was more expensive than everything I owned. It felt like stepping into another world, one where money changed the rules. Though I was fairly certain that shutting down a department store in one of the busiest cities in the world was an extravagance reserved for the ultra-elite.

Alida disappeared behind a door, while an extremely chiseled guy in a black suit offered me a drink from a silver tray.

"Beverage?" he asked, somehow reminding me of Dylan.

A twinge of sadness that felt like regret spasmed in my gut. *Had I been clinically stupid to dismiss the boy who carried my luggage, so I could chase after the one who ghosted me?*

"I'm good," I finally replied to the guy, who was still staring at me. "Thank you."

"Eva!" Alida called out from the other side of the wall. "Where are you?"

I followed the sound of her voice to another room, where luxurious whites and golds met beveled mirrors and parquet wood floors. She was standing beside a rack that had twenty or so dresses hung on it.

"Well, come on," she said. "Start seeing what fits. You can take anything you want. Anything. Everything." She was holding a black dress out at me.

At what price, I wanted to ask. I didn't want to be indebted to her, but I also didn't want to be the only one at the dinner in jeans.

Reluctantly, I took the dress out of her hands and walked behind a curtain to change. As soon as I knew she couldn't see me, I checked the price tag and almost choked: £9,295.

I held it away from myself as if it were a grenade about to explode. Petrified I was going to break it and have to buy it.

"Is it on?" Alida called out.

"Not... yet."

As I went to walk out to give it back, I remembered how she'd acted toward Nicole and Elizabeth in the car. Alida was the type of person who expected to get her own way. It seemed wiser to comply now so I could use her trust when I needed it.

"Okay, I'm putting it on *but* you can't buy this one because —" I said, stepping out.

"Valentino," she said. "Beautiful."

"It's too expensive."

"Does it fit?"

"Sure," I said. "But that's not the—"

"Perfect. We'll take it," she said to the woman who was hanging on her every word. "Next!" she called out to me.

"Woah. Wait a second," I said. "No. This is too much. I can't let you." My plan to comply was going completely out the window.

"Eva, these are just gifts. Accept them as such."

"With all respect, I highly doubt that."

"I'll have Vivian write up a letter for you. The clothes will be yours free and clear."

I took a breath, thinking it over. "If you really want to give me something, give me honesty. That would mean more to me than any piece of clothing," I said, trying to give her what I was asking for.

She looked conflicted, as if the truth wasn't something she was prepared to negotiate with.

"If I do, then will you let me spoil you? You are, after all—"

"Let's see how good the honesty is first," I said, skeptical. "But you have my word, I'll try on at least... two more dresses."

She turned to the woman helping us. "Let's also pick her out some ready-to-wear options. Saint Laurent, Chloé, Burberry... well, you know, and pack them into a nice suitcase for her."

The woman disappeared so quickly that I didn't have time to stop her.

Alida turned back to me. "I'd like to see the Chanel next," she said with a cheeky grin.

"And I'd like to know what Nicole was referring to in the car when she said 'both sides' of the family."

I could see her bristle but I didn't care.

She pointed to the curtain and I obliged.

"My sister Katalin, my brother Alexander, and I are the last of the Dubois family. A very, very old bloodline whose lineage spans several nobilities throughout Europe. Terence, and his brother Liam, inherited their grandfather's company Atlantic Mining and Minerals in the seventies when it was worth next to nothing. They were able to turn it into what it is today."

"So you brought the status, and he brought the money?" I asked, stepping into the dress. The cut of it I could get behind—floor length, long sleeve, high neckline. If it didn't have a metallic floral appliqué all over it, I might have actually felt comfortable wearing it.

"We've been fortunate to bring many things to each other's lives," she said. "The fact that we were able to help both of our families in the process was a bonus. For them, mostly."

I walked out to show her the dress.

She stopped speaking, staring at me as though I'd just turned into a swan.

"Breathtaking," she said. "Just breathtaking."

She made me try on a few more dresses, while alluding to friction between Terence, who chairs the company's board, and his brother Liam. Nicole's father.

As we wrapped up, Alida confidently walked towards the elevator. "Have everything sent to the house," she said to no-one, knowing it would still get done.

Attempting to please her, I told her I'd wear one of the dresses, but accepting the other clothes was out of the question. The fear of being blindsided by owing them something was just too great.

"Is it money you don't trust?" she asked as we descended floors. "Or just me?"

"A little column A, a little column B," I said. "You haven't earned my trust, and I haven't earned your money."

"You earned it by being born," she stated factually. "Tell me, is there really such glory in refusing a reward when given it? Don't cut your nose off to spite your face, dear," she said. "Especially when you have a such a beautiful face."

We were back at her house within minutes, pulling through the gates into the circular driveway. Nicole and Elizabeth, who were in "desperate need of a cocktail," ascended into the house without so much as a glance behind them.

"I've sent someone to your room to help you get ready. Top of the stairs to the left."

"My room?" I asked, defensive.

"It was your mother's," she replied. "I figured you'd like it best. You're obviously welcome to stay the night."

"I have to be back. A friend's waiting on me," I lied, again. It was becoming a reflex when I didn't want to commit to a situation, and I wasn't mad at it.

As we walked through the entrance, I could hear voices out in the back garden. It must have been where the party was because I couldn't see anyone through the foyer.

"I have to greet the guests," said Alida. "And give them my apologies for being late. You'll come down when you're ready?" she asked and told me.

"Sure," I said, taking a few steps up the staircase.

"Eva, you're going to feel beautiful," she called back. "Trust me!"

"I thought we already established, I don't."

"You will, dear!" She winked, disappearing down the hall. "Soon enough, you will!"

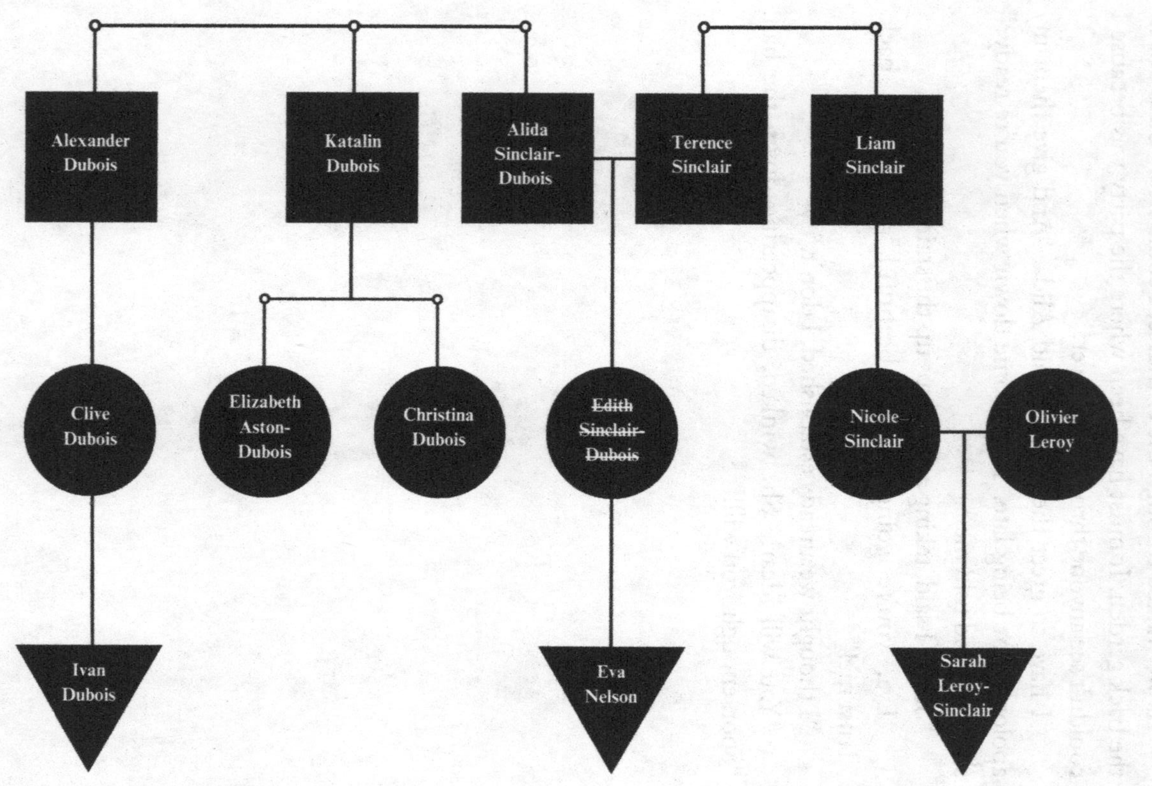

Alexander Dubois
Katalin Dubois
Alida Sinclair-Dubois
Terence Sinclair
Liam Sinclair
Clive Dubois
Elizabeth Aston-Dubois
Christina Dubois
Edith Sinclair-Dubois
Nicole Sinclair
Olivier Leroy
Ivan Dubois
Eva Nelson
Sarah Leroy-Sinclair

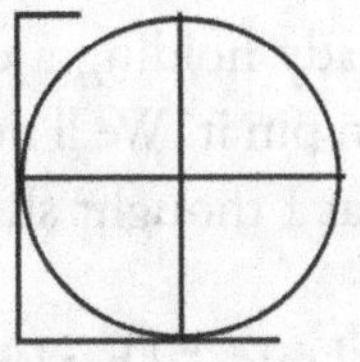

SEVENTEEN
I WANNA BE ADORED

My mother's room was unlike any in the house, as if it didn't belong. Untouched by the outside world, it was a time capsule of her life. As though when she left, the door had stayed shut forever.

Flicking on the lights, a messy tapestry of photos caught my eye. Pinned directly into wooden panels that took up the far side of the room, their presence stood out as a defiant act of protest.

They showed a different side to Edith than the one displayed in Alida's photographs. Relaxed and happy, she looked like someone who didn't care what people thought; her clothing so baggy, it almost swallowed her whole. Most of all, she looked fun. Like someone I would've been friends with.

"Knock knock," sang out a man from behind me.

I turned to take in his artificially frozen face. His voice, the only part of him that retained any animation.

A petite woman with red, curly hair trailed him.

"I'm Oscar, this is Ange," he said hurriedly through pursed lips. "She'll get your outfit ready while I do your hair and makeup."

"It's fine," I said. "I'm more than capable of putting on—"

The woman was already holding a dress up against me. "I'll need to see this on so I can pin it. We'll need to alter it a titch," she said, or at least that's what I thought she said. Her accent was so strong I needed subtitles.

'Uh, that's not... no," I said. "That isn't the dress I chose."

The gown was adorned with shimmering clear crystals that covered every inch. Cascading to the floor, its excessive weight and flashy design were exactly why I'd told Alida to put it back—it didn't seek attention, it screamed for it.

"This is the only dress we have," she said. Looking up, petrified. "Is this not the dress?"

"*No*," I said, trying to stand my ground, while also reminding myself that she was just doing her job. "No, thank you."

"It's a beautiful dress," said Oscar, who already had my hair in a pony and was combing the ends.

I pulled it out of his hands.

"Yes, I can see that, but it's not really my style," I said as politely as possible. "Are you able to ask Alida where the other dresses are?"

"She's out at the party," he replied. "With all the other guests." He looked down at his clothes, pulling on his sweatshirt. "I can't go out there and interrupt her, wearing this."

I looked at my own clothes. *I knew the feeling.*

"Everyone's very dressed up. There's dignitaries down there," said Ange, her accent getting thicker by the minute as though her anxiety was pushing her into a different dialect.

"Look out the window at what they're wearing. This dress is perfect. Honestly," he added, looking hopeful he might persuade me.

"Fine, whatever," I said. The people pleaser in me couldn't look at their terrified faces any longer. "Just please, don't make me stand out. I want to blend in."

"Okay. But if you don't want to stand out," said Oscar, doing his best to smile, "you probably should've picked a different dress."

I stared at him like I wanted to slap him. Instead, I relinquished control, letting him slather makeup on my face and scrape my hair back into an updo that if pushed, could be described as... not bad.

It wasn't until I caught my reflection, as I made my way down the staircase, that I truly wanted to bolt. The glittering, look-at-me dress was the opposite of blending in. Flashy on the hanger, it was alarming on my body, emphasizing every curve.

"Eva!" I heard Terence proclaim. I'd already descended too far into the party to retreat. An elderly couple who had been standing with him turned to appraise me in a way that made me feel like livestock entering a cattle auction.

"You look..." said Terence, starting to get emotional. "Ravishing. Truly."

"Thanks," I said, diverting my attention to the string quartet, and then to the crowd. "That's a lot of fancy people."

Candles lit up the heavily-manicured garden, where forty or so people were mingling, sipping cocktails from crystal glasses. Thousands of fresh flowers suspended overhead formed a see-through canopy, impressively shielding the guests from the rain while still managing to reveal the night sky above.

"Yes," he said, joining me in assessing the guests. He was wearing the same symbol Alida wore. A circle, cross and triangle inside a square. "Tough people, too," he said, more seriously than I was expecting. "And then there's your family."

"They're not my family," I said. "I don't know them."

"I'm not sure they'll care," he said in a way that made me think he was referring to more than petty pleasantries. "A word of advice. Be on guard. And hide that necklace."

"What?" I asked. "Are you being serious?"

"It's a very precious stone and families love to fight over them, especially this one."

"They're welcome to try," I said, gearing up internally for an attack.

"Or you could place it out of sight," he suggested. "It's no coincidence that people who go looking for trouble often find it."

"True," I said. "Or I could just leave?" This 'dinner party' was beginning to sound more like an ambush.

"Let me hold onto it for tonight," he offered. "You have my word, I'll return it."

I raised an eyebrow. *Did he think I was completely naïve?* "Your word doesn't mean very much to me, especially after you tried to buy it not even—"

"*Words*," he stressed, "mean a very great deal around here. Remember that."

"This is ridiculous," I said. "I—"

"I hope you're not frightening the girl, Uncle Terence," said Elizabeth.

"Though she does appear rather unflappable," added Nicole, appearing from out of nowhere. "But I'm sure time will tell."

"You've met your cousins, I understand?" Terence asked me.

Before I had time to answer, Nicole had thrown another jab: "Alida's given her a fighting chance, I see," she said, looking my dress up and down but addressing Terence.

"It's a *designer*. Whose name I can't pronounce," I replied, with the nastiest expression I could muster. "And you can speak directly to me, considering I'm—"

"Nothing my brother didn't do for you," Terence interrupted. "Or that you didn't do for Sarah, for that matter." He was still being polite but his demeanor had turned. It was guarded, protective almost. "Visiting my granddaughter on the other hand, in an attempt to dissuade her from joining us tonight, does seem like something the board might want to look into. Perhaps even take disciplinary action against."

"Our apologies, Uncle Terence," said Nicole. "We were just overjoyed to meet her."

Her eyes landed on my necklace, long enough for me to regret not hiding it.

"Exactly. We all slip up, every now and again," added Elizabeth with mock sincerity.

The terrible two were joined by a third. "Lizzy, can you still call it a slip up when you've spent half your life on the floor?" She was younger (and shorter) than the other two, with sun-kissed red hair that framed a porcelain complexion. Her hourglass figure and natural beauty gave her the look of a classic Hollywood starlet, but her infectious demeanor made her relatable.

"Christina..." Terence began to introduce her.

She intercepted, holding out her hand to shake mine. "It's so special to meet you," she said. "I flew in as soon as I heard." She was wearing a low-cut black dress that showed off her ample cleavage. Large but elegant jewels lined her fingers. A reoccurring family theme.

"Of course you did," sneered Nicole. Then turned to look at me. "Be wary of this one, she was obsessed with your mother."

"Sad to watch, really," added Elizabeth. "I wonder if the revival will be as entertaining."

I was still forming words when Christina struck back.

"Jealousy doesn't suit you," she remarked. "Any more than your new gentleman friend does." There was an air of threat in her voice. "He's a little young, no?"

"Keeping tabs on me, sis? How sweet," replied Elizabeth. It was the furthest thing from a sibling dynamic I'd ever seen. Alarm bells were sounding. *If surveilling your own sister wasn't out of the question, what was?*

"Eva!" boomed Alida, breaking the tension. "You look more exquisite than I ever could have imagined." She hugged me and whispered in my ear. "I promise I'll answer every question you have about tonight. Just promise me you'll fight like hell."

I always do, I thought to myself, while also trying to figure out how hyperbolic she was being.

"That's enough, Alida," said a glamorous woman in her late sixties. She had arched eyebrows, soft eyes and a defined bone structure that hinted at the beauty of her youth. She spoke in a thick Eastern European accent. "Come. It's time to eat," she said.

As everyone turned, I slipped my necklace off as discreetly as I could.

"My sister Katalin," introduced Alida. "Elizabeth and Christina's mother."

"A pleasure," said Katalin, then put her arms around her daughters to usher them away.

"Aunt Alida," Nicole offered, her voice dripping with feigned sweetness. "Allow me to walk you and Uncle Terence to your seat."

"It would be our pleasure," Alida replied. Though I could tell it was the last thing she wanted.

"I'll just walk myself," I muttered. "Seeing as it's only thirty feet."

Amusement crept across Terrence's face, as we made our way to the tables at the garden's edge. In the center was a long rectangular one set for thirteen, surrounded by smaller, circular tables that each sat six.

While everyone was distracted I searched for somewhere to hide my necklace, when I realized my safest option, was walking in front of me. Before I had time to overthink it, I dropped the crystal into Terence's hand. Perhaps not the wisest decision, but I'd rather lose it to him, than the terrible two.

"One chance," I whispered to him, completing the exchange. "Don't make me regret it."

He registered what it was as we arrived at the table. Nodding in what I took as agreement, before taking his place at the head of the long table.

To his left was a man in his seventies, who I assumed was Alida's brother, Alexander, based on his high cheekbones and trained posture. Next to him was his son, who I recognized from the Atlantic Mining and Minerals' website. His name was Clive Sinclair and he was rumored to be next in line to take over the company. He was in his late forties, and wasn't mentioned in a single article online without the precursor 'playboy.' Beside him was his son, who looked around my age and had the kind of cut features that belong on a cologne ad.

Alida, who was sitting on the other side of Terence, pointed to an empty seat next to her. As I walked around, the three men stood up.

"My brother, Alexander," she said gesticulating toward the older of the three men. "His son, my nephew, Clive, and his son, Ivan."

I had no idea how I was going to remember anyone's name, and the speed at which the violinist kept rapidly changing notes wasn't doing anything to help me focus.

"Hi." I waved. Trying not to get overwhelmed.

Katalin sat next to me, with Elizabeth and Christina next to her.

Toward the other end of the table was Nicole and her father, Terence's brother, Liam Sinclair. He was a burly man with a muscular upper body and permanent no-nonsense expression. Next to them was Nicole's replica, twenty years younger. She was effortlessly beautiful, with piercing blue eyes and alabaster skin so smooth it looked as though it had never seen the sun.

"Liam and his granddaughter, Sarah," Terence whispered, winking at me before knocking on the solid wood tabletop to draw everyone's attention. "Good evening," he called out. The entire room fell instantly silent. "Please take your seats for dinner."

I wondered what it felt like to have that kind of power, to command so much respect from people that they hung on your every word. The final member of the table arrived, finishing a phone call as he kissed Nicole on the cheek. He took a seat across from her, and Sarah, who I assumed was his daughter.

The quartet began quietly playing a new piece, as thirteen waiters simultaneously arrived to deliver colorful starter salads to our table. As I took a bite, I noticed Sarah watching me, before flicking her attention back to her food, cutting up a tiny piece of tomato and placing it into her mouth as though each chew were exhausting.

It wasn't until I scanned the room that I noticed how eerily silent everyone was, as if by orchestrated design. It was unnatural to have so many people in such an intimate space making barely any noise—the gentle scrapes and clangs of silverware against bone china, the only audible sound.

As I looked back to my unusually tasty salad, I noticed a man at the table opposite me who looked identical to a member of the Royal family. Across from him, I could've sworn, was a musician from the seventies nicknamed 'The Walking Sin.' Or at least that's what I remember my grandma calling him. On the table next to them was a man in white robes, who looked like Middle Eastern royalty. His diamond-encrusted Rolex peeked out from under his sleeve.

I wondered if they really were the individuals they resembled. I couldn't work it out. *Did the ultra-wealthy all just hang out, automatically introduced to one another once their bank accounts hit a certain threshold?*

Servers reappeared to take my plate, and the food I wasn't finished eating.

Terence raised a glass of wine. "It is my duty, and a task I am humbled by, to call this meeting... this family, to order."

The pageantry was comical, and yet no one laughed.

"Tonight we celebrate a very special guest." I looked around the room to find the 'dear family friend' whose birthday it was, thinking it strange that the person of honor wasn't seated at the main table, when it sounded like Terence had said my name.

"It is my great honor to welcome my granddaughter, Eva."

I felt myself sink, wanting to hide. The barely chewed lettuce

I'd just swallowed was doing backflips in my stomach. I looked around to assess the unwanted attention of everyone in the garden only to see that aside from our table, everyone else was still eating their food, oblivious to the words coming from Terence's mouth. It felt like a consolation of sorts, easing my anxiety enough to take another breath.

"In accordance with *In Unio* lore and ritual, I open the floor," he said, bowing his head.

'*Law and ritual*,' I thought to myself. *What the hell have I gotten into?* Accepting the invitation to dinner was starting to feel like a serious mistake.

Across from me, Nicole began speaking, "For reasons that are obvious, I call to challenge Eva's seat at this table."

I was in a trance, left without speech. It was my greatest fear realized: being somewhere people didn't want me to be. I froze, a panic building in my chest.

"On what grounds?" Terence asked as though he were reading news he didn't care for.

"Precedent," she snapped. "We have the majority, *In Unio* has—"

"Nicole!" Liam warned. The first time I'd heard him speak.

"This *family*," she said, raising her voice back at him. "If the majority of this family aren't in favor, she cannot proceed."

"Is that the only motion set before us?" inquired Terence, speaking quickly, like he wanted it to be over. I looked around the table, everyone content in their silence, further illustrating how alone I truly was.

"Uh, whoa," I said. "No."

I stood up, if only to find my courage.

"I have no idea what's going here, but you can all keep it. I don't want any part of this."

"That works for us," said Nicole. "You're welcome to leave the way you—"

"*ENOUGH*," bellowed Terence, using the full power of his

voice. I looked around the garden and when no one else noticed or acknowledged his outburst, I felt my body move from suspicious to certain: something insane and, frankly, disturbing was taking place. It was starting to become too obvious to ignore.

"Conference will commence until the hour. You will each have time to present your case to the nominee." He knocked on the table and with immediate effect, the party and its noise resumed.

Not wanting to waste another moment, I lunged toward Terence, whispering aggressively in his ear. "My mother's necklace," I demanded, holding out my hand.

"Of ear or not at all!" insisted Liam Sinclair.

I looked up, surprised. *Was he kidding?* Anger brewed across Terence's face.

"I just want my necklace," I asserted, loud enough so that everyone could hear. I was through conforming to the rules of their elitist charade. I wanted what was mine, and to be out of there. "Though I'm not sure how that concerns you," I added, staring Liam dead in the eyes. I wanted him to know that I didn't fear him, though perhaps I should have.

"Watch that she doesn't end up like the other one," he seethed.

Terence almost knocked me over, leaping toward him.

It was Alida's voice that intervened. *"We are in conference,"* she said. "Is now not the time for private counsel?"

"As long as it doesn't break lore," said Katalin. "It will be reflected in trial if she's guided more than as is written."

"Then it's settled," she said, moving to where I was standing next to Terence.

"One, two. No more than three," said Clive, like a mischievous riddle.

"I'll go," said Alida, moving toward the other guests.

"What the hell is going on?" I asked. "You people are..." I didn't know how to put into words what I was witnessing. It felt as if I'd stumbled into the middle of a choreographed dance and I was the only one who didn't know the steps.

Terence stood tall, pulling me aside. He held my shoulders as though they were the helm of a ship. "Listen to me," he said in a rushed whisper. "In less than an hour, a vote will be cast that determines your future. I'd hoped there would be more time to prepare you. To ensure that you were ready. But I know in my heart you already are," he said.

"What are you talking about?" I asked, trying not to laugh, or cry.

"We believe in you," he said. "We believe you can do this, or we wouldn't let it happen. We wouldn't risk losing you." I was trying to keep up but his words were melding together, making me feel like I was in physical danger. The fear of it weighed down my chest.

I shrugged his hands off me.

"Okay, I'm done with this, and you," I said. "I am done with this whole insane family." It felt good to finally verbalize what I'd been wanting to say since I'd met them. I just wished I wasn't wearing a twenty-pound dress and could make a quick escape. "Just *give me* my necklace."

"The vote is permanent," he said, fear overtaking his eyes. "If you leave or vote no—"

"Time," yelled Elizabeth, satisfaction filling the upper decibels of her voice.

Terence looked to her, then to Alida, who had reappeared nearby. She nodded to him, clarifying his non-verbal question.

"You promised," I reminded him, attempting to return his attention to me.

"And I maintain that promise. It shall be returned before the night is—"

"*Time,*" repeated Elizabeth. "You wouldn't want to be the cause of a disqualification."

Terence relented, turning away from me.

I was about to follow, but Elizabeth stepped in front of me, blocking my path. "The truth is, I was best friends with your mother," she declared. "Nicole and I both were. We were inseparable," she said proudly. "She was spunky, just like you. Hated all of this. Not sure she'd want any of it for you and that is the honest truth."

I felt like I was swimming fully dressed in a sea of confusion.

"Why are you telling me this?" I asked, backing up. "I'm already leaving."

"*Good. Then leave*," she said. "There's absolutely nothing keeping you here."

She was right, necklace or not, I didn't belong there. So I did the smartest thing I'd done in days, and fled back toward the house—bumping a waiter full of drinks on the way.

I'd almost made it to the front door when I saw Alida standing in front of it.

I didn't know how she'd gotten there so fast, but my brain didn't have the capacity to care. I just wanted her gone.

"Please get out of my way," I said.

"Do you understand?" she asked, panic etched into her face. "If you walk out that door, there's no coming back. There's nothing we can do. If you leave tonight, you can never be part of this family."

"You're incredible," I said, disgusted at the conditional way she operated. "So much for, 'we want to get know you.'"

"It wouldn't be our choice," she said, anguished. "Our hands would be tied."

Nicole arrived by my side. Her presence changing Alida's demeanor.

"A vote will be cast," Alida stated.

"So I've heard," I replied, frustration building. "You know, you should consider taking up a hobby. Y'all clearly have too much time on your hands."

"We *believe in you*. Do you understand what I'm saying?"

asked Alida, repeating what Terence had said. "*You can do it. You're more than capable*—"

"You're leading, Aunt Alida," said Nicole. "You ought to be careful."

"*You* ought to be careful," she snapped back ferociously. It made her appear dangerous in a way I wouldn't have thought her possible. "You may have succeeded in scaring her away but I am not going anywhere," Alida warned. "And my memory is good and long, dear. *Good and long.*"

"Well it's almost time anyway," said Nicole.

Alida turned to me. "We believe in you," she said, finishing her sentence. "I'm asking you now to believe in us."

"Time," said Nicole, with vengeful resolve.

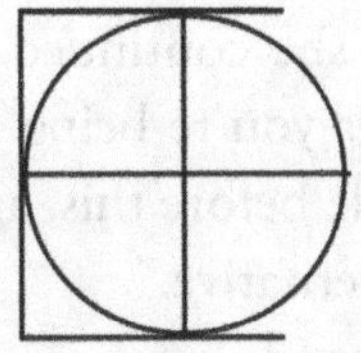

EIGHTEEN
STRING QUARTET NO. 14 IN D MINOR

Conflicted, as though she wanted to say more, Alida complied by stepping aside.

"I love you," she added, "even if right now, that's too hard to trust."

She was gone before I had a chance to register her words.

"I've done my research," said Nicole, not even giving me a second to recover. "You're a smart girl. Well-written, well-argued... *almost* well-educated," she said as though she was trying to be kind. "So I'm going to be as straightforward with you as lore will allow." My brain still couldn't decipher if they meant law or lore.

"Your *arrival*," she continued, like she was referring to an atrocity of war that happened long ago, "pushed my son from his rightful place in this family. For obvious reasons, that's not something I can allow. I'll play by the rules, of course, but I won't stop until your presence here no longer jeopardizes ours. Do you really want to live amongst that?"

I managed to sneak a foot or two closer to the door as the man I assumed was her husband approached. He spoke with a thick French accent.

"Almost time," he said.

"I'll level with you," she continued. "*Go*... Not because you don't want to be here, or you're being told to. Go, because I'm sure your life was tolerable before this, and it will be after. I can't say the same about the alternative."

"Time," said her husband.

She smiled and retreated.

I used the elapsed seconds to walk the additional two feet to the door. I was about to open it when I realized her husband hadn't said a word.

I turned back.

"You're not gonna stop me?" I asked.

"Mieux vaut être seul que mal accompagné," he said.

I stared at him. Perplexed. "I think we both know I don't speak French."

"It is better," he said, "to be alone than in bad company."

"Company you've chosen to be around," I said, without thinking. "I guess they can't be all that bad?"

"They're worse," he said, with a cheeky sneer. "But my son, no matter his shortcomings," he added, mockingly like they were in competition, "should be here."

Alida's brother, Alexander, appeared behind him. Straightening the cuffs of his sleeve that poked out of his bespoke suit. Nicole's husband eyed him before returning his attention to me.

"The decision is all yours," he stated. "If you leave now, no one from this family will ever bother you again. Of that, you have my word."

Good. Great, I thought. All I wanted to do was leave. To run back to my normal life. It might not be perfect, but at least it operated in a way I understood. At least I could count on things I knew to be true.

I opened the front door and walked outside as Alexander said: "Time."

Nicole's husband looked at him, nodded and left.

"I'm your great uncle," said Alexander, moving toward me as

I debated returning inside. The cold prickling my exposed skin. "I'm not sure what that really means. Only to say that my parents were your great-grandparents. As though shared blood is supposed to bind us in some way."

"Well it doesn't. DNA may link us, but that doesn't mean we share any kind of connection," I said.

"True," he chuckled.

"What do you all want from me?" I spat, finally asking a question that had been circling my mind. "Like, *actually want?*"

"Stay," he said. "Take the seat that is rightfully yours. The test is nothing to worry about. I did it at thirteen."

"Is that how I get out of this unscathed?" I asked.

He looked at me like he was scrutinizing a business deal. "I'm not sure such an option exists."

"You clearly managed?" I asked, trying to ascertain the severity of his statement.

"Careful planning and trusted allies."

"Careful, Father," said Clive entering the room, devilment in his voice. "If I'd been Liam... or Sarah..."

"Hush," he said to his son before returning his focus to me. "I am loyal to your grandparents, and my sons are loyal to me. You have our vote."

"Time," said Clive.

"You're family, Eva," Alexander concluded. "You belong here."

Having anyone tell me I belonged anywhere hit hard. It struck a chord, one that I was sure he'd knowingly aimed for.

Clive took off his overcoat and handed it to me as Alexander walked away.

Declining it wasn't an option. I was so cold I was starting to shiver.

"The good news is you're over halfway through," he said. He was charming and he knew it. I could see why gossip magazines were so infatuated with him.

"So I have to hear from everyone at that table?" I asked in disbelief, as I wrapped the luxurious fabric around my shoulders.

"You don't *have* to do *anything*," he said without judgment.

"But if I leave, I'm never allowed back, correct?" I said like it was the most ridiculous thing I'd ever heard.

"Correct." He smiled.

"What is this, some kind of cult or something? What's with all the rules?"

"Lores and rituals."

"Of the family?" I asked.

"Yes," he said. He held the 'e' a millisecond too long for me to be satisfied that his answer was the complete truth.

"And?" I asked.

He laughed uncomfortably, like perhaps I'd caught him.

"I can't say," he said.

"Sounds like a cult to me," I replied. "Or a secret society. That would certainly explain the guy out there in the garden who I'm pretty sure's a very famous musician."

"He may well be."

"Who's *dead*."

I didn't expect to shock him, someone so familiar with these bizarre gatherings, but I'd anticipated more of a reaction. He paused briefly, his expression tinged with amusement, as if debating whether to indulge me. At the last moment, he decided against it.

He exhaled, shifting his tone. "Was there a question in there?"

"Is there any point in me asking any? Are you even going to tell me the—"

"Time." Ivan had appeared beside his father.

"Stick around, seriously. You're gonna fit in great around here," said Clive before stepping aside for his son. The constant changeover meant every conversation was interrupted right before I was able to get to the bottom of anything useful. Like I was being drip-fed information. Never enough to enlighten me; just enough to antagonize my addiction for answers.

Ivan was better looking up close, his onyx-black eyes glistening in the entry lights. He was around Max's age, but his disposition felt younger. More unaffected.

"Firstly, if you're planning on hitting or slapping Sarah, I'd appreciate a heads-up. Tonight's already been the most eventful one of these I've ever been to, and missing that would be a tragedy from which I may never recover."

This family gets more nuts by the second, I thought.

"I have no impending plans for physical violence, I'm afraid."

"Alas," he responded, turning back, perhaps to see who was coming next. As he did, I saw a small tattoo behind his right ear. It was of the circle, square and triangle symbol.

"What's the symbol?" I asked.

"I can't say," he said.

"What's the test?"

"I also can't say." He grinned, taking pleasure in the discourse.

I scoffed. "*What is wrong with you people?*" I might have raised my voice a little. But it didn't seem to faze him.

"What *can* you tell me then?" I said, almost giving up.

"We're all very eager to see if you'll survive."

"Survive like *live*? Your grandfather said he passed it at thirteen?"

"He did."

"So it's not serious then?"

"He was raised in this family, he had predisposed knowledge."

"Shouldn't I be entitled, then, to that same information?"

"He discovered things organically."

Ugh. I exhaled out of frustration.

"You're telling me to stay, but you're not giving me any reason to."

"Well, there is the obvious reason…"

I looked at him blankly. "Spell it out for me."

"You'll never have to worry about money again."

"Oh, *that*. Money doesn't do it for me," I said.

He smirked condescendingly. "Well, does it 'do it' for the people you love? Your family, your friends. I assume you have friends? Charities and causes that matter to you?"

Of course I did. There were a million things I'd want to do if I had their level of money. Take care of my grandparents, for one, so they never had to worry another day in their lives.

"At what price?" I asked, earnestly.

"None. It's rightfully yours," he said. "Your mother was next in line to inherit everything. You could easily take over this family, if you wanted to. That's what's got everyone losing their minds."

"You can put them out of their misery. I don't want it," I said. The risk far exceeded the reward.

"What *do* you want, then?" he asked. "A scholarship at NYU? Done. An internship at *The New York Times*? Sorted. Financial freedom? It's all yours."

"I get the point," I said cutting him off before I was tempted. "Am I supposed to be impressed you did your research?"

"Everyone wants something, Eva. You just need to figure out what that is."

"Answers," I said without thinking. "All I want is answers. Like to begin with, who are you all? And who was my mother? It's like everything I knew about her was a lie. Can you just tell me something truthful about her? Like what made her run away, was it because of all this stuff?"

"That I don't know," he said. "But I do know none of those answers are out there. Leaving only gets you farther away from them."

"Absolutely right," said Katalin, walking up gracefully beside him. "And, time."

"Stay safe," he said, departing. I wasn't sure if it were a farewell or an omen.

Katalin moved toward me, her chiffon dress bellowing in the

wind. She must have been cold, but she didn't show it. I couldn't imagine someone of her refinement ever would.

"He was telling you the truth," she started out. "The farther from this family you go, the further you'll be from the truth you seek. But it's imperative you ask yourself, what you have to gain. Will this knowledge, however hard, bring you the happiness you so desperately crave?"

"You're going with ignorance is bliss?" I retorted. "That's your big sell?"

"No sell, just an alternate way of looking at things. Name a fact or a piece of knowledge that gives you as much joy as believing that, if you put a fallen tooth under your pillow, a fairy will visit and leave you a gift. Reality is rarely kind, and yet so many people desperately chase after it."

I considered what she was saying. She seemed sincere, but she was Alida's sister. I had no way of knowing if she were an ally, or one of the people my mother was running from.

"If I stay," I asked, "what do you have to gain?"

She smiled at my question. "So like your mother," she said, studying me. I was beginning to tire of hearing it. "If you stay and fail, nothing. If you stay and succeed, a great deal."

"And what do you get if I leave?" I put my cards on the table and asked the question we both knew I was leading to.

"Nicole's challenge is not just about her son. It's part of Liam's grand coup d'état to overthrow your grandfather and the family members who have aligned themselves to him. I have forever been the balance, choosing to side with my sister. A vote against you and your grandfather would signal a tear from him, and allow Liam to succeed."

"Why, after all this time, would you do that? To your sister?"

"Because I promised your mother I would," she said, her stare so intense it made the hairs on the back of my neck stand up.

"Why would my mother—"

"Time," announced Sarah, as she walked outside, a devilish look on her striking face.

"You didn't ask me what I'd risk losing if you chose to stay."

"Time!" Sarah insisted.

"What?" I asked, as quickly as I could. "What would you lose?"

"*You*," said Katalin, sadness flashing briefly across her face before she glided away.

"What's she talking about?"

"I can't say," answered Sarah coyly. "Why is it you haven't left yet?"

"Excuse me?"

"You've been threatening us with it for long enough, haven't you? You don't want people to think your words don't carry any weight. Attention seeking is such a juvenile act."

The glow of the moon reflected off the tops of her cheeks, brows and nose, further highlighting the prominent angles of her face.

"I have no interest in taking what's yours," I said.

"And yet, here you stand." Her loathing was peeking through the seams of her carefully composed façade. "I suggest you run along back to America and find solace in the fact that at least your pathetic life is your own. You don't belong here."

My insecurity latched onto the words, but I wouldn't let them break me. Instead, I raised her bluff. "Then why are you so afraid I'll stay?" I asked.

"I'm not afraid," she laughed. "You're the one who should be afraid because every option that exists through that door involves me. And if you somehow manage to keep your life, I will personally make sure it's torturous."

I analyzed her face, fury steaming off every inch of her. *How seriously should I take what this person says as the truth?* Her behavior felt inflated, but there was no lack of conviction in her eyes. She wanted me gone, and was prepared to threaten and intimidate me to achieve that.

"I can't imagine you're acting this psychotic over your brother because that would require you to actually have the human emotion of empathy, so I'm just going to assume—"

"You can assume all—"

I held up a finger. "I wasn't done speaking. You'll know when I'm done speaking because words won't be coming out of my mouth." I took a breath to get back on track. "*I think* you're scared I'll pass whatever test they're about to give me and I'll vote against your grandfather. What I can't work out is why that's so important to you."

I paused to make sure she wasn't going to cut me off again. "But if I do decide to stick around, I'll be sure to do some digging."

"Time," said Liam Sinclair, arriving on cue. He was slightly shorter than my grandfather, but had the same broad shoulders. He looked like a man who didn't stop until a job was done, and done well.

He rested his hand on Sarah's shoulder.

"I tried," she said to her grandfather. "But she's as thick as a brick."

He appeared deep in thought, as she returned into the house.

The wind rustled through the towering trees as ominous clouds, hanging low in the sky, threatened to unleash more rain. I had no idea what I was doing still standing there, but I felt cemented in place.

"You must think we're horrible people," he said. Pausing, no doubt for dramatic effect. "Rightly so, I suppose. My comment earlier was out of line. I apologize."

"You mean the one about me ending up like my dead mother?" I clarified, wanting to confront him to his face with his own words. If I had to listen to his phony apology, the least he could do was be explicit about it.

"Yes," he said. "That was callous."

"An abundant trait on your side of the family. Sarah, Nicole… and you, have all threatened my life in a matter of min—"

"You scare them, or at least your presence here does; they don't play well when cornered."

"Thank you for your honesty, I guess," I replied. Part of me wasn't being sarcastic. He may have been blunt, but at least he seemed to be more candid than the others.

"Let me walk you back inside," he said. "It's clear that you'll be partaking in the vote this evening."

"No, I—"

"Something's keeping you here," he said. "Curiosity, perhaps? I can tell you from experience that it's rarely worth it."

"Do you think it's a coincidence," I asked, trying to maintain my composure, "that the people who keep telling me it isn't worth it, are the ones who have the most to gain by my departure?"

"The question you should be asking is, why are the people telling you to stay so comfortable *risking your life*?"

"Risking my life?" I repeated back to him in disbelief.

Maybe it was how he said it, or the gravitas he exuded, but until that moment all the threats leveled against me had felt cunningly veiled. Liam's words, however, stood out—too blatant not to take seriously. Reaching a breaking point, I had to draw a line. "This is insane," I said. "I'm done."

I didn't doubt that he was manipulating me for his own personal gain, but he'd just raised the bar higher than I was willing to go. There wasn't a single cell in my body prepared to *risk my life* to solve a puzzle I had closure on years ago. I couldn't do that to my grandparents. Not when they'd already lost so much.

I took Clive's overcoat off and handed it to Liam.

"You win. Enjoy your revolution."

He grinned, resolute.

I descended the garden steps toward the gate, making it as far as the hedges when I heard Christina yelling my name.

"Eva, wait!" she sang out. "For heaven's sake, don't make me run in these heels!"

I stopped. Not because I cared about what she had to say, but because she struck me as the type of person who wouldn't rest until she caught up with me.

Without a jacket, the evening's chill had begun working its way into my bones, causing my muscles to tighten and relax in quick succession in an attempt to raise my body temperature.

As she finally reached me, she attempted to regain her composure.

"Before I start," she said. Her intonation was musical, unlike the rest of her family. "I need you to know that I truly... that I'm on your side. No matter what that turns out to be."

I exhaled, not believing her, not disbelieving her. I didn't have the energy to care.

"My horrid sister, was, in fact, right about one thing," she continued. "I adored your mother. She was the sister I wished I'd had. I can't remember a time when I didn't look up to her. She said and did all the things I wanted to do, but never quite had the courage for."

She started to get emotional. I was fighting a similar urge.

"A quality you apparently have in spades," she said, shrugging off her public display of emotion.

I bristled, uneasy. I wasn't about to let my guard down with anyone from the Sinclair family. No matter how tempting it was to know more.

"All that to say, I feel like I owe her, even still. To protect her memory, and now to protect you."

"Look, thank you," I said. "But it's freezing and I really gotta get back."

She laughed, passive-aggressively. "You don't make it easy to get in, do you?"

My blood wanted to boil over. "It's been a really... *long...* night," I said through gritted teeth that were starting to chatter.

"I do understand. And I am sorry, to make it any longer," she said, by all appearances legitimately remorseful. "I can't imagine how hard it's been, but..." She took a deep breath. "I had some people look into your mother's accident."

"*What?*" I asked, infuriated. "Why would you do that?"

"Because I... I couldn't make sense of it."

I wasn't sure if I was imagining it, but my vision seemed to be warping in and out. Tiny spikes of static sparking under my skin.

"Did you know that it was never investigated at all? The police ruled it an accident at the scene."

I was trying to focus on her eyes. Her breathing. Trying to spot any tell that would reveal her angle. "Why would it need to be investigated?" I rhetorically asked. "The road was icy and they were driving too fast for the corner."

"And yet the driver didn't turn the wheel to avoid the very large tree."

"He *turned* the wheel," I said, getting defensive of my father. "*It was too late!* That's how they got themselves wrapped so well around it instead of exploding straight into it!" I hadn't meant to raise my voice but I wasn't backing down. "Why are you bringing this up? Haven't you all tormented me enough tonight?"

"Time!" Liam called from the steps of the house.

Christina looked nervously back to him.

"It's time for the vote," she said, walking backward. "You have my support, in whatever form you want it."

"Is that everything you found?" I asked, unable to resist.

"The police photos of the accident show a straight line of skid marks leading to the tree." She was speaking hurriedly as Liam walked towards us, I assumed to monitor the conversation. "The only curve was at the very end. It would seem that either someone in the car purposely tried to drive into that tree and panicked, or someone fixed it so they couldn't turn the wheel."

She spun toward Liam, then ascended into the house.

I could feel my lungs trying to betray me, my body losing its ability to process oxygen. I gripped my hands tightly, digging my nails into my skin. I needed to feel something other than the shock of Christina's words. I needed to not collapse in their flowerbed.

Liam approached. "Still here, I see."

I couldn't bear looking at him. I was struggling to remain upright.

"Final call," he said. "You have been duly notified."

He left, walking back into the house.

The vote was about to happen, with or without me. I wanted to flee to safety. To remove myself from a situation that I knew could cause irreparable harm, but I couldn't deny that the final hook, cast out by Christina, had sunk its way into my flesh.

I didn't know what to think, or who to trust. I didn't even know if I could trust myself, or whether the panic working its way through my body was overriding logical thought altogether. I did, however, believe them when they said that whatever choice I made would be permanent. That if I walked away, it would be for good—a thought that only minutes earlier filled me with comfort, now filled me with dread. But was that exactly what they wanted? Was I playing directly into their hand?

It came down to a question of what I could live with. And the one thing I *couldn't* live with was unanswered questions. Especially ones with the potential to haunt me forever. So for better or worse, I picked up the bottom of my egregiously heavy dress, and ran as fast as I could back inside.

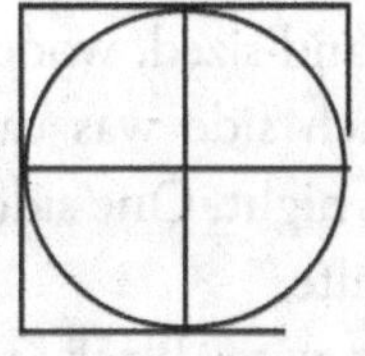

NINETEEN
UPRISING

I climbed the front stairs in one swift movement, landing unsteadily on the sky-high stilettos Alida had bought for me only hours before. Within seconds, I was marching across the perfectly manicured grass as Christina, Liam and Sarah were taking their seats at the long table. The other guests were scattered nearby in private discussions of twos and threes, unwise to the political battle happening directly in front of them.

As I approached the table and scanned the faces of the twelve people who supposedly shared my DNA, I grappled with the knowledge that one of them held the key to figuring out what had happened to my parents. It hadn't clicked until I saw Terence register my presence that if their death hadn't been an accident, one of them could've been responsible. I was gravitating directly into the lion's mouth, willingly choosing an uncertain future.

Terence stood up, reaching for Alida's hand to alert her to my arrival. Knocking loudly on the table, he declared: "Conference is concluded."

Slowly, reluctantly, I took my seat.

"In silence, as it is written, we will cast our votes in favor of Nicole's challenge."

In front of us sat a hand-sized, wooden paddle. Antique, but in pristine condition, each side was carved into the geometric symbol I'd been seeing all night. One side charred black, the other bleached grain, almost white.

Terence cast the first vote: black, rejecting his niece's challenge. Alida followed suit, placing her paddle dark side up, gesturing toward me as she did it. Her brother Alexander mirrored her, also choosing black, followed by his son and grandson, Clive and Ivan.

Liam was the first to break the pattern, choosing white in support of Nicole. She, her husband, her daughter, and Elizabeth voted next in synchronized succession. An attempt, I assumed, to demonstrate their alliance's power. All three choosing white.

It was Katalin, though, who blindsided the table when she also turned her paddle light-side up—a move that left Terence and Alida barely able to conceal their shock. Analyzing their faces, I tried to decipher the authenticity of their reactions. *Was Katalin using this opportunity to get rid of me? Or was she trying to protect me, per her alleged promise to my mother?* It was a touching story, but I couldn't work out how it could've been true, unless she'd known about me before my mother's death.

Christina held the penultimate vote. If she were to choose white, Nicole would win and my vote wouldn't matter. Instead, she turned her paddle black, separating herself from her family and putting the decision firmly in my hands. *Did that mean I could trust her?*

I looked around at the twelve sets of anxious eyes, waiting for my decision. Black would overrule Nicole, white would mean I could go home.

Spinning the handle of the paddle between my fingers, feeling the grain twirl against my skin, I realized how exhausted I was. Both physically and emotionally. I wanted answers, but I didn't know if I had the strength I needed to take the family on—then, or for the rest of my life.

Resigned to giving up, I almost did, when it dawned on me that it would be the first time in my life that I'd backed down due to fear. That wasn't something I was ever prepared to do. So I flipped the paddle down, black side up. In favor of my own personal bravery, and in favor of the truth.

Almost as soon as it landed, Terence was knocking on the table. "*The challenge is unsuccessful!*" he said swiftly, with overt smugness. "But I assure you, it will not be forgotten."

I looked to Nicole and her 'side of the family,' awareness setting in that I'd drawn a line in the sand that I wouldn't be able to walk back. I didn't want to be their enemy, but as Delilah would've said, 'sometimes you gotta be a villain in someone else's life so you can be a hero in your own.'

"Eva, it's my great honor as the head of this family to offer you a seat at this table, and with it, a position on the Sinclair-Dubois family council. Do you accept your position, knowing that if you do, you are accepting your birthright and the privileges that come with it? Not all of them will be gifts, and you will be challenged by your peers, as you have been tonight, and are required to do further, in accordance with lore and ritual. Do you swear to love and protect this family, forsaking all others?" I wondered how anyone seated before me had ever taken the same vow. "And accept a future of abundance, though death may be the remedy of failure?" he added.

Before I had time to object to his disclaimer, he concluded, "Finally, do you, my granddaughter, child of my child, accept your place in this family?"

"Sure," I said quickly, so I didn't have a chance to talk myself out of it. "Why not?" *After all, could I ever really call myself a journalist, if I didn't have the conviction to search out my own truth?*

Everyone began clapping, even Nicole and Elizabeth. I glanced across the garden, the commotion once again going unnoticed by all the other guests, as though they'd been told to ignore us.

Terence and Alida reached out for one another's hands, smiling at their victory in a way that made me question whether it was also mine.

"As it is written," he announced, "you shall prove your choice, by selecting your *vulnus mortale*."

"In English?" I asked as three men in suits, English butler types, appeared carrying large wooden boxes. They varied in dimension, but all sat at the same height once set upon their designated plinths.

"Please select a box," instructed Terence.

Confused but playing along, I walked over to the box closest to me. It was the middle-sized one of the three, about ten inches in length, with a gold clasp closure on the top. Glancing at Terence for approval, I opened the heavy lid.

Inside, nestled in dark green velvet, lay a small dagger. Engraved on the seven-inch blade was an opalescent full moon, flanked by two crescent moons.

I looked to Terence again, and when he nodded, I moved on.

The second box, wider yet similar in size, slid open to reveal an antique revolver that looked as though it had been scavenged from a shipwreck at the bottom of an ocean. Aged, but intricately designed, its body was a blend of gold and silver metals, overlaid with brass and mother of pearl.

Moving on I approached the largest box, unlatching its simple, rustic clasp. Inside, a crescent-shaped knife with a white handle shimmered in the candlelight. It was so thin and razor-sharp, it looked capable of taking someone down with one lethal strike.

Terence's face remained stoic, offering no guidance. Neither he nor anyone at the table gave any indication of how the contents of the box were to be used. *Was it a ceremonial... gift? Or had they truly lost their minds and were attempting to... arm me with a weapon?*

With no intention of actually using it, I gestured in the direction of the revolver. The knives I could (and probably would) accidentally cut myself with. A rusty gun, not so much.

"Let it be so," said Terence unreadable, walking toward me.

I tried to catch Alida's attention, but she was fixated on something inside the house—Christina too, was preoccupied, perched above her headrest, attempting to catch tears that fell down her cheeks. Liam was the only one who looked me in the eyes, as though he were being respectful.

Arriving by my side, Terence retrieved the revolver from its box, popping open the cylinder. Checking the chamber, he looked up to me and said, "*Fortis fortune adiuvat.*"

Had the Latin phrase not triggered thoughts of Max, I might have realized what was happening sooner. Rather than handing me the gun, Terence cocked it and aimed squarely at my head.

Instinctively, I leaped backward, stumbling onto one of the boxes and pushing it off its plinth. Regaining my balance, I twisted into a sprint. But the thickening density of the wind around me made it feel like I was stuck in hardening glue.

I managed to turn back to Terence, as the click of the firing pin sounded, the snap of the blast sending jolts of terror rippling through my body.

Flinging my arms up in front of me in a futile attempt at protection, I noticed Alida still averting her eyes. In that moment, I understood: I'd been betrayed by my own grandparents.

As she finally looked up, I felt the bullet sear through my skin; my last thought vengeful, hoping my death would at least haunt her forever.

After that, everything went silent...

Still.

Slow.

Labored.

Dark.

So dark, it was as though light didn't exist. As if it couldn't.

Warmth had enveloped me. A sense of calm, like I was being held by someone who wasn't going to leave.

Exhausted from a life of being brave, I let myself relax. Releasing into my fate, perhaps far too easily, until a rising heat began scoring at my skin—alerting my body to the consistency of the atmosphere that surrounded me.

To the scarcity of oxygen.

The limitation of air.

I tried to push out in front of me, but my hands collided with a solid barrier, the motion triggering pain in my shoulder where I'd been hit. Groping for the wound, I found nothing but a slight abrasion from where the bullet must have grazed my skin.

I felt relief, if only for a second.

Panic infiltrated my body as I discovered that the barrier enclosed me on all sides, even above where my head lay.

Frantically, I banged my hands, but whatever encased me refused to move. Each violent pound of my fists dragged me further into horrifying consciousness.

I screamed, as alarm took hold. The absence of an echo confirming the confinement of the space.

"HELP!" I pleaded desperately. "HELP ME! HELP!"

I was gasping for air. My throat already raw.

"Please, *please please!*" I cried. "*HELP!*"

I kicked and hit against the solid force around me, but nothing would budge, except tears that burst uncontrollably from my eyes. I was teetering on the edge of a panic attack from which there would be no return.

"*HELP!*"

I knew that increasing my heart rate would only kill me faster, but communicating that to my body felt like an impossible challenge. I exhaled sharply, attempting to slow my rapid breathing, but I couldn't overpower my quivering diaphragm.

Instead, I tried to focus on colors—sky-blue immediately emerging in my mind. My brain's feeble attempt, no doubt, at tricking me into believing I was free, but the thought of open spaces only underscored my captivity, and the sense of imminent suffocation I faced. Complete terror infected every area of my mind.

Colors, Eva, I internally yelled.

Cobalt.

Teal.

Aquamarine... you have to control your breathing.

I forced myself to imagine I was in the ocean. The cool water lapping over my hot skin, each wave floating me further from hysteria.

Gently I tried to sip the air—taking slow, feeble breaths between sobs—careful not to overwhelm my lungs, or overuse what little supply I had left.

Lapis.

Indigo.

Azure.

With each intake of oxygen the hyperactive beating of my heart began to decrease, until I was composed enough to reach out again.

Letting my hands drift slowly in front of me I felt around the smooth, polished material. Tiny imperfections raised and lowered my fingertips, as I tried to discover what I was encased in.

It was the corners that gave it away. Age had created notable gaps and uneven joints, but it wasn't the comfort I was hoping for. None of the ways the wood had buckled over time suggested a way out.

I tried to feel around more, but my head began to pulsate. Bolts of pain branched across my temples and into the back of my skull; I'd been holding my breath again.

Breathe, you idiot. You have to breathe.

There was no more than an inch of space between my nose

and the thick wood surrounding me. Six inches maybe, above my head. The box was so narrow that I couldn't reach past my thighs without knocking my shoulders against the side panel. I didn't want to believe I was in a coffin but couldn't deny the obvious conclusion.

I felt the urge to scream again. To cry. To give up. The realization of where I was, threatening to permanently override my body.

Sapphire.

Navy.

Cerulean.

I tried to calm myself as tears free-flowed from my eyes.

Denim, turquoise, midnight.

I pushed up, this time with all the force I had.

Nothing. The wood moved slightly, but it was too heavy to lift and seemed to be anchored in place. My only solace was that nothing came in, even when I raised the surface higher. Not a fleck of dust or dirt, allowing me to convince myself at the very least that I hadn't been buried.

I tried to go over the details I knew for certain. The last thing I remembered was Terence firing the gun. He was so close to me though, less than fifteen feet away. If he'd wanted to hit me, he could have.

This had to be part of their test. Their insane, cultish ritual.

Anger bubbled as I forced myself to stop crying. It was costing too much air.

Pull it together, Eva. If it's a test, then there has to be a way out.

I exhaled slowly, reexamining my surroundings with my fingertips. There were no hinges or metal work on the inside. Nothing seemed to slide or move, and there weren't any compartments or grooves that would indicate any kind of cutouts.

"Alida gave her a fighting chance, I see."

Recalling Nicole's words to Terence, I turned my attention

toward my dress, feeling around for anything that might help me escape.

The crystals were attached by nylon, which I considered unpicking, but I couldn't work out what use it could have. There was nothing in the material across my chest or inside the straps that looped over my shoulders either. It wasn't until I ran my fingers over the zipper under my right arm that I found a potential tool: thick metal boning.

Pulling the zip down to its end, just above my hip, I dug into the material to push the metal out through the bottom seam. It slid out easily, barely tacked in place. *Was it left by the seamstress at Alida's request?*

Holding it with the fingers of my left hand, I repositioned it with my right, careful not to let it drop. It was far less rigid than I'd expected, ruling out any hope I had of using it as a lever. Instead, I wondered if I could trace the lid's opening to find what was holding it in place.

The air was thickening even more, signaling that my time was rapidly running out. With a trembling hand, I held the metal at the intersection of the top joint, using my other arm to push the lid up. The boning easily fit; allowing me to drag it around, alleviating any fears that I was nailed in. It sent a wave of optimism over me as I slid it down toward my waist, especially as I felt it collide with something metallic.

I pulled the boning back and forth on the barrier to see if it could be moved, but it was stuck in place. Retracting the wire, I doubled it up, hoping it would provide more leverage against the obstruction, but it still wasn't strong enough, buckling uselessly.

I doubled it over again, but to no avail. Each attempt, the external force overpowered the one between my fingers.

The hope I'd felt moments ago was rapidly fading. I wasn't sure how much longer I could hold myself together. *I needed to get out; I needed to breathe.*

Frustration surged through me as I repeatedly rammed the

wire against the metal, foolishly hoping for a miracle when one occurred—the wire slipped through to the other side of the gap, accompanied by the unmistakable sound of a clasp being unlatched.

Excitedly, I pushed up in front of me, expecting the wood to have been released, but it didn't move.

I pushed again, harder. Still nothing.

Moving my hands to where I had just been working, I pushed once more. This time, the wood raised slightly, enough to fit a finger through. There still wasn't any light, but feeling air on the other side soothed my fear of running out of it. A realization then struck me: if there was one clasp, there might be more.

Quickly, I dug around the left side of the dress, finding the sister piece of boning. Extracting it, I inserted it into the gap in seconds, my fingers working automatically from muscle memory.

Sliding it up above my head, I managed to reach higher this time, maneuvering my left arm completely upwards. Sure enough, the wire encountered another lock. Bending the metal upward as before, I pushed it outward, the clasp opening on the first try. The ting of metal, the sweetest noise I'd ever heard.

I pushed up against the wood, which this time created enough space to fit my whole hand through. Cold wind rushed at my face as I lifted it up toward the opening, taking rabid inhales of air. The immediate rush of oxygen overloaded my body, sending my already woozy mind spinning even more.

Letting the euphoria wash over me, I felt the silky air settle on my skin and with it, the optimism that I might just get out alive. The box was still being held together by additional latches, but at least I knew how to unlock them.

Pushing up with my left hand, I squeezed my right arm through the opening, to see if I could reach the latch around my waist. Splinters of wood dug into the soft skin of my upper arm, but adrenaline masked the pain.

Feeling around the outside of the box, which was carved in

ornate detail, I found a third latch that unclipped immediately with the flick of my fingers. I repeated the process on a latch above my head, until there was enough space to squeeze my torso through.

I'd almost pulled myself through when I discovered that the box was sitting atop a stone or marble ledge—the drop-off just six inches from the side of the box.

Swinging my legs out carefully, I let one dangle down to gauge the distance to the next level, but nothing was within reach. Hoping the sound could tell me something, I tapped my foot but all I heard was an echo.

Taking a chance, I lowered myself to whatever was waiting below and found the floor not even four feet down. Hesitantly I let my full weight onto it, stretching out my arms as far as they could go.

My hands met nothing but empty, unsettling space.

The floor was rough and damp, like sandstone or some kind of unpolished rock. Loose sediment scratched loudly as I slid across its surface, dragging my left foot to my right, and so on.

Moving cautiously, I swept my arms out in front of me, searching for something to hold onto. I knew I had to keep moving forward, to figure out how to escape, but the terror that something was lurking in the darkness almost paralyzed me in place.

I couldn't bear knowing what, or who, was waiting next.

Don't go there, I thought, blocking it from my mind. *That's not going to help*. I stepped forward again, this time more quietly, trying to minimize any noise that might give away my location.

Swiping my arms methodically, I navigated the dark space until I touched something that made me recoil.

Immobilized by dread, I braced myself for something to jump out at me. When nothing did, I swiped my arms again, this time with closed fists.

They grazed a coarse material that felt exactly like the floor.

Without thinking, I lunged out and found a solid wall. Leaning on it, I raised myself up on tiptoes, trying to reach the ceiling, but nothing was within reach.

I returned my heels to the ground, and moved my hands across the coarse stone, searching for clues. For a door, a window, *anything*... but it seemed like there was no way out.

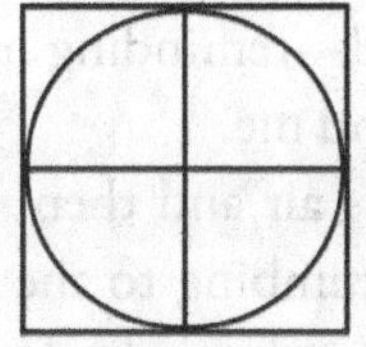

TWENTY

SKIN

Within three or four feet, I found a corner. The discovery propelled me forward, and I continued around the room trying to find the next one. It was double the length, perhaps even fifteen feet, before I came upon it. Eventually I reached the third corner, and then finally the last.

What I still couldn't find was a door, or an exit.

Kneeling on the ground, I began to check the floor by methodically crawling across it. The cold stone numbed my knees, which were becoming scuffed and bloody from the crystals on my dress.

Finding nothing other than the base of the wooden box, I searched around it for compartments or latches, but there was nothing but smooth marble etched with a design.

The only place I hadn't looked was above me.

Pulling myself up on the platform, I placed a foot on top of the box. My quads shook uncontrollably as I attempted to find balance in the dark.

I crouched down low to find my center of gravity, my fingers gripping the carved wood—reminding myself that, if I fell, it was unlikely anyone would find me.

I raised an arm in the air and then slowly tried to stand, my legs on the brink of succumbing to the exhaustion and fear that had been circulating through my body for what felt like hours. Just as I almost reached full height I slipped, my left foot sliding off the edge. Instinctively, my right hand shot up, fully extending and searching for something to grab onto. Relief washed over me when it found what it was looking for: the stone ceiling. My open palm pushed against it for support, allowing me to regain balance.

I let my hands run over the surface, walking as far as the length of the box would allow. Reaching the far end, a sense of hopelessness began to take hold as I discovered nothing there. Frustrated, I slapped my hand against the wall. The sudden movement caused the box to shift slightly from under me, revealing the tiniest fleck of light.

Managing to jump down before I fell, I grabbed onto the side of the box, then tried to push it farther off the platform, but it wouldn't budge. I tried again, pushing it with my shoulder, but it still wouldn't move.

I fell back against the wall panting, almost giving in to despair when I remembered what Alexander had told me. He'd done the test when he was thirteen. *Thirteen*. There was no way any thirteen-year-old could move a coffin. There had to be another way. I wasn't lacking strength; I was lacking logic.

I reached out to find the lid and ran my hands across it until I found the closest latch. Unclipping it, I worked my way around until all the hinges were open. Pushing the lid off, it slammed loudly to the floor, making me jump, even though I was anticipating it.

Wedging myself between the wall and the wood, I extended my legs out, easily pushing the box from its podium.

As soon as it crashed, light escaped from underneath. A slice of faded gold crept out from where the coffin-shaped box had sat.

My eyes struggled to adjust, the sudden brightness burning my corneas.

I blinked hard, reopening my eyelids to take in a long set of stone stairs that led off farther than the light reached. Energized by the discovery, I pulled myself up onto the marble, then slid down into the crawl space. As I took one last look at the solid stone tomb that had entrapped me, I was enveloped by gratitude. Thankful I hadn't been able to see the doorless or windowless room, or I might have spiraled beyond control.

The material of the walls was the same as the outside of the Sinclairs' house. Pale sandstone, inlaid and mortared with intricate detail, which suggested I was either still in their house or somewhere close to it.

As I traveled farther the tunnel narrowed, the stairs became shorter and shorter until they transitioned into a completely smooth surface. I had no choice but to get down on my hands and knees and crawl the rest of the way. The candlelight from behind me flickered ominously, growing dimmer the farther I moved away from it.

Before long, I was plunged back into darkness. Too far in to see behind me, and no light ahead as the tunnel wove deeper and deeper. I stopped to catch my breath, my hands starting to match my bloody knees, as I tried to distract my mind from thinking about how easy it would be for the stone above me to cave in.

Driven by fear I pushed forward even faster, until a bend in the tunnel revealed a beam of shimmering light.

I hurried toward it, crawling as quickly as pain would allow, when a large opening came into view. I stopped abruptly, allowing my eyes to adjust, just in time to see that I was on a ledge with a forty-foot drop below.

I paused, allowing my mind to process what I was seeing. Blurs at first, turning into shapes. Outlines, followed by depth and detail.

Rich colors.

Large crystals.

An underground chamber, at least five stories deep.

It looked more like Krypton than a cave. Crystalline structures covering the ceiling, giving the sense I was inside an enormous geode.

Across from me were other platforms, each of which connected to their own tunnel. It was too dark to see into them, but it was clear from their orientation that they led well beyond the Sinclair's property, perhaps even the street.

Black and white marble tiles on the floor depicted the same circle, cross, triangle and square symbol I'd been seeing all night. Two-story wood and glass shelves surrounded the ground floor of the space, filled with various items, most of which I couldn't make out.

I needed to get closer, so I reached out for an iron ladder that extended down. My traumatized muscles shook violently as I gripped onto the metal, the unfinished surface digging into my raw hands.

Pulling myself off the platform to place my weight on the first rung, it felt as though my legs might collapse. I steadied my footing, trying to summon the courage to transfer myself entirely, when something caught my eye: a way out. In the far corner of the chamber was the glass elevator shaft that led directly to the main lobby of the house.

Closing my eyes, I carefully descended the ladder, nervous sweat making my bloody hands even more slippery. It didn't help that the dress, which not only weighed me down but kept getting tangled under my feet, was making each step more treacherous.

When I finally landed on the solid floor, so much relief washed over me that I almost started laughing. Worried it would be followed by more crying, I took a deep breath, the largest of the night, and let the exhale remove some of the fear residing in my body. I repeated the process, trying to calm the constant tremors that had been running through my aching muscles for hours.

Releasing my grip from the ladder, I took a few steps back and surveyed the glass-fronted cupboards in front of me. Clusters of various shades of purple caught my attention—at eye level was a compartment filled with differently shaped crystals labeled *Amethystus*. Above that, glass jars contained other purple preparations, such as powders, *Amatistus De Pulvis*, and liquids, pastes and gels.

I glanced around the chamber, taking in the contents of the walls. They were stocked high to low with jars and boxes, ampules and beakers, all containing a diverse array of items—from dried flowers and herbs to precious stones, liquids, and tinctures of varying consistencies. In between the different shelves stacks of leather-bound books could be seen: Some individually displayed behind temperature-controlled glass, others meticulously lined up and organized in rows.

In the room's center, a raised platform held a large table that showcased various instruments. An oversized gold pan, a crystal mortar and pestle, and two glass flasks connected to one another by a tube, resembling a more elaborate version of the distillation kits I'd used in chemistry class.

On the table was a stand, which was home to a large antique book. The solid gold cover was embossed with the circle, cross, square and triangle symbol. Below it, two words: *In Scientia*.

I scanned the room, wondering if finding the book was part of the test. The full moon's glow, visible through a skylight a hundred feet above my head, illuminated it as if under a spotlight.

Considering opening it, then deciding against it, I ran over to the glass elevator and examined the keypad, which required a four-digit code. I was contemplating whether the code could be in the book, when I recalled the passwords that Terence's assistant had provided over the phone. One in particular, seemed worth trying: my mother's birthdate, 0406.

I entered it electronically and was surprised when the keypad transformed into a menu that allowed me to call the elevator.

I extended my hand to press the button, but something held me back.

Hovering my hand over the button, I couldn't help but reflect on how far I'd come, all the events that had brought me to this point. I'd been shot at and locked in a coffin, *inside a freaking tomb*, and yet I was no closer to finding answers about my parents. What had it all been for?

I looked back to the platform, and to the book titled *In Scientia*.

Knowing that most of the English language was derived from Latin, it seemed reasonable to assume that 'Scientia' had something to do with science, which I knew translated directly as knowledge. *How could I so easily turn my back on the very thing that had lured me there in the first place, especially when I was so close?*

I rushed back to the book and carefully peeled the cover open, revealing a weather-worn page adorned with at least a thousand characters and symbols, handwritten in ink. Some I recognized, like the letters P and A. But the context made no sense. In English at least.

I shifted my attention to some of the other symbols—a Q that curved upwards, an X with a dot hanging over its middle, and two sets of parallel lines intersecting one another, resembling an off-center hash sign. Some looked more like hieroglyphics, rather than letters, like a large O with a wave symbol tucked inside it, or a miniature pyramid alongside a sickle blade.

Intently studying the page, I tried to decipher meaning from the shapes, which seemed as if they belonged on rune stones or some other ancient artifact.

In search of clues, I turned to the next page, but it was blank.

The page after that was blank, too.

And the one after that.

As I flipped through the entire book, I realized that all the pages were blank except for the first one. Returning to it, I attempted to refocus.

Tilting my head, I attempted to view the symbols from a different perspective. If the tail of the *Q* were upside down, perhaps certain letters should be read that way too. After studying it from all sides until I felt myself growing dizzy, I searched the drawers of the workspace for something to write with, just in case it was as simple as a substitution cipher.

I tried every variation of a substitution I could think of—a simple shift where A becomes B, a reversal shift where Z becomes A, and even a Caesar cipher, where each letter is shifted by a fixed number of positions.

I looked for repetitions of symbols that might indicate a double letter, usually the easiest way to decode something because there aren't many words containing them. But nothing. There wasn't a single pair anywhere on the entire page. Apparently the author was smarter than the kids in Spring City who used to write secret letters about me.

I wanted to explode. *How was I expected to read it?*

I felt stupid, and angry.

'*Fight like hell. We believe in you.*' Alida and Terence's voices circled my head. I wanted to scream.

"I give up! I'm done with this!" I yelled at my own echo, slamming the front of the book shut. I wanted to kick it but I wasn't sure I could get my leg that high.

"*In Scientia* can suck it," I muttered, as I walked back to the elevator. "And so can all of you!"

I'd gotten three steps away when it hit me: *In Scientia*. It was Latin.

Remembering a trend in the late 18th or early 19th century, for secret societies and fraternal orders to hide a cipher's key in its title, I realized the Latin word for knowledge could itself be the clue.

Swiftly, I transcribed the Latin letters I recognized

T-O-B-E-G-I-N-D-I-S-T-I-L-B-Y-V-A-P-O- R...

I felt a rush of exhilaration—the first time in days I'd experienced anything close to happiness. I didn't know if it were still part of the test, but it was clear that it was supposed to be uncovered.

Looking at the glass distillation kit in front of me, I wished I could turn back time to pay better attention in chemistry class. Thankfully all I had to do was distill wine, which just meant heating it up and collecting the condensation. The composition of which I was fairly certain was straight alcohol.

Next it called for me to *add one part crushed Arabia Felix frankincense*.

I found some rock-shaped crystals of the hardened tree sap on a shelf near some dried herbs, next to a liquid that looked like honey. Then it asked for *one part lava salt from the tunnels of Mount Vesuvius* and *two parts powdered holy wood from the Middle Americas*. I found jars of it with the label *Australis*, which I deduced meant Australia.

The preparation finished with equal parts: *soil from the ring of fire* and *emerald dust*, both of which sounded made up, considering one referenced hell and the other was a rare gem. Then I remembered that the Sinclairs traded in precious stones and minerals, so if anyone would have an abundant supply, it would be them. Nevertheless, I felt enormously guilty throwing a handful of the expensive stones in the mortar and pestle so I could grind them up.

Finally, I had to combine all the ingredients with the vapor, which I did in the gold pan and, *with the spark of jaspre, ignite it to see*.

There were two large pieces of red and brown crystal already on the desk that I gathered were jasper, but what I hadn't realized was that they had the ability to spark like flint rocks.

Clumsily, I banged the two crystals together. The friction of which caused a tiny bolt of electricity to erupt.

I did it again. This time, with more power.

And again.

The sparks were getting bigger, the closer I got to the mostly dry powder mixture.

With a whoosh, the compound combusted, sending my hair flying behind me. The force of the chemical reaction almost knocking me off my feet.

Dark green smoke began to float and twirl upward, ascending high into the chamber. I didn't know if it were dizziness from being so close to the powder, or inhalation from the smoke, but my heart began racing out of control—my vision distorting.

As I struggled to focus, I suddenly realized an invisible force field had formed around me, encapsulating me in a bubble-like barrier. I could only make out fragments of the room through the thick atmosphere that blurred my view, but nothing looked how it should. Waves of energy appeared to rise out of every object in the chamber. Some were translucent and fast-moving, warping and gliding freely, while others lagged groggily behind, like waves unfolding in the ocean, or sticky drips seeping and curling lazily.

I focused more intensely, trying to discern the cause, when I felt my whole body spasm as if the hallucination were short-circuiting my brain. I reached out in front of me to grab onto the table, but the barrier that was surrounding me held me back. Worse, the pocket of air seemed to be shrinking with every inhale I took.

I held my breath for as long as I could, before my hands began to cramp; my knees buckling, taking me to the floor. Based on past panic attacks I could tell I was mere seconds from blacking out.

I begged the ground for help, tears streaming down my face, as I slammed my fists into the tiles.

I wanted to cry out, but I couldn't risk losing the air.

My vision faded as all the energy in my body crumbled like dry sand.

With the last of my strength, I threw my head back, gasping for oxygen. My chest collapsed in slow motion as gravity tried to swallow me whole.

That's when I felt him.

Max.

His warm touch, the smell of rose and sandalwood on his skin.

I could feel him wrapped around me, pushing me forward. Urging me on. *Guiding me.*

I tried to open my eyes to see where he was but was engulfed by a feeling of weightlessness, the same way I had when we'd kissed. Warmth spread from behind my navel throughout my chest, like a twinkle of happiness being set alight.

I might have felt at peace if it weren't for the tremors surging through my body. I couldn't tell if they were coming from me, or vibrating through the crystals on my dress—I forced my eyes open just in time to see vapor release from them, as if the molecules were reverberating so fast they had to escape.

It was in that moment that I understood what to do, like the knowledge had been there all along. I somehow had to create a chemical reaction of my own, in order to tear myself out of the invisible barrier that threatened to suffocate me.

I imagined the pores of my skin opening to absorb the vapor, transferring the energy from the crystals through my arteries, veins and capillaries into my hands, where I tore at the thick sack that bound me.

As I did, the room came back into view in vibrant high definition. I could feel myself collapsing, but there wasn't an ounce of fear in my body. Seeing the energy move so freely around me allowed me to comprehend the connectedness of every single element on Earth. Making me see that nothing was final. That energy is never destroyed, only repurposed.

As though this new knowledge couldn't live in the same space as the fear of dying, the driving force behind my panic attacks, I took the largest inhale of air I could take. A millisecond too late.

As I was passing out, I saw Terence and Alida rush toward me from the cover of darkness, followed one by one, by the other ten members of my new extended family.

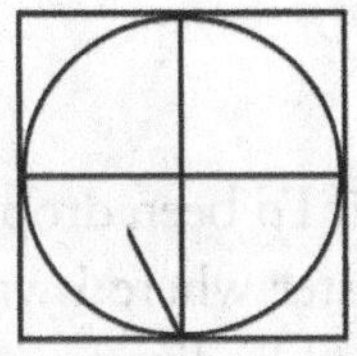

TWENTY-ONE
WHERE THE LIGHT GETS IN

*H*e has a freckle just under his left eye. I hadn't noticed it until we were at the diner. He was talking about wanting a certain kind of love and I was avoiding looking into his eyes for fear I might drown in them. But the longer I looked at it, the more I wanted to reach out and touch it—to kiss it.

As I sit in front of him now, I can't understand what I've done. He's looking at me angrily, his piercing eyes trained in my direction, but he won't say a word. The furrow between his two brows looking even more distinct. I wish it would disappear, as it does before he smiles, or on the rare occasions when he laughs. I want to make him laugh now, but it feels like he's looking through me. Impossible to catch his attention, no matter how hard I try.

I reach out to grab his hand, our fingers interlocking, like a puzzle finding its missing piece. But he doesn't move, or register my touch. I try to say his name, but I can't speak. My words, soundless, like they never happen at all. Without warning, he pulls away. As though he's falling... backward. As though I'm falling backward... I try to reach out. To hold onto him, but I can't grasp his hand.

I'm falling too far.

Too hard.

Too fast.

I woke with a jolt, as if I'd been dropped ten stories. Catching my breath, I tried to register where I was—the brightness of the morning sun temporarily blinding me, as an unfamiliar ceiling came into view. My mind felt crunchy, like broken gears.

"Ssh... Eva, darling," said a voice with the distinct accent of Alida Sinclair. "Just rest now," she said, stroking my head. "Rest."

I tried to push her off, but my arm went limp. My body still asleep.

"Get off me," I managed to mumble, dragging my hand to my chest, feeling the soft cotton pajamas I was wearing. *"Ew, you changed my clothes?"*

"Ssh," she said. "You're okay—"

"I know I'm okay," I declared, fully opening my eyes.

Alida's version of a concerned face stared back at me.

I was beyond weak. My muscles atrophied from exhaustion, intensifying my confusion with reality. *"What time is it?* My flight—"

"Isn't until later this afternoon," Alida reassured me.

Terence appeared, out of the shadows no doubt.

"How are you feeling?" he asked, attempting to appear worried.

"Since you tried to shoot me?" I asked. That much I hadn't forgotten. My energy was starting to return, and the anger was helping. *"Wonderful."*

"I'd never intentionally hurt you," said Terence.

"Go slowly," warned Alida, as I tried to sit up on the bed. Blood rushed to every nerve ending, memories from the previous night flashing too quickly in my mind to comprehend. I didn't feel scared, but something was telling me I should be.

"Don't tell me what to do," I replied, coughing up a lung. I closed my eyes and tried to focus on what I needed. "One of you better start explaining," I said, rubbing the bridge of my nose where the headache was the worst. I was starting to remember waking up in coffin, thinking I'd been buried alive.

"Eva," said Alida, in a tone that screamed she was trying to reason with me. "There's—"

"You have about five minutes before I have the strength to put my clothes on and walk out of here," I said. "When I do that, I won't ever be coming back."

Eva, *please*," she repeated.

"There are certain things you don't know about the world," interrupted Terence.

"I doubt patronizing me is gonna help."

"I'm trying to explain," he said sternly. "There are certain things *that most people* don't know about the world."

He looked at me like he was unsure of how to proceed.

"Such as?" I asked.

Alida reached her hand over to hold his, the same way my grandparents do in times of distress. Strength in numbers, I guessed.

"I apologize," he said. "This is... difficult. Your mother should have been the one to have this conversation with you."

I averted my eyes, not wanting to give him the satisfaction of knowing I was affected by his words.

"Well, you have about four minutes and thirty seconds to figure it out," I said, as cold as I could. I wanted him to know I wasn't interested in nostalgia of any kind.

"As I told you before, I come from a family with a very long history," began Alida. "My ancestors can be traced back to a time before even the Roman Empire. With that history has come vast wealth, and vast knowledge."

"That knowledge is the most important thing we have," added Terence. "Any of us."

"*In Scientia*," I mumbled, repeating the book's title, wanting to prove I wasn't completely ignorant.

"Yes," she said, with a smile. "Although largely ceremonial, the book you worked out of last night contains our family's greatest secrets. History and formulas, passed down from generation to generation."

"The pages were all blank," I rebutted.

"The book will look very different the next time you see it."

"Formulas for what?" I followed up before they had a chance to say anything else. "What did you have me do? Was it the smoke that made me hallucinate? Where do all those tunnels lead?" I had so many questions, I didn't know which to ask first.

Terence reached for the glass of water next to my bed. "May I?" he said, picking it up as he asked. One of my least favorite things people do.

He rested the heavy-bottomed tumbler on his palm as though he was presenting it to me. "What do you see?" he asked.

I sighed, well and truly done with tests of any kind. "A puppy," I quipped.

"And now?" he asked, ignoring my sarcasm.

As I looked down, the clear liquid started crystalizing in front of me, cracking and shrinking slightly away from the sides of the glass until it was a single, solid piece of ice.

I was stunned, the realism of the trick giving me goosebumps.

"What the hell was that?" I asked.

"What do you think it was?" he replied. The contents of the glass slowly turning back into liquid.

"Everything on this planet is made up of atoms. This you know, yes?" Alida asked.

I nodded, somewhat insulted, and equally confused as to where they were going.

"Well, water is made up of hydrogen and oxygen atoms, and by changing the order of how they're arranged inside the glass, your grandfather is able to transform its state," she said, throwing me with her knowledge of chemistry.

"Sure, but... a chemical reaction like that requires external energy," I said. Speaking the words 'chemical reaction' reminded me of the previous night, but I couldn't remember what.

"Precisely!" Terence exclaimed, opening his left fist to reveal a large ruby in his palm. "I used the energy from this to induce the reaction."

I didn't know how to rationalize what he was saying.

"What? How?" I questioned, before immediately adding, "No, you didn't. That's impossible."

"Do you not remember what you saw last night?" Alida asked me, before immediately turning her attention to her husband. "Did it not work?"

"Did what not work?" I asked, feeling like I was turning invisible.

"It worked," Terence reassured her with certainty. "She's choosing not to see it."

"How?" probed Alida.

"This is crossing into insanity," I interrupted, peeling back the covers of the bed. My legs were starting to feel like they might be able to support my body weight.

Terence held the glass of water again on his palm.

"What do you see?" he asked again, this time instantly turning the water into ice.

"A magic trick."

The frustration of not being able to get up and run out of the room was pushing me to tears.

"It's no trick," said Terence. "What you *think you're seeing*, is actually happening."

"Magic, seriously?" I laughed. "That's your big secret?"

"That word assumes the incantation of supernatural forces, or the command of nature. We don't call upon anything, nor do we command," he said.

"However, there are people in the world who can do that," added Alida.

"We merely transmute the energy, working with what is already there."

"Alchemy has been disproven, decade after decade," I scoffed.

"Yes. Among other things that are also true," he said.

My mind was reeling. I felt like I'd fallen into an alternate dimension, an Alice-esque vortex where everything was upside down. As I attempted to process it, trying my best to analyze it rationally, Terence turned the ice back into water like he was the feature at a carnival show. But this time as he did it, I saw something I hadn't before: As the ice started to melt, I saw the energy within it move. What was previously tightly packed with tension, loosened into a free-flowing state. The liquid itself didn't change, just how it was packed and organized, like the energy was tightening and contracting.

I looked up to Terence's face. He could tell I'd seen it.

"I don't understand," I said, as tears started to fall. But as I said it, I recalled the sensation of absorbing the energy from the crystals the night before. It wasn't just a hallucination, as my logical brain wanted me to accept.

"I think you do," said Terence.

Wherever I looked in the room, I could see hidden dimension and detail. Waves of energy revealing qualities and components invisible to the naked eye. I blinked hard, taking a deep breath, trying to rid my mind of it, but that only forced the feeling inside. It was as if I could visualize how the energy within me moved, metabolized, silently operated without my command.

"What have you done to me?" I asked him, seething with anger.

"Nothing," said Terence, with a sigh. He sounded disappointed, like he'd expected me to react another way. "It's what we *undid*."

"What gives you the right to mess with my head like this?"

I moved to the other side of the bed and managed to get up. As I did, Terence and Alida followed.

"Eva, please rest a little longer. We'll leave you alone, give you some time to recover," she offered.

"*I'm fine*," I insisted, unsteady on my feet as I walked over to the dressing area where my clothes were neatly folded. "I just wanna get out of here."

I grabbed onto the wall for support, the rippling movement around me threatening to take me down.

"It was your choice," said Terence. "Every step of the way."

"*Excuse me?!* How could it have been my choice when I didn't know what I was agreeing to?" The rage helped me stuff my feet into my shoes, and put my leather jacket on over the pajamas. As I stood back up, blood rushed to my head like I was about to pass out again.

Alida rushed over, placing my mother's necklace in my hand.

"Here, take this," she said.

I looked down at the jagged crystal and immediately felt better, like someone had turned off a strobing light.

"It cloaks your energy, effectively turning off your ability to see," she explained. "Use it, until you get your strength back."

"So that's why you took it from me?" I asked dumbfounded. "Not because you were worried someone would steal it but because it was—"

"I didn't lie to you," said Terence. "It is a very valuable stone. Almost fifteen carats of untreated pigeon-blood ruby."

"But yes, it's a barrier to the metaphysical," Alida confirmed. "We were worried it could hurt you when it was time to do the ritual."

"We hoped taking it off might help, but it had been on for too long—its energy and yours had melded together, requiring an immense amount of force to break through. That's why your grandmother gave you the dress. To give you a source of energy to unbind yourself with."

"Don't ask how many diamonds were on that—" Alida remarked.

"Why would my mother...?" I almost asked, before stopping myself. I knew exactly why she'd want to create a barrier around me and I'd stupidly walked right though it. "It was keeping me away from you," I said. "Wasn't it?"

"No," Terence insisted. "We don't know that."

"Your mother might not have known. When the necklace cloaks your energy, it works by closing you off from the metaphysical world. But we think your body reacted so violently because it couldn't handle being bound when you're clearly so able to see," said Alida.

"With the right knowledge, anyone's able to do what we do, but after generation upon generation of *In Scientia* being passed down, through your side of the family especially, you're genetically predisposed to be more skilled at it," he said.

My mind was racing a million miles an hour.

"She changed her name," I stated. "And told my grandmother to give me that necklace. You knew that, and you knew what it was going to do, and you deceived me into doing it anyway."

"We had to make you see. The longer you walked around not knowing, the longer you were exposed," she said.

"I was fine for seventeen years."

"Were you?" asked Terence, with unnerving insight.

"As soon as you reached out to us," said Alida. "You were even more vulnerable to being targeted."

"By who?" I asked, remembering the feeling I kept having of being followed. Perhaps I wasn't as insane as my insecurities tricked me into believing.

"We needed you to be able to see, to understand everything, so you could protect yourself," said Terence.

"You locked me in a box and tried to shoot me in the head," I spat.

"The ceremony is our coming-of-age tradition. Ancient tests that date back to the fourth century. They demonstrate a person's readiness for adulthood and, in turn, their formal introduction to *In Scientia*," Alida explained.

"You mean the book that contains a ton of critically important information that could actually help mankind, but like everything else in this world, is kept locked away by elites who *don't actually need it*?"

"It is not solely our choice. Lore dictates that we must practice in secret," said Terence.

"What *lore*?" I asked, finally getting confirmation they meant traditions and information passed down through generations. "And who exactly is the governing body enforcing it? Next you're going to tell me there's some kind of Ministry of Magic?" I joked.

"Admittedly some rules are our own, but the most important stem from a peace agreement between your ancestors and a collective of clerics known as *The Praesidio Sancti*," explained Terence. "They consider themselves to be God's true representatives on Earth."

"And, of course, there are the laws that are bound by the universe," added Alida.

I paced back and forth in the room, trying to comprehend what they were telling me.

"This can't be real," I said. "This has to be some elaborate—"

"We assure you, it is real. Very real. As are the dangers," warned Terence.

"Of what, priests? They're gonna force me to recite Hail Marys?"

Alida's voice had a sense of personal passion as she said, "These men are the direct descendants of those who fueled multiple holy wars over five centuries, including the medieval heretic trials, which saw tens of thousands perish. They are not to be toyed with."

"Lucky, then, that I'm not trying to," I said. "Not that God's done a whole lot for me, but I'm certainly not on his, or their, opposing team," I said, thinking about what my grandparents would say about all of this.

"There weren't always sides," said Alida. "It began in 313 AD when Constantine converted to Christianity. Aiming to stabilize a fracturing Roman Empire, he harnessed religion to unite the masses under a singular faith. With it, he took the concept of individual power or the worship of multiple gods, and directed it toward a singular god. One whose teachings could be controlled."

"The real conflict came with Emperor Theodosius I, seventy years later," Terence interjected. "He began the suppression of paganism by closing temples, outlawing rituals, and removing altars and statues."

"Pagans?" I asked, like I didn't want to know the answer.

"Some would call themselves that," Alida replied. "Back then, it referred to anyone who didn't adhere to Christianity, including indigenous and polytheistic religions."

"Those once revered for their extraordinary abilities or knowledge became targets of the Church's expanding authority," said Terence.

"Why not fight back?" I asked. "If they're the ones with the power?"

"Some did," said Alida. "Achieving brief victories. But revealing your power is akin to showing your hand in a game of poker; you can only do it once and the game is over. Then, you must either fight or hide, and that can only be done for so long."

"The clever ones," continued Terence. "Hid in plain sight. Openly following the rules, while preserving their secrets, even through the Dark Ages, a time when much of the ancient wisdom was lost and destroyed. That is, until a series of wars in the 11th century changed everything. Religious leaders sought the help of those they'd formally admonished in battles over the Holy Lands. Leaning on heretics for new ways to heal and weaponize themselves, they sought advancements in medicine, astronomy, botany, or what we now call chemistry."

"Some complied—idealists who believed in promises of peace," Alida's eyes darkened. "But when the wars were won, and the formulas were stolen, the heretics who hadn't been killed were forced back into the shadows."

"That wasn't enough for some, though," added Terence. "A group of ultra-conservative men formed *Praesidio Sancti* to root out their former allies, launching relentless campaigns across Europe and the Americas, from the Spanish Inquisition to the witch hunts in Massachusetts. This persecution persisted for centuries until the descendants of those ancient practitioners, weary of loss and betrayal, finally united."

"This union," Alida concluded, "brought together thirteen families from across the globe, each a custodian of profound arcane knowledge. Their collective power was so immense it forced the *Sancti* into a clandestine accord known as *In Unio*—a treaty that allows the thirteen families to continue their practices in utmost secrecy, in exchange for staying out of public and political affairs."

They both stopped talking and stared at me. As if looking to see how I was handling all the information.

"Well, I guess that settles it. I'm certainly not dreaming or hallucinating, cause that's all... far too detailed for my brain to have made up," I said, still in hopeless shock.

Alida moved closer to me and put her hand under my chin to lift my face to hers.

Instinctually, I pulled away, but gave her what she wanted by meeting her eyes.

"Haven't you ever felt it? Like there's more out there? More than you know?" she asked. Apparently the question was rhetorical because she didn't wait for me to answer. "Of course you have. It's the feeling you get walking into a cathedral, or listening to a grand piece of music. It's your body knowing there's more to experience than what's before it, more to life than what it sees. It's what brought you here. *It runs strong in your veins.* I felt it as soon as I saw you." She smiled. "You are right where you belong."

"Why did she run away?" I blurted out, as a barricade to actually addressing her. "If you want any kind of relationship with me, you'll tell me the truth. There can't be any more secrets."

She was conflicted, hesitant about how to respond.

Terence stepped forward. "It was my fault," he said, tears reddening in his eyes.

"Terence—" said Alida, her voice breaking.

"It was," he continued. "I was too hard on her. We fought and I pushed her away. I saw what she had in her. The talent, the power. I wanted her to take over the family after me. She was a true leader. One of the smartest people I've ever known," he said. "That is, until I met you."

I gave a polite half-smile, but I wasn't going to let him manipulate me again. "You said she'd run away before," I stated, unwilling to let the topic go without more information.

"She was mostly just exercising her freedom. Your mother had certain obligations she had to fulfill," said Alida.

"Such as?" I asked. "The time for vague platitudes is over."

"University, learning the family business," said Terence. "On top of her *In Scientia* studies."

"Sure, that sounds like a lot of pressure. But something must have happened for her to run away again," I pressed, knowing there was more to the story.

"If you have something you'd like to ask us," suggested Alida, "please do."

"Did you cause my parents' accident?" The words flew out of my mouth before I fully comprehended their severity. Instant regret rose on my face as looks of pain spread across theirs.

Terence hung his head. "We would never. We could never," he said. "Edith was our life. We would have gladly traded ours for hers."

"You don't think very much of us," acknowledged Alida.

"I don't know you," I replied, which was the truth. And I wasn't sure I wanted to. "And considering your actions since I met you..."

Stillness crept over the room, so quiet, I could hear my own heartbeat.

"My flight's in a few hours," I said. "I should go," motioning for the door.

"Wait," said Terence. "I can't bear to see you walk out of here thinking such terrible things about us."

"Well, unfortunately, that's not something you have any power over."

I knew I was being harsh, considering how forthcoming they'd just been—albeit a day too late. "Look, I don't know what to believe anymore. About anything." I was so emotionally exhausted, I couldn't even cry.

Terence walked over to an antique hutch and retrieved a large, shiny box. It was made of dark wood that had been stained black, with an ornate gold clasp on the front. "For you," he said.

"Another gun?" I asked seriously.

He shook his head as I observed the box. "I... don't want any more gifts."

"This is not a gift," Alida interjected. "This, you have earned."

Reluctantly, I unclasped the box, still in Terence's hands, and lifted the lid.

Lined in purple velvet, it framed a leather-bound, quarter-sized version of *In Scientia*. Embossed in gold lettering was my name, 'Eva Nelson-Sinclair.' Beside the book, a necklace with a pendant—the circle, cross, square, and triangle symbol set in diamonds, identical to the ones Nicole and Sarah wore the night before.

"The treaty dictates that while our magic must remain secret, we are to identify ourselves with this symbol. There are penalties if you are caught practicing without displaying it," said Terence. "It's very important that you understand that."

"Go on. Take them," encouraged Alida.

I looked at the box, aware that I didn't have the energy to argue. Reluctantly, I slipped the necklace into my jacket pocket and tucked the book under my arm.

"The second rule dictates complete autonomy of the original thirteen families. The *Sancti* fears the power we'd have if we shared our knowledge," Terence explained. "That's why your mother and I fought, and why she ran away to America. She had fallen for a young man from the Mendoza family. His father and I, in an attempt to protect them, were forced to break them up."

Alida stepped forward. "His father took him back to Spain, and we had to inform Edith. That was the last time we saw her. We managed to keep track of her until she met your father," she said, with obvious regret. "Not even a year later, I felt her leave us," she continued, echoing her earlier remark about my mother's death.

I must have looked confused because Terence added, "When you sense energy as we do, you're able to tap into those closest to you."

I nodded like I understood but in reality, I didn't.

"Do you…" I began, careful with how I phrased it to avoid revealing my source. "Do you believe her death was an accident?" I asked.

Terence nodded. "Christina showed us the evidence she gathered," he said, indicating my effort to conceal her identity was in vain. "But there's no reason your mother couldn't have stopped the car herself, especially with the amount of power she possessed."

"What if she was wearing the necklace?" I asked, trying to piece together everything I'd learned.

"She could easily have taken it off," Terence replied.

"She was in active labor," I said.

Alida almost laughed. "She would have had it off quick smart, trust me," she clarified. "Your mother was powerful beyond belief."

"What if those *Sancti* guys found out about her relationship?" I asked.

"That's not how they operate," said Alida. "If they'd been discovered, there would have been a formal hearing."

"The truce has been in place for hundreds of years. Nobody from their side, nor ours, would jeopardize that. Murder is an act of war no one wants," stated Terence.

"Right," I said, half to them, half to me. "So there's really nothing you can tell me about her that helps, then?"

"Helps, what dear? The pain? That never goes away," said Alida.

"Nothing, it doesn't matter," I replied, uncomfortable. "Anyway, I should really go."

"You'll take our town car," she instructed. "To your hotel and to the airport."

"No," I said. "I'm more than capable of—"

"I insist," she said, with extreme sincerity. "And if there's anything else you need, you have our number."

"We'll give you your space," Terence added. "After all, it's a lot to absorb. But we'll be checking on you."

"Is that a threat?" I asked, thrown by his tone.

"No," he chuckled. "I know better than to threaten you. It's merely my way of saying that you're not alone. We're your family, and you will always have a place here with us."

I acknowledged his words and then turned away, fearing I might believe the sentiment if I stayed any longer. I didn't trust either of them, but all I'd ever really wanted was to not feel alone.

"Eva," Terence began. "One last thing. The books you gave us...?"

"Oh," I replied, remembering the lie I'd come up with. "I bought them from a used bookstore last week," I said. "Sorry."

"Ah." Terence smiled in a way that made me think he was covering.

"Looking for something?"

"No," he said.

"Your mother's copy of the book," interjected Alida. "No more secrets." She smiled, looking to Terence and me.

"I don't have it," I said. "If I did, perhaps I wouldn't have been so clueless last night."

"Yes," Terence agreed. "It always made me laugh that the knowledge is given after the test."

Just as I was about to leave, Alida marched over and grabbed me in an embrace. I resisted the urge to wriggle free, not wanting to return the gesture but also thinking better than to forcefully reject it.

As she was letting go, she whispered in my ear. "Your mother would have been so proud." I pulled away, nodding to her and Terence.

I didn't know how I felt about them, if I felt anything at all. But I couldn't deny that we shared more than just blood; our immovable grief an unbreakable link.

The car took me to the hostel, where I quickly ran inside to pick up my suitcase. I knew I'd be a couple of hours early to the airport, but the thought of being alone with just my thoughts scared the hell out of me. I kept cycling through shock, denial and anger over everything I'd been through and everything I'd learned, struggling desperately to convince myself that it couldn't be true.

As we pulled into Heathrow Airport, I tried to push any and all thoughts from my mind. It was futile trying to rationalize the irrational, especially when sleep deprivation was making it difficult to even remember my own name.

My phone, having automatically connected to the airport's Wi-Fi, dinged with incoming text messages. One was from Delilah, asking how everything had gone, another was from my grandma:

> I hope you know how much we love you, and I hope you can forgive me. I love you always. Call us as soon as you can. We can't help but worry.

Guilt coursed through my body like a thousand tiny knives. She may not have known what she was doing, but she had done the right thing. She'd protected me, and with good reason.

> Of course I forgive you. I hope you can forgive me. Everything's okay. I love you too. I'll call you tomorrow x

I hit send as the car stopped, only to find we were in front of a large British Airways sign.

"I don't think this is the right terminal," I said, while searching for the flight itinerary on my phone. "I'm flying—"

"Your grandparents had your flight rebooked, Ms. Nelson," replied the driver, his accent almost too Cockney to be real.

"*Seriously?* What is wrong with them?" I asked, frustrated.

"It's a direct flight, ma'am. First class," he said, with a face that begged, *'please don't get me in trouble.'*

"Sure," I conceded. "Whatever's easiest. Thank you."

I was in no mood to complain, nor, I realized, should I. Deciding to just accept the gift that most people would envy, and deal with the consequences later, if there were any.

Thankfully, I only overanalyzed my decision for about four minutes into the flight. My 'seat' was actually a small pod, which I converted into a fully horizontal bed as soon we reached altitude.

As I drifted in and out of consciousness, my mind wandered aimlessly into thoughts of Max. I tried to stop myself, knowing how much worse it would feel when I woke up and he wasn't there, but I couldn't resist.

The allure of him was just too great, and my exhaustion was just too strong.

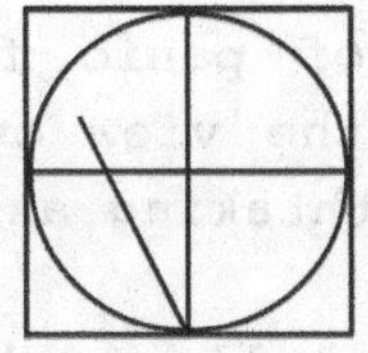

TWENTY-TWO
LUNA CAPRESE

On my worst days, I've often thought about the Horace quote: *"Without love and laughter there is no joy; live amid love and laughter."*

Almost as soon as I read it, I wanted to erase it from my mind. It felt like a flammable ember sitting right behind my ribs, daring me to believe that life could be something more, when I knew it couldn't… at least not for me. It was the same way I felt when I was with her; hopeful, and I was determined to do anything I could to forget that feeling. Even if it meant seeing them.

I landed at Napoli Airport at 11:30 A.M., and was on the ferry to Capri by one. Forty minutes later, I was standing in the doorway of my grandparents' house, a stone villa built into the mountains of the Italian island overlooking the Gulf of Naples. Even under the cloud of panic from the previous week's visitors, the view over the turquoise ocean was as breathtaking as the first time I saw it.

I rang the doorbell and heard a yell from inside — something in Italian that I couldn't understand. Before I had time to decipher it, the door flung open to reveal my grandfather, a look of shock upon his face.

"Massimo!" He rushed at me, scooping up my face to pull me in close. "You're all bones. Are you eating?"

I wanted to say the same thing to him. He looked significantly older than last I'd seen him, time seemingly moving quicker between each visit. His gentlemanly refinement, however, was steadfast. Standing over six feet tall, Omar demanded respect with just his presence. He was shoeless in an off-white linen outfit, that made his tanned summer skin appear even darker.

"Massi!" I heard my nonna shriek from within the house. "What's he doing here? Is he in trouble?"

"He's all bones, Isabella!" he shouted back.

"Grazie, Giddo," I said, calling him by the Arabic name for grandfather to honor his Egyptian heritage.

My nonna appeared in the hallway behind him, silhouetted by the bright sunlight. Even in her seventies, she was still as beautiful and glamorous as ever. She lunged toward me, her high cheekbones leading the charge.

"Max!" she exclaimed, forcefully kissing both cheeks. "He is handsome! That's what he is!"

"*Come on in, come on in!*" my grandfather sang.

The scent of bougainvillea, carried by the salty ocean breeze, enveloped me as I walked through the house, triggering memories I wasn't prepared to address.

Gazing out through the sliding glass doors, I took in the view of the island's most famous landmark: Faraglioni, a three-rock formation that juts out off the coast. As I did, a knot of anxiety tightened in my stomach, the thought of breaking the news to them weighing heavily on me.

"Tell us," Nonna asked, as we ate lunch outside by the infinity pool, the water's edge vanishing into the horizon. "Are you hurt?"

"No, Nonna," I said. "Nothing like that." I'd worn a crew neck sweater to cover the wound on my chest, hoping they wouldn't clock the indentation of the gauze through it.

"Have you been using your gift?" asked my grandfather, hopeful.

"Omar!" my nonna scolded him. "He's made it clear how he feels. This visit won't be like the last."

He winked at me like he expected to get caught. "People change their minds, amore. That is one of the only joys of age."

"Stop it," she implored, worry strewn across her face as she searched my eyes to understand why I was there. "Something's wrong, that's for sure," she said. "Look at him! He's heartbroken. *What happened, Massi?*" she asked.

When I didn't say anything right away, she teased, "Who is she? I'll have her killed."

"Nonna!" I said. "Don't even joke."

"What joke?"

"Please," added my grandfather. "What more could they do to us?"

"You know exactly what they could do," I seethed.

Sadness danced across both their faces. A sorrow like ours, only ever a moment away.

"Sorry. I just…" I didn't know how they'd ever understand. "They paid me a visit. The *Sancti*," I said, bowing my head.

"With reason?" Nonna queried with alarm.

"No," I lied, avoiding her gaze.

"*Massi*," she said.

"It was an accident," I replied. "I…" The truth was, I had no excuse. Anything I said would be a lie. That's why I didn't know how to explain it.

"Start with how you met," offered my grandfather, a mischievous smile upon his face. Knowing without knowing.

I looked out onto the horizon, the sun beginning to set, and tried to think of how I could possibly summarize Eva Nelson in a way that would do her justice.

I told them about the park, and the jazz club, and the kiss. That we began to fly, spiraling twenty feet in the air, our connection emitting waves of neon energy. A bright orb of power, lighting up the Manhattan skyline.

"The twin flame," said my grandfather.

"Omar," warned Nonna. "Don't start with that nonsense."

He ignored her, continuing his thought. "The ancient Greeks believed that when a person met their soul mate, it would result in an alchemical reaction. For most it's just a spark…"

"Stop with the fairytales. There are serious matters at hand," my nonna interjected.

"Fairytales?" he mocked. "Plato might've begged to differ."

"You're saying the *Sancti* saw you?" Asked my Nonna, immediately back to business.

"No, they felt the energy surge… I guess. It was clear they didn't know much," I replied.

"Or, that's what they want you to believe. You have no idea of her family?" she asked.

"I researched her, I swear. She has no connection to *In Unio*. I checked before I even… I'm sorry," I said. "I can't believe I let this happen. I didn't want to involve you, but I didn't know where else to go."

"*Never, ever,*" my grandfather said, his voice becoming stern, "apologize for coming home."

"If she's unaware or inexperienced, as you

suggest, it's likely that when you both let your guards down, your powers became unstable. What did you tell the *Sancti*?" asked my nonna.

"That I only just met her. The truth. And that I must have got carried away."

"Massimo…" she said, looking heartbroken. "You took responsibility? When your life was at stake?"

"They didn't know what happened and neither did she. It *was* my responsibility," I said.

"How could it be?" she asked. "Twenty feet in the air? That is not your power."

"I know… I do. But you should have seen how shocked she was. She had no idea."

"If they knock on my door, you best believe I will tell them the truth," she said.

"Nonna," I protested. "She's done nothing wrong."

"Then let the *Sancti* decide that for themselves. You've had your fair share of those murdering zealots for a lifetime. We all have."

"Hush," my grandfather urged. "No one is telling them anything." Then he turned his attention to me, with a sympathetic stare. "You understand that you can't see her again?"

"Yes. I know."

"For so many reasons, but the biggest…" His voice faltered as he spoke. "That you would follow in your father's footsteps."

"Giddo, please," I said. "I know that. That's why I'm here, I need to know how to erase my memories of her so I can be sure that we never—"

"Oh my goodness, you're in love with her?!" my nonna exclaimed.

"No. I told you, I don't even know her. I'm just trying to do what is right. By everyone."

"You shouldn't be thinking of her at all," my nonna said, flushing red. Then added, before I had chance to respond, "You do realize that if she has even distant lineage, and they find out, it will be the death of us all. Whether you remember her or not, Massimo. Next time they will not be so forgiving."

Her words dug a hole in me. I'd never seen her so enraged. "I understand. I do," I said. "I'm sorry."

"So am I," she replied. Finally brought to tears, she stood up and left the table.

I rose to follow her. "Nonna, wait—"

My grandfather grabbed my arm. "Leave her be, Hafeedee," he said, using the Arabic word for grandson. A term he reserved for when he really wanted me to listen. Instantly, I felt like a small child, reminded of the care he'd given me after me parents' deaths.

"I'm sorry," I said. "I don't know how it happened. I don't even date. I keep to myself. I… I let my guard down. There was just this overwhelming feeling that I had to be close to her. That things would be better, bearable even, if…"

He lifted my chin. "You can't be sorry for falling in love. It is the single greatest thing on Earth," he remarked, getting overcome by his own words.

"It wasn't love," I insisted.

"Massimo, if we are not honest with ourselves, how are we ever to make the right choice? We have to look at all the information, objectively."

I nodded, unsure of what to say.

He gazed at me with unconditional love so heavy it hurt. Compounded by the love he had for my father, it was more than I'd ever known what to do with.

"Mind if I take the boat over to Marina Piccola?" I asked, needing to break away.

"Your father's favorite beach."

"Was it?" I asked sincerely. I had no memory of that. I just knew it was mine.

He smiled. "*Quando il gatto non c' èi topi ballano,*" he said, which I understood as 'the mice dance when the cat is away.' "Be careful, Hafeedee."

I spent the last few hours of daylight in the sea, floating above the density of the waves that gently lapped against my body. It felt like nothing else existed… except maybe her. I balanced thoughts of hoping she was okay against the bitter reality that her safety depended on staying away from me.

There was no point in wishing she were beside me. No point in imagining what it would be like to be holding her, to be kissing her, in the Mediterranean Sea. I knew nothing could ever happen between us, and I had to firmly accept that.

Before bed, I spoke briefly to my nonna, reassuring her that everything was resolved. I promised to stay away from Eva and, if necessary, do whatever it took to protect what was left of our family. I believed what I was saying, too — that I could walk away from her and make the right choice, the logical one. That I could let my rational brain call the shots. However, as I drifted off to sleep, my mind rebelled and flooded me with images of her as I wrestled with the sheets.

In my dream she was fighting with people, crying. The look of heartache was plastered upon her face. I wanted to reach out and wipe the tears off her cheeks, to comfort her as she wept, but before I could, she sprang to life, fighting like a cornered animal in a dark abyss. She was surviving in a way I knew all too well, and I ached for her to know I was proud.

It wasn't until I saw *In Scientia* that I realized what I was seeing might be more than a figment of my subconscious. Somehow, I was with her. Aware I was asleep, I knew that what I was witnessing couldn't be a creation of my own thoughts; it was a world unknown to me.

As she read from the book, I refrained from engaging, but when she started gasping for air, it felt as though I were losing my own. My ability to breathe dependent on hers. She was choking, drowning, in a Kevlar-thick blanket of energy, and needed to break through. To harness the energy of the crystals surrounding her so she could tear a hole.

I sat down behind her, urging her elbows forward, pressing her hands through the energetic fabric that bound her. As she did, I felt her consciousness fade, and with it, whatever link we shared. I awoke, startled and covered in sweat. I inhaled deeply, to fill my lungs with air. The realization of what I'd just seen terrified me.

I pulled on my trousers and ran into my grandparents' room, knocking furiously as I entered. *"Giddo, I know who she is! Giddo!"* I called out.

He flicked on the lamp as my nonna — annoyed at the mention of her, no doubt — rolled over into her pillow, groaning.

"Get me my robe," my grandfather requested. I retrieved it from the hook and handed it to him.

He rolled out of bed slower than the moment required and followed me into the kitchen, the moon partially illuminating his face. "Tell me, Massi. What is worth raising the dead?"

"She's elemental. Stones and earth metals, I think," I said, delivering the news that could be our death certificate.

"But… how?" he asked, fear stricken for the first time since I'd arrived.

"I don't know. Her parents are dead, and her living grandparents don't have any ties to *In Unio*."

"How did you discover her magic then?"

"I saw her, just now, in my dreams… it felt like I was with her. She must have found the other side of her family." As I said it, I realized. "That means she's their responsibility now."

My grandfather scrutinized my eyes, inspecting them in a way only possible for someone with our gift. Giddo and Nonna weren't permitted to practice anymore, punishment for aiding and abetting my parents, but I could see his mind working overtime trying to connect the dots.

Without a word, he strode down the hallway and into his office leaving a void that beckoned me to follow. As I entered the room, he switched on an antique light, then selected a volume of poetry, leaving it hanging off the bookcase.

"Close the door," he instructed. Systematically, he removed another book from the shelf, and then another, until a soft click announced the opening of a trap door in the wooden floor. He knelt down, pulling it open to reveal a bronze hand imprint nestled within.

"Come," he called out. "Put your hand in."

"What's it going to do?" I asked, wary. "You know you're not allowed to keep anything secret anymore, Giddo. It was one of the conditions—"

"*Hand. In,*" he said, firmly.

I crouched down and did as he requested, my hand almost perfectly fitting inside the cold metal, which disintegrated upon contact. A section of the stone floor crumbled away, revealing a circular staircase that led into a dark room below.

"What was that?" I asked, examining my hand, still recalling the sensation against my skin.

"An illusion crafted to open at our bloodline's touch. Some of your mother's best work," he said fondly, descending the stairs as I grappled with the complexity of the illusion.

Trailing my grandfather down the tunnel, I silently prayed that I hadn't inadvertently led the *Sancti* to Italy. Having them discover us where we were would be fatal.

The stairwell led to a candlelit room with book-covered walls. Two leather armchairs and a solid wooden countertop stood in the center. My grandfather opened a drawer and pulled out a large leather-bound volume that I remembered seeing when I was younger: *In Scientia*. He placed it on the table with a thud, opening it to a section titled *Elementum*.

"Sinclair-Dubois," he announced. "Alida Dubois and Terence Sinclair. They have the *In Scientia* for precious stones."

I moved beside him, eager to see for

myself. On the family tree, beneath Terence and Alida's names, was Edith Sinclair, which matched the online searches I'd done.

"That's her mother, I think," I said. "Her first name was definitely Edith."

"If that's true, then your girl is not only part of their family, she'll be on their council. This is…" He paused. I didn't need him to say "very, *very* bad," but he did anyway.

He walked over to a dusty bottle of grappa and poured some into a tulip-shaped glass. Sitting in one of the leather chairs, he took a sip in contemplative thought.

"You learned of this in your dream, you said?" he asked, as I took the seat opposite him.

"I thought it was a dream."

He exhaled loudly, the sound intensifying my guilt. "When a person loses their arm, or their leg," he began, "they can experience phantom pain from it for years. Sometimes, even, for the rest of their life."

"Okay," I said, not following.

"When you meet your other half, your soulmate, and connect in the way that you and Eva have, your body remembers their energy. When it's truly powerful, your energy has a way of reconnecting with theirs."

"You think she's my…?" I couldn't even say the word, let alone comprehend it.

He nodded. "It's a cruel irony that she should be from an *In Unio* family. But such is the game of life."

I dropped my head, trying to accept the finality. Once and for all.

"I could see it in your eyes, the moment you walked through the door. I was hoping it would be lust, but this seems unequivocal," he said. "You could run away together, hide? If you're clever, they might not find you for a while. There are worse fates."

"How can you even suggest that?" I asked, hurt he'd think I was capable. "I would never do anything that puts you or Nonna in harm's way."

"What of the harm you cause yourself? A life without love is no life at all. Especially once you've felt it so strong."

"I'm not even 20. I'll meet another—"

"And what if you can't forget what it felt like to know her? You can dissolve the memories, but erasing the feeling that something is missing—"

"*Then I'll learn to resent her, because I will either way.* Do you really think I could be happy knowing I put you back in danger? After everything my father put you both through. And for what?"

"*For love, Hafeedee.* You know that. *For love.* He loved your mother, and I supported him then, like I will support you now," he said, emotion filling his eyes.

"No. I would never make such a selfish choice," I declared, rising to my feet. "I don't want to talk about it anymore, and I don't want to be down here. If the *Sancti* knew you kept—"

He stood too, gesturing for silence with an outstretched hand. Reaching behind him, he retrieved a book from the shelf and extended it toward me, "Take your book. You might be needing it."

"Stop it," I said through gritted teeth.

"There is no shame in using what we know. Those fanatics made you believe it was wrong, but it's who we are."

"No, those are my thoughts. It's an infection that destroys the natural order—"

"Order that was created by people," he pushed. "You're not interfering with the natural world any more than humans do when they breathe."

"*Then why does everyone who uses it end up dead?!*" I spat out, not realizing I felt that way until I heard myself say it.

"That has been your only experience," he said with pity in his eyes. "That is not always the case. Our people lived peacefully for hundreds of years."

He drained the remnants of his drink, before giving me a gentle look. "Tell me Massimo, what happens when water in a puddle dries?"

"It evaporates," I said, extending him one last bit of rope before I left.

"Si, evaporatus. The process of liquid becoming gas. But the water vanishes, does it not? Yet it's not called magic. Why?"

"Because it's been proven, by science." I was losing my patience.

"Magic is just a label for things that

people can't explain. Or don't want to explain because its existence threatens their beliefs," he said.

I opened my mouth to argue, but he cut me off before I could. "We each get one life," he said, pausing. "One chance to do something great. Your nonna and I have done that, many times over. Now it is your turn. We'll stand by whatever choice you make."

He held the book out once more. Its leather was unblemished, in perfect condition.

"I doubt Nonna would appreciate you speaking for her," I said.

At that, he chuckled. "There's not a single choice I make where I don't think of your nonna. We operate as a team. She supports this," he insisted.

"How? How could she?" I inquired sincerely, knowing her feelings toward the *Sancti* and *In Unio*.

"I'm only tough because I love you," said Nonna, from the doorway. I turned around to see her in her nightgown. "He doesn't speak for me, but yes, from time to time I allow him to do the heavy lifting. Especially at four in the morning."

"You heard everything?" I asked.

She pointed between herself and my grandfather. "One soul, two bodies," she said. "Or just too many years being together."

Approaching me, her expression softened, perhaps at the thought of her greatest love.

"Listen to me. Only you, in your heart,

know what is right for you. Anyone else's opinion is tainted by their perspective," she said. "You can't, and shouldn't, trust it."

"There is no choice to make, Nonna," I argued. "Not where your lives are concerned, and that is the end of it." I could feel anger swirling within me, the conversation the furthest from the one I wanted to be having. Then or ever.

Undeterred, my nonna continued. "You're almost a man now, an adult. So I won't patronize you by claiming I know better. Instead, I'll trust what you say. But if you change your mind, my only request is that you allow me to meet her. I can't imagine any person who would ever be good enough for you and your brilliant mind, but if you believe it, I'm sure I'll see it." She moved close enough to rest her hand on the side of my face as she repeated my grandfather's sentiments: "After all, there are worse things than death."

She kissed me on the cheek, as my grandfather comforted her, wiping a tear from his own eye.

I left Italy the following day, deluding myself into feeling better. Knowing more information about her filled me with a false sense of confidence that I was better prepared for the level of threat I was bound to face. As if understanding the gravity, not just for me but for my grandparents, could help stave off the gnawing feeling tugging at my chest. The one that told me I was already tail-spinning out of control.

All my worst fears were bubbling to the surface, but one undeniable truth stood out. The best thing I could do for everyone I loved, including her, was to disappear.

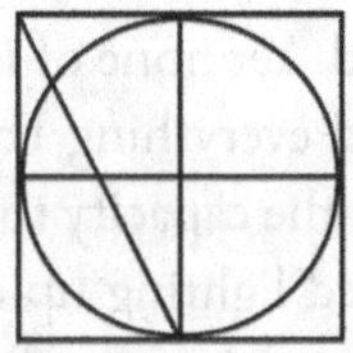

TWENTY-THREE
HAPPIER THAN EVER

"Ma'am. *Ma'am*," yelled a voice in my head.

I was hanging out with Max again (in my dreams), when it felt as though an earthquake had struck.

"Ma'am. The plane is landing, *Ma'am*?"

"No!" I screamed in the flight attendant's face as I woke up. She was bent over me, shaking my shoulders. "Sorry," I mumbled, groggy and out of it.

She held a button down that raised the bed into a seat, before stomping back to take her own. With one eye open, my body involuntarily slid upright, alerting me to the other first-class passengers who were staring at me like an intruder who'd just broken into their living room.

"First time on a plane," I shrugged, with a sarcastic half smile.

I was drained. Physically, emotionally... idealistically. Every bone and muscle in my body wanted to give up. But as the wheels gripped the asphalt runway of JFK, I forced both eyes open and grabbed my phone to take it off airplane mode.

Peering out at a shade of grey different from what I remembered leaving just four days ago, my mind was overrun with all the change that had happened. Yet none of it felt real. I was detached, as if my body had shoved everything I'd witnessed into invisible compartments until I had the capacity to process them.

As notifications started lighting up on my phone, I clutched the red rock that hung around my neck, realizing it was the only thing still holding me together.

I quickly swiped past a text from my carrier welcoming me home, and one from Delilah:

Can't wait to see you. Text when you land!

Before finding a message from Dylan:

Wanna grab dinner tomorrow night before Delilah's play thing? Just as friends, no funny business... even if you try!!

If I had the energy, I would have laughed, or at least smiled.

There was nothing from my grandma, but I interpreted it as her respecting my space, honoring my promise to call her. I didn't even have a full second to process the thought before I saw the subject line of an email that immediately put me on high alert: *Plagiarism*. It was from Mr. McKenzie:

Dear Ms. Nelson,

I regret to inform you that your recent assignment, titled "The Woman Who Helps Them Die," was flagged by the school's moderating company as being almost 100% plagiarized.

In accordance with Anderson's Plagiarism Policy, we can only award marks for the original content of any assignment.

Since the vast majority of your work has been identified as plagiarized, you will receive 0% of the total possible mark. This reflects the percentage of the assignment that was identified as your original work...

I wanted to hurl my phone. The article must have been online somewhere, and the plagiarism software thought I'd stolen it. The problem was that to clear my name, I'd have to admit to submitting an article I'd previously written.

It wasn't enough that I'd just discovered everything in the world was a complete lie; I was also at risk of failing the only thing I cared about that could give me an actual foundation in life. It seemed both trivial in the grand scheme of things and yet monumental. Sure, I could technically freeze the entire school (or at least all its water, *I was fairly certain-ish*), but failing Advanced Journalism for plagiarism would be the reddest of flags for any journalism program, especially NYU.

I panicked the entire way off the plane and onto the concourse, with what little energy I had left. Not even the sight of a man in a black suit holding a sign reading: Ms. Nelson-Sinclair-Dubois could snap me out of it. I told him to mark me as collected so he'd get paid, but that I had another ride. That wasn't my name, after all, so I opted for the train and subway instead.

It wasn't until I saw the skyline while going over the Williamsburg Bridge that I felt like there was a chance I'd be able to figure it all out. New York was still the only place in the world I wanted to be... my eternal escape. Just like it had been my mother's, apparently. Perhaps it was a misguided sense of assurance, but there was something about the vibrancy of the city that made me feel like anything was possible. I wondered if that's how she'd felt, too.

DELILAH WASN'T in the room when I got back to Anderson. It was close to two in the afternoon, and I decided the best thing I could do was to clear my head with a nap before responding to Mr. McKenzie's email.

On brand, I woke up at four the next morning, dehydrated and disoriented. I'd been so tired that I didn't even dream, instead floating around in a state of nothingness. Instinctively, I reached for my phone, squinting against the harsh brightness of the screen.

McKenzie's email was still open, and instead of swiping it closed like I wanted to, I rationalized that it was better to rip the Band-Aid off. I copied in Sheila Marshall, in case I needed a witness—at least I'd learned something from my encounter with the Sinclairs' lawyer.

> *Dear Mr. McKenzie,*
> *Thank you for your email.*
> *I'm understandably alarmed and upset to be accused of stealing someone else's work and passing it off as my own. I would appreciate a meeting at your earliest convenience so that we may clear this up before it incorrectly enters my record.*
> *Miss. Marshall if you're able to join, I'd appreciate it?*
> *Thank you,*
> *Eva.*

I knew I was being unnecessarily antagonistic, but rage was overriding reason.

Lying back, staring at the popcorn ceiling above me, I thought of what Alexander's grandson, Ivan, had said about the family's connections. That I could have an internship at any paper I wanted, or a place at any college. Instead of inspiring me, it made me recoil. *How would I ever dig myself out of my crumbling insecurity, if I knew I was there unfairly? Worse, how could I live knowing I'd stolen something that rightfully belonged to someone else?* I wasn't looking for a golden ticket, I simply wanted access to the same opportunities as everyone else.

McKenzie replied a few minutes before our 10 A.M. class, confirming we could meet afterward, and Miss. Marshall agreed. All I had to do was endure another egotistical monologue for an hour and fifty-five minutes before I could present my case.

Miss. Marshall showed up just after the bell rang, as kids were still filing out of the room. I was waiting at the back until she got there.

"Eva, hi," she said, waving. "Patrick, how are you?"

"Good, good," McKenzie responded with a brisk nod, then turned to me, his grin not quite reaching his eyes. "Eva, come on down."

I took two steps forward and wanted to run ten steps back, grabbing my necklace for moral support.

"Well, you asked to meet with us," he said, as I was halfway there. His words feeling like a spotlight.

"I didn't plagiarize anything," I said, trying to find my big girl voice. "The assignment I submitted was my own. I wrote every word. If any configuration of those words matched the works of other people who have already been published, then it was strictly done by accident." I knew I was speaking like a character from a legal drama, but I didn't know how else to get my point across.

"The website provides a report, Eva," Miss. Marshall pointed out. "It showed it was 100% plagiarized."

"From what source?" I inquired.

She hesitated. "Pardon?"

"From which author did I steal the work?"

She exchanged a glance with Mr. McKenzie, who reluctantly sat down at his laptop and started typing. With a smug look on his face, he clicked the mouse, the printer spitting ink.

He distributed the pages to the three of us, as I scanned through them, landing on the last.

"98% of the article was taken from a newsletter titled, '*The Dunnington Doula of Death*,'" I said, wishing I hadn't gone so hard on the alteration.

"So?" retorted McKenzie. "You challenged your standing here for two percent of a grade?" Miss. Marshall's face dropped as she looked farther down the page.

"I wrote that piece," I said. "Look at the original author. Eva Nelson. It was published in my old school's newsletter."

He scanned the page, calculating his approach as he spoke.

"This doesn't change anything. You didn't write the article for this class," he declared, his condescending tone heightened. "The assignment was to—"

"The assignment was a human-interest piece, which I submitted. All that report proves is that I'm lazy, not that I've stolen anything. How could I possibly steal from myself?" It was my only angle, and I had to argue it.

"And you're proud of that kind of behavior?" he questioned, as though it were the most deplorable thing he could imagine. "Learning hinges upon honesty, Eva. What integrity is there—"

"Integrity?" I scoffed. "I'm seriously supposed to stand here and be lectured about integrity from a teacher who'd rather tell a student to give up than help them?"

"Eva, rules are rules. The assignment had a deadline and I wasn't prepared to extend it. Do you think the print deadline of *The Washington Post* gets delayed when a journalist is overwhelmed with their workload?"

I felt bad. If only for a split second.

"But I'm not a journalist yet, am I? And this isn't *The Washington Post*. I'm a high school student, at a new school, who wants to learn. Do I think that article reflects my aptitude? Absolutely not. I know I've made mistakes, but I did meet the deadline—"

"With stolen work—" he tried to interject.

"With lazy work," I corrected him. "I would never steal someone else's—"

"It's beside the point, I'm afraid," said McKenzie, packing up his things dismissively. "Unfortunately, the assignment has already been flagged in the system, so technically there's nothing that either of us are able to do. Should you wish to appeal the decision, you can argue your case in front of the plagiarism committee but be warned, if you're unsuccessful, you will receive an F for the class."

I wanted to tell him that he could *shove his grade and his class*. That I'd happily argue in front of any committee that believed submitting used work was the same as stealing someone else's, but I didn't know if I had the conviction.

I looked to Miss. Marshall; her encouraging eyes offering support, if not sympathy. Something about it softened me. Reminding me that while everything I was defending was the truth, I'd also gotten myself into the situation because *I hadn't done the work*. I was the one who'd allowed myself to get distracted by a boy. Sure, it felt like destiny was bringing us together, but I was the one who actively pursued it. That was on me and I knew the bigger I made the situation the uglier it was going to get—and I wasn't sure I had the heart, or the belief, in what I felt was right.

"I need some time to think about it," I said, heading out the door before they could say anything else.

I tried desperately to be present for my next class, to make up for the guilt I was feeling for not giving Anderson the attention it deserved, but every time I did, I was brought back to the bitter aftertaste from my encounter with McKenzie. Instead, I let my mind wander to thoughts of magic and crystals, and a world that made even less sense.

It felt so fantastical that by the time class was over, I'd almost convinced myself I'd made the whole thing up—easier to accept I was crazy than powerful. The doubt lingering until I got back to my room and confirmed the existence of *In Scientia*.

Spending the rest of the afternoon glued to it, I learned about the history of the original thirteen families and the three branches of magic they mastered: *Elementum, Mentis* and *Spiritualis*.

I discovered I was part of *Elementum*, the study of magic

derived from the Earth and the elements present within its atmosphere. It encompassed nature, water, weather and, in the Sinclair-Dubois family's case, metals and gemstones. It was represented by the triangle in the Symbol of *In Unio*.

Mentis, represented by the square, referred to matters of the mind. It included illusion, implanting thoughts, mind reading, mind control and the ability to manipulate space and time. *Spiritualis*, on the other hand, pertained to only two things: connection to spirit represented by the cross, and divination—the practice of reading energy to predict the future, represented by the circle.

It wasn't until I came across various formulas, most of which seemed too fantastical to comprehend, that an idea started to form.

Reflectere Campus, or Reflective Field, was a formulation to reflect light around the caster, allowing them to move unseen. It was a simple preparation that involved 'anointing' a piece of quartz crystal with oil from sun-dried roses, then rubbing it to create friction. The movement was meant to generate heat, releasing a gas that established a reflective aura.

Delilah had some crystals on her bedside table, one of which was a citrine quartz, according to an internet search, and I had face oil that was made of roses. I lathered some on the crystal and tried reciting the words in the book.

"Lux... anfractus... ad visum."

I was sitting in front of our floor-length mirror, watching with anticipation as nothing happened. Over and over again I tried, feeling more and more foolish for having thought it would work, until I realized I was still wearing my necklace.

Unlocking the clasp, I slid the chain's ends apart and tucked it into my jacket pocket. As I lifted my head, my mind surged with an overload of information, a brain freeze overwhelming all my senses.

Placing both hands on the ground, I tried to stabilize myself, extracting sorely needed oxygen from the air. "*You've got this, you've got this, you've got this,*" I encouraged myself.

I took another large breath, this time imagining it calming my frayed nerves. Slowly, I peeked around the room.

The afternoon sun had saturated everything in light: the white walls, white bedding, white ceiling, each bouncing light into a playground of multi-colored convergence. Rainbow refractions zipped around the room, the energy pulsating as if it were alive.

As I attempted to stand, water molecules rose and fell in front of my face in a state of harmonic dependence. Dizzying my senses, I fell into the wall—I may not have been moving, but the world around me was and my body couldn't process it. I reached into my jacket pocket to retrieve the necklace, when something on the shelf next to me caught my attention.

It was a small aloe vera plant in a white pot, its thick, spiked leaves spiraling upwards. I'd never really noticed its beauty before, nor the precise geometry of its spiral. Now, however, I could see energy cycling in and out of it, particles rising and falling in a delicate dance around its orbit. It was more subtle than the free-flowing energy around the room, but as I drew closer, the details became clearer. The plant was microscopically filtering the room, drawing in carbon dioxide and releasing oxygen that seemed to float directly towards me.

I was in such awe at the miracle of the process that I actually started tearing up. I was witnessing something that I knew existed, but had never been able to see before, directly challenging my skeptical heart. In that moment, I realized what a gift I'd been given. How fortunate I was to experience what so many other people couldn't. I wondered how different the world would be if everyone could see what I was seeing. If selfish-by-nature humans could directly witness the visual impact of how plants aided their lives, perhaps they'd be worshiped more than gold.

Inspiration crashed over me like a wave, bringing with it the realization that this was the answer I'd been unwittingly searching for my whole life. It was a way to tell the truth, to help people, to ensure I left the world better than I found it so no one else had to suffer the way I had.

I pushed off the wall to stand upright, battling the enormous weight of gravity and the nausea swooshing in my stomach. Rubbing my thumb back and forth over the citrine in rapid succession, I began reciting the words I already knew by heart:

"Lux anfractus ad visum, *lux anfractus ad visum.*"

Within moments, I could see sparks of energy being released as the electrons within the citrine were becoming charged. The silica within the stone was reacting with the rose oxide to create a vapor, which was being absorbed by my skin. It was turning the rock, and my hand, invisible.

Amazed, I gazed into the mirror across from me, as my arm and sleeve started slowly disappearing. Along with my shoulder. Then my neck. Then my face. I should've been panicking, but I was too exhilarated with possibility.

It was by far the strangest sensation I'd ever experienced; knowing I was standing there, yet unable to see my own reflection. My ears tingled, perhaps as a warning bell, but nowhere near loud enough to stop me.

I paced the room, trying to think of where I should go, or what I should do. I considered sneaking into McKenzie's office to change my grade, or exploring the newsroom of *The New York Times*, but I didn't know how long the invisibility would last and I didn't want to get caught suddenly reappearing somewhere I shouldn't be. Especially in an office full of journalists.

Instead my mind, or rather my heart, were suckered into thoughts of Max. Of where he might be, of what he might be doing...

Then it struck me so embarrassingly hard I wanted to slap myself: how he'd interacted with the man in the park, instantly pacifying him; how he'd asked about my grandparents; *how I'd passed out in his arms*. Foolishness flushed my cheeks and then anger overtook everything. Without a second thought, and with nothing but my jacket and Delilah's piece of citrine, I bolted out the door.

I hadn't gone far when I nearly tumbled down the staircase. The inability to see my own feet as I attempted to lower them onto each step presented a coordination challenge I wasn't sure I'd ever be equipped for. It felt like walking down a broken escalator backward, my brain fighting the preconceived notion it knew too well.

The overwhelming sensations I was experiencing indoors, however, paled in comparison to what awaited me outside. Exiting the building I was engulfed by an avalanche of movement, information bombarding me from all angles.

Quickly discarding the plan I had to walk, I jumped into a taxi that had pulled up to the curb.

"City Hall Park, please," I instructed the driver, the closest monument I could remember near the downtown highrise Max had taken me to. It was his 'favorite place' after all, if anything he'd told me had been the truth.

Turning around, the driver looked at me confused, before turning back and accelerating.

We hadn't even got a block away before he turned the wrong direction. "Hey. City Hall's back there!" I exclaimed, rapping my hand against the partition to catch his attention. He glanced in his rearview mirror, then looked over his shoulder, before slamming his foot on the brakes to an attention-grabbing stop.

He cast one more glance at me before leaping out of the car screaming, "Tener que ir al babalao!"

It took me a very long, slow second to realize why.

I'd been so focused on ignoring the energy whizzing around me that I'd forgotten the state of my body. Crimson washed over me, not that anyone could see.

I was at a loss for what to do. Opening the door wasn't an

option with the driver outside causing a scene, especially since people on the street had begun to stop and stare.

As I tried to figure a way out, I glanced down at my hand, horrified to discover that I could see it. Stress surged in my chest, making me question how much my body could actually handle, before I pulled out the citrine and started rubbing it again. My hand instantly disappearing.

I looked up in time to see the driver climbing back into his seat, slamming his door shut behind him. A cloud of dust swirled towards me, right into my nose.

Holding my breath, I fought the urge to sneeze as he spun around like a startled cobra, coming face to face with me through the partition.

"Achoo."

"I know I heard something that time!" He looked petrified, banging his hand on the plexiglass as he yelled.

"Stop it!" I yelled back, out of impulse. To my surprise, he did.

Looking outside the car, his performance was attracting more onlookers, some of whom were filming on their phones. He made the sign of the cross on his forehead, chest and shoulders, and I knew I had no choice but to strengthen my commitment.

"I won't hurt you," I said. As I did, I noticed Santeria beads on his dashboard and hoped his faith in things he couldn't see would fall in my favor. "I just need you to drive to City Hall Park and everything will be okay. Please," I requested, speaking as calm and non-threatening as possible.

The taxi driver shut his eyes tightly and opened them, as if he could blink away the hallucination.

"I'm going insane..." he muttered to himself, squishing his face up against the partition to check the floor.

When he couldn't see anything, he turned back around and accelerated up the street. I figured I'd make a run for it on the next block, when he did a U-turn over a crosswalk to head south toward my destination. I smiled to myself and closed my eyes, trying to give my nerves a moment to rest.

We'd gotten halfway there when he started babbling.

"I didn't mean to cheat on her, I swear. It just happened. She's always miserable. Nothing's ever good enough. She—"

"Woah, okay, let's not go blaming *her* for *your* crappy choices," I blurted out defensively, momentarily forgetting the whole invisibility thing again. Fortunately, it bought me the rest of the ride in silence to concentrate on not being sick. The movement of the car and the information of everything around me was threatening to short-circuit my brain.

As we neared the park, the driver pulled over, his face pale and clammy, probably just as mine looked.

"Tell your wife the truth. Maybe she'll understand," I suggested.

He made the sign of the cross again.

"She won't," he replied, his head bowed. "She's too good of a woman."

"Well, that's for her to decide. We all deserve the dignity of the truth," I said, opening the car door and running out before he had a chance to ask me more questions I didn't have the answers to.

Laser-focused, I dashed across the park toward the building I'd last seen from the back of Max's bike. The limestone-colored tourelles on the tower's corners glistened in the sunlight as I pushed through the heavy gold and glass doors.

Bypassing the doorman was simpler this time, though the stairs and ladder proved far worse. When I got out through the manhole, using all the body strength I had, and Max wasn't there, I felt like I might finally be sick. The bird's eye view showcased an explosion of energy I couldn't possibly process, especially against the deluge of disappointment rising in my throat. It was like stepping into Jackson Pollock's New York, without a single tether to the ground.

I took shelter on the stone floor, regaining my strength while the wind gently whipped my hair around my face. I watched, mesmerized, as different streams of air intertwined. The symphony of it calmed me, as I let the invisibility wear off before attempting to climb back down.

Disappointed, I pressed the elevator call button, but as it lit up, I felt an unmistakable magnetic pull. I swung around to face the door behind me, leading to the penthouse apartment.

Temporarily frozen, I listened for any kind of sound. Then, without thinking, I strode over to the door and knocked on it. *Loud*. Five times.

From inside, I heard movement. The rustle of fabrics, followed by footsteps.

The suspense both petrified and excited me.

I went to knock again, when the door opened to reveal a model-tall woman with naturally highlighted brunette hair. She had a perfect smile and distinct eyes that elevated her out of being cookie-cutter pretty.

"Can I help you?" she asked, almost seductively. Though I could imagine anything she ever said would sound that way. She was the epitome of everything I wasn't: bouncy, sparkly and cool. If I wasn't feeling nauseated before, I certainly was now.

"Max?" I managed to get out.

As soon as I said his name, my heart sank, realizing who the woman might be to him if he was there.

"He's out," she said, confirming my worst fears. It meant he'd lied about so much more than I realized, and yet somehow that didn't soften the blow.

"Guess that's what I get for turning up unannounced," I said, trying to downplay play it. "Tell him Eva stopped by?" I asked, backing away.

"You're Eva?" she exclaimed, her face lighting up.

"Uh, yes. That's me," I confirmed, feeling slightly better that he'd at least mentioned me.

"It's so great to finally meet you!" she said, reaching out to hug me. Her hair smelled like she used too much conditioner. I couldn't help but like her.

She stepped back, sadly just as pretty up close. "It's so crazy, I didn't even know he had a sister until a couple of weeks ago," she revealed, like a heavy-handed punch to my face.

My legs felt broken, just like my heart surely was. Moisture burning my sinuses.

"Are you okay?" she asked. "Did I say something wrong?"

I couldn't find words. I just shook my head. The anxiety of forcing my way into Max's life had become a stark reality. I'd chased and chased, and was still chasing, ruining another girl's life in the process.

"I am *so* sorry," I whispered unable hold back the tears any longer. She looked horrified, and with good reason. "It was great to meet you, but I've gotta go..." I couldn't even finish the sentence or think up an excuse to leave. I turned around and slammed my hand against the elevator button. Barely holding myself together. My body wanted to heave, but I wouldn't let it break free.

"Damnit. I can't do this," said Max, his husky voice reviving me like a defibrillator placed directly on my chest. I turned around to see the brunette dissolving into thick, iridescent smoke.

Standing twelve feet behind her was him.

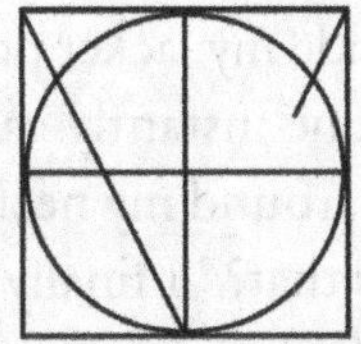

TWENTY-FOUR
COLORBLIND

He stopped my heart, and my breath, more beautiful than anyone I'd ever seen. As if my newfound clarity made him even more dazzling.

Light drenched his crystal-brown eyes making his thick, black lashes stand out even more; the cherry in his lips summoning the memory of when they were close.

If I weren't so violently mad, I might have fallen even more in love with him right then and there. Instead, I launched forward with the fury of an army—the electricity of my anger propelling me toward him, as if I were flying without an engine.

I don't remember falling down and blacking out. I only remembered seeing his face, and then feeling him cradling my head.

"Not again," I managed to get out.

I felt him chuckle.

"Get off me."

He obliged, pulling my head up to remove his arm and replacing it with a pillow from his couch. As the room came back into focus so did the throbbing in my head, the vividness too much to bear.

293

I slipped my hand inside my jacket pocket to retrieve my necklace. The touch of the stone instantly calmed my system, enough to be able to clasp it back around my neck.

"What. The hell. Was that?" I finally managed to get out. *The fainting portion of my life had better come to an end soon*, I thought.

"An illusion. What are you doing here, Eva?" he snapped. "Tell me you didn't just walk in the front door?" It appeared he was also mad.

"*Seriously?*" I replied. "You're seriously gonna say that to me after what just happened? After *everything* that's happened?" My annoyance was affording me the energy I needed to sit upright. "Yes, I walked in the front door—"

"Oh my God," he exclaimed, suddenly standing and pacing across the room. "*You shouldn't be here.*"

"What's the big deal?" I said, flinging my arms up in the air. "Are you really that insulted by my presence?" I was starting to feel like day-old sushi.

"Anyone could have seen you come in, or... or expel a plume of neon smoke in my living room!" he said, walking over to look out the windows before hastily closing the thick floor to ceiling drapes.

"I expelled smoke?" I asked. "From where? Also, I wouldn't be here if you'd *returned so much as a text.*"

"It's not safe for you," he barked, but I wasn't done.

"I knew you had to be involved in all this. I knew it!" I said, even though I hadn't known until just minutes earlier.

"What part of *it's not safe* don't you understand?!"

"I made myself invisible, alright? No one saw me!"

My words seemed to appease him enough to relax slightly. He looked away from me as I stared at his pensive face.

"So, who's the brunette?"

I thought I saw him roll his eyes. "I told you, an illusion."

"An illusion for what?" I asked, my mind running amok with less than favorable ideas.

"To keep people away," he corrected me.

"I imagine she gets some people to stay," I quipped.

He took a breath, I assumed because he was feeling guilty for being so rude.

"It's a manifestation. Of the beholder's fears."

"Oh," I retreated, thinking back to how perfect she was. "*Oh*... well, I mean. I wouldn't say she's like my *worst* fear."

He took a seat on his aged leather couch and, for the first time since I arrived, I took in his apartment.

It had polished concrete floors in every visible room, with random pieces of modern art propped up against the stark, white walls. The only element of depth in the space came from black velvet curtains. "So, this is your place? It's nice. A little cold and serial killer-y, but ni—"

He shook his head. "Did they really not tell you?"

"Apparently not if you have to ask me," I blurted out, rising to my feet. I felt like a child sitting on the ground and his tone wasn't helping. Peering down the hall I could see two suitcases, both halfway packed. "You going somewhere?"

"*The rules*," he said, his face falling, laced with dread. "Where's your symbol to start with?" he probed. "You're not displaying it." He stood up swiftly to spin me around, searching, I guessed, for the necklace Alida and Terence gave me.

"The necklace? Oh... I guess I forgot," I admitted, confused. I assumed it was ceremonial. "I didn't realize they were serious."

He fell silent, turning away from me.

Somehow, I knew I'd crossed a line.

"Don't get me wrong, I'm all for rules," I added. "Like never let a friend eat alone. I love that rule."

"Don't belittle this," he said, seething without facing me.

"Max... that's not what I meant."

He turned around and unbuttoned his shirt to reveal the

Symbol of *In Unio* freshly branded into his skin, the sharp points of the triangle, cross and square, melding with the jaggedly cut circle. The muscles of his chest and shoulders taut with rage.

"This isn't a game," he said, tears brimming in his eyes.

I had no words. The image of him so vulnerable stripped my vocabulary of meaning. Instead, I stepped forward, getting close enough to touch him.

He flinched, almost retreating, but before he could, I placed my hand on his chest. My ice-cold fingers thawing against his skin.

He closed his eyes, inhaling the moment.

"Who did this to you?" I asked.

"The *Sancti*," he said. "Guardians of the Holy. They enforce *In Unio*, the treaty of magic. Didn't they tell you anything?"

I let my fingers trace his color bone.

He pulled back. "I'm sorry," he said, buttoning his shirt. "This can't happen."

"What can't happen?" I inquired, mostly earnest.

"Stop it. You're not as interested in me as you think you are," he grunted.

"Because you know me *so* much better than I know myself?"

He looked me dead in the eye. "I'm not some cool, interesting guy being coy or whatever. I'm... broken, okay? *Damaged*. I ruin anything I get near. You're not missing out—"

"We're all damaged, Max," I said. "I don't pretend to understand how yours feels, but it doesn't scare me, so if you're trying to push me away—"

"Your family gave you *In Scientia*," he said. "That much I saw—"

"So you *were* there? I wasn't sure if I'd imagined it."

"Then you know that the families are forbidden from alliances, or interacting in any way. I'm from a different family to yours," he said.

"Isn't that a good thing?" I joked.

"*You're not listening.* There isn't a world where we could ever be together. The *Sancti* would never allow it, especially when it comes to me." Pain scarred his face more than any branding iron ever could.

"We don't have to broadcast it," I offered as a suggestion.

"The Sancti are fanatics, incredibly adept at what they do. They have a hold on everything—from churches to politicians, in every corner of the globe. Nowhere is safe from them. Their network, their influence, it's limitless."

"Surely there are ways around it. My *In Scientia*—"

"You don't get it, Eva. *They killed my parents*! My mom and my dad were from different families, and they thought they could hide it too. Instead they were murdered, right in front of my face."

His words reverberated around the apartment, and right through my heart. I felt horrific.

"I'm so... sorry," I whispered. "I didn't—"

"It's not your fault. None of it is. It's mine. I'm the one who should've known better. I'm the one who should have stayed away." His voice trailed off, leaving stillness hanging in the air.

"So that's it?" I asked, a lump forming in my throat. "I just leave and never see you again?"

"*They'll kill us both, Eva*. And our families, if they ever caught us together. They've been waiting for the chance since I was born. In their eyes, I shouldn't exist."

"Well, thank God that you do," I said, trying not to cry. Then I realized. "I'm putting you in danger being here, aren't I?"

He looked heartbroken. "Believe it or not, I was trying to protect you by not contacting you."

"It's not like I made it easy" I said, embarrassment pummeling me. "I practically stalked you."

"Practically?" He teased, before getting solemn. "I figured you'd lose interest."

"I'm not that girl," I said.

"I know." He nodded. "Relentless."

He fell silent again, and I knew it was time to leave.

I just needed to figure out how I was going to walk.

We stood staring at each other for what felt like hours, shadows from the setting sun our only marker of time. It seemed neither of us could say or do anything.

Then a question came to me, one that I knew would bug me if I didn't ask it. "That day in the park... when you helped that man... why did you do it? When you had so much to lose?"

He paused.

"I wasn't thinking, honestly. I... I was distracted by you, I guess. I could feel you watching me, then before I knew it I was trying to calm him down."

"How?" I asked. "How do you do it?"

"By taking over his mind," he confessed, sounding ashamed.

He looked like a little boy who'd been taught to hate the person he was, and it chipped away at my heart just that little bit more. I wanted to wrap my arms around him and somehow turn back time, to shield him from ever getting hurt.

"What a beautiful gift," I said. "That you can help people in that way."

"I wouldn't know," he replied, dismissing the thought. "I've only ever done it a handful of times. It's not... who I am."

"Of course it's not. We're not our actions, they don't define us. They're just something we do."

"What do you mean? We're exactly our actions."

I almost giggled out of frustration. I couldn't get enough of him.

"There must be something about it you don't hate?"

He gazed off, trying to find a truthful answer.

"I don't know... my mother's powers were in illusion. She could make people believe good things had happened to them by implanting happy memories," he finally said, his voice softening.

"That's... incredible. How could you ever think of that as being bad?"

"She could also make them forget," he said, his face turning dark.

"Every coin has two sides, but that doesn't mean..." I felt myself trail off. "Wait, you can erase people's memories?" I asked, the thought making my stomach drop.

"Yes," he responded. Like he understood incorrectly, what I was about to ask.

"Don't you *ever* do that to me," I said, getting closer to him. "Promise me. No matter what happens. You won't *ever* do that to me." My voice was barely a whisper. I knew if I spoke too loud I would start to cry.

He struggled to respond.

"I promise," he nodded.

"I mean it. I *never, ever* want to forget knowing you."

My voice was breaking, telling me it was really time to go.

I got two paces away before I heard him call my name. "Eva?"

I didn't want to look at him, but I knew I had to. The realization that it might be the last time I ever would, haunted every part of me.

Reluctantly, my eyes found his.

"Thank you. You made me feel something I've... only ever read about in books. Ones written centuries ago."

"You blinked."

"No. I most definitely did not."

It was real, I thought. *And it had been all along.*

"Rare and fleeting," I said, tears rolling down my cheeks. "Goodbye, Max."

Knowing that if I didn't leave then, I never would, I walked out of his apartment and into the elevator.

Every step felt like a mistake. As if I were getting farther and farther away from where I was meant to be.

I didn't even bother hiding it, letting the barrage of tears flood my face. The sympathetic eyes of strangers, New Yorkers no less, cast over me in conciliatory glances. I knew I looked crazy, but I couldn't have cared less.

It was close to midnight by the time I got back to Anderson, debilitated from a day of twists and turns, emotionally devoid, having lost the strength to feel anything.

Delilah appeared as I walked into the common room. She was holding my phone and hers. "*Where have you been?!*" She looked like she'd also been crying.

"What?" I asked, confused. I didn't even know what day it was.

"I've been looking for you for hours. Dylan's out searching the streets," she said, looking horrified.

"Oh, sorry," I mumbled.

"*I almost called the police, Eva!*"

"Well, I'm fine. I was saying goodbye to Ma—"

"*Are you kidding me?* You were out chasing that guy again?" she asked, infuriated. "You didn't even take your phone."

"What's the big deal?" I shot back. "I was only gone for a few hours. Like, I appreciate the concern. I do, *really*. But I'm not a child," I added, trying to stand up for myself.

It clearly was not the time.

"Got it," she said. Hurt rippled across her face. She picked up her leather jacket from the sofa, and put it on. "I'll remember that next time," she said, heading toward the door. "My rehearsal went great by the way. Really appreciate you being there to support me."

She slammed the door so hard, the echo of her disappointment lingered long after she left. I was frozen in shock, the realization of how badly I'd messed up almost too much to bear.

I ran after her, shouting down the stairwell. "Delilah, wait! I'm so sorry... wait!" But she was already gone.

I stood there, helpless. I'd selfishly hurt someone who'd shown me nothing but kindness, and I had no idea how to make it right. It felt like everything was falling apart. Like I was careening down the side of a cliff and no matter what I did, there wasn't anything I could do to save myself or the people I cared about.

I was on the verge of returning inside when I heard footsteps hurrying up the stairs. Lifting my head I saw Dylan, his face flushed and sweaty, as if he'd been sprinting across half of Manhattan. Probably because he had.

His face brightened when he saw me.

"I'm so sorry!" I said. "I really, really didn't mean to—"

"As long as you're okay," he interrupted sweetly. "That's all that matters."

"Thank you," I replied, feeling insipid.

He stepped closer. "You are okay though, aren't you?" he asked, tentatively.

"No. But it's not your problem. At all. I'll be fine," I said, perhaps trying to convince myself.

The concern in his eyes made me feel even worse. I wanted to tell him that I wasn't who he thought I was, that I was a fraud, unworthy of anyone's attention, especially his.

"Have you eaten?" he asked, the question surprising me. I hadn't thought about food in what felt like days. "No," I said, miserably. Trying not to cry. "But I'm not hungry."

Naturally, he ignored me. "Come on, let's order some Chinese."

He ushered me back into the girl's common room, where I laid on the couch in a quasi-state of catatonia. Dylan sat on the ground, with his back against me ordering food on his phone

"You really don't have to stay," I murmured. "I'm okay. If anything, you should go find Delilah and make sure she's okay. I'm sure I'm the last person she wants to hear from."

"She's fine," he replied, flashing his perfect smile. "I already checked. She's with Katie."

"Good," I sighed, burying my face in my hands. "Uh, how am

I ever going to fix this? It was so important to her, and I…" couldn't stop myself from crying.

"Eva, it'll be okay. People mess up. I think she was mostly just worried about you."

"I know. That's what makes it so bad."

"Just apologize and everything will be back to normal. I don't think D's the type to hold a grudge."

"I hope not," I said meekly.

"She said you went to London?" he asked, a tone of surprise to his voice, but I could tell he was just trying to change the subject to take my mind off it. "When?"

"I got back yesterday," I said. "I met my mother's parents."

If Delilah had already told him, he didn't let on.

"Woah, that's big. How was it?"

"Ummm…a lot?" I said, wondering how to articulate even the understandable parts.

"They must have been so proud," he prodded. "Soon to be an Anderson grad."

"It didn't come up, actually," I said. The idea of school, let alone graduating from it, felt so distant. "I might need to go back to Spring City," I continued, trying to be pragmatic. "I don't think I'm cut out for it."

"That's insane, no," he exclaimed. "You're not dropping out, Eva. You've worked so hard to get here."

"It might not be my choice," I said, recalling my meeting with McKenzie. "I think I'm going to fail Advanced Journalism. How's that gonna look on my college applications?"

"So you write some creative essays about the learning process, going back to basics. About how life's not about failing but growing from it, blah blah. Admissions committees eat that stuff up."

"It's not just that," I admitted, deflated. "I'm gonna fail other subjects, too, I think. And I'm not sure I have the energy to be able to fix it." I knew I sounded like I'd given up, but that's because I had.

"Well then, I'll help you. I can tutor you in whatever you need. You can pay me back in 10 years when I'm having a nervous breakdown doing my surgical residency."

I let out a small laugh. I didn't have the strength to fight him, so I tried to accept his kindness in the manner it was being offered.

Tears still escaped my eyes sporadically as I stared at him, contemplating how different life would be if he represented a different part of it.

He seemed to sense my thoughts. "I want you to know," he said, "that I'm here as your friend 'cause I care about you."

Not quite the direction I thought he was heading in.

"I appreciate that," I responded, the realization dawning on me that I'd turned him off me too, like I had everyone else in my life.

"But that doesn't mean I've given up hope," he said, dimples appearing at the side of his mouth. "Respectfully, I'm gonna hold onto that for a little while longer."

I didn't know what to say, or if there was even anything I could say. It was perhaps the right sentiment, just at the wrong time. I had to admire his resolve though. In a world of people always looking for something better, it felt impressive to be so decidedly chosen.

By the time the food arrived, I could barely keep my eyes open. But I knew if I didn't eat I'd be awake within hours, starving.

I'd managed about three mouthfuls when Delilah burst in, panic stricken.

I sat up, placing my plate on the coffee table. "Delilah, I'm so sorry. I—"

"Stop, this is way bigger than us." She held up her hands in surrender, a look of deep concern on her face. "Your grandma called. Your grandad's been taken to the hospital."

The words knocked the wind out of me.

"What happened?" I asked, fearing the worst. "Tell me he's okay?"

I felt like a little girl again. A child, bouncing on my grandfather's knee. Memories of him sneaking me chocolate before dinner. Always on my side. Always looking out for 'his girls.'

"She doesn't know. I told her I'd get you to call her on the way. I've got a cab waiting downstairs," said Delilah, acting like my guardian angel.

I got up and headed straight to the door.

"Shoes, babe," said Delilah.

"Sorry," I mumbled, turning toward our room to get them. As I put them on and grabbed a coat, I saw *In Scientia* on my bed.

I paused, then picked it up, along with the necklace the Sinclairs had given me. I didn't know how, but if there were a way to help my grandfather, even if it meant putting my life in danger, there wouldn't be a choice to make.

I tucked the book under my jacket as I walked down the hallway, finding Delilah and Dylan talking in sympathetic whispers. They followed me downstairs to the taxi, where Dylan argued with the driver about taking us two and a half hours interstate. After multiple backs and forths, and a promise of a fifty-dollar tip, he finally relented and the three of us climbed into the backseat.

My hands shook as I tried to find my grandma's contact in my phone. She picked up on the second ring.

"Eva?" she asked, her voice soaked with tears.

"Is he okay?"

"They're saying he's critical but stable right now," she said, repeating what she'd been told. "I don't really know what that means, but they seem to think it's positive. They've just gotta figure out what's wrong with him, cause they don't right now and—"

"What do you mean they don't know?" I interjected, frustration mounting.

"They're doing everything they can, so there's no point causing a fuss," she said, her way of telling me not to arrive guns blazing. Then she broke down. "He's had two seizures, Eva. And they're saying at his age..." She couldn't continue and neither could I. I'd never felt so helpless.

"We're leaving the city now. I'll be there as soon as I can," I assured her, as we entered the Holland Tunnel. "I love you. We'll figure it out," I said. I just wasn't sure I believed my own words.

TWENTY-FIVE

BELLS IN SANTA FE

I tried to fall asleep in the taxi so I'd be doing anything other than thinking—after all, it was close to 2 A.M.—but every time I closed my eyes, I was jolted awake by different images of my grandfather. It was almost certainly guilt, I realized somewhere between New Jersey and Pennsylvania, the scenery morphing from laneways to dense foliage. The last words I'd said to my grandpa were "not now." He'd been there for my first words in this world. I couldn't let those be our last. If they were, I'd never forgive myself. My body went rigid at the thought.

I tried to push it from my mind as fast I could; this wasn't about me or my feelings. It was about him. And it was about her's. My adoring grandmother, who had loved everyone who came into her orbit unconditionally, including me.

I glanced over at Delilah and Dylan, who were asleep, leaning on each other, before I quietly pulled out *In Scientia*.

Using the light from my phone screen, I flicked from page to page, looking for anything to do with health or time, removing disease or reversing it. But most of the information concerned manipulating material and light, or transferring energy and transmuting vibration. It seemed that even *In Scientia* had its limits;

the magic of the human body elusive, even to the members of *In Unio*.

It was damp and cold, and close to dawn when we arrived at Tower Hospital. Opening the taxi door at the place where I was born felt oddly full-circle, as if the moment held a significance I hadn't yet grasped. I dismissed the thought, rationalizing it as fear trying to feed worry, as I ran through the automatic glass doors and headed for the Emergency Room.

Grandpa was in the Intensive Care Unit, where Gran stood vigil at an observation window. She was so focused, I thought nothing could disturb her. But, when she heard my footsteps and turned to see me, she burst into tears and pulled me into a hug.

She spoke into my neck, through sobs that inflamed my guilt. "We've missed you so much, Eva," said my grandma, in a way that laid bare her vulnerability. "I'm so sorry."

"No, no," I said, breaking. "*I'm* sorry. I shouldn't have acted that way, and I shouldn't have…" I wanted to tell her the truth but I couldn't risk putting her in danger. "I shouldn't have stirred up the past. You were right. It's better left alone."

As I finished, my grandmother's attention was captured by someone behind me.

Father Michael, the priest from our local church, approached with a paper cup of coffee for her.

"Thank you, Father," she said.

"My pleasure," he responded.

I barely acknowledged him, my gaze turning to my unconscious grandfather who lay covered in tubes and wires that connected him to various machines. I couldn't escape the priest's musty odor though, which took me back to sermons past where he preached devotion above all else. It felt particularly bitter now, as I watched the life slip from one of the most righteous people I'd ever known.

He must have sensed the hostility, or perhaps just noticed my turned shoulder.

"I should probably get back," he said to my grandma. "But you have my number if you need anything."

"Thank you, Father," she replied. "It means a lot that you came."

"I'll pray for you all," he said, departing. "Good night, Eva."

I turned to look at him, amazed he'd broken tradition by actually addressing me. If he was willing to ease the tension I knew my gran was feeling, it was time I did the same. "Thank you for coming, Father Michael," I said. "It means a lot to my grandma." It wasn't original, but it was the best peace offering I think of.

"Of course," he said. Before adding, unable to help himself. "Our door's always open."

As he left, I walked over to Delilah and Dylan, who were respectfully keeping their distance.

"Nothing new," I informed them. "You guys can go if you want to? Take my card and get a cab—"

"We have nowhere else to be," Delilah replied. "Unless you'd rather we left?"

"No," I said. "I like having you guys here." As exposing as it felt to say it out loud, it was the truth.

Two doctors arrived to enter my grandfather's room—a tall, freckled man in his late fifties, and a stern woman whose gaze seemed to analyze every detail of the room photographically. My grandma followed them in, so I trailed behind.

"Dr. Carlson, this is my granddaughter Eva," she said.

Ignoring pleasantries, he nodded toward me before returning his focus to the papers in his hand. The female doctor approached my grandfather to examine him. "Pupils remain reactive," she noted, shining a flashlight into his eyes. "How long since his last seizure?" she inquired, making a note on her iPad. According to her name tag, Dr. Kamari Chaudhary was the ICU Director.

"Over forty-five minutes," said Dr. Carlson. "But his stats keep dropping."

"And you're sure there's no history of diabetes?" she asked Dr. Carlson as though she doubted his accuracy.

"None. And the labs aren't showing any abnormalities—," he was saying before I interrupted.

"So you have no idea what's wrong with him?" I both questioned and stated. I could see my grandma tense up, her squinting eye telling me to behave. Even now, when her husband's life was at stake, she still wanted to maintain politeness.

"We're running more tests," replied Dr. Carlson, his evasiveness speaking volumes.

I felt powerless, until I remembered that I wasn't, entirely.

Slipping my mother's necklace off, a familiar head-rush overpowered me, sending a searing pain into to the front of my head. I held onto the back of a chair to steady myself before glancing over to my granddad, wishing I hadn't.

His heart pumped lethargically under his crinkled, dehydrated skin. Diminished veins and arteries struggling to keep up. I approached him, tears streaming down my face, as I placed my hand on the right side of his chest where there weren't any wires

"Let's rerun blood count, amylase and lipase, and—"

"Ssh…" I said, without meaning to.

My grandma immediately interjected: "Eva, don't be so—"

"Sorry," I apologized, "but it's just, what's here?" I asked, holding my hand above his abdomen. I could see the area was stiff, tense, as if the organ below it was in distress. As if, the cells were under a tremendous amount of pressure.

No one was answering me. "Please," I urged, looking up. "What's here?"

"Ribcage, liver, pancreas…" Dr. Carlson listed off, like he was trying to appease a bratty toddler.

"The liver," I said. "There's something wrong with the—"

"And this is based on?" he asked, skeptical.

"A feeling," I admitted without thinking. "Intuition," I added for clarity, but their faces showed it wasn't helping my case.

"Did you give him something?" asked Dr. Chaudhary mistakenly confusing my help as guilt. "We need to know everything to treat him properly."

"She wasn't even there," said my grandma, valiantly jumping to my defense without missing a beat.

Dr. Chaudhary considered both me and my grandma, then turned to Dr. Carlson as she was leaving. "Add another hepatic panel," she instructed, catching my eye before walking out the door. "That's for the liver."

My grandma waited for Dr. Carlson to leave before speaking.

"They don't have a clue what's going on," said my grandma. "Do they?" She looked smaller and more terrified than I'd ever seen her. As if her body had shrunk when my grandfather's had. Like their life-forces were irrevocably linked.

Words escaped me, so I just hugged her. Voluntarily, without trying to wriggle out.

"I'm so glad you came," she said. "He's going to be so jealous when he wakes up and finds out how much time we got to spend together without... him." She'd clearly caught herself off-guard, verbalizing something she probably hoped never to think.

As she cried on my shoulder, tears collecting on my shirt, I looked down to my grandfather's hand. There was a faint, reddish dot where blood cells were gathering. Energy congealing to heal the area.

I pulled away from my grandma to look closer.

Leaning over his hand, it was evident that it was a puncture wound. I knew ordinarily that wouldn't be unusual—a patient in hospital with an injection mark—but under the skin, I could see molecules slowly decaying, turning a darker hue, and he'd only been in the hospital for a few hours. It didn't make sense.

"Did someone give him an injection?" I asked. "On his hand."

"Probably from all the tests," she said, confirming my original thought.

"No, it's turning purple," I insisted. "What was Granddad doing before he started seizing?" I asked, eager to piece it together.

"I told the doctors everything, Eva. He came back from the grocery store around five. We watched TV, ate dinner. Then he started seizing around 11pm, just as we were getting ready for bed."

"Why were you up so late? On a Monday night?" I asked, instinctively. "Oh, never mind," I added, realizing that it was probably because they knew I'd gone missing.

"Father Michael stopped by—"

"Huh?" I asked, acid invading my mouth. "Why was *he* at the house?"

"He was doing the rounds and wanted to check in on us," she said.

"Doing 'the rounds'!? *What does that even mean?*" I couldn't tell if I was overreacting, just on high alert when it came to members of the church considering the fresh lacerations I'd seen etched into Max's skin, or if I really found it suspicious.

"Well he had another priest in town and he wanted to show him around. It was nice, is what it was," she said, momentarily distracted by a nurse who entered my granddad's room to check his vitals.

I couldn't shake the feeling that something wasn't adding up, and I was almost sure it wasn't paranoia. My gut was screaming at me and if I'd learned anything from my trip to London, it was that I had to trust it.

Rationalizing that if I were quick enough, I might be able to catch up with Father Michael before he drove away, I ran out of the room, darting past Dylan and Delilah in the hallway, before leaping stairs two at a time to get to the lobby. The faster I sprinted, the more the urgency within me swelled.

As soon as I dashed through the sliding glass reception doors, I saw him in the distance. He was walking toward the top section of the hospital parking lot, built on a hill overlooking the main tower.

Getting closer, I noticed two other men getting out of a black, vintage car to greet him. One was shorter, with unkempt red hair that glowed under the streetlights still lit from the previous night. The other was thinner, lankier. His silhouette reminding me of the priest in London, when it all clicked. *The reason my grandfather, who'd never even been admitted to hospital before, was unconscious with a mystery illness. And why random priests kept popping up on the streets of New York and the alleyways of London.* They were members of the *Sancti*, and it seemed they'd been following me for some time. Perhaps, even, my entire life.

As the understanding unfolded in my mind, a wave of tension engulfed my body. It was the most violent form of anger I'd ever experienced: the kind of hysterical fury that empowers mothers to overturn vehicles to save their children.

It exploded inside me, directed firmly toward the men on the hill. The people who had tried to kill my grandfather, who had been spying on me for years. I inhaled the cool dawn air in an attempt to stabilize myself, feeling the frigidity radiate through my body. It gave me a sense of control I didn't know I had, my body acting as a conduit from the Earth below me to the air around me. My feet drawing power through the solid cement, the current becoming magnetized to my walk.

As the three of them turned to look in my direction, wisps of vapor—cobalt blue, black, purple, and red—began whirling around me in rapid succession. In response, the irises of the priests glowed white, as though light was being channeled through them. Their sights locked on me.

It didn't feel like a choice I'd consciously made, when I felt myself propel toward them, as though my body were more buoyant than the air. I soared high, fast, the electricity through my feet growing more intense the higher I rose. Smoke and glare radiated outward, lighting up the dawn sky.

I was a mere second away from colliding into them, our energies poised to explode in some cataclysmic event I couldn't fully comprehend, when I heard the throaty growl of a familiar motorcycle.

In my peripheral vision, I saw Max speeding across the parking lot, then up the hill to where the men were standing.

Zipping behind them, he skidded off his bike to run toward me, arms extended. Making it clear that if I wanted to hurt them, I'd have to go through him.

He hadn't needed to revert to heroics. The sight of him alone disarmed me. As though I'd been re-tethered to reality.

To consequence.

To conscience.

To love.

I let myself free-fall, gliding into him—his arms absorbing the momentum from my body.

Part of me resented being held. Being lifted up and simultaneously stopped by someone I couldn't love. The other part relished the feeling of being in his embrace, nestling myself into a home I never wanted to leave. It was fate. This time I was sure of it.

I opened my eyes to see the priests, who had been blown off their feet, struggling to regain their footing. "By the authority of *Praesidio Sancti*, I am placing you under arrest," announced the eldest one, making his way back up into a standing position.

"For what? No one was harmed," said Max, as we approached the men who'd tried to murder my grandfather.

"*What did you do to him?!*" I screamed at Father Michael. "I saw the injection mark. Tell me what you gave him!" He ignored me, his attention fixed on the short man who seemed to be in control.

"We have you, on exposure of—"

"Everyone will have forgotten as soon as we leave here," interjected Max. "I made sure of it as I drove through."

"If you've tampered with our minds—" said the younger one I'd recognized from London.

"Look around you," challenged Max. "Do you see anyone watching?" It was true, there were people scattered around the hospital entrance, but no one was looking in our direction.

"You're colluding, just like your par—"

"No," I interrupted him, before he could finish the accusation. "He was stopping me from murdering you. That's it, and as soon as you tell me what you did to my granddad, you won't see us together again. *Ever*."

"It's too late," said the eldest one. "You're both to accompany us back to the Vatican City, where you will await trial." As he spoke, he pulled handcuffs from the side of his belt.

"Wait," I shouted. "Max, show them the video."

"What video?" demanded the younger priest.

"The video of Father Michael, injecting my grandfather," I said, gesturing to Max, who wasn't picking up on the hint. Hoping he would, I retrieved my phone from my back pocket, scrolling through photos to pull up one of my granddad in his living room. I handed it to Max.

"Before I left for school, I bought cameras for my grandparents in case I needed to check in on them," I explained as I took the phone back to present it to the priests.

I wasn't sure if Max had fully grasped what I was asking him to do, but as trepidation began to mount, I realized he had—he'd created an illusion of footage.

"If this got out," I said, shock rippling across all three of their faces.

"It's on me alone," interrupted Father Michael. "A senile priest accidentally injects—"

"I'm not talking about the news. I'm talking about the members of *In Unio*. Your actions hardly constitute playing by the rules. I'd imagine it would change how a lot of people feel about the treaty."

"This is blackmail," said the younger one. "The *Sancti*—"

"Yes, it is," I agreed. "But the Lord gave us critical thought for a reason, no?"

He was about to continue his argument when the leader held up his hand to stop him.

"I was unaware that my colleagues behaved in this way," he said, acting genuinely shocked, whether it was true or not. "It is not... how we operate."

"And yet here we all are," I said.

"But..." He paused, no doubt for dramatic effect, a grave look falling over his face. "Should either of you cross the line again, or should you be seen together, leniencies will no longer be extended. This is your final warning," he declared with pompous regard.

"No, this is *your* final warning," I replied, smoke and vapor beginning to swirl around me again. This time though, I was in control. As if feeling it in my muscles before had given me a roadmap of how to recreate it.

"*Careful! Lest you be seen*," said the younger priest, his eyes glowing white once more, daring me into a fight.

"Attack my family again and the last thing you'll be worried about is whether I'm seen," I said, taking a step toward them. As I did, I caused the ground under us to tremor slightly. Just enough to make them unsteady.

I didn't want to start a war, but the last thing I was prepared to do was be bullied by three men. "I don't know your world, and after everything I've seen over the past week, I'm not sure I care to. But it turns out, I have access to some pretty powerful magic—I mean, look what I can do without even trying."

"*Stop!*" the old priest exclaimed as I got within a foot of him.

"No, but seriously," I quipped. "I barely even read the book."

"We won't be threatened," he barked, fear in his eyes.

"I'm not threatening you, I'm informing you. I'm not a

person you wanna push. Leave me alone, and I will happily do the same."

"We—" he tried to come back at me.

"You!" I pointed a finger in his face. "Are all *dismissed*."

Making the ground quake just a little harder, I turned my back on them to return to the hospital. It must have frightened the youngest one because I caught him slipping as they scrambled back into their car. I hoped they were headed directly to the Vatican City, and for his sake, they were taking Father Michael with them.

"Incredible," said Max, shaking his head in disbelief. "You're incredible, Eva Nelson."

It was impossible not to smile. Even with everything happening, hearing him say my name still made me giddy.

"My grandpa," I said, drawing focus back where it belonged.

"What's wrong with him?" he asked as he ran after me down the hill. "Did they really inject him with something?"

"He wouldn't have admitted to it if he hadn't. It was a hunch, and he confirmed it," I called back. "The doctors don't know what's wrong with him, but when I had my hand on his body, it felt like it was his liver." Not that I had any clue what that meant. I could see and feel energy more now, but aside from creating smoke clouds, I still didn't fully understand how to manipulate it. It made me think of the Sinclairs and whether they could help, either through their powers or their financial means. I just didn't trust that they wouldn't make the situation worse, if there were even a chance it would benefit them.

"Do you think it could've been poison?" he asked. "That's what the liver—"

"Wouldn't that have shown up on blood tests?" I countered, as we hurried back into the hospital.

"It wouldn't if modern medicine doesn't know it exists."

Before the elevator doors had completely opened on my grandfather's floor, I'd already charged out to the nurses station to find his doctors. A brunette, who looked as overworked as my body felt, was typing nonchalantly at a computer.

"Hi. Excuse me. Could you please page Dr. Chaudhary? It's about my grandfather's condition—"

"In surgery," she said, without looking up, hinting at an uphill battle.

"Can you page her anyway? It's really urgent. I think I know what's—" I tried to get out.

"What's the message?" she asked, finally meeting my stare. I could tell she had no intention of actually helping me.

"Forget it," I said, swiftly walking away to avoid an inadvertent display of magic. Max followed, so I flicked some of my anger toward him. "You couldn't have persuaded her?"

"No," he replied flatly, not offering any further explanation. Or perhaps trying not to antagonize me.

It wasn't until I saw Dylan and Delilah still standing outside my grandfather's room that I understood how Max's presence might make Dylan feel. I wasn't sure if Delilah had filled him in, or if he'd seen us on account of Max's stupidly loud motorbike, but my empathy for him surged. If only he knew it would likely be the last time Max and I ever saw one another.

"This is Max... my friend," I said. Realizing it was the sad truth. The boys nodded toward one another with polite but protective regard.

Delilah's face was strewn with equal parts surprise and guilt. She hugged me, whispering in my ear, "I might have called Max looking for you when I didn't know where you were, *so* sorry."

"You never have to say that word to me," I said, pulling back so she could see my sincerity.

There were so many things I wanted to express, so many words that remained unspoken. Yet Delilah seemed to understand all the same, nodding with the kind of comprehension that only a true friend can offer. We were lifers and we both knew it.

"How's gramps? Any change?" I asked.

"None," responded Dylan. Eager to prove his worth. "His vitals are the same, and the doctors haven't come back yet."

"Thank you for being here," I said, my gaze shifting from Dylan to Delilah, then to Max, and finally resting on my grandfather's bed through the observation window.

"I'd love a minute alone with my granddad. Do you think one of you could take my grandma for a coff—" I tried to ask before Delilah and Dylan simultaneously offered an eager "of course," exactly as I had hoped.

I softly tapped on the door, opening it to find my grandma's weary face longing for sleep.

"Do you want to go home for a bit?" I asked, knowing what the answer would be.

"No, no," she said. "I'm happy wherever he is."

My heart ached. "My friends are going to the cafeteria for some coffee. Do you want to stretch your legs?"

Understanding exactly what I was asking, as people often do in times of crisis, she gave a small nod of acknowledgment.

As the three of them went downstairs, I closed the blinds and Max walked over to my grandfather's bedside.

"Gramps, this is my friend, Max," I said.

"Nice to meet you, sir," Max said, making me want to tell him I loved him even more.

Approaching my grandfather, I pointed to a specific area on his torso. "Can you feel it? Right here, it's tenser, almost like it's blocked or cramped. It feels like a stitch that wraps around..." My words faltered, my limited knowledge of human anatomy insufficient to describe what I was sensing.

Turning to Max, I noticed his silent, astonished stare. "What?" I asked.

"I can't feel or see any of that. That's... extraordinary," he said, a mix of awe and disbelief in his voice.

"Oh." I just assumed everyone's magic worked the same way.

"Well, it's here. I think," I said, pointing self-consciously along the midpoint of his torso.

Max continued to look at me, his thoughts seemingly adrift, perhaps pondering an alternate version of our lives. I sensed it because I was wishing for it myself. But there was more to his distraction, a deeper pain I'd seen before: guilt over his magic.

"Are you okay?" I inquired, gently.

"Yeah," he said, snapping out of his trance. "There's something I could try. I don't know if it'll work, but..."

I placed my hand on his. "You don't have to."

"It's okay."

He leaned down next to my grandfather's ear and ever so quietly started humming a modulation between three notes.

I could see the vibration of the sound, radiating out from his lips, covering my granddad and even me. It sent chills down my spine, my body melting, releasing, as was some of the tension in my grandfather's body. As though all his bodily functions were slowing down.

"That's all I can really do. It's just buying us time though. The liver's a filter; if it stops working, the poison will travel through the rest of his body," he said. "I'm sorry. There's only so much I know how to do."

"It's okay," I said, remembering. "Maybe there's something I missed."

I found my jacket in the corner of the room, and with it my copy of *In Scientia*. Whipping the book open, I found what I was looking for almost immediately, as if I could read the energy of the pages. They seemed to flick to my touch, as if gravity was helping me find what I was seeking.

"*Movere Calor*," I said out loud. "That's to do with conduction, right?" I could see from the diagram that the preparation involved the transference of energy from one vessel to another in order to contain it.

"Yes, to move heat, or in this case, energy," he said.

"Could it work?" I asked.

"I don't know. I'm sorry, I don't know anything about your magic."

He continued humming, as I read aloud.

"It says, energy can be moved, and subsequently trapped elsewhere. The material has to be more dense. It suggests... diamonds. *Of course,*" I said, sarcastically.

Fortunately, the necklace Alida and Terence had given me had a couple of carats worth of diamonds in it. I placed it stone side down on my grandfather's bare skin, directly above his liver.

The next step called for external energy to fuel the reaction. I didn't need to finish reading the sentence to know what it meant; retrieving my mother's necklace.

Holding the dark red, raw crystal in my hands, I understood what I had to do. It would mean learning to permanently see the world differently, exposing myself to the *Sancti* in the process. But for a single day longer with my grandfather, it was a sacrifice worth making. I had to believe it was exactly what my mother would have wanted, too.

I closed my eyes, concentrating on conducting the energy from the necklace to disperse it into the diamonds. Heat flared in my hand, as I opened my eyes to witness the stone's color drain, the charge passing from one side of my body through to the other with electrocuting intensity.

I must have looked possessed because Max looked on, concern etched on his face. "Eva?" he asked, his tone laced with worry. "Are you—?"

Before he could intervene, I channeled the vibrational force down toward my grandfather's abdomen. As I struggled to maintain the connection against the increasing heat within me, the diamonds began vibrating, magnetizing the substance from his liver up through his skin.

The door opened with a *pop*, as Dr. Chaudhary came in reading from a chart, oblivious to the scene in front of her. I pulled the necklace off his body to stop the energy transfer, as Max hid the book under his jacket.

"You're certain he wasn't administered anything?" Dr. Chaudhary inquired, glancing at the computer monitor by his bed. A nurse trailed behind her, wheeling in a tray laden with syringes and vials.

"I actually think he was. I tried to tell the nurse at the ER desk, but I don't even know what it could have been," I said, starting to panic that they were going to give him something to treat a problem that I'd already fixed and the combination would be fatal.

Then came the sweetest sound I'd ever heard—a cough, from my granddad, as he tried to use his dry throat to speak.

"Eva?" he croaked, dazed and groggy.

Grasping his hand, I choked back tears. "Gramps," I managed to utter.

"Raymond!" exclaimed my grandmother, rushing into the room as if she'd sensed his recovery from several floors below. "You scared us," she said, kissing his face multiple times.

Dr. Chaudhary used a flashlight to check his responses, but she hadn't needed to. I could already see him recovering, his system moving and circulating freely, like a boulder had been removed from a backed-up dam. Delilah and Dylan observed from the doorway, as I threw a thumbs up to say he was going to be okay.

"You all... made such a fuss," said my grandfather with a raspy voice.

My grandma pulled back. "That's the thanks I get?" she joked.

"Eva, quick. Tell me everything you told your grandma," he urged, his speech not his own. "I don't want to miss out."

"So, you were listening?" I asked, wondering how conscious he was.

"Distantly," he replied. "Romeo can sing." A chuckle escaped him, leading to another bout of coughing. Max blushed, sheepish.

"Alright, he needs rest," announced Dr. Chaudhary, attempting to clear the room. "And we'll need to do more tests."

I hugged my grandma, who wanted to stay behind, and walked everyone else out.

Delilah and Dylan had ordered a car to take them back to the city, which was waiting as we exited the building. As they left, I followed Max across the parking lot. The morning sun now brightly shining, clearing away the last of the overnight dew.

I stopped a few feet short of his bike.

"I can't do the whole goodbye thing again," I admitted, my legs dragging behind me. "I just... I can't, ya know... Also, I love you," I said. "So there's that."

It felt cathartic to say it out loud, even though I knew it didn't matter. I wasn't expecting to hear it in return, nor did I need to. It was about saying it because I felt it. Because I finally had the courage to.

He dropped his gaze, conflict blanketing his face.

"Before you say anything," I added quickly. "I only said it because I wanted you to know. As ridiculous as that sounds, having only had one date."

"And a very memorable kiss," he interjected. "No one can take that away from us."

"That I won't argue," I quivered, trying not to cry. "I'm just saying it because you deserve to know."

"I do, I know," he said.

"Oh yeah?" I asked, kind of offended by his arrogance.

"Yeah," he said, assured. "You have a very special way of making the people you love feel loved. I'm lucky... to have experienced it."

Bittersweet irony washed over me: I'd found a love so star-crossed that no amount of magic could spare us from it.

"Maybe in another life," I said.

"Maybe," he agreed.

Before he could say or do anything else, I left. Unable to bear dragging the moment out any longer.

It certainly wasn't the ending I'd imagined, but the door had finally shut, and I hoped the closure that came with it helped ease my aching heart. It felt agonizing to leave him, even more so to not look back, but I did it clinging to the knowledge that the memories of him were better than never having known him.

I prayed to the stars that he was just a chapter in my life, and not the whole story. That someday I'd find another Max who would make me feel again like nothing else in the world mattered but us.

TWENTY-SIX

AS TIME GOES BY

Raymond John Nelson passed away from liver failure on the 25th of November, despite the best efforts of his doctors, and the scope of *In Scientia*.

Departing the world in peace, he was surrounding by those who loved him most—my grandma and me.

I was lucky enough to spend his final weeks beside him, asking him every day what he was grateful for, what he was excited about, and what he was proud of. No matter how many times he answered, his first response to every question was always me.

Delilah surprised me when she visited for the funeral, orchestrated by my grandma no doubt, correctly sensing I needed a shoulder to cry on. Even on her darkest day, she still concerned herself with my well-being, over her own.

It was easier to acclimate myself to seeing the vibrations of everything around me than it was to accept that I'd never see Max again. Most days it felt like a punctured lung: possible to get by, but only barely. Granddad never took my word that 'Romeo' was just a friend, even trapping me into conversation about him not long before he passed.

"Friends make the best kind of partners," he declared one afternoon, completely out of nowhere.

"Thanks, Grandpa, I'll remember that," I said.

"If not Romeo, then the other?" he probed, hopeful. "Puppies grow into loyal companions too you know," he added, with a laugh that turned into coughing.

"How about neither," I said. "I don't need a man."

"You don't need *anything*," he agreed. "I believe that you, my dear Eva, are perfect. Exactly as you are."

"Well, thank you—"

"*But* there may come a day when you'll find that companionship is often the safety net we need to be even more daring." He was trying to speak my language, and I appreciated every word.

Living back in my old room, in the house I'd tried so desperately to escape from, was surreal. But there was nowhere else I would have rather been. I soaked up every moment I could with my granddad, while making sure my grandmother felt supported in every way. It felt like the most important thing I've ever done.

The time also gave me space to process everything that had happened. After weeks of soul searching and trying to figure out what I was supposed to do next, I had to confront the events of London: an experience I'd tried desperately to disassociate from as soon as I landed back in the States.

Call it intuition (or foreboding) but I knew I hadn't heard the last of the Sinclair family. I hoped they got the message from my abrupt departure that I wasn't a threat to them, but I doubted it would keep them at bay for too long. I'd have to face their world again, sooner or later, but for the time being I had enough real-world problems to figure out.

At the top of my list was Anderson. I'd been taking classes remotely and working on make-up assignments, but I had to decide whether I wanted to go back. The problem was, I wasn't sure I did. College didn't even seem like a certainty anymore.

The second weekend of December, I'd arranged to take the

train into Manhattan to rectify a past mistake: missing rehearsals for Delilah's play. But when I got to the girls' dorm, she had a look on her face that told me she had other things in mind.

"Okay, so don't hate me... promise?" She was wrapped in a towel, applying mascara in front of the common room mirror.

Before I could reply, Dylan appeared behind me in the doorway. He was wearing a suit with a bow tie—a picture of charming awkwardness.

"Oh, sorry," he said, hastily covering his eyes and looking away. "I'm early."

"Seriously, Dylan? Relax. You've seen me more naked in clothes."

Hesitantly, he withdrew his arm from his face, properly seeing me for the first time. He beamed, and without thinking he grabbed me in a bear hug.

"Eva," he gushed. "It's great, *really great*, to see you." His slight Southern accent was coming out

I couldn't help but giggle like a tween. *Gross*.

"It's only been a few weeks," I said.

"Six," he corrected me. He looked different in a suit. Older. More assured.

"*Wait*," I said. Turning to Delilah. "What am I gonna hate you for?"

"We're going to a formal," she said, looking at me through the mirror.

"What?" I queried. "*No*. No, we're not."

"Yeah. Yeah, we are," she said, like the conclusion was forgone. "We already talked about it."

"*I* didn't talk about it."

Dylan smiled uneasy, hiding a box he was holding with what looked like two peony corsages.

"Actually, come to think of it," I added. "I did talk about it. To you both. And I said *I wasn't going*—"

"That is true," said Dylan, trying to support me. "You did say that. But your grandma—"

"My grandma?" I was starting to spiral slightly. I'd reached my limit with deception in all its forms. Even the kind-hearted type.

"Your gran and I have stayed in touch a little," said Delilah, moving over to where I was sitting on the couch.

"You have?" I asked, knowing how much that would've meant to her.

"She's been a little worried about you."

Ouch. Not what I was expecting.

"And so have I."

"We," added Dylan.

It completely blindsided me, I thought I'd been doing well. I guess some pain is just impossible to bury.

My pride wanted me to be angry, but the genuine concern on their faces told me how much they cared. "And you thought the best way to cheer me up was by taking me to *winter formal*?" I asked, incredulous.

Delilah laughed. "Well, no. But I did think it could help with getting into NYU."

I'd forgotten about the article Annabel had asked me to submit, but the mere thought of it reignited my sense of cynicism.

"How, though?" I asked, remembering how much tickets were. "My gran better not—"

"She did," interrupted Delilah. "She insisted... I'm sorry," she said, clear she was starting to lose courage in the idea entirely. "She said your grandad would've—"

"*Ah*," I said, "don't say it. I get it."

Dylan chimed in, attempting to break the tension, "My parents just really wanted me to have the experience," he said, turning embarrassed at his omission.

I felt terrible, mostly because of how much money everyone had spent—especially my grandma—but, I reasoned, I'd feel far worse if I wasted it.

"This was a trap," I said.

"Totally," Delilah agreed.

"I have nothing to wear," I stated flatly.

A grin slowly appeared across her face. "So you're coming?"

"I have nothing to wear," I maintained, my expression accidentally matching hers.

"Then come with me, little lady, 'cause I pulled out options," she said, grabbing my hand and skipping off into the bedroom.

Hung across the top railings of her bunk bed and mine were various dress options, each demanding a level of confidence I didn't possess.

"Do you have anything more...?" I was trying to find the right words.

"Amish?" she suggested.

"Covered," I said, simultaneously.

She walked over to her wardrobe and opened the double doors, before walking over to my side and doing the same. "Is there anything in one of these?" she asked, stepping aside to reveal four large suitcases crammed inside.

I'd forgotten all about Alida's 'gifts,' if that's what they were.

The irony was poignant.

"You know, there just might be," I said, pulling one down and opening it. "But you wouldn't wanna wear..."

The Chanel dress was on top. Even crumpled, it was stunning.

"That's... not?" Delilah asked, in disbelief.

"Yup."

"Some trip," she said, as she bent down to almost touch it. "Can I?" she asked.

"Of course. Take the first pick," I offered.

"No," she replied, outraged. "I could *never*."

"Oh, but you can," I encouraged her. "And should. Especially as they're going back tomorrow."

She picked up the metallic dress and held it against her body like a baby. "*Bonjour, belle. Je m'appelle Delilah*," she said to the dress, before looking at me, perplexed. "What? She only speaks French."

WE ARRIVED at the hotel where the formal was being held an hour late. According to Delilah, however, this meant we were right on time. A handful of other students, dressed in gowns and suits, were exiting limos as our taxi pulled up.

In front of us, a girl with over-sprayed curly hair posed with her date for photos. The professional photographer had an assistant holding an extra-large light box, the flash of which kept intermittently popping. The spectacle had drawn a crowd of tourists eager to see a celebrity. Little did they know it was just a high school dance.

"Is this compulsory?" Delilah asked the photographer's assistant as we approached.

"*No*. This is where *my* photos are being taken," said the girl with curly hair, as though it was something to be proud of. "I'd rather die than have the same background as everyone else."

Delilah nodded as though she agreed, then took out her phone and took a selfie of us with the hotel in the background. "Oops, now we have it too," she said.

The girl didn't seem to find it as funny as we did.

The room itself was nothing short of dramatic. Archways adorned with intricate paintings reminiscent of the Italian Renaissance framed the space, but the real showstopper was an elegantly-tiered antique chandelier, which hung above the center of the dancefloor.

Standing atop the opulent staircase that overlooked the party, our mouths hung slightly agape. We were a long way from where any of us grew up.

"Wow," I said. "It's like... epic."

"It's only The Terrace Room," said a voice from behind us. It was Ciara, a girl from my Politics class, accompanied by none other than Annabel Monteith herself. "You should see the Grand Ballroom, it's so much nicer."

"Will you give it up? It was three times the price," Annabel interjected, who was basically wearing a chandelier of her own. "People were already complaining about how much tickets—"

"Yeah, well, this gives me Florida. And that makes me sad," said Ciara.

My eyes flicked to Delilah, and then to Dylan. Both of whom were having trouble suppressing laughter, which only encouraged mine.

"Oh, hi Eva," said Annabel, as if just noticing me. "So glad you decided to come." Awkwardly, she kissed me on both cheeks. *We're not in France*, I wanted to scream.

"You look stunning," she said. She genuinely seemed to mean it, which somehow made me feel better about owning her old uniform.

"Oh my god, did I not just say Valentino's everywhere right now?" Ciara asked Annabel, my excitement deflating.

"Shut up, Ciara. It's chic and you know it," she turned to me, "ignore her, her parents never taught her to socialize."

"What's your excuse?" I quipped, accidentally snapping the olive branch she seemed to be extending.

Ciara walked off, clearly bored with the conversation.

"Do you, like, think I hate you or something?" Annabel asked. "'Cause I really don't."

I looked to Delilah and Dylan. "Can I meet you down there?" They understood, disappearing down the staircase and into the crowd.

"If you don't have a problem with me why won't you let me write for *The Advocate*?" I asked, trying to be direct.

"I told you, if your winter formal piece is better than Portia's, I'll publish it. And I will. I wasn't lying when I said the other features were already given out. Mr. McKenzie made me allocate everything at the end of last year when I got the job. He said every student had to have at least one article printed otherwise their parents would complain."

"So what, because I don't have parents I don't count?"

"What? No," she said, indignant. "At least I don't think so... that would be horrible. It's probably cause you're on scholarship and—"

"And what? I don't have a right to complain because I'm not paying for it? I should just be happy with whatever I get?" I asked, feeling more frustrated than I should have been.

"That's not what I meant." She took a breath, trying to get back on track. "I agree, it's messed up that you don't get a piece. I promise, I'll do whatever I can to use what you give me."

She looked sincere, like she was trying. "Thank you," I said and I meant it.

"Of course," she shrugged, as we both looked around the room.

Delilah and Dylan were jumping up and down to a pop song I didn't know, the sight of them instantly lifting my mood.

I had no idea what I'd write, if I were even capable of doing so. But I knew that if I felt passionately enough to argue about it, when I could have been hanging with my friends, then it must have been important to me in some way.

Annabel descended onto the dance floor, as I started properly surveying the party. It was extravagance at its most excessive.

A thought came to me, so I pulled out my phone to Google it. Anderson was a private school, but it received tax credits from the state government *'as long as equity and inclusion quotas were met amongst graduating students.'*

Immediately, I began drafting a piece in my head:

Anderson Preparatory held its annual Winter Formal with opulent fanfare this past Saturday, at The Plaza Hotel across from Central Park's lush expanse. No expense was spared for the *lavish event, which was open to all students provided they could afford the $350 price tag.*

Hundreds of long-stem white roses filled the room, creating an ethereal glow, while students danced and showcased this season's latest designs from the runways of London, Paris, and Milan.

"You have to stand out," said Lara Barnett, 15, who wore an $11,000 Dolce and Gabbana chiffon dress. "The last thing you want is to be like everybody else," she added, filming herself being interviewed to post on her TikTok.

Hors d'oeuvre's of wild leek pancakes and lamb chop lollipops, were passed around by white-gloved butlers, while the band 'Don't Look At Me' performed covers from a pre-approved list of profanity-free pop songs.

"We wanted to make sure everyone could have fun, even the younger kids," said Kerrie Baker from the Parents and Teachers Association. "They don't need to be unnecessarily exposed to adult themes." In an unrelated reminder, our next lockdown drill is scheduled for this week. Remember: Locks, Lights, Out of Sight kids.

Edward DeLuca and Chloe Shin were crowned Snow King and Snow Queen, breaking hearts across the ballroom as they 'hard launched' their budding romance. Nika Dyzla, who hired her own photographer for the event, astutely observed: "They're the perfect couple because they're the same level of hot."

However the real crowning moment of the night may have come from the silent auction, which managed to raise over $300,000. Not for a charity though: for the refurbishment of the school's own ballroom, which is used for exams four weeks out of the year. Money well spent, I say.

All in all, the Winter Formal was the perfect representation of everything Anderson Preparatory is: a shiny façade so bright it almost detracts from the real issues that matter. Like the carbon it took to fly in the out-of-season flowers from Ecuador, which at the time of writing were already wilting, or the financial strain it took on less affluent families, just so their children could be included in the experience.

It would seem the icy night under the stars was much like the rest of Anderson: subject to catches. Like the scholarship students who are given a free ride, but are kept from ever actually participating in the extracurriculars that matter. Were it not for inclusive teachers like Ms. Marshall, those kids might be forced to think of themselves as mere tokens, used to beef up diversity statistics to qualify for state tax breaks, and nothing else.

Fortunately there are people who want to change the status quo. People like this paper's editor Annabel Monteith who, by publishing this article despite potential repercussion, proved that diversity in ideology and economic status are not only welcomed, but encouraged.

Perhaps if enough of us follow suit, and stand up for what we believe in, we'll finally understand the power that lies within us all: change is ours to make. All we have to do is Advocate for it.

I had no idea if she'd actually print it, but it felt good to have cared enough to want to write it. To have cared for something other than losing my grandfather, or losing Max.

Locating Delilah and Dylan hovering near the dessert tower, I negotiated my exit to the dorm so I could write up the piece. After, that was, I joined them for two dances.

Back at my desk, having just finished what I felt was an acceptable first draft, I noticed a stack of mail. Sifting through a bunch of college brochures, my attention was drawn to a thick courier envelope topped by a handwritten letter simply addressed to *Eva*.

There was no return address, no stamp.

Cautiously I opened it.

Inside was a flier for the *Casablanca* screening in New Jersey, the same one the doorman from the jazz club had given me.

I pulled out my journal to find the original inside the cover.

Unfolding it, I compared the two. They were almost identical, except... upon closer inspection, some of the letters in the one I was sent were brighter than the original. Intrigued, I pulled out a pen and began to circle them.

M and *E* from *movie*.

E from *dinner*.

T from *starts*.

M from *pm*

E from *live*.

I was buzzing, excitement radiating through me. The event was that night, but it had started at 7 P.M. on the other side of the city, and it was already almost ten. Even if he was the one who invited me, I couldn't imagine he would've stuck around for three hours.

But it was worth a shot.

I sprung up out of my seat, almost hitting my head on the bunk above me, and was out the door hailing a cab faster than it normally took me to get out of bed.

One arrived within seconds, and before I knew it, we were pulling off the causeway into New Jersey City.

There was a busy hospital I'd found on Maps, a fifteen-minute walk from the screening.

Rushing into the emergency room, I made a beeline for the restroom, where I pulled out a piece of citrine and turned myself invisible. If anyone from the *Sancti* were still following me, I didn't want to be responsible for leading them to him.

I let the effects wear off, as I walked into Liberty State Park, just before 11 P.M. Four hours after the event had started.

String lights were suspended over a vacant waterside lot, which was filled with two-person tables adorned with Moroccan candle-lamps. The poster of the movie was being projected onto the side of an old train station, where I assumed the movie had been shown earlier.

Disappointment gripped me as I scanned the crowd. Only a

handful of people were left, still dancing on a parquet wood floor. As if on cue, the female singer started belting out a rendition of "*As Time Goes By,*" making my solitude feel even lonelier.

"May I?" a familiar voice asked, its sound turning me to jelly. He was wearing a white dinner jacket with a black bowtie. Classic Bogie. "Have this dance?"

"Only if I can lead," I said, grabbing his hand and drawing him in close.

We swayed to the music, mesmerized by the lights twinkling above us. As the title song from the movie came to a close, he nestled into my ear, his warm breath caressing my skin. "Would it be too clichéd to say, 'here's looking at you, kid?'" Max asked.

"Not if you're the one who's saying it," I replied.

We continued dancing. The music echoed across the harbor, the Manhattan skyline shimmering behind us.

It was perfect. Even more enchanting than I could have ever dreamed.

Until I remembered.

"Wait, is this safe?" I asked, concerned about any risks he might have taken. "What if someone sees us?"

"I sent a decoy uptown," he replied, looking smug.

"You used magic?"

"No. I hired a guy to dress up like me," he said, his pride evident that he'd managed it without breaking the rules. "I had to do *something*. It's a special occasion."

My heart sank. "Oh," I said, understanding. "This is a one-time thing."

He couldn't answer, or he didn't want to. Instead, he tried to pull me in closer.

"Why come, Max?" I asked, earnestly. I didn't want to create conflict but I'd only just stopped crying myself to sleep every night.

"Because I couldn't not," he said, matter of fact. "Are you sorry that I did?"

I looked up, wanting to kiss him, but not wanting to pass out.

"How is this fair?" I asked, my voice laced with frustration. "We've done nothing wrong."

"I have a feeling the *Sancti* don't care about what's fair."

"They killed my grandfather, Max. An innocent man. A good man, who did nothing wrong his entire life."

"I know, I'm sorry," he said, but he didn't need to. I could see it on his face. "That's why I tried to stay out of your life in the first place. Anything I get near—"

"It wasn't your fault," I cut him off. "I've known Father Michael since I was a child. They've been watching me my entire life."

It was as if I could see the weight being lifted from his eyes.

"I'm still sorry," he said.

"For what?"

"Eva, if I never came into your life—"

"Come on," I said, finding the courage to say how I truly felt in the actual moment. "Let's stop pretending we ever had a choice. Some things are... fated."

"And yet..." he said.

The singer belted out the last line of the song, *"as time goes by."*

"You really think they'll stop us forever?"

"They outnumber us three hundred to one. They have the power to."

"*We* also have power," I urged him.

"*Don't*, Eva. It's dangerous to even think like that," he warned, anger to his tone. "You've seen what they do to innocent people. I've seen what they do to the guilty."

He tried to pull me in close again. This time, I let him.

"So, what does that mean?" I asked. "For us?" I could hear the self-preservation in my voice but I didn't care.

"I don't know," he admitted. I looked up to see his face darkening. "But we have the rest of tonight. Is that enough?"

"I guess it has to be," I replied. The only response that felt truthful.

He rested his hand on the side of my head, and held it to his chest.

I could hear his heartbeat, steady and reassuring, as we swayed without music.

Thump, thump. Thump, thump.

In that moment, I knew how fortunate I was. I'd experienced a love that so many spend a lifetime searching for. Then, just as the band introduced the final song, I let the boy I love kiss me, under the moonlight of a clear New York City night... and this time, I remained fully conscious.

I WOKE EARLY the next morning, with sunlight breaking in through a gap in the curtains.

Crawling onto my hands and knees to close them, I accidentally pulled too hard, sending the entire rod crashing to the ground.

"*No!*" screamed Delilah, as if boiling water were being sprayed on her. "That lighting's homophobic, make it stop!"

I leaped out of bed, attempting to rehang the curtain when she got up to help.

"Meh," she grumbled, swatting the rod out of my hands when she realized the height involved. "New plan: Brunch. It's so early we might actually get a table somewhere decent."

I let my mind adjust to the idea of staying awake, as my eyes gradually adapted to the bright light.

Grunting in agreement, I grabbed my towel from my desk and headed for a shower, inadvertently knocking all my mail to the floor in the process. *This is going to be a long day,* I thought.

"Get. Later," I muttered, walking out the door.

With renewed strength from the hot water, I dressed in my

own clothes and re-attempted the stack of unopened letters while Delilah finished getting ready.

"Know what this is? I asked holding up the heavy courier package.

"No idea," she replied. "I haven't snooped."

Sitting down at my desk, I pulled on the precut tab to open the cardboard. Inside were keys and a handwritten letter, paper-clipped to a thick document.

Eva,

We respect your need for space. It was a lot for us to ask of you, but now there are no secrets between us. Know that we'll be here when you're ready.

Enclosed, please find the deed to your mother's apartment in New York City. Along with all necessary information to access your trust fund.

Do whatever you want with it. It's yours, free and clear. No catches, no conditions.

Your loving family, if you'll let us,
Alida and Terence

I convinced Delilah to make a pitstop on the way to the restaurant, going via the address listed on the paperwork: *13 Central Park West.*

As our taxi pulled up outside the building's Art Deco façade, a knot of unease tightened in my stomach. *Had the driver been unusually attentive, or was my imagination playing tricks?*

"Okay, what is this?" Delilah asked, as the grand structure loomed before us. "Do you actually know people who live here?"

"Well..." I began, my voice trailing off. The sight of a priest stepping out of a taxi behind us caught my eye, reminding me I wasn't completely paranoid. "Wanna come in with me? I can catch you up on my trip, so brunch can be all about you," I said, eager to distance myself from potential prying eyes.

We paid the fare and made our way inside. The doorman, recognizing the address, escorted us to a private elevator that opened directly into the penthouse suite.

Stepping into the apartment, the vastness of the space felt staggering. It seemed to stretch endlessly, room after room, with towering windows offering an unobstructed, panoramic view of Central Park. High ceilings were accentuated by antique crown moldings, complementing the natural light that bathed the entire space.

"Again, I ask," Delilah said. "*What. Is. This?*" She was looking out at the view as I walked into the kitchen, where I found a gift basket filled with expensive chocolates and gourmet snacks. Delilah followed me in, picking up the card, which had my name on it.

She looked at me. "Why does this have your name on it?"

I didn't know how to explain it.

"Okay... how about this?" she suggested. "I'm gonna run downstairs and grab us coffee because I know words aren't your friend before it, and you can tell me how you're a freakin' princess or whatever."

"I'm not a princess," I said. "But yes to everything else." Delilah laughed and left for the elevator, leaving me alone in the apartment.

I continued to explore the apartment, my thoughts drifting to my mother.

I wondered which room would've been hers when I found myself in the main bedroom suite. My attention was captured by a purplish hue emanating from behind a panel in one of the two apartment-sized walk-in closets.

I approached the panel, letting my fingers glide over the smooth wood, searching for the source of the light. The carpentry felt like it was solid until a sharp splinter pricked my finger, leaving a small smear of blood on the wood.

Before I had a chance to wipe it off with my sleeve, the panel opened with a creak.

Inside, I found a familiar sight: a copy of *In Scientia*. Beside it lay another diamond necklace, intricately designed with the Symbol of *In Unio*.

I picked them up, assuming they were my mother's, when a letter fell out. It seemed to be the day for them.

It was addressed to 'My Baby Girl.'

My hands began to tremble, as I unfolded the pristine pages.

My darling child,

It is my dearest hope that you never read this letter. For if you do, it will mean that I was not able to share them with you myself, but there are a few things you need to know:

One, I love you more than I have ever loved anything in this world. Myself included. As soon as I felt you grow inside me, I knew that you were special in ways that not even you will be able to comprehend. Your existence is a miracle, and the greatest love I'll ever know.

Two, your father and his parents are all the family you'll ever need. My affection for your dad is only eclipsed by my love for you. To know him, and his kindness, has made my life infinitely more beautiful than I ever thought it could be. I'm happy in a way I once believed was out of reach. I pray you'll be just as lucky in your life.

Three, there are things I cannot commit to paper for fear of them falling into the wrong hands, but please trust that everything I've done has been for you and your safety. Even, and especially when, blood wasn't thicker than water. Remember, no one controls your destiny but you. No matter what the holiest of men try to convince you —tablets can break, empires have crumbled. Your fate resides in you.

Trust your intuition, my beautiful girl. It will never lead you wrong.

Mum x

Every emotion I'd ever had about my mother came rushing to the surface: pain, loss, love, anger, abandonment... fear.

My knees weakened as I heard the elevator doors slide open. Rushing into the kitchen, I found Delilah unpacking grocery bags from a bodega.

"Is everything okay?" she asked, noticing the tears streaming down my face.

I shook my head. "My mom..." was all I could get out.

She immediately dropped everything and wrapped me in a hug.

"You're alright," she said. "*You got this*, remember."

My tears free-flowed.

"What can I do?" she asked. "Is there anything?"

I pulled back to look at her, attempting to order my thoughts. My mother's letter was a warning. But of what? I didn't know. All I knew was that I couldn't do it alone. I needed to trust someone, and my gut was telling me that person was Delilah.

"I don't even know where to start," I said, saying the words out loud, a release of their own.

"The beginning's usually a good place," she joked, sweetly.

Taking a deep breath, I gathered my thoughts.

"Okay…" I said, trying to figure out how to explain the unexplainable. "What do you know about magic?"

ACKNOWLEDGMENTS

~~I may never win any acting awards, so here it is...~~

First and foremost, thank *you* for reading. For your time, ~~your money,~~ and your support. It means the world and is a privilege I don't take lightly.

To my Mum and Ian, and my Dad. Thank you for letting me follow my artistic dreams. Your belief in me, even and especially when mine faded, pushed me on. To my sister Zoey, thank you for giving me some of the best notes, and reminding me who I was writing for. To Heidi, Brodie and the rest of my family, thank you for always cheering me on, even from afar. ~~Please stop telling everyone I was a brat.~~

To Will, thank you for reminding me to write the book I wanted to read, and for making me feel safe enough to do so. To Kelly, for providing so many years of honesty, I believed you when you told me it was worth pursuing, and to Claire, for advocating for my writing long before I deserved it. Your reactions to the first draft gave me the drive to make it through the many that followed~~, and if people hate this book, you are all to blame.~~

To some of my nearest and dearest; Essy, the realist who never wavered in her support, Brytni, who showed up with her whole heart as she always does, and Cassandra, my eternal optimist who always believes in love... and me. To Hope, who saw the magic reminding me it was there, and Stefanie, who fired me up from the very first read. To Darci, who reminded me to relax cause *if it makes you happy, it can't be that bad,* and to Kate, whose sound magic inspired so much of *In Scientia*'s. To Nick, who's given me more opportunities than anyone in my career, especially as a writer, and to Zac, Christina, Zelda, Rachael, Liz, the Zumbados and Sarah, who inspire me always. To Kelli, Nika, Chelsea and Lexie, for providing an unconditional home in Jersey, and to Tam, Earl, JL and Tom for welcoming me so wholeheartedly. Your warmth will inspire me always.

To Todd Slavkin, whose enthusiastic feedback gave me the confidence to keep going, and to the rest of my *Shadowhunters* family; Kat, Dom, Berty, Tessa, Em, Will, Kim, Jade, Matt, Harry, Chai, Anna, Alisha, Nicola, Darren, Brian, Sydney and Javier, (breath) thank you for feeding my delusion that writing a novel was a good idea. And to Taylor, the first person I pitched the idea to, thank you for helping me navigate the minefield that is young adult tropes. I hope I haven't made the internet mad.

To Alissa, who fights for me daily, and Alex, who encouraged me to publish the novel my way—your backing helped build my bravery. To Josh, who didn't laugh when I told him I wanted to write a book, and Ann, who deceived me into thinking I could. To Tatijana, for reading my manuscript when I took six months to read your screenplay, and to Caroline, who approached my work with so much compassion and care, it gave me permission to do the same. To Elizabeth, for guiding me down the treacherous path that is publishing, and Bailey, thank you for pretending my incessant questions weren't annoying.

To Tez, for always lifting everyone around you up, and introducing me to Deb, who is too perfect to be real. Both of you are a light to me and so many. To Ari, for making it seem easy to trust your intuition, and to Jessica, for helping me identify it in the first place.

To David, my literary angel, thank you for saving me from myself, and to Marina, Isra and Davina, for approving my translations. To Mr. Jenkins and his AP Literature class, for their incredibly insightful and occasionally unnerving critiques. To

Alexandra, for reigniting my love of reading, and Sally for teaching me the importance of not over-explaining jokes. ~~Not that I've learned.~~ To Andrea, for teaching me how to listen to my inner critic so I could eventually turn it off, and to Ellen, for making me understand that if you make the same choice, you'll always remain in the same place. To Jackie and Oxfam, for always guiding me and reminding me what's truly important, and to Moyo, KC, Brooke, Darren, Blaine, Amy and Michelka for loving me the exact way you always have.

To the heroines who inspired Eva; Buffy, Max, Prue, Piper + Pheobe (~~fine,~~ and Paige), Sabrina, Nancy (and Sarah), Lorelai Gilmore (x2), Katniss, Clary, Bella, Lizzy Bennet and Hildy Johnson, thank you for your service. You walked, so Eva could run / fly.

Finally, to the fans I've been lucky enough to meet as an actor, and the ones I haven't. Thank you for caring enough to pay attention to the things I do. Without your support, none of it would be possible. This book's for you.

~~Last, and certainly least, I'd like to thank my year 11 English teacher who told me I wasn't smart enough to be a writer. Just one question for ya: *How do you like them apples, Miss?*~~

About the Author

Luke Baines is an English-born Australian actor, writer and producer. He's best known for his work on the Netflix/Freeform fantasy drama series *Shadowhunters*, which earned him a Teen Choice nomination.

Luke also starred in *The Girl In The Photographs*, directed by Nick Simon and produced by Wes Craven, and in David Robert Mitchell's A24 feature *Under The Silver Lake*, which premiered at the 2018 Cannes Film Festival.

His other film credits include *Untitled Horror Movie*, Syfy Channel's *Truth or Dare*, *The Ever After*, *As Night Comes*, *A Dark Place* and Disney's *Saving Mr. Banks* (even though he was cut out of it). His TV credits include, Marvel's *Agents of S.H.I.E.L.D.*, *The Mandalorian* and *Nancy Drew*.

He is an ardent supporter of Oxfam, which seeks to end injustices that cause poverty. Luke holds a Bachelor of Communications (Business) from Bond University, Australia.

In Scientia marks his debut as an author.

For more projects and updates, visit: www.lukebaines.com